T0301160

SEVEN DAYS

SEVEN DAYS

ROBERT RUTHERFORD

HODDER &
STOUGHTON

First published in Great Britain in 2024 by Hodder & Stoughton
An Hachette UK company

1

A CIP catalogue record for this title is available from the British Library

Hardback ISBN 978 1 399 72639 9
Trade Paperback ISBN 978 1 399 72640 5
ebook ISBN 978 1 399 72641 2

Typeset in Plantin Light by Manipal Technologies Limited

Printed and bound in Great Britain by Clays Ltd, Elcograf S.p.A.

Hodder & Stoughton policy is to use papers that are natural, renewable and recyclable products and made from wood grown in sustainable forests. The logging and manufacturing processes are expected to conform to the environmental regulations of the country of origin.

Hodder & Stoughton Ltd
Carmelite House
50 Victoria Embankment
London EC4Y 0DZ

www.hodder.co.uk

For Nic. Chesney Hawkes lied –
he isn't the one and only. You are.

Prologue

FLORIDA, 2011

Manny knows that the only way that he walks out of here is if the other guy doesn't. He sees it in the other man's face. A look he's worn himself more times than he cares to remember. Lips drawn into a thin line, narrowing of the eyes. That singular focus that comes with knowing there's only one outcome.

He reaches into the pocket of his jeans for the switch-blade, fingers closing around the handle. The first time he registers that something is wrong is when he flicks his wrist to open the blade. There's a clumsiness to it, like he's a bottle of whiskey deep, relying on sheer muscle memory.

'You walk outta here now, or you'll never walk again,' he shouts at the man, even though he's only six feet away.

No answer. Something glints by the man's side, making Manny's eyes flick down. Just for a second, but it's long enough. The man doesn't so much move as flow towards him. Manny hadn't bothered to turn the kitchen light on, so the dark shape that lunges at him might as well be shadow.

Manny stabs, aiming at the guy's face, but even as he does so, he feels the sluggishness of his efforts. Might as well have concrete flowing in his veins. It's like everything's on slo-mo, for him at least. Not so much his attacker. The man leans to one side, stepping in to slap a palm against Manny's knife hand. The blade slices through the spot where the man's head should have been. Manny tries to reverse the blade, bring it arcing back down, but it's like his head is pumped full of cotton wool, and his hand won't obey fast enough.

The man's hand snakes around Manny's neck, pulling his head down as he slams a knee up and under his ribs, driving the air out with such a force that Manny hears a wet snapping sound before the pain lances through his side. He drops like he's been shot by a sniper. Tries to howl in pain, but can't even draw breath. It's like he's suffocating. Takes a few seconds to realise that the weird gargling noise is coming from him.

One hand clutches his side, the other goes to slash with the switchblade, but there's no strength in his fingers and the knife tumbles harmlessly to the floor. The man swings a foot at it, sending it skittering away out of sight. The pain in Manny's side is a fluid thing. The first flash was hot and white, but already it's being swept away by adrenaline, morphing into something else, a dull ache, throbbing with a drum beat all of its own.

His head feels like an over-shaken snow globe. This isn't a fight he's going to win with his fists. Not unless he can buy a little time to recover.

'Look man,' he rasps, squinting up at the man staring down at him. 'Whatever this is, I'm sure we can work something out.'

The words come out in ones and twos rather than complete sentences as he tries desperately to catch his breath.

He knows that face. Has seen it recently, but can't quite place it. Disgruntled customer, maybe? Manny usually cuts a little of this, and a little of that into his product before he sells it on. Sometimes baby formula, sometimes a little creatine. Could be he'd just been heavy-handed with his extra ingredients, and the dude had a shitty high.

'Look, I don't usually do refunds,' he wheezes, forcing a smile. 'But I can make an exception.'

The man squats down a foot away. Manny tries to rise up onto one elbow, but it's like pushing up through treacle. He feels the man put a hand on his chest.

In through the nose, out through the mouth. Manny lies back, repeats the mantra, desperately trying to find a rhythm, but his breathing is like a misfiring motor. He notices a warmness for the first time. At first, he thinks it's just from the exertion, but it's spreading outwards across his whole body. Like he's being wrapped in a warm blanket. The harder he fights it, the deeper he sinks, as if the carpet is swallowing him up. Manny goes to speak again as the man leans in close.

'Let's … look man, I just wanna …'

Words run together, jumbled, borderline incoherent.

The eyes that bore into his might as well be glass marbles for all the emotion they contain. Manny's head feels heavy, like it's made of stone, but he manages to force his gaze down to the man's hand, remembering that it had been holding something that twinkled in the light.

It's more ice pick than blade. Four inches of steel tapering to an impossibly fine point. Manny wills himself to reach up, slap it out of the man's hand. Can't be more than twelve inches from his face, but might as well be twelve miles. It's as if someone or something has short-circuited his brain, stopping any orders it sends to his body.

The man studies him for a moment, then flicks the pick around with practised ease, until it's pointing at Manny's left eye.

'You've got to pay what you owe, Manny. I'm here to collect.'

Chapter One

Monday – Seven days to go

Pain sears through Alice's foot as her toes connect with the heavy wooden chair leg. The words sneak out through gritted teeth before she can stop them.

'Bloody hell!'

She doesn't even need to see the disapproving look on her mum's face to know it's there. What qualifies as swearing is a long-time bone of contention. A battle she knows she'll never win. Even so, she cringes inwardly at the apology that follows on autopilot.

She pivots, Mum's arm still round her shoulder, and lowers her into the armchair.

'You get yourself away,' Mum says, even before Alice can straighten up.

It comes out sounding more like *your-shelf.* Even now, four years on from the stroke, there are markers it laid down. Mum jokes that it makes her sound like Sean Connery, but the bravado is just behind closed doors to a safe audience of Alice and her younger sister, Fiona. With anyone else, if you know where to look, the self-conscious tells are there. The way she digs one thumbnail into the edge of the other, worrying at it.

More than once Mum's drawn blood, as if the pain will keep her sharp.

'Plenty of time Mum,' Alice says, even though she needs to leave in five minutes, tops. She reaches down, easing her mum forwards a few inches to slide an extra cushion behind her back for support.

'Shona'll be here soon,' Mum says shooing her away with one hand. 'Go on, away you go.'

These morning exchanges are regular as clockwork, part of the fabric of Alice's life. Feel borderline scripted at times. She loves her mum, although there are layers to it. Some of them best left alone for everyone's sake. Her carer, Shona, has patience that goes on for days. Enough that it makes Alice feel lacking in that department at times.

'Fiona says she'll swing by this afternoon,' Alice says, smoothing out the creases in her skirt. 'I'll pop in on my way back home later.'

'I'll be fine,' her mum says, a little terse even by her standards.

Alice wishes she had her mum's confidence. Too many times to count she's popped in to find a trail of destruction where Mum has tried to reclaim her independence. Doctors have said she'll likely never regain the full use of her left foot or right arm, both victims of the stroke that nearly killed her. It's enough that she warrants Shona being here five days a week, with Alice and Fiona covering the weekend shifts. Doesn't stop Mum making a cup of tea with her one good hand. Getting it back to her seat intact is another matter entirely.

It's an endless see-saw of emotions for Alice. There are days where she wishes her mum had gone into the assisted living facility the doctors had suggested, for both their sakes. Others where the mere thought of it makes her feel like a candidate for world's worst daughter. God knows it would be the easier option, for her at least. It isn't as if this is their childhood home, stacked with memories that she wants to cling on to. That house is four thousand miles across the Atlantic, and most of the memories there are ones she's happy to forget.

Alice bends down, planting a kiss on her mum's forehead.

'See you later Mum.'

Alice grabs her bag as she heads out into the hallway. She hears the soft purr of her phone vibrating somewhere in the depths, and rummages around until her fingers close around it.

'Just leaving now,' she says, tucking it under her chin, bag in one hand, the other pulling the door closed.

'Your house, your mum's, or did you stop somewhere else last night?'

The playful insinuation is enough that Alice can picture the twinkle in Moira Wilkinson's eye as she asks the question.

'I'll take the fifth amendment on that one.'

'You're not in the good old US of A now, counsellor,' Moira says, swapping out what Alice thinks of as her posh Geordie accent for a butchered American one.

Ever since she came home from the States four years ago, Moira has never let her forget the lingering accent she brought back with her. It's long gone now, unless she's speaking to one of her friends back in New York, but that doesn't stop her assistant from poking fun when it's just the two of them. Moira's been at the firm since Alice was in nappies, and that kind of tenure buys you a level of tolerance in certain circles.

'I'm just getting in the car now,' Alice says, heels clacking as she walks down the street towards her car. 'Be with you in half an hour. Remind me who my first meeting is with?'

'Mr and Mrs Williams at nine-thirty,' Moira says without missing a beat, 'but you might want to get an extra shot of espresso on your way. Fiona's here, insisting on jumping the queue.'

Alice's brow creases at the mention of her little sister. Since the twins came along, Fiona has lived her life by their routine to a level of precision that would put a drill sergeant to shame. Quick check of the watch shows it's a few minutes after eight. Why the hell is her sister at her office instead of shovelling breakfast into a pair of four-year-olds?

'What does she want?'

'Beats me,' Moira says. 'I told her to call you instead, but she said she'd rather wait. Whatever it is, she's going to owe you a new carpet the way she's pacing.'

Alice thanks Moira for the advance warning and heads out into early morning Whitley Bay traffic. Seagulls drift overhead, circling in search for scraps. The faint hint of salty sea air drifts through the open car window. Pale October sunshine sneaking through gaps in the clouds is just for show, not warmth. Alice smiles to herself, savouring these little pieces of the jigsaw that make up her home town. Worlds apart from the melting pot of her old life in New York City.

She forgot to ask Moira if Fiona's alone, or whether Jake and Lily are there with her. For a split second she has an image of the pair of them scribbling pictures of stickmen on the walls of her office. It'd almost be worth it to see Moira's reaction. She makes her usual resolution to pop round and see the kids more. Somehow, she has acquired the mantle of cool Auntie Alice, even though she feels like she barely gets to see them between work and looking after her mum.

The journey to Newcastle is death by a thousand traffic jams. Alice joins the treacle-slow procession of commuters that crawls along the Cradlewell bypass. She can't help but people-watch as they inch along. Everything from full-blown car karaoke to stoic silence as people get their game faces on for another day in the office.

Hers is a stone's throw from the river, and as she winds down towards the Quayside, the dull green curve of the Tyne bridge arcs over the water like a raised eyebrow. The water beneath is millpond calm, barely flowing.

A flash of light on the south bank catches her eye where early morning sunlight glints off the Sage concert hall. It crouches on top of the riverbank, a giant collage of glass and steel. It's all so different from the Newcastle of her childhood. One she can only remember in snatches. She was nine when her life was uprooted, transplanted from northern nirvana to the muggy humidity of her father's home town of Orlando, Florida.

All Dad's doing. A fresh start he'd said. A homecoming, for him at least. Painting pictures of sunshine and theme parks. The truth was a little more tarnished. Always was where Dad was involved. Something he was happy to bend into a shape that suited. Is he still there, she wonders? Shacked up with *her*, while the mother of his children spends her days trapped in a body that did its level best to throw in the towel four years ago.

Alice hasn't spoken to him since she was twenty-one. The same day her mum finally kicked him out fourteen years ago. He tried an olive branch a couple of times in the months that followed, but the stubbornness she has inherited from him wouldn't let her accept his half-hearted apologies.

It's almost ten to nine by the time she parks up and walks through the doors of Shaw, Finnie and Co, tucked away behind the Crown Court. As soon as she sets foot inside, she sees Moira making a beeline for her, like a sprinter from the blocks, albeit far more elegant. Moira dresses to impress, with a seemingly never-ending procession of outfits. Alice has joked that she only wears them once then throws them away. Fact of the matter is, Moira isn't here for the money. Her husband Steven works Monday to Friday at a London hedge fund. She could walk out the door now and never work another day in her life, but that's just not how she's wired.

'I've made up a nine o'clock for you, so she'll have to be quick,' Moira says with a wry smile.

Alice can't help but smile at how protective Moira gets, even if the opposition is her own sister instead of another solicitor.

'Everything okay with your mum?' Moira asks, voice softening. She lost her own not long after Alice joined the firm. She's never one to overshare, but Alice remembers her talking about how hard it was at the time to juggle her own life, while helping her mum towards the end of hers.

'She's on good form,' Alice says, flashing a practised smile.

'I'll leave you to it,' says Moira after the briefest of pauses.

Alice watches her go, then looks down the length of the building towards her own office. An opaque strip runs through the middle of the glass wall, like a layer of buttercream in a cake. Floating above it, the top of Fiona's head bobs backwards and forwards like a brunette iceberg as she walks back and forth.

Alice puffs out her cheeks as she heads towards the door, half expecting to see two pairs of four-year-old legs running along the length of her office, but when she opens the door, it's just Fiona. Her sister is cut from a different cloth. Four inches shorter than Alice's five six. Dark hair a far cry from Alice's own sandy curls, which she's wearing scraped back.

Her sister stops pacing when she sees her. There's something about her expression that troubles Alice. Something she can't quite read.

'Morning,' she says, trying to inject a level of cheeriness she doesn't feel. 'To what do I owe the pleasure?'

'You might want to sit down,' Fiona says after a beat, with a look that speaks of nothing good to follow.

'What's up? Are the kids okay?' Alice asks, hearing a note of panic in her own voice.

'What? Oh, yeah, they're fine. It's nothing to do with the kids.'

'Where are they?'

'With Trevor, but that's not why I'm here.'

The corners of Alice's mouth turn down at the mention of the kids' dad and Fiona's on-off boyfriend, like she's just sniffed sour milk. Back playing part-time parent by the sounds of it. She sees Fiona clock her reaction, but for once, her sister doesn't bite.

'Why are you here then?'

Fiona slips into a seat beside Alice's desk, gesturing for her to do the same. Alice sighs at the theatrics of whatever this is. She shrugs, then slides past Fiona. Fine, she thinks. She'll play the game until Fiona is ready to get whatever it is off her chest.

Alice lets her bag slide off her shoulder and drop by her feet, then leans back into her seat.

'I've got a nine o'clock,' she says, glancing at her watch to emphasise the point.

'They're going to kill him in seven days,' Fiona's words fall out at a hundred miles an hour.

'What?' Alice says, forehead folding into a spider's web of confused creases. 'What are you talking about? Who's going to kill who?'

'Dad. They're going to kill Dad.'

Chapter Two

Monday – Seven days to go

'Whoa, back up a minute,' Alice says, brain scrambling to make sense of the grenade Fiona has just lobbed her way. 'What do you mean they're going to kill him? Who's going to kill him?'

Fiona looks at her like she's a five-year-old who's just asked the same question for the fortieth time.

'I mean they're literally going to kill him a week today,' she says, leaning in with heavy emphasis on the *kill*. Her eyes are tinged pink, like she's been crying.

'Who's they?'

'I got a call this morning. He's on death row. They're going to stick a fucking needle in him in seven days.'

Alice huffs out a loud breath, head swirling like a stirred pot, and places her palms flat on the table. 'Wind it back for me, Fi. Who told you this? Have you been in touch with him?'

She doesn't mean it to come out like an accusation, but that's exactly how it rings in her ears.

'What? No, I haven't spoken to him in years. Mariella called me this morning.'

It's a name Alice will forever associate with a rift that opened up in their lives, one she still feels to this day.

'And what? She just called out of the blue to catch up on old times, then drop in that Dad's on death row? What the hell is going on, Fiona?'

Dozens of questions jostle for pole position. Dad's been in prison before, so that part doesn't come as a shock, but death row? Only way he's got there is murder. Murder, for Chrissake! Who has he killed to get there? Executions are years, not days in the making. How long has he been sat in a cell? Fiona's words have tipped the world on its axis, and she opens her mouth to ask all of these questions and more, but instead she just sits there dumbstruck.

'Dad didn't want us to know.' Fiona fills the silence. 'Still doesn't according to Mariella. He made her promise not to try and find us, but there's only a week left. She cracked. Found me on Facebook and said she needed to speak. Said it was life and death. Guess she wasn't kidding.'

'And is that it?' Alice asks. 'She lets us know, then what? I mean Jesus, Fi, if it's even true, then he's literally killed someone.'

'What do you mean if it's true?' Fiona snaps back, her eyes wide with surprise. 'Who's going to lie about something like that?'

'They've both got form,' Alice fires back. 'Managed it well enough when they were sneaking around behind Mum's back.'

'For fuck's sake Alice, our dad is going to die.'

'He's not been our dad for a long time.'

The coldness in her tone surprises even Alice herself, and she sees her sister wince.

'I know he hasn't been a great dad,' Fiona begins, and Alice has to stifle a laugh. 'And I'm not saying we'd ever play happy families, but he's going to die, Alice. Surely that trumps any shit you're still working through from your childhood?'

You. You're still working through. Not we. Inference being that Alice is the one with the problem.

Alice swallows down a hundred snarky replies. Dad's where all her frustration springs from, not Fiona. Well, mostly Dad. Either way, arguing with her little sister isn't going to get her the answers she needs.

'Have you told Mum?' Alice asks.

'Not yet,' she replies.

'But you're going to?'

'She's got as much right to know as we have,' Fiona says with a stubbornness Alice has heard a thousand times growing up.

'I don't know that it's a good idea, Fi,' Alice says, feeling what could be the faintest warning tremors of a migraine lurking.

Fiona was only eight when their parents split. Too young to remember the half of it. He had already done a stretch inside before Fiona was born. Two years for theft. She's also too young to remember what came after that. Alice can though. The years of late-night yelling drifting through bedroom walls. Nights when Dad wouldn't even come home. Alice is still amazed that Mum ever found the courage to leave him. Even when she did, it was like cutting out a parasite from its host.

Takes a long time for the marks to truly fade, if they ever do.

'If I was her, I'd want to know,' Fi says, and Alice knows that she's going to tell Mum no matter what she says.

'What did *she* say then?'

Fiona exhales, long and slow, like the last puff of air from a deflating tyre. Alice waits her out while she gathers her thoughts.

'She said that he was arrested back in 2011 for killing a guy back in Florida, but he swears he didn't do it.'

Alice almost laughs at this, but catches herself. 'Oh well if he swears …'

'Don't be like that,' Fiona snaps.

'Like what?' Alice asks. She feels twin currents of anger and nausea. Her dad. A murderer. Not only that, but choosing now, of all times, to swing a wrecking ball back into their lives.

'This is serious, Al. They've got him in a place called Raiford, in Florida, and he's getting a lethal injection next Monday. Apparently, his solicitor has washed his hands of it.'

'Attorney,' Alice interrupts.

'Hmm?'

'Solicitors over here, attorneys over there.'

Fi gives her an arched eyebrow at the pedantic pick-up.

'Sorry,' Alice says, trying to take a little of the heat out of the situation. 'And was that it?' she asks, seeing Fi's nose crinkle in disapproval at how dismissive that sounded. 'I mean, was she literally just calling to tell us? Or is this his way of trying to get us to talk to him?'

'He doesn't know she called,' Fiona says.

A silence settles over the office as the two sisters stare at each other. Fi looks like she could tear up at the drop of a hat. For Alice, the news feels more like a cold compress across her chest. Numbing. Hard to feel after all these years for a man who couldn't feel enough towards his own family to keep them together. All the same, it's a peculiar sensation.

'She'd like to talk to us,' Fi says finally. 'Both of us.'

'And say what?' Alice turns her nose up at the thought.

'She says he's innocent. Says the police got it all wrong.'

'And what are we supposed to do about that?'

'I don't know,' Fiona spits back. 'But are you really telling me you're okay with knowing what's happening and not giving a damn whether he dies or not? He was a shit dad. Is that what you want to hear? Yes, he was shit, but that doesn't mean we should be fine if he dies.'

Fi's getting louder now, and Alice needs to bring her back down off the boil before colleagues and clients hear every sordid detail. She leans forward, places one hand over her sister's.

'You're right,' she says. 'I might not want anything to do with him, but I don't want him dead either. I just don't know what we can do for him, or her.'

Even now, she can't bring herself to say Mariella's name.

'We're not the only ones who are going to lose him, Alice,' Fiona says, sniffing loudly. 'You do what you want, but I'm going to talk to her again. I think you should too, but you please yourself. You always do.'

Alice counts to five in her head. Doesn't react to the jibe. Tries to wear the thirteen-year age gap like a big sister should. Take the moral high ground and not bite.

'Can I think about it?' she asks finally.

'Don't think about it too long,' Fiona says as she gets up. 'Or he'll be gone by the time you decide.'

Chapter Three

Monday – Seven days to go

As the door shuts behind Fiona, Alice closes her eyes, pinching the bridge of her nose between thumb and forefinger. Dad's face flickers into her mind. A version of him that hasn't existed for fourteen years.

A thought hits her head on, making her eyes snap open again. She powers up her laptop, does something she swore she'd never do. Opens Google. Types his name into the search bar, along with a few other key words.

Jim Sharp. Florida. Murder.

Unlike Fiona, she left his surname behind not long after she saw him last, switching to Mum's maiden name instead. Logan. Her finger hovers above the mouse button, afraid of what headlines might pop up. Only for a second though, before curiosity makes her click. And what she reads sends her falling, spiralling down a rabbit hole she thought she'd left in the past. It's all true. Her dad is a killer. Sad thing is, knowing that doesn't make him sink any lower in her estimation. You can't go any lower than rock bottom.

Chapter Four

Monday – Seven days to go

It's all there in glorious technicolour. Every major newspaper in the state has run with it. There hasn't been an execution in Florida since 2019, so it's getting its fair share of tabloid inches.

His mugshot stares out at her, a world away from the face she remembers. Gone is the rakish smile. The face she sees now just looks sad, like a kicked puppy. One who has lost the will to fight back. Dirty blonde hair like flattened straw. The wear and tear around his face is more canyons than creases. He's fifty-seven but could pass for late sixties, signature death row orange T-shirt hanging loose on his skinny frame.

Looks can be deceiving, she reminds herself. He might look the part of a wrongly accused prisoner, but Dad has always been good at putting on the face he needs the world to see to get his own way. Ted Bundy would get his fair share of swipes right on Tinder these days, but doesn't mean he'd make for a great first date.

She clicks on an article in the *Miami Herald*, and starts to read.

The man he killed was a small-time drug dealer out of Miami by the name of Manny Castillo. Popped his carotid with a single puncture wound if the prosecution is to be believed. And believed they were, by every single member of the jury. Alice flicks through half a dozen more articles, every single one of them laying it out as a slam dunk. Enough physical evidence to convict him many times over. His prints on a glass at the scene. Traces of cocaine on him that matched a batch they found at Castillo's place. A cocktail of other drugs in his own system that no doubt fuelled what happened that night. And as if all that wasn't enough, Jim Sharp had enough of Castillo's blood on the shirt he was wearing when they woke him up to arrest him, to double as a Jackson Pollock painting.

He denied it back then at trial, and at every appeal hearing in the eleven years that followed. Though what else would a man say when he's scheduled to be put down like a mangy animal?

Alice isn't sure how long she sits there staring at her computer screen before there's a knock at the door. It's more of a token gesture from Moira, who breezes in without waiting for a reply.

She starts rattling off the running order for Alice's day, but stops a few seconds in, tilting her head a few degrees.

'Everything okay?' she asks.

Alice nods, flashing what she hopes is a convincing smile, but Moira must see straight through it.

'Mr and Mrs Williams are due any minute. I can get Nicola or Sharon to see to them,' she says.

'Honestly Moira, I'm fine,' Alice says, but the attempt to sound fine falls far short of bright and breezy.

'Anything I can help with?'

'Wouldn't even know where to start if I'm honest,' Alice says, head still on spin cycle from Fiona's whirlwind visit.

Moira closes the door behind her, and steps closer to the desk.

'Tell me if it's none of my business,' she says, 'but speaking as a little sister myself, I know how much of a pain in the arse we can be. Truth be told, I pride myself on it. I'm sure that gap between you can feel like thirty years never mind thirteen at times. Whatever it is will pass.'

Alice wavers for a beat, determined to keep this morning's revelation to herself, but something has taken root inside, an anger that he's found a way, however dramatic, to work his way back into their lives. She has long since boxed up the part of her life that includes him, stashing it away in a dark corner. She was so angry at him for so many years, and pretending he doesn't exist has been the easiest way to deal with it.

Fiona is making a mistake if she thinks the call she got was nothing other than a 'by the way, thought you'd like to know'. Despite what Mariella told her sister, Dad has probably put her up to it.

Then there's the elephant in the room. Death row is as serious as it gets. Twelve people have sat on a jury and put her dad where he is. The fact that her father has killed someone washes over her like a wave breaking, and she finds herself telling Moira what little she knows. Keeps most of the backstory of her childhood to herself, sharing just enough to underline the fact he was a shitty dad.

Anger blooms as she talks, prickling in her flushed cheeks. But underneath it, there's a surreal sense of pity at the thought of him sat in a tiny cell, counting down the hours. What must be going through his mind right now, knowing that he only has days left? Is he remorseful, sat there tallying up his regrets? Is she one of them?

Moira sits quietly soaking it all in, poker face giving nothing away. When Alice has finished, she leans in and takes Alice's hand between hers.

'There's no right or wrong answer here,' she says, giving Alice's hand a squeeze. 'If you want to keep him in your rear-view mirror, nobody would judge you.'

'But?' Alice prompts.

'But this isn't an ordinary decision as to whether or not you let someone back in. Most families fall out. Difference here is that in seven days' time, this is getting taken out of your hands. Now, I'm not saying you have to believe he's innocent. You don't even have to talk to him. But right now, at least you have the option to. After next Monday, that's off the table. Whether you're okay with that,' she shrugs, 'only you can decide.'

'Fourteen years,' Alice says, as much to herself as Moira. 'I don't even know who he is any more.'

'Neither does Fiona,' Moira says. 'And maybe her spectacles are more rose-tinted than yours could ever be. But grief is a fickle thing. Lost my Nan in my early twenties. Cantankerous old bat of a woman. Still cried at her funeral. I'm not saying you'll shed a tear for him, but everyone takes losing a parent in their own way. Might be that Fiona came here first instead of your mum's because she doesn't know how she feels, and needs her big sister in her corner.'

Had she been so busy surrounding herself with enough flashes of failed fatherhood that she failed to see the real reason Fiona came here instead of heading to Whitley Bay to see Mum?

'You think I should do the call with Fiona?'

'I think whatever you end up doing, it'll be the right decision,' Moira says, and stands up.

'Guess I just need to decide what the hell that's going to be then,' says Alice, followed by a 'thank you'.

As silence settles back over her office she wonders what it must be like being cooped up in a cell, knowing that in seven days, you'll cease to exist. He ceased to exist for her a long time ago already. Will she feel differently about him after this? Will she feel anything? She'll find out soon this time next week.

Chapter Five

Monday – Seven days to go

'Thanks, Fi,' Alice says, hands curling around the coffee cup that Fiona offers. 'Sorry if my reaction wasn't what you were expecting. It's just more … complicated for me.'

'Sorry if I ambushed you.' Fiona returns the olive branch. 'But there wasn't exactly a subtle way to break that kind of news, you know?'

Something hard digs into Alice's backside as she sinks into the sofa. She reaches behind her and pulls out a plastic toy soldier.

'Sorry,' Fiona says, leaning forward to take it. 'Jake's obsessed by them. Little buggers get everywhere.'

There's the briefest of pauses, where Alice pretends they're just two sisters, catching up. Nothing more serious to pick apart than Trevor's efforts to get back in the good books, or Alice's disastrous foray into the world of online dating.

They have flashes of that, but their parents' choices that left them an ocean apart, have put paid to any chance of anything closer than what they have. The combination of a thirteen-year age gap, and the willingness to ignore a herd of elephants in whatever room they happen to be in for Mum's sake, makes for what can be an awkward coexistence at times.

'I googled him Fi,' Alice says, diving headfirst back into this morning's maelstrom. 'What they say he did, it sounds pretty brutal.'

'I googled too,' says Fiona. 'He says he didn't do it though. You hear about these miscarriages of justice all the time. I watched that thing on Netflix last month about the Central Park Five. I know he's no angel, but …'

'The stories I read,' Alice cuts in, 'they found his DNA at the scene, Fi. Dad even had the guy's blood on him.'

'If he says he's innocent, I believe him,' she says, practically pouting.

'Because he's never lied about anything before,' Alice says with a roll of her eyes.

'You're not exactly perfect on that front,' her sister snaps back. 'Doesn't mean I'd believe you'd kill someone.

'What's that supposed to mean?'

'Like you don't know?'

'Jesus, Fiona, I didn't come here to fight,' Alice says, forcing down her impulse to lash back. 'You turn up and lay that on me first thing in the morning … It's just a lot to take in, you know?'

Fiona's glare could sour milk, but she only holds it a second longer. She lets out a loud sigh, shoulders sagging.

'I just … it freaked me out when she called. You know how much I hate surprises, even the good ones, and this …' she pauses, searching for the right words. 'This is a pretty shitty surprise. All these years, the times I tried to reach out to him, I thought he was ignoring us. But he was in prison that whole time.'

They have phones in prison, Alice thinks. This is typical Fiona. Even now, her image of Dad is like one of those photos with the background blurred out. Just the central image in full focus. Fiona's is of a dad Alice wishes they both had, but he was never cut from that cloth.

'I don't know if I can talk to her,' Alice says, staring out through Fiona's living room window, wishing she wasn't cooped up inside. What she'd give to lace up her trainers and clear her head with a five-miler along the coast.

'Up to you. I am though,' says Fiona with a shrug. 'I don't want to wake up next week and hate myself for being too stubborn.'

The veiled jab in Alice's direction doesn't go unnoticed.

'I'd just rather speak to her with my big sister there beside me,' Fiona adds, slipping in a sucker punch that Alice, for all the layers she's insulated herself with, still feels digging in right under her heart.

How would it feel to have a conversation with the woman jointly responsible for breaking her family apart? To watch her tears spill out as she talks about the unfairness of it all? Alice feels her hackles rising until she sees the look on Fiona's face. It's as if all the usual brashness and bravado has been stripped away, paring her back to the eight-year-old girl who had blamed everyone but her dad for the break-up, and the move back to Whitley Bay that followed a few years later.

So many times since she left New York to come home, Alice has beaten herself up for not finding a way to reconnect better with her little sister. She'd been twenty-three and starting her dream job as a criminal attorney in

Manhattan. Fiona had only been ten, and not able to process why her big sister didn't want to make the move back across the Atlantic with them when their mother decided to return to the UK. Is it really worth adding another black mark against her name just to stay principled? There must be something of her indecision in her expression, and the hope that sparks in Fiona's eyes is the clincher.

'Fine, you win. If you want to speak to her, I'll be there with you. Can't promise I'll say much, but I'll be there.'

Fiona practically drops her own cup on the coffee table and launches into a hug that takes Alice by surprise. She flinches a touch as her sister's arms wrap around her, but only for a split second before returning the squeeze.

'Let me know when, and I'll be here.'

They keep the hug going for a five count, until Fiona pulls away, dragging a palm down her cheek, trying and failing to catch the stray tear before Alice can see it.

'Thanks Al,' she says folding her arms across her chest.

'I'd better get back to work,' says Alice. 'Call me when you work out a time with her.'

'Oh.' Fiona looks a little sheepish. 'I've kind of already done that. I'm FaceTiming her at two. You can just work from here while you wait if you like?'

'Jesus.' Alice exhales, 'You don't mess about, do you?'

'No point in faffing around with the time he has left,' Fiona says, uncrossing her legs, and standing up. She points to Alice's drink. 'Top-up?'

Alice feels a sensation in her stomach like she's just crested the first hill on a rollercoaster. No getting off the ride now.

Chapter Six

Monday – Seven days to go

Alice's eyes flick between the iPad on Fiona's kitchen table, and the clock on the far wall. The speed the last thirty seconds tick off, she's seen paint dry faster.

'Thank you for doing this,' Fiona says, reaching out to tap the screen.

'You said that already,' Alice replies with a nervous smile, like she's fixing bayonets to receive an enemy charge.

A melody warbles from the speaker as they wait for the call to be accepted. Alice has only actually seen Mariella Serrano in the flesh once. That was all it took to bust up a nineteen-year marriage. She'd been the one to see her dad's hands all over another woman. It was Alice that told their mum. Alice that Fiona had blamed for the carnage that followed.

She's spent the last couple of hours trying her best to work from Fiona's living room, but all the while imagining how this call will go. How it will feel. The cocktail of emotion from earlier was confusing enough; now that it's here, there's a nervous ache in her gut, like she's shrugging off a punch from hours back. What would they be doing if he was in a UK prison? Could she bring herself to see him in person? She's still focussing on that, hating the jangling nerves, when the call connects.

The face that snaps into view looks every bit as uncomfortable as her own. Wide-eyed, chewing on her bottom lip, the dark mane of hair Alice remembers now streaked with grey. The shadows under her eyes speak of sleeplessness. Big brown eyes like pools of infinite sadness. The room behind Mariella is a drab grey. Sums up the mood of the day, Alice thinks to herself.

She can't help but glance at the smaller window overlaid, containing her and her sister. Polar opposites looks-wise. Fiona has their mum's high cheekbones and almond-shaped eyes, framed by hair black enough to pass for tar. Whereas every time Alice looks in the mirror, she sees echoes of her dad's rounder face, the same ski-slope of a nose, and hair the colour of hay. Wishes they'd inherited the other way around.

'Hi,' says Fiona, holding up a hand like she's the new kid at school greeting the class. 'I'm Fiona, and this is Alice.'

Alice finds herself mimicking her sister's gesture on autopilot.

'Thank you so much for agreeing to speak,' Mariella says softly. 'I know this must have come as quite a shock.'

Alice catches the nervous laugh before it gets out. Instead what escapes sounds more like some kind of weird tic. 'That's one way to put it,' she says.

So much for her plan of letting Fiona do the talking.

'I know what you must think of me. The way things happened with your father and me. I just want you to know, he has never stopped loving you girls.'

Alice grits her teeth but says nothing.

'How is he?' Fiona asks.

Mariella shakes her head. 'Not good.'

'How often do you get to see him?'

'I've been staying with family, up here near Raiford. They're gonna let me see him every day for an hour between now and …' her voice trails off. 'Now and Monday.'

Alice wishes for Fiona's sake that she had the patience to do a softer version of this chat, but she has no desire to sit here and make small talk with the woman, no matter how tragic the circumstances.

'What happened to his attorney?' she asks. 'Why did they walk?'

The directness of the question seems to snap a little life into Mariella. She blinks and sits up a little.

'They had an argument. Jim, your dad, he wouldn't tell me what about. That was last Thursday, and the lawyer quit on Friday. Said there was nothing else he could do. Said it's a fight we can't win.'

'And you think he's wrong?' Alice asks.

Mariella shakes her head slowly from side to side. 'About winning? I'm not stupid. I know the odds are stacked against us, but I can't give up on him. I know he wouldn't if it was me in there.'

Ironic, thinks Alice. He gave up on her and Fiona easily enough.

'If he didn't do this,' Fiona chirps up, 'then who does he think did?'

'I've asked him that a hundred times,' she says. 'He'd had a few drinks after work. Says he can barely remember a thing from that night.'

Alice remembers only too well what her dad's version of a few is. This is starting to feel like a mistake. A waste of time. She isn't here for herself though, she reminds herself. This is the only chance to give Fiona closure on where their dad has been all these years.

'What kind of defence did his lawyer run with at the trial?' Alice asks. 'If Dad can't remember anything, how does he know what he did or didn't do?'

Mariella glances at her watch. 'He'll explain far better than I can,' she says, and her words send something clicking into place deep in Alice's subconscious. It's like her body realises what's about to happen before her brain catches up.

'Wait,' she says, her frown carving furrows in her forehead. 'Where are you calling from?'

Mariella's smile is somewhere between confused and nervous. 'The visitors' centre at Raiford. Your dad should be here any minute.'

Chapter Seven

Monday – Seven days to go

Alice whips her head round to look at her sister, but instead of shock, she sees sheepishness. She knew. She was expecting this. Alice opens her mouth to speak, when she hears a tinny buzzing sound through a speaker. Somewhere off screen, a door clicks open.

Alice's cheeks flush like she's stepped into a sauna. This isn't happening. Can't be happening. There's a squishy feeling in the pit of her stomach, like worms wriggling in a bucket.

She instinctively goes to rise, but feels Fiona's fingers dig into her thigh.

'Please.'

Fiona's whisper is borderline begging.

On-screen, Mariella shuffles over to one side, pulling across a chair, legs scraping like nails on a blackboard. Gives Alice goosebumps even from four thousand miles away.

And then he's there on screen. He stands, paused for a moment, and she wonders if the connection has dropped. Looks like he's staring directly into her eyes. She wonders if he even recognises them after fourteen years. Only stays frozen that way for long enough for him to process what he's seeing, and it's clear this is as much a surprise for him as it is her.

'Hey Dad,' Fiona says, and Alice knows without even turning that her sister is a heartbeat away from a flood of tears that could float an ark.

'Fiona?' he says softly, looking from the screen to Mariella and back again, then, 'Alice?'

Some things don't change. His voice is soft, whistling the second syllable of her name in an accent that's a mash-up of South Florida, with a little Georgia thrown in around the edges.

Last time they spoke it was Alice that had the most to say, more shouting than talking. Tearing a strip off him for the situation he had put her in, having to tell Mum what she saw. She remembers the look in her mum's eyes that day, like someone had snuffed out a light. Right now, there's none of that heat. It's like her brain has slipped into neutral.

'I told you I didn't want this for them,' he says to Mariella, with a hard edge to his voice. 'I caused these girls enough pain over the years. This shouldn't be how they remember me.'

Alice can't help the corners of her mouth turning down at that one. As if the memories they have of him are precious enough to safeguard. The fun-time dad that used to take them to the beach and the fair has long since been buried under layers of disappointment.

'It's too much, Jim,' Mariella says. 'I carried this on my own for too long, and they have a right to know.'

'That wasn't your story to tell, honey,' he says, but there's no venom in his voice. He's just staring at them, eyes flitting back and forth like flies looking for a place to land. 'But maybe this way I get a chance to apologise before it's too late.'

As if a few platitudes will gloss over the cracks. Alice's lips press together into a tight line, but everything she's harboured towards him these past fourteen years, longer in fact, seems just out of reach. All the anger, the resentment, the pure bloody frustration that he couldn't have put them first when it mattered.

Maybe it's got something to do with the sad figure he cuts as he slides into the seat beside Mariella. Like a boxer slumping onto his stool, but all she feels in this moment is pity. That passes the instant he slips an arm around Mariella's shoulder. Alice sucks in what feels like her first good lungful of air since the call began, and tries her best to press the emotional reset button.

'I'm sorry you girls have to see me like this,' he says. 'This isn't the kinda family reunion I'd have chosen.'

It's his lame attempt at humour that makes her snap.

'You think that's what this is, Dad?' she says, with just a hint of emphasis on the last word, so it slips out sarcastically. 'You had fourteen years to choose a better one.'

'And I've been in here for eleven of 'em,' he says.

'Stop,' Fiona snaps. 'Just stop. I'm sorry I didn't tell you he would be here, Al, but I didn't think you'd have stayed, and I need you.' She reaches across and grabs Alice's hand, squeezes it tight, like she'll fall if she lets go. 'I need you here now, and I'm going to need you when …'

She leaves the sentence hanging, as if it's bad manners to bring up someone's execution date.

'She's right about one thing though, Dad,' Fiona says. 'You should have told us sooner. We could have helped.'

'Don't see how, pumpkin,' he says, the pet name slicing through a decade and a half of absenteeism. 'They got me pretty good.'

'We could have found you a better lawyer,' Fiona ventures.

Jim Sharp shakes his head. 'It weren't the lawyer that put me here.'

No, thinks Alice. That was all you. Stabbing a man in the neck.

'Let's just say once the police had me, they didn't look too hard for anyone else. I've been sat here waiting for the needle ever since.'

'And that's what happened, is it?' Alice asks, sounding more cross-examining lawyer than daughter. 'Someone else killed him?'

'As God is my witness,' Sharp says, raising a hand like he's swearing on a stack of bibles.

'From what I read, the prosecution case was pretty tight,' Alice says.

She almost adds that she's seen plenty of long sentences handed down in cases with far more doubt, but he already looks whipped. He nods, a single slow movement, gaze drifting, thousand-yard stare fixing on the desk in front of him.

'I don't blame them you know, those people on the jury.'

His voice is quiet and his eyes flutter, lost in one of a thousand bad memories.

'They just done what they thought was right. Damn, the evidence they had against me, even I might have voted to convict.'

The laugh that comes out is high-pitched, nervous. Like a guy trying to break the ice on a date. She waits him out. Lets the silence grow, swelling around them, squeezing until it wrings the words out.

'I didn't do it,' he says, emerging from behind the bank of foggy memories. There's a hint of steel in his voice now. 'I didn't kill that man, but I suppose you get that a lot in your line of work. Assuming you're still a lawyer that is?'

'Occupational hazard,' she nods in agreement.

'I mean, I never even met him for Chrissake, why would I kill a man I don't know?'

Alice wants to tell him that he wouldn't be the first, and wonders, for his sake, if there's more to his story than a 'you gotta believe me'.

Instead she goes with, 'I read in the papers that you don't remember what happened that night.'

'What do you remember, Dad?' Fiona butts in, acting like a buffer to stop them squaring off.

He walks her through it as if it happened in a parallel universe, to another version of him. One who made better choices perhaps. The night it happened comes back to him now like a series of stills, he says. Snapshots of one bad decision after another.

'Work and me, I mean real work, we ain't never got on so well,' he says with a sheepish shrug. 'But I was trying to make a go of it all the same.'

'Car wouldn't start, so I needed a little something to unwind while I waited for the tow truck. Ended up at a bar, and one drink turned into five or six. Then this guy comes and sits next to me at the bar.'

He looks off camera, frowning as if he's trying and failing to visualise the scene in the bar eleven years ago.

'We started shooting the breeze about being underpaid and overworked. He bought me a couple more beers, and I …' he breaks off, face puzzled as he draws a blank. 'After that, next thing I remember is waking up on the floor, hearing someone hammering on a door. Barely opened my eyes when they came steaming in, pointing guns at me like I was in any fit state to do anything but lie there.'

The detached way he's described it at times makes it sound like it happened to someone else. An out-of-body experience that, from the way he's talking, isn't over yet.

'The police never found the guy from the bar.' Mariella steps into the silence he leaves behind. 'They say they looked, but …' She throws her hands up in exasperation.

'Is there nothing you can remember about him?' Fiona asks.

Sharp shakes his head. 'Not a thing.' His face screws up, voice rising, somewhere between anger and frustration, like his brain is a frozen computer that refuses to reboot. He breathes in deep. In through the nose, cheeks puffing as he exhales, coming back down, emotion leaching back out. 'I've not always made good choices. You girls of all people know that. Bad might even outweigh the good if I reckoned up. Me and the booze ain't a good mix. Never were. But there ain't no amount of liquor could make me do what they say I did to that man.'

'Tell them about Grant McKenzie as well,' Mariella says.

It's a name Alice recognises from the articles she's read.

'The homeless guy you said was on the street that night?'

Jim Sharp nods slowly. 'Disappeared before I went to trial.'

Alice decides it's time for some tough love. The kind she'd give if she was advising on the case.

'Even if they'd found him again to testify, that kind of statement doesn't sit well with juries. I read a quote from the bar owner, saying McKenzie always had a bottle within reach. Would have been too easy to pick apart on the stand. Too vague.'

For vague, read the worse-than-hazy recollection of a man who had already been a half-bottle of whiskey deep that night, not to mention the hundred that had probably come before it.

'But he saw your father leave.' Mariella leans towards the camera, eyes shining with a mix of anger and tears. 'He saw the other man too, the one from the bar.'

'He saw a man he thinks *might* have been Dad,' Alice corrects her, 'then disappeared himself. Never testified in the trial. From what I read, the police did an appeal at the time for other witnesses, but nobody came forward, and that was almost a decade ago, Mariella. Memories fade fast.'

'What about hiring a private investigator to find both of them?' Fiona asks, getting animated now, going into solution mode, leaning forward in her seat like the time that's passed has been forgotten and forgiven.

'We had a guy take a look before it went to trial,' Sharp says. 'But these guys cost money, and I ain't had a whole lot of that in a while.'

'Is that what this is?' Alice asks, things snapping into focus. 'You're here cap in hand?' She knows how harsh that sounds given his circumstances, but she can't help but give free rein to every ounce of anger inside.

Sharp turns to look at Mariella, then back to Alice, his face creased in confusion.

'What? No. I didn't even know I'd have a chance to talk to you girls, much less asking for any help. You ask me, I don't deserve either.'

Part of Alice wishes he'd put up more of a fight. She's not used to this version of him, all apologies and admissions. It's throwing her off balance.

'From what I read, it wasn't just booze you had that night,' she says, even as she feels her need to lash out dialling back a notch. The articles I've looked at from back then say you had fentanyl plus a few other bits and pieces in your blood as well.'

Statement of fact, not a question, but he picks it up as if it is.

'Never done drugs in my life,' he says firmly, as if the lab reports are in dispute.

'Then how do you explain what they found?'

'I can't,' he says, very matter of fact.

'Police also found three grams of cocaine in your pants pocket that came from a stash Manny Castillo had at his place. How else could that have gotten there if you didn't know him?'

'I don't know,' he says again, sounding frustrated now. 'Never touched that stuff in my life. I'm a drunk. Was a drunk,' he corrects himself, 'not a drug addict.'

'Reports say that it was a drug deal gone wrong,' she continues. 'That you'd had an argument, didn't want to pay, weren't happy with the product, something along those lines. Just because you can't remember, doesn't mean it couldn't have happened.'

'He's not on bloody trial now you know?' Fiona interrupts. 'Why are you being like this?'

'That's all right, honey,' Sharp says. 'She's got every right to be angry with me, me not being around to raise the pair of you.' He looks back at Alice. 'Amazes me they think I'd be able to see straight, let alone cut a man's throat,' he adds, and somewhere in Alice's head a cog turns.

From what little she's had a chance to read of Manny Castillo, he was a nasty piece of work. Stood trial for murdering his girlfriend three months before he died, but managed to walk thanks to a screw-up with the forensics. The mugshot she'd seen online had showed a man much younger and fitter than her dad. Castillo had been twenty-nine, and the very definition of the wrong side of the street. Had enough of a reputation that he should have been able to handle a drunk like her dad without breaking sweat.

'And how did you get home?' she asks, picturing the state his clothes would be in. Hard to blend in if you look like you work in an abattoir.

'I already told you,' he says, a frustrated zing in his words. 'I don't remember a damn thing! Car was in the shop so I figured the guy from the bar helped me out.'

It's circumstantial, and no surprise at all that it didn't convince a jury, or any appeal judge. She realises with a start what her subconscious is doing. She's trying to convince herself that he deserves to be where he is for more than just being a crap dad.

She's never worked a death penalty case, but ten years as a practising criminal attorney in Manhattan before she packed up and came home to look after Mum has left her with a better bullshit detector than most. Helped her find holes in cases involving everything from theft to murder, and the old defence attorney in her is seeing threads you could pull on.

A cab is unlikely given the state he was in, and with his car out of action, the only options left would have been hitching a lift or walking. No way anyone picked him in in that state. As for walking, sounds like it's a miracle he made it up the stairs to his apartment, let alone staggered the eight miles from Manny Castillo's place without being spotted by anyone, or picked up on CCTV.

'I know how it sounds,' he says, no edge to his voice now. 'And I don't blame you if you're sat there thinking I'm a murdering sonofabitch.' He leans back in his chair, a man with all hope squeezed clean out like a tube of toothpaste. 'I've not always been the best daddy, and I've made my fair share of mistakes. Lord knows there's been times when I just don't have the energy to fight this, but then I think of Mariella, little Anthony, and both of you girls too. How I'll never get a chance to make it right if I don't try. I'd give anything for a chance to put things right, with all of you. Thought that I might not get a chance breaks my heart.'

'Dad, who's Anthony?'

Calling him that feels awkward, ill-fitting even after all these years. But that's the least of her worries as her brain jumps ahead, joining dots she hopes she's misread.

Jim Sharp's face breaks into a nervous-looking smile, and he glances across at Mariella. 'You didn't say nothing?'

'Say nothing about what, Dad?' Fiona asks.

'Anthony's my son,' he says. 'Your baby brother.'

Chapter Eight

Monday – Seven days to go

It's like she's stepped into an icy pool. Same sharp intake of breath. Split second of panic as she tries to pivot, to readjust to the new reality his words have just slung at her. Beside her she hears Fiona stammering out more questions.

'Brother? Since when?'

It's like the air in here has taken on weight and form, clogging up her chest. She slaps both palms against the table, pushing up and away. It's too much. She can't breathe.

'Alice?' Fiona calls after her as she heads for the door.

'I need some fresh air,' is all she manages, then she's out in the narrow hallway, pulling the front door open hard enough that it bounces back on its hinges as she strides out. She sucks in lungful after lungful.

She's spent so many years rebuilding what her dad broke in her, learning to trust other people again. And now he slips back in, like a drunk driver T-boning someone at a junction.

Fiona's street is a quiet row of terraced brick houses. Quiet as a disused movie set. It's literally a stone's throw from Mum's house, as well as her own. Three points on a neat little triangle. Alice wonders how her mother will react to this. She'll do her best to steer Fiona away from telling her, but she knows her little sister, always the more impulsive of the two of them.

Alice perches on the raised front step and sits, head in hands, staring at the postage stamp of a garden. She hasn't smoked since she moved back from New York, but boy could she do with one now. She's not sure exactly how long it's been by the time Fiona follows her out.

Alice doesn't turn around as her sister shuffles down into the space beside her. Fiona's the one to break the silence.

'I didn't know anything about a brother, I swear.'

'You should have warned me he would be there, Fi,' Alice says, tone as hard as granite.

'Would you have stayed if I had?'

'Not the point and you know it.'

Another silence, punctuated only by more sniffs from Fiona.

'You're right. I'm sorry.'

'That thing still on?' Alice jerks her head back towards the house.

'No, he had to go. Mariella only gets him for an hour a day.'

'Is that it then?' Alice asks.

'Don't tell me there's not even a tiny part of you that thinks he could be innocent,' Fiona says, turning to face her. 'The way you started grilling him like you were in court.'

'DNA doesn't lie, Fi.'

'Neither would Dad. Not about this.'

'I know you weren't born the first time he went to jail. I was five, but I remember enough. That time was for theft. This is way more serious. You need to face up to the fact that our dad is not a good man.'

'He swore to me,' she says, 'on our lives and Anthony's, that he didn't do it.'

'Fiona, I—'

'He's got nothing, Alice. No money. No time. Remember when you worked in New York. You used to tell me about the pro bono stuff they'd let you do? How you loved that part of the job the most because you were standing up for the people who had nobody to fight for them. Well that's Dad right now.'

'I can't represent him, Fiona. I'm not licensed in Florida.'

'You don't need to be his lawyer to help him.'

'And I haven't got a couple of grand stuffed down the back of the couch to hire a PI for some kind of Hail Mary.'

'You don't need to hire one. Aren't you still friends with the one at your old firm? What was her name again? Sandra something or other?'

'Sofia, and yes I am, but I'm not asking her for help.'

'It's fine. I've already said I'll send them money anyway,' Fiona says in a haughty tone.

'Where are you going to get that kind of money from?' Alice narrows her eyes, dreading the answer.

'Trevor can lend me it.'

Fiona might be young, but she knows how to fight dirty. Alice wouldn't spit on that man if he was on fire for the way he treats her sister. But he's the father of her kids, and Fi keeps wiping the slate clean for him. She was only seventeen when he got her pregnant, and Alice just wishes Fiona had taken more time to work out what makes a man worth being with, before Trevor Biggs waltzed into her life. She'd tried telling her back then that just because he was the twins' dad, didn't mean to say he was right for her. But Fiona is nothing if not stubborn. Who knows, maybe a good psychiatrist would stick some sort of father figure label on it. Say she'd sought out a replacement for the one who had abandoned them both.

'I know you hate him,' Fiona continues. 'And you can hang on to that all you want. But I'm not going to let your hang-ups decide what kind of man I should be with. Not as if you're much of a relationship expert anyway, is it?'

'What's that supposed to mean?'

'I mean Trevor's my type, and you've got yours.'

'Which is?'

'Emotionally unavailable, career-focused, not likely to settle down for at least a decade.' Fiona counts the points off on her fingers. 'It's like you pick 'em to make sure there's no danger of anyone sticking around.'

'You can hardly talk,' Alice fires back. 'Trevor is a …'

'Oh will you forget about bloody Trevor,' Fiona snaps. 'This isn't about him, it's about Dad. So what if it's a one in a million shot? We have to try. Hating him for leaving doesn't carry the death penalty.'

'Fi, I just …'

'If you won't do this for Dad, then do it for me,' she says. Alice winces as the emotional cheap shot lands. 'Do it so I can look my kids in the eye when they're old enough to ask about their grandad.'

Fiona doesn't wait for a response. Just stands up and heads back in. No histrionics, no slamming of doors. Alice's head spins like she's stepped off a fairground ride. Somewhere behind her eyes, a base note thud of a headache finally kicks in.

Fiona's plea still reverberates around her heart. Set against it, though, is the fact that every emotional low point she can think of traces back to her dad. The two years when Mum had to work two jobs to avoid losing the apartment back in Orlando when Dad got sent away for burglary. Nights when Alice had to read Fiona's bedtime stories loud enough to drown out the muffled shouting when he came home drunk.

Alice remembers parents' evenings at school, the ones he turned up for anyway. How she'd look at the other dads. See the way they looked at their kids, pride positively radiating from them, while her own kept checking his watch, wondering if he'd make it to the bar for the big game kicking off.

Fiona's right about one thing though. All of that might add up to being a crap parent, but the punishment he's facing now is nothing to do with those crimes. She thinks of Lily and Jake. Of what they might think of her when they're older if she doesn't lift a finger now. And the brother she now has, as innocent in all of this as her niece and nephew. How old is he? Does he know she exists or has he been kept in the dark too?

So many reasons to do what Fiona is asking. Only one not to. She pushes up from the step, shaking her head in annoyance. Decision made. A fresh wave of anger rolls in across her, goading her to hate Dad all the more for being the architect of so much pain.

Chapter Nine

Monday – Seven days to go

Telling Mum is hard, but not as hard as Alice had anticipated. She lets Fiona do most of the talking. Watches as this new reality soaks in. Eyes widening at finding out the father of her children is a convicted murderer. But it's the mention of a son that seems to hit home most, sending a ripple of something across her features. Regret? Betrayal?

When Fiona has finished, Mum just sits there, speechless for once. When she eventually speaks, there's a flatness to her voice as the shock settles over her.

'He always had his demons, your dad did, but I never saw this in him. Are you sure he did what they're saying? Could it be one of those what do you call them, miscarriages of justice?'

Alice shakes her head slowly. 'I don't think so, Mum,' she says softly. 'From what I read it sounds pretty open and shut.'

Fiona arches an eyebrow. 'You've had a look though?'

'Just at the news reports, Fi,' she says, faintest of edges to her voice, hoping her sister isn't going to turn this into a two-on-one tag team.

'Surely he can appeal though?' Mum asks. 'He's entitled to do that at least?'

'He's been doing that for most of the last eleven years,' Alice says. 'It'd take a miracle to save him now.'

As she says it, she glances across to Fiona, seeing something in her eyes that borders on begging.

'Then that's what we'll pray for,' Mum says softly. 'Whatever he's done, nobody deserves to die like that,' she adds, one thumb pick, pick, picking at the skin on the other.

A brief smile flashes across Fiona's face. How can Alice stand alone in the face of so much willingness to forgive? She checks her watch. Almost three. That makes it nearly ten in the morning New York time.

'Quick call to make, then I'll do the cuppas,' she says, rising to her feet. She's used to her little sister getting her own way, but there's nothing smug about Fiona right now. She just looks … relieved.

Alice heads into the kitchen, grabs a glass of water, and settles in at the table. She props her phone up against the vase that sits in the centre, and taps to make her call. Despite everything that's happened today, a smile as wide as the River Tyne creases her face when Sofia Marquez pops on screen.

'Hola amiga,' Sofia says, flashing a smile of her own in return, with teeth straight out of a dental commercial. 'Is this you calling to tell me you've finally come to back to town to buy me the drinks you owe me?'

'I wish.'

The image wobbles as Sofia sets her own phone down and flops down into a high-backed chair, flipping her legs up to rest her feet on the desk. Sofia Marquez is second generation Mexican-American, hair as black as crow feathers, pulled into a severe ponytail. She still looks every bit the FBI agent; dove-grey suit pants, powder-blue shirt. It's the footwear that sets her apart. She has a seemingly infinite range of Converse, many of them personalised courtesy of Etsy.

Today's pair sport the Miami Marlins logo on either side, said fish arching itself around stitching on a baseball. Comfort over style, and as she challenges anyone who questions her choices, they should try chasing down a suspect in formal footwear before they raise an eyebrow over her fashion decisions.

'To what do I owe the pleasure then?'

Where does she even begin, Alice wonders? Must be something of her dilemma showing in her expression, as Sofia's eyes narrow while she waits. Alice has never been one to air her dirty laundry. Sofia is as close a friend as she made in New York. It's more than just a work friendship too. Alice had moved to the city with her best friend from college, Gail Lonsdale, the pair of them planning to take New York by storm. That dream had lasted three years, until Gail had been killed in a hit-and-run on a trip back to Orlando. In the absence of her own family, Sofia had been the shoulder Alice had cried upon.

She had blamed herself, having been due to head home with Gail only to cancel thanks to a stomach bug. Told herself if she'd been there, things would have been different. She'd have found a way to save her best friend. Couple of years' worth of counselling hadn't rid her of the guilt. She wore it like a twisted keepsake even now.

Still manifests in bad dreams and panic attacks. She can keep it at arm's length most of the time, but when it hits, it hits like a tidal wave.

Alice opts for a slimmed-down version for now.

'And he thinks that this mystery guy from the bar is the ace up his sleeve?' Sofia asks when she's finished.

'Yes, maybe, I don't know.' She throws her hands up in exasperation. 'Honestly, this is more likely to turn out to be a wild goose chase, but Fiona will never forgive me if I sit on my arse and do nothing.'

'I do this, you come to Manhattan before the year's out.'

Statement, not a question. Alice's smile returns at the prospect. The thought of a week away feels like heaven right now. The thought of slipping away from doing the early morning trips to Mum's, even just for a few days, washes over her like a guilty pleasure.

'Deal,' she says, and it feels good to have something to look forward to. 'And in the meantime, if you happen to have any contacts down Florida way that do pro bono …'

'Gimme a couple of hours,' Sofia says.

Alice makes good on her promise of cuppas, and when she walks back through with three cups and a packet of biscuits on a tray, it's as if none of the last few hours has happened.

Mum is chatting away, Fiona leaning forward in her seat, hanging on every word. Mum must have just dropped a punchline because Fiona tips her head back laughing. It's a little too loud though, a few decibels above nervous.

'What've I missed?' Alice asks as she hands out the cups.

'Ah, Mum was just telling me about the time Dad bought a truck load of Louboutin shoes from a guy he knew. Thought he'd won the lottery 'cos he paid peanuts for them. There was a burst pipe in the storage unit he had them at and turned out the red soles were just sprayed on. Place looked like a crime scene with all the paint running off them.'

Alice manages a smile, but it's skin-deep only. Typical Dad story, always trying to make a fast buck. One of the reasons he'd moved them from the North East to his home state of Florida in the first place. He'd always had a knack of sniffing out the wrong crowd. Now's not the time to tell funny stories about him though. Feels too much like the kind of tale someone would drop at a wake.

Hey, remember when Old Jim screwed up again?

Not the kind of conversation she needs right now, so she excuses herself after five minutes, saying she has a few conference calls to do from the car. Once outside though, she walks right past the car, keeps going until she hits South Parade, and follows the downhill curve all the way to the Promenade.

A brisk breeze whips white caps onto the waves that roll in towards the beach. Alice reaches the railings that look out over the North Sea, leans forward, arms draped over them, and closes her eyes. Stands like that for a full minute, focussing on her breathing. In through the nose, out through the mouth. Every exhalation feels like she's shedding a layer of the heavy cloak her dad's revelations have draped over her.

Even after all these years, the loss of her best friend is like an open wound. A chink in her armour that a series of crippling panic attacks had slipped through in the aftermath. She hasn't had one since she left New York City, but today was pretty damn close. From the moment she found Fiona in her office this morning, the pressure in her head has been a rising barometer. Dad's casual mention of a brother she never knew existed had leaned in hard, crowding out what little headspace she had left.

Mum and Fiona see her as the strong one. Diamond-hard and unbreakable. Maybe she had been before the accident that robbed her of her best friend on a night out that she herself should have been at. Would it have happened any differently if she'd been there? Could she have seen it coming? Pushed Gail out of the way?

It had left her feeling all alone in a city that can be as intimidating as it is exciting. Maybe she'd have left there eventually even if Mum hadn't had her stroke.

Alice opens her eyes, takes in the full sweep of coastline. The lazy arc of sand that curves away from Whitley Bay, all the way along to St Mary's Island, where the lighthouse stands proud, like a gleaming white chess piece. She starts to walk towards it, past a row of seafront cafés.

It's a typical northern autumn day, October sunshine still bright enough to be a spotlight, making the sand seem to glow against the dull blue tide. The wind slips its cool fingers down the back of her neck. She picks up the pace, striding past the row of sculpted metal sandcastles, until the dome of the Spanish City comes into view, gleaming white like a mini Taj Mahal. It's all changed so much since she was a kid. Memories from back then are happier than the ones that followed, but that's not saying much.

As she turns inland up towards the few remaining amusement arcades, she makes a pit stop at Di Meo's for a two-scoop tub of cookies & cream. Almost feels like she's putting distance between herself and the family shitshow. Almost.

She stares at herself reflected in the chilled glass cabinet, watching huge dollops of ice cream get carved from a mini-mountain. Mum keeps telling her that she'd blow away in a strong wind. Dad used to say she'd fill out when she grew up but the willowy frame is here for the long haul.

When she hangs left past the Playhouse theatre, she can't help but remember the Christmas pantomimes that Mum and Dad brought her to here back in the day. Some of the few memories of him that still feel remotely positive. Her thoughts are dragged back kicking and screaming to a prison cell four thousand miles away.

Would he have ended up there if he and Mum had stayed together? Had she inadvertently set him on that different path when she told Mum what she'd seen? No, you can't live your life by a string of what-ifs. What happens next though is anyone's guess. She wouldn't put it past Fiona to be pricing plane tickets by the time she gets back though.

Alice heads back into Whitley Bay town centre, parking herself up on a bench for a while to check in with Moira. Satisfied that the office hasn't crumbled, Alice meanders back along Whitley Road, taking her time to try and unravel the tangled ball of thoughts. Isn't sure what label she'd put on her feelings right now. It's nothing like the anticipation of grief she imagines if it were her mum or Fiona. But it's not nothing either. No need to give it a name just yet.

When she walks back into the living room, the only sign either of them has moved is the fresh packet of biscuits on the tray.

'Fiona's popped fish and chips in the oven for us,' Mum says.

'Do you not need to get back for the kids?' Alice asks.

'Trev's bringing them here,' says Fiona. 'Should be here any minute.'

Rock and a hard place for Alice. She'd happily never set eyes on Trevor again if she could help it. The way his eyes slide over her like she's a tasty snack even though Fiona is in the room. Flip side though is she gets to see Jake and Lily. Bonus is that with them around, the Dad-related chat should be kept to a minimum.

The only place she can't escape it is in her head. That's where, in the darkest corners, the thoughts that whisper loudest live. The ones she can never say out loud in present company. Ones that say maybe it's a shame they couldn't have found out about all of this seven days from now. Ones that say her newly discovered brother's best chance at a happy childhood might be one without Dad in it.

She can't decide what's worse. Having these thoughts, or not feeling the need to apologise for a single one of them.

Chapter Ten

Monday – Seven days to go

Jake and Lily blow into the house in a whirlwind of limbs and laughter. Trevor saunters in behind them, nodding a hello, letting his eyes linger longer than they need to. He makes Alice's skin crawl, and she wonders if it's just a family trait to have the worst taste in men. What Fiona sees in him, she'll never know. He's more her age than her sister's, belly hanging over his belt like icing running off a cake, and hair that's millimetres away from being a mullet.

'Auntie Alice, Auntie Alice, look at this.'

'Auntie Alice, do you want to draw with me?'

The requests come in machine-gun fast. Barely time to think let alone answer each one. Their energy is infectious, and Trevor's lecherous gaze is quickly forgotten. Alice revels in her role as cool auntie like she was born to play it, although part of her knows it's fuelled by the guilt of not seeing them as often as she should.

She's halfway through a game of noughts and crosses with Lily when a sobering thought hits her. It's the twins' birthday this week. They'll be blowing out their candles, making a wish, while their grandad's clock counts down his remaining hours. The confluence of it all is unsettling.

She shakes it off, accidentally on purpose puts her cross in a spot that lets Lily win, and anchors herself back in the room. Bad enough they barely see her, that she should waste that time getting distracted by the memory of a man she hasn't seen in fourteen years.

No sooner does Fiona start plating up in the kitchen, than Alice's phone purrs. Sofia. Alice makes her excuses, and heads out into the back yard, popping a pair of AirPods in.

'You seen my email yet?' Sofia asks, cutting straight to the chase.

'Nah, I've been too busy getting my arse kicked at noughts and crosses by a four-year-old,' she says. 'What's it say?'

'What am I, your secretary now?' Sofia laughs. 'Open it up while we talk. I'll give you the highlights.'

Alice swipes back to her home screen and taps to open her inbox. Sure enough, there it is, received twenty minutes ago. First thing she sees is a series of bullet points covering the timeline of arrest to present day.

- *Manny Castillo murdered Feb 11 2011*
- *Jim Sharp arrested Feb 12 2011*
- *Jim Sharp convicted August 26 2011*
- *Jim Sharp confirmed execution date October 26 2022*

It's a reminder of just how meticulous and structured Sofia is. Doesn't extend to her home life, from what she remembers of Sofia's place the times she's been over for dinner. But her ability to dig through a heap of data the size of Mount Everest, and distil it down to a selection of choice morsels is priceless.

Next is a string of attachments. A quick scan of titles shows arrest report, forensics, toxicology, the works. She starts to click into them as Sofia rattles through a summary at a pace, wincing as she flicks past crime scene photos. Not the kind of thing she wants to dwell on.

At the time of his arrest, other than the stint inside Alice already knew about, her dad had nothing more than a few traffic tickets. Not that this was any indicator of guilt or innocence when it comes to murder, but for the kind of story the prosecution built their case on, a drug deal gone wrong, you'd usually see a trail of breadcrumbs leading up to it.

'You think I'm crazy for even looking, don't you?' Alice asks when she's finished.

'Thought that for years.'

'Like I said earlier, it's more for Fiona than me. At least this way I can say I tried.'

'And in this case, you're absolutely right to,' Sofia shoots back, catching Alice off guard.

'What's that supposed to mean?'

'I mean this one might not be as lost a cause as you think.'

Chapter Eleven

Monday – Seven days to go

'There's the circumstantial bits you talked me through yesterday, sure,' Sofia says. 'Could your dad have overpowered Castillo? Sure. You pump enough booze and coke into someone, they'll take on King Kong and have a fighting chance. Does the toxicology report support what I see at the crime scene? Not so much.' Sofia wrinkles her nose.

'How so?'

'The wound to Castillo's neck was made by something real sharp. Single wound, so something that slid right in, popped him like a piñata. They never recovered the weapon. Question is, do we believe that your dad had the presence of mind to ditch the knife somewhere nobody finds it, but forgets to change his shirt?'

'Did that come up at trial?'

Sofia nods. 'His attorney tried to argue that, but the prosecution objected for speculation and the judge agreed.'

'What about his journey from the scene back home?'

'Another thing that doesn't sit right. Castillo didn't live in the best of neighbourhoods. No CCTV in the building itself, or around the entrance. Don't get me wrong, there's plenty around the further out you look. You can barely fart in any major city without it being caught on a half-dozen cameras these days. They looked in a one-mile radius, then it got a bit half-hearted after that. I plotted the cameras they looked at on a map though, and for your dad to have avoided them all, there were literally two routes he could have taken, neither of which made sense.'

'How do you mean?'

Sofia tells her to open one particular attachment, and up pops a map of Manny Castillo's neighbourhood.

'You can see where I've marked Castillo's apartment,' she says. 'And the red line is the direction your dad would have taken if he walked back to his place. Blue dots are cameras they checked the footage on, and the black lines are the two routes that avoid them.'

Alice sees a pair of dark lines snake in and out of streets on screen, both heading away from the supposed safety of home, before they double back.

'Again, the caveat of anything is possible, but they'd have us believe that he was so amped up that he commits this heat-of-the-moment crime, yet just happens to have the perfect escape route plotted. You can't back both horses there.'

'You think they missed something?'

'Not here, no,' she concedes, 'but it would have bugged the hell out of me if it was my case. Feels like this was just too nice and gift-wrapped for them to consider anything else.'

'None of that touches the foundations of their case though,' says Alice. 'The blood, the fingerprints on the glass.'

'No, it doesn't,' Sofia agrees. 'And again, I'll preface this by saying it might be nothing, but the toxicology is all wrong for how they spun it.'

'In what way?'

'Doesn't add up. They claimed it was a coke deal gone wrong, and fair enough, they found coke around your dad's nostrils, and on a bank note in his pocket. Doesn't stack up against the rest of the toxicology though. There was barely any trace of coke in his system, nothing near what you'd expect if he'd actually done a few lines.'

'You're saying he hadn't used any?'

'Some maybe, but not as much as the prosecution made out. Then there's the rest of it. They found traces of fentanyl. If you're on a coke binge, you're a race car on the tracks. The rest of that stuff is the equivalent of slamming on the brakes. Doesn't make sense that he'd be doing both at the same time.'

'What did they say about that at trial?'

'They didn't.'

'Seriously?'

Sofia shrugs. 'Bigger fish to fry. My guess is they had tunnel vision around the blood and prints. Besides, unless you're an expert witness, or expert user, it's the kind of thing that could slide past you.'

'Still largely circumstantial though,' she says, then sees something in Sofia's expression that hints at more.

'You know me. All about saving the best for last,' Sofia says. 'The other stuff that showed in his bloods, it's an unusual combo. What's really unusual is that they both had the exact same mix.'

'Both? You mean Castillo as well?'

Sofia nods. 'So, I took it one stage further, and had a look for any other cases where this, or a similar combination of narcotics showed up.'

Alice feels her pulse quickening, a sense of something about to click into place. Sofia isn't one for hyperbole. If she thinks Dad's isn't a lost cause, then there'll be substance to it. And what's good enough for someone like her is generally a good enough ripcord to reach for.

'And there wasn't another one like it in the entire continental United States,' she finishes, and her words are a needle, pricking a bubble of anticipation Alice hadn't realised was there.

'I called in a favour with a friend from GALE,' Sofia continues, 'and they found one in Europe though.'

And just like that, the rollercoaster is heading up again.

'GALE?' Alice asks. Not a name she's familiar with.

'Global Agency for Law Enforcement. They're a multi-country taskforce, with cross-border jurisdiction in any member state.'

'How similar are we talking?'

'Same drugs in killer and victim, same single puncture wound to the carotid. No murder weapon found and same defence of "I didn't do it" when they found him passed out at his place after an anonymous tip-off. Only real difference is this guy has a record as long as my arm.'

'Where was this? When?'

'Paris, France. Little over two years ago. Guy by the name of Alain Dufort killed a man called Viktor Semenov.'

The possibility still feels too big to wrap her arms around, but she asks the question anyway.

'How likely is it that the same person committed both killings four thousand miles apart? That's a tough sell without anything more substantial.'

'Agreed,' says Sofia. 'It'd be great if there was some kind of harder link between the cases like, say, if someone had been involved in both.'

There's something in her tone that makes the hairs on Alice's neck stand up.

'What are you saying?'

'Look at the arrest report for your dad.'

Alice riffles through the pages on her desk, searching for the right one, but there are dozens, spreading out like a messy deck of cards.

'Just tell me already.'

Sofia drops a name, and it's like Alice has trodden on a landmine, thoughts scattering like shrapnel. A name she's seen just moments earlier. An Orlando PD detective. The same man who arrested her dad has put someone else behind bars for practically the same crime, thousands of miles away. The lawyer in her shouts loudest, tells her this can't be a coincidence.

Former Orlando detective, now serving agent with the GALE Paris field office. Luc Boudreaux.

Chapter Twelve

Monday – Seven days to go

Her thoughts tick over like an idling engine, conjuring questions, looking for a weak spot.

'And this detective, Boudreaux, how does someone end up swapping Orlando PD for Paris?'

'That'll take a little more time,' Sofia says.

'But he's responsible for this Dufort guy too?'

'Uh-uh,' Sofia says. 'Not directly, not that I can see anyway. He works in people trafficking now from what my contact says. Part of the same unit though.'

In Alice's line of work, coincidences are rarely what they seem. Since she requalified as a solicitor on this side of the pond, she doesn't have the same opportunities to pull witnesses apart in court, but she's seen enough coincidences fall apart when prodded with the right questions.

'I tried calling Boudreaux,' Sofia continues. 'He shut me down in under two minutes. Said he had nothing else to say that wasn't on file already. Better news on Alain Dufort though. My contact said they could get us a Zoom interview with him if we want it.'

'Is this crazy, Sofia, Boudreaux aside, to think that a murder committed while my dad was already on death row has any connection whatsoever? Even just saying it out loud sounds stupid.'

'You want reasonable doubt. Here it is. We have a detective involved in two unusual cases, with way too many similarities. A missing drinking buddy who could vouch for your dad's movements, who didn't come forward, not even to help save his life. A very specific cocktail of drugs in killer and victim in both cases. The odds that four men on opposite sides of the Atlantic decided to party with the exact same combo, and two of them then meet their fate courtesy of a carbon-copy MO?'

Alice's mind whirrs around like an overactive hamster on a wheel. This was meant to be about pacifying Fiona. Being able to lay old ghosts to rest without any chance of 'what-ifs' when he's gone.

'Things add up like this, you start to prise open that window of doubt,' Sofia adds. 'I say we poke Boudreaux and Dufort with a stick, see what else we can rustle up. I've still got more documents to review from the original case files. Give me one more day with them, and I'll set up the two calls day after tomorrow. What do you say?'

Alice's head is adrift on a current, battered by the twin winds of past and present colliding.

'Yeah,' she replies eventually, 'let's do that. Can you send me copies of the rest of it too?'

They agree to touch base first thing New York time tomorrow, and Alice ends the call. She heads back inside, feeling a little punch-drunk. Where does she even go with this? She isn't her dad's attorney. Has no desire to be. But the call with Sofia has left her with a sense of uneasiness.

Fiona must have been listening for the back door, because Alice is barely halfway down the length of the galley kitchen when her sister appears at the other end, closing the door behind her.

'Well? Was that her?'

Alice nods, deciding how to play it. As intriguing as the parallels between the cases are, the last thing she needs right now is Fiona seeing this as a get out of jail free card for Dad.

'Yep,' she nods. 'There's a few things she's going to look into.'

Fiona's face crinkles in disbelief. 'That's it? Uh-uh, you're not fobbing me off with that. You've got that look on your face. Not quite pissed off, but not exactly dancing for joy.'

'It's complicated, Fi,' Alice tries, but her sister won't let it drop.

'And I'm not the same age as my kids, Al. Now's not the time. If it's bad, just tell me. Don't sugar-coat it.'

Fiona's tone rankles her, like she's an employee being ordered about, not an older sister calling in favours on behalf of a man she would rather had just stayed out of her life. To hell with it. She gives Fiona the full rundown, opens Sofia's email, lets the screen linger a little longer than necessary on the crime scene photos, then feels instantly bad about it when she sees Fiona's face pale.

Behind them, the kitchen door opens a crack, and a small face appears.

'Maaaam,' Lily says in a pleading tone. 'Can I have some cake now?'

'In a minute sweetheart,' Fiona says. 'Go and finish your dinner first.'

'But I finished it already. Can I …'

'I said not yet.' Fiona snaps this time. 'Now do as you're told.'

Lily retreats with a bottom lip jutting out like a ledge in protest.

'So, what do we do now?' she asks Alice when the door clicks shut again.

'Now we wait and see if this Dufort fellow will speak with Sofia.'

'And the policeman? What did you say his name was?'

'Boudreaux.'

'He can't just ignore us, surely?'

Alice almost smiles at her sister's innocent indignation. If only all problems could be solved by being as self-assured as Fiona.

'He can do whatever the hell he wants, Fi. Not like we can just go knock on his door and refuse to leave till he talks to us.'

Fiona folds her arms, and the look she gives is pure insolence.

'Why not?'

Alice can't help but laugh at her sister's naivety. Imagines her sat pouting in a waiting room like she's claiming squatter's rights.

'Because you just can't.'

'We'll see about that,' says Fiona.

'Fi,' Alice says, no attempt to disguise the parental tone in her voice. 'Whatever you're planning …'

'I can be there and back in a day. Two tops if he makes me wait.'

'Don't be bloody stupid,' Alice snaps. 'If there's anything to find, Sofia will dig it up.'

'From thousands of miles away?'

'It'd be a waste of time and money.' Alice tries a different tack, knowing how stubborn her sister can be when she sinks her teeth into something. 'Besides, who's going to look after the kids? It's half term and Mum can't exactly keep an eye on them, and everyone else will be working.'

'It's fine, Trev will take a few days off.'

'And literally sit them in front of the TV the whole time,' Alice says, frustration adding a few decibels.

'Small price to pay when it's literally life and death,' Fiona counters.

'Will you listen to yourself?' Alice says through gritted teeth. 'You do realise it's 99 per cent nailed on that he killed somebody. Literally stabbed them to death.'

'At least you admit there's a one per cent chance he didn't,' Fiona says with a smugness that rubs against Alice like sandpaper.

'You're not going,' Alice says, feeling the fight slipping away from her.

'You can't stop me.' Fiona turns on her heel to head back into the dining room.

'Wait,' Alice says, hating the desperation in her own voice. Knowing that if her sister walks back through there she'll start making arrangements with Trevor. Never mind the fact that Trevor doesn't deserve the trust she puts in him; Fiona in Paris would be a car crash. Way out of her depth. Best-case the detective ignores her. Worst-case, she's stupid enough to try and bluff her way into a prison to speak to a man who, as far as they know, has no connection to her father.

'What? You gonna tell me how stupid I am? How I should grow up and be more like you? Not giving a shit whether a parent lives or dies?' Fiona's words are darts, designed to hurt.

Alice feels like she's teetering on the edge of a precipice. Doesn't want to lose her sister as well as her dad, for all she feels disconnected to the prospect of the latter. What other option does she have?

'I'll do it,' she says, words tumbling out before she can talk herself out of it.

'Do what?'

'You can't leave the kids and disappear off to Europe. I'll go to Paris.'

The angst in Fiona's face melts away, replaced by a grateful smile – but not before Alice spots a flash of something else. Takes her a second to decipher it, but she's pretty sure there's a glint of satisfaction. Has she just been played? The thought that her twenty-two-year-old sister might have rounded her up like livestock gets her hackles up, but there's no way to reverse back out of this cul-de-sac without repercussions that'll last long after Dad is dead.

'You're the best, sis,' Fiona says, beaming now, and whirls around, disappearing into the dining room, leaving Alice alone with her thoughts.

Is she really going to do this? She doesn't see a way out if it now. So much to plan. Meetings to cancel or switch to virtual. Flight and hotel to book. All for what is almost certainly nothing more than an exercise in family loyalty. Well, at least to the people she still considers family.

Chapter Thirteen

Tuesday – Six days to go

Despite her head feeling battered by storm winds, or maybe because of it, Alice falls into one of the deepest sleeps she's had in ages, filled with vivid flashes of memory. A trip to Daytona Beach the year they moved out to Florida. That had been a great holiday. A happy island in otherwise uncertain waters. The dream was pretty true to life, all save the last part. Instead of bundling them all back into the old Cadillac Eldorado convertible he had apparently won in a card game, this version of her dad had turned and walked into the waves without so much as a goodbye. Her nine-year-old self had shouted at him to turn back, tried to follow him even into water way colder than Florida surf had any right to be, but every time she tried, she was picked up by a wave and dropped on the beach like driftwood.

It was vivid, the kind of dream that takes a few seconds to reorientate yourself back into the world. Alice's throat is dry, tight, as if she's been crying, and she reaches for the water by her bedside, gulping down half the glass. Her bedside clock reads four fifteen. Two hours before her flight.

She swings her legs out of bed, trudges to the bathroom and runs the shower as cold as she can bear. She's had the presence of mind to pack a small carry-on last night, so as soon as she's dried and dressed, she grabs a banana and bottle of water that'll pass for breakfast, and grabs her car key from the hallway table.

Percy Road is deathly quiet as she pulls out and follows the coast around. She winds down her window, listening to the rhythmic pound and retreat of the surf that seeps into the car from the beach below. Took her a little while to fall back in love with the North East when she came home, but it's worked its way bone marrow deep again. Would she move back to Manhattan now, she wonders, if, God forbid, anything happened to Mum?

If you'd asked her that for the first six months, maybe even twelve, it would have been a toss-up. But as much as Manhattan excited her at times, the North has a way of reeling its prodigals back in. The countless walks along miles of coastline and stretches of beach that are food for the soul. They soothed her, at a time when life felt like a snow globe rolling down a mountain. Mum's stroke had come right after a less than memorable office romance turned bad. That, plus the sad echoes she still felt from the space in her life where her best friend should be, meant the homecoming acted as a form of therapy. Slowly but surely it ground the New York varnish away. If home is where the heart is, hers is buried in the beaches of North Tyneside, and the rolling hills of Northumberland.

Forty-five minutes later she's checked in and waiting in line for coffee. Moira has ruthlessly rearranged Alice's diary for the next few days, including leaving a completely clear morning today, so Alice can focus on the task at hand.

Sofia's brownie points balance is at an all-time high too. She's arranged a tour guide in the form of her GALE contact, an agent by the name of Eva Monteiro. Between Sofia and Monteiro, they've managed to wangle Alice a visit with Alain Dufort. Whether she gets to speak to Boudreaux after that remains to be seen.

Her phone buzzes with two early-morning texts from Fiona in quick succession. The first is an audio file, the second a message that makes Alice shake her head.

Recorded the chat with Dad yesterday. Thought it might come in handy.

Reliving that emotional ambush is the last thing she wants to do right now, if ever. All the same, she plays nice, texting back a thank you.

The flight takes around an hour thirty-five, all of it dedicated to her dad and Alain Dufort. Thanks to a window seat and privacy screen on her MacBook, prying eyes aren't a concern, and she pores over the files that Sofia has shared.

She opens those relating to the Frenchman first. Dufort is no stranger to prison. The phrase 'career criminal' always strikes her as a misnomer, as if it's something you might have chatted through with your guidance counsellor instead of law or banking, but it fits here. With three previous custodial sentences, and time in a juvenile facility before that, Alain Dufort is not exactly a model citizen.

His offences have escalated over the years, along with his climb up the ranks of organised crime. From petty theft to drugs, then stepping up to assault before he peaked at murder. Dufort's victim was no angel either. Viktor Semenov had moved to Paris from St Petersburg for a job in construction, and had been arrested earlier that year after he'd put his girlfriend in hospital. The details of this investigation aren't included, but Semenov hadn't been charged, even after his girlfriend had her life support machine switched off. His and Dufort's lives had no intersection that the gendarmerie could find, until the night of the murder.

Semenov was found in a boarded-up bar, served up on the counter, carotid artery leaking like poor pipework, blood pooling out in place of spilled drinks, a dark, tacky waterfall. Unlike her dad, Dufort had been found at the scene, slumped in a dusty booth, half-drunk bottle of vodka cradled like a sleeping baby. When police arrived after a tip-off about a break-in, they found an ice pick coated in Semenov's blood sat atop a stack of paper towels.

Toxicology could have practically been copied and pasted from Manny Castillo's. A mind-bending mix of fentanyl and midazolam. Enough, Dufort's defence argued, to make it unlikely that he would have had the coordination to attack Semenov in anything other than a child swatting a piñata kind of way. Apart from the puncture wound to Semenov's artery, the dead man didn't have a mark on him. Certainly nothing to suggest the drink and drug-fuelled tussle the French police hung their case on.

Just like Dad, Dufort insists he's innocent. He'd been on a night out with friends, none of whom recalled seeing him leave. The last activity on his phone had been a text exchange with an old flame he'd been flirting with again. Nothing between his disappearance and being rudely awakened by officers slapping cuffs on him.

Alice opens the notes app on her phone, tapping in questions as they float to the surface. Some for Dufort, some for Boudreaux, some for both. She's on a second read-through of Dad's file by the time the captain announces their approach into Charles de Gaulle, and she pauses to glance out of the window at Paris creeping towards them. Patchwork quilts of green fields gradually give way to a more industrial palette as they flirt with the northern edge of the city.

The Seine snakes off to the south, a flash of sunlight making it shimmer like tinfoil, and Alice wishes that her first visit here could have been more about browsing a city that's steeped in so much history and culture. A voice whispers in her head that a big part of this trip is about her though. It's not just her chance to be the big sister that Fiona needs to see her through this. Dad went to ground after she outed his affair. Left them all to fend for themselves, and never looked back once to see if they were okay. If she's being brutally honest with herself, she doesn't expect anything other than confirmation of what the jury has already decided. Proof that her dad is as bad a man as she thinks, worse even. She's carried so much anger with her for so long, maybe in a twisted way, that this will be the closure she needs.

Alice drifts through arrivals, and out into the morning sunshine. Sofia has arranged for Agent Monteiro to meet her here, but Alice can't see anyone who resembles the headshot Sofia shared. A row of black taxis stretches along the road.

Alice checks her watch. A little early thanks to a tail-wind. She has a number for Monteiro and starts to scroll through her contacts, but looks up as a Mini Cooper the colour of caramel ice cream bumps up onto the kerb. She recognises Monteiro despite the oversized mirrored shades, and hair bouncing around her shoulders rather than scraped back like in the picture she's seen. She looks a lot better put together than Alice feels after her early morning start. Hair so dark it seems to absorb light. Olive skin and dark brown pools for eyes. Thirty-something at a guess, but hard to stick a pin in exactly where on that scale.

'Miss Logan.'

Monteiro strides over, hand outstretched. Alice takes it, trying to inject a touch more joie de vivre into her tired smile than she's feeling.

'Agent Monteiro. Thank you so much for helping me at such short notice.'

Monteiro shrugs. 'It's nothing, and please, call me Eva. Unless I'm arresting you, the agent thing makes me feel like an extra from *Men in Black*.'

Eva smiles at her own joke. Sofia didn't say how she knows Eva, but Alice takes an instant liking to her. How much has Sofia shared, she wonders. Eva opens the boot and she throws her bag in before sliding into the passenger seat. Paris is at the tail end of a warm front, and the jump in temperature from North East England is enough to make her unbutton her jacket.

'You need to catch up on sleep?' Eva asks, hint of an accent, Portuguese at a guess given her surname. 'We have forty-five minutes, maybe an hour drive to La Santé.'

'La Santé?'

'The prison where Alain Dufort is. Then we go from there to the NCB.'

'NCB?'

Feels like the in-flight recycled air has wrapped a wet towel around her mind.

'National Central Bureau. It's what we call the unit where we work with local police. You want to speak to Agent Boudreaux, yes?'

Alice nods. 'Yes, yes, you know him?'

Something shifts, a micro-expression. Gone in a heartbeat, but enough to confirm she does, and not necessarily in a good way.

'I know him, yes.'

Nothing elaborated. Alice files it away for now.

'Is he expecting me?'

Eva shakes her head. 'Sofia, she says not to mention to him. Says it will be better that way. I know he is there for a task force meeting this morning though. We go to La Santé first, and then plenty of time to get to NCB. Maybe you even want some breakfast in between, yes?'

The very mention of food makes Alice's stomach gurgle like a blocked drain.

'That sounds perfect,' she says, thinking she could do with something now to settle the nerves fizzing away like an Alka-Seltzer.

It's as if Eva can read her mind. Either that, or her stomach was loud enough to be heard over the car engine.

'There is a little bakery along the road from La Santé, if you prefer?'

Alice nods enthusiastically, taste buds tingling at the thought of fresh pastries.

'What's Agent Boudreaux like? To work with I mean?' she asks, testing the waters as they merge onto the motorway and wind their way south towards the city. It's a three count at least before Eva answers.

'He's a good agent,' she says non-committally, short and to the point, as if anything more might be an overshare. Doesn't really answer her question either.

'Have you worked on many cases with him?'

'A couple,' Eva admits. 'Enough to know he does not like surprises.'

'You mean like lawyers flying into town to ask him questions?'

'When you put it like that,' Eva says, deadpan, 'he'll love you. You'll be fine.'

Alice can't help a little nervous laughter. 'Any tips on getting him onside?'

Eva thinks it over for a beat. 'Just be straight. Ask what you need to ask, no bullshit.'

Alice is pretty sure Boudreaux isn't going to like her questions regardless, but she hasn't been on the go since before sunrise for nothing. She's faced down countless lawyers on both sides of the Atlantic. Ones hell-bent on sending people to a ten by eight cell for crimes they hadn't always committed, full of righteous indignation towards anyone who dares oppose them. Even so, she can feel her subconscious building this up, threatening to hijack what she's here to do. She can't let this overwhelm her to the point she has a full-blown panic attack.

They settle into stilted small talk, landscape around them becoming steadily more built up. Finally, forty-seven minutes, two croissants and a double espresso later, La Santé hoves into view. The contrast between the French prison and the pictures of Raiford she has googled couldn't be more apparent. Unlike Raiford, miles from the nearest big city, La Santé is smack bang in the middle of civilisation. A walled city in its own right, towering stone walls thirty feet high. There's something about that featureless facade that's every bit as bleak as the flatlands of Florida.

It isn't an establishment Alice is familiar with, but a quick search along the way dates it back to the mid-nineteenth century. Home over the years to the highest profile of prisoner, the likes of Carlos the Jackal, infamous terrorist back in the seventies, as well as a handful of prominent Nazi collaborators. There hasn't been an execution in France since 1977, but La Santé has seen its fair share. Its walls have a presence to them, a weight that extends beyond bricks and mortar. One that speaks of a life inside being no kind of life a human should have to endure. Still, more of one than her father has left. No matter what kind of misery manifests inside, most will still get to walk out again eventually.

Even though Alice knows she'll be one of those people she can't help but feel the walls close in around her as she crosses the threshold. Folding her into their grip.

Chapter Fourteen

Tuesday – Six days to go

Even with Eva's credentials, it's a slow, laborious process from pavement to prisoner. When the door opens, though, it's as if somebody has hit fast-forward. No time to collect her thoughts. Dufort sits, silently staring at her from behind a table bolted to the floor, handcuffs looped round a ring set into the surface. French-Algerian origins according to his file. Thirty-six years old, but life, or prison, hasn't been kind to him. Maybe both. A milky film covers one eye, canyon-like scar carving a path down his forehead towards it. Pre-prison injury, or the cost of staying alive in here? His hair has been taken right down to the scalp, a patchy Brillo pad, like he's sat for a blind barber.

His one good eye locks on to her, as if he can sense she's the non-law enforcement officer of the two. Easier pickings. Glint in his eye like an animal sizing up prey. Not the first time Alice has been in a staredown though, and she meets his gaze head-on for a three count. Dufort's mouth twitches, and the smallest of nods tells her she's passed the first hurdle.

'I'll call you when we're done,' Eva says to the guard who stands against the far wall, crisp white shirt straining at the buttons around his gut, face like he's sucking on a lemon.

'Mes ordres sont de rester ici.'

Alice doesn't speak French, but his tone translates well enough.

'Vos ordres sont ce que je dis qu'ils sont,' Eva fires back, switching to English as she sweeps her jacket back to reveal the handle of her SIG Sauer pistol. 'Now give us the room. He's not going anywhere.'

The guard glowers at her, but only for a second, knowing that other than over his prisoner, his authority in the room is non-existent. Alice nods her thanks to Eva as the sullen Frenchman exits stage right.

Dufort regards the pair of them with a shade of uncertainty now. Alice takes the initiative, striding forward and sliding out one of two plastic chairs that remind her of school days, and taking a seat in front of him.

'Mr Dufort, thank you for seeing me,' she says, like he's granted her an audience. Manners cost nothing though. She lays out the stretched version of the truth she'd agreed last night with Sofia. No way she's about to admit to this man that it's her own father's life on the line. Easier if this doesn't come across as personal.

'My name is Alice Logan. I don't know how much you've been told about why you're here, but I'm a lawyer. Without your help, a man is scheduled to die in six days.'

He folds a pair of hairy arms across his chest as she slides a business card across the table to him. Swirling sleeves of ink ripple across forearms, lips pressed into a tight line of distrust as he eyes up her details embossed on eggshell. She presses on undeterred.

'There are some unusual similarities between your case and his. And,' she huffs out a loud sigh for effect, 'well, I'm clutching at straws but I always say the only place coincidence belongs is in the dictionary, so here I am.'

She leans back in her chair, hard plastic edge digging into her back, spreading her hands wide, shrugging in a 'what the hell am I doing here' kind of way. Dufort is a statue, eyes only for her now, oozing indifference. He holds the silence for a few more seconds, then looks over at Eva.

His face creases in confusion. 'Je ne comprends pas l'anglais,' he says with a shrug.

The inference is clear in any language. He hasn't understood a word she's just said. She gives herself a mental slap for not checking first, but since touching down this morning, it's felt like she's never quite stepped off the travelator at Charles de Gaulle, being hurried along a road while she's still getting her bearings. Quick glance across to Eva for help. The agent looks pissed off, glaring at Dufort. The two lock eyes in a Mexican stand-off that lasts a heartbeat, Eva with a gaze that could bore a mineshaft, before Dufort's face creases into a broad smile, with more of a low rumble than a laugh.

'I am just playing Miss Logan. I speak pretty okay English,' he says, heavily accented, doubling down on vowels, coming out as *Ee-ngleesh*. 'Un petit peu, a little bit.' Dufort holds his finger and thumb a centimetre apart. Alice flashes a nervous smile at Eva, shuffling through the dozen questions she'd so carefully crafted on the plane.

'I do not get many visitors, especially not such a lovely pair as you two, non?' His eyes flicker up and down, scuttling across her like black, beady bugs, and she forces herself not to grimace. 'This client of yours, he is innocent too, yes?'

Another chuckle – low, like a motor idling – at his own attempt at a joke. Alice lets it slide past her. She needs to control the conversation. Steer it back on track.

'That's what I'm hoping you can help me find out,' she says.

'And this concerns me how?' he asks, nonchalant, a man without a care in the world.

Alice is loath to share any more than she has to. Any sloppy investigative work on her dad's case doesn't mean a free pass for Dufort, though that's a straw she suspects the man across the table will try and clutch at. All the same, she has to start somewhere, and gives him the headlines of her dad's case, the similarities in toxicology, investigators not looking further afield than the suspect served up on a plate for them.

'The mix of substances in your bloodstream was identical to those in Jim Sharp's, all the similarities in the crime scenes, it makes me ask questions, you know. Whether those investigating had confirmation bias.'

His puzzled look tells her he isn't following.

'Whether they actually investigated properly, or whether they started to interpret the evidence in a way that fitted what they'd already decided had happened.'

'You are saying they have set us up? Me and this Jim Sharp?' Again, with the elongated vowels. *Jeem Sharp*.

'No, no, that's not what I'm saying at all,' Alice says. 'Nobody has set anybody up, or planted evidence. None of that. What I mean is that police officers can sometimes get fixated too early on an outcome, a suspect. Then they start to see evidence and facts in a way that supports that theory, and rule out anything else.'

'So, if you are saying that the police, they do nothing wrong, then why are you here? I am important man, places to go, people to see. This means nothing for me.'

Dufort bellows something in French over his shoulder. The door opens almost instantly as if the guard has been pressed up against it, eavesdropping, but Eva dismisses him before he can set foot inside with a flick of her wrist.

'What I'm about to tell you, Mr Dufort, isn't proof of any wrongdoing,' she says, choosing her words carefully. 'But you're more than welcome to share this with your own lawyer if it helps. One of the agents on the team that arrested you, they used to be a detective in Florida. They also worked on the case that put this client on death row.'

That gets his attention, a narrowing of the eyes, spotting a tiny window of opportunity to exploit.

'And this agent, you are thinking he has this bias, yes?'

'Maybe, yes. That's what I'd like to explore,' Alice says with a shrug.

'And if I help you explore,' Dufort says, leaning as far forward as his restraints will allow, 'what will you help me with?'

Even though there is a good four feet between them, a stale sweaty scent wafts over, speaking of too-long days in too-small spaces. No mistaking the twinkle of pending negotiation in his eyes.

'I'm not licensed to practise in France, Mr Dufort.'

'And my case is in France, not Florida, yet still you have come a long way to speak with me,' he says pouting, as if she's caused him offence.

From the file she read on the flight, France is all the better for having Dufort locked up, even if, by some quirk of fate, he is innocent of this most recent infraction. Not her place to judge though she reminds herself. The day she starts doing that is the day she has outstayed her welcome on this side of the legal table.

'I can't promise anything Mr Dufort, but in return for any help you can give, I'll be sure to pass on anything that might help you to the French authorities.'

He runs his tongue across yellowing teeth the colour of ivory, tilting his head to one side, weighing up what to do.

'Okay,' he says finally. 'We have a deal, non? You have a face I can trust.'

The hand he holds out to seal the agreement only stretches so far, like a dog on a short leash. Alice stares at it like it's a live wire for a beat. She's about to override her instinct to keep her distance when Eva cuts in.

'Enough already with the flirting, Dufort. We find anything, we share.'

Alice watches in silent thanks as Dufort withdraws his hand, clasping it back with the other. He raises his eyebrows.

'What do you want to know?'

Alice relaxes into it, working her way through a series of questions around the night of his arrest, the officers that brought him in, what he remembers of events leading up to waking up in the bar. This is her comfort zone, where she slips into a flow state. Forgets who the supposed client really is, and that she's carrying the weight of her sister's expectation of miracles to be worked.

'Nothing, and I am no stranger to a good night out,' he says, again with a leering look that makes her skin itch.

'Forgive me for asking, Mr Dufort, but the drugs they found in your system, are these substances you have taken before?'

'I could not even spell them, let alone take them,' Dufort says. 'Sure, I do a little coke sometimes, who doesn't?' Another eyebrow raise, as if to say what are a few grams among friends. 'But nothing like what they say they found.'

'So how did they get there?'

Slow head shake as he considers her question. 'I'd say ask my friend Viktor, but I hear he's not too talkative these days.'

Again with the gallows humour. It's wearing thinner than the already wafer-like veneer it started with. Less than five minutes in a room twice the size of Dufort's cell and already the walls are pressing in.

'Look, I won't pretend I'm a nice guy, a gentleman you take home to meet your *maman*, but this is not how I do business. Not sloppy like this,' he says, like murder is an art form to be practised, perfected, proud of. 'I don't know, maybe someone slip something in my drink. I have enemies. You are telling me this agent, he does not investigate properly, I can give a long list of people who are happy to see me in here.'

Alice is about to ask what feels like an improbable question; whether Alain Dufort knows her dad, or has any connection whatsoever to Florida, when the door behind him opens, guard emerging like a troll from under the bridge.

'We're not done,' Eva snaps at him. 'You interrupt again, I'll be speaking to your superiors.'

His face splits into a smug smirk. 'By all means, Madame. The warden, his name is Monsieur Touissant. I have a message from him for Miss Logan.'

'Message for me?' Alice frowns. She hasn't even spoken to the man. What kind of message can he possibly have for her?

'Oui, Mademoiselle. He ask me to tell you that Agent Boudreaux is waiting in reception for you.'

Chapter Fifteen

Tuesday – Six days to go

Alice's palms feel as if they've been greased as she marches back along the maze of corridors, following the guard. She walks shoulder to shoulder with Eva.

'How the hell does he even know I'm here yet? I thought you said you hadn't said anything?'

Eva glares at the accusation. 'And I have not.'

They walk the rest of the way in silence, through corridors with walls thick enough to double as soundproofing. The fact Boudreaux is here is both worrying, exhilarating and terrifying, all twisted into one gnarly knot deep in her stomach. Clearly, he's here on the offensive, forcing the meeting on his own terms. Which begs the question, how did he know a meeting was on the cards? No time to waste speculating now though, as they round the final corner, out into a sparsely furnished box of a room that passes for reception in the visitors' centre.

Luc Boudreaux is facing away from her, wearing jeans and a jacket. He whips his head round as Alice and Eva come through the final doorway, and Alice comes face to face for the first time with the man who helped put her dad on death row.

Boudreaux is in his early forties. Looks more dock-worker than detective. Messy mop of dark hair, top two buttons popped on a white linen shirt, and scuffed suede Caterpillar boots. He's a head taller than Alice, maybe around six feet. A little heavier-set around the lower half. Cyclist's legs rather than a runner's build. Intelligent hazel eyes set into a weathered face. Hint of a scar tracing a track through his stubble. An altogether fascinating face that she finds herself staring at a second longer than she should.

Alice has done a few dry runs in her head as she flew over the Channel. Planned how to approach this as a lawyer, not a daughter. Maybe she hasn't shrugged off the oppressive feel of La Santé. Maybe it's because she still doesn't quite believe in this mission of mercy last-minute dash bullshit that Fiona has guilt-tripped her into. Or it could be the way he seems to be studying her. Whatever it is, she hesitates a beat, step faltering, and scolds herself as Boudreaux steps forward to meet her.

'Miss Logan,' he says, offering a hand after a brief pause.

'Agent Boudreaux, what a surprise to see you. I was going to come and find you after I was done here.'

'So I gather,' he says, giving nothing away as to how. 'Well, this saves you a trip, although if you'd picked up the phone, I could have saved you a much longer one.'

Alice gives a polite smile. 'I wasn't sure you would take my call.'

Boudreaux looks past her towards Eva, something passing between them that Alice can't decipher.

'I'll wait in the car for you,' Eva says, exchanging nods with Boudreaux on her way out.

'Let's get some fresh air,' Boudreaux says. 'I always find these places claustrophobic.'

They pass through the gates, back out onto Rue de la Santé, chill breeze slipping its fingers down her neck, promises of a cold winter to come. Alice spots Eva climbing into her car a hundred yards down the street, but Boudreaux starts out in the opposite direction at a slow, ambling pace.

'I know you've come a long way to see me,' Boudreaux says, glancing across at her. 'That PI yesterday, she's yours?

'Sofia Marquez, yes.'

'Well, like I told her yesterday, Jim Sharp, that's a watertight case right there.'

Alice tries to place his accent. The way he pronounces his words, 'that' coming out almost like 'dat'. Cajun maybe, with a name like his?

'As I recall, we had DNA, blood, prints. Ain't no good comes of poking the bear so close to his date.'

Date. Like Dad's meeting someone for drinks in six days.

'What happened to the other lawyer?' he asks.

He may be well connected enough to know Alice had come to town, but he assumes that she is just a lawyer, and nothing more. Makes it easier if he doesn't throw any family ties back in her face. Not for the first time, she's glad she took Mum's maiden name.

'Jim didn't say much about that,' she says. 'He did have a lot to say about his case though. Things that were missed.'

Boudreaux's face splits into a wide grin. 'Missed? Enlighten me. We must have been too busy collecting all those fine forensics samples that proved he did it. Why don't you tell me exactly what we missed?'

'You mean apart from the eyewitness you guys lost?'

'Oh, the homeless guy?' he says, sounding genuinely amused.

'That's the one.'

'Not our fault he disappeared, but with the evidence we had, wouldn't have made much difference having a drunk on the stand even if he had turned up.'

Alice doesn't know Luc Boudreaux well enough to say whether any shortcomings could be skill or will. Could he have bagged his current job if there were a lack of basic investigatory ability? What she does know are a few titbits about him that she found courtesy of Google on the journey here. Time to drop a few in to the conversation like depth charges. See what floats to the surface.

'From what I've read, you don't have much luck even with the witnesses you do find.'

She sees a flicker of annoyance. Knows she's landed a blow. The story she'd read was from a few years after her dad's arrest. A high-profile murder trial against a local Orlando crime boss called Mario Higuita, that had fallen apart after allegations that a witness was coerced into making a statement by police. Boudreaux and his partner at the time, a twenty-year veteran by the name of Danny Allan, were thrown under the bus by a witness they tracked down who initially testified that he'd seen Higuita pull the trigger. Claimed later that detectives had bullied him into testifying, saying they'd plant drugs on him if he didn't. Nothing was ever proven, but it cast a long shadow that Boudreaux had to cross an ocean to come out from under.

End result was that Higuita walked, and the other main witness against him, a twenty-six-year-old by the name of Nancy Killigan, was found face down in the river a few weeks later. Boudreaux still carries her death with him like an anchor around his neck. If he'd done a better job, Higuita would be behind bars, and Nancy Killigan might still be alive.

'If you mean the Higuita trial, I was cleared of any wrongdoing,' he says, with no warmth in the smile he offers. All teeth, nothing around the eyes. 'What I said about Sharp still stands. That one's a tight case.'

'That's a matter of opinion,' Alice says, folding her arms.

They're four feet apart, but it feels like a pre-fight face-off, nose to nose. The staredown stretches into seconds.

Boudreaux breaks first. 'Maybe, but last time I checked, it wasn't just mine that put him where he is. Twelve others agreed with me.'

'A judgment's only as good as the evidence it relies on.'

'And?'

'And you could wallpaper the courtroom with what was missing.'

'Please! Only thing that could have made that stronger was a confession.'

'Did you even look into the drugs in his system? You don't buy those from any old street corner.'

'What does it matter where he bought 'em?' Boudreaux counters, taking a half-step towards Alice, hands buried deep in pockets.

'Do you even know why I've been in there?' Alice asks, gesticulating at the towering walls of La Santé. 'Who I've been to see?'

Boudreaux puffs out an exasperated sigh through pursed lips. 'How the hell should I know? And whoever it is, makes no odds to me, or to Jim Sharp.'

'There's a man in there serving life for murder, a murder that's practically the same as the one you pinned on Jim Sharp. A man who had the same cocktail of drugs in his system that should have made him more likely to cut a fart than a throat. Another convenient name served up on a plate so neat and tidy that nobody gave any other possibility a second glance. A paint-by-numbers investigation just like you did with Jim Sharp, that any half-decent cross-examination could poke holes through.'

Alice sees something flare in Boudreaux's eyes.

'And of course, a judge would see that for the objective argument it is.'

It's as if the surrounding street is fading away, giving her the kind of courtroom tunnel vision you get when sparring with a witness.

'You're honestly telling me you're happy to fritter away a man's life knowing there were avenues you could have explored, even just to close them off, if you're so bloody sure of yourself? A man's life is worth that courtesy at least.'

She surprises herself with the last line. Not that she says it, but that she means it when it comes to her dad. That the swell of ill-will her dad's name usually sends rising to the surface is less somehow. Like she's forgotten for a moment that it's him, rather than a client, waiting to be put down like a stray.

'All right, look,' Boudreaux says, tone all business now. 'I came down here 'cos I thought it'd save you a trip to the office. You know, speed things up so you can turn around and catch an earlier flight. Do I blame myself sometimes when things go south? You're damn right I do. That doesn't mean I'm a shitty detective, or that I don't work my ass off to make sure the right people pay for what they do. Jim Sharp was every bit as good a bust as Mario Higuita, and you poking your nose in with a few extra questions after all these years don't change that.'

There's a bite to his voice when he mentions his old case. Alice wants to press him more on it. Feels that anything he wants to avoid talking about means there's something worth talking about. If he cut corners on one case, who's to say he hasn't done it again?

'And no matter how hard you say you worked your ass off on your old case, you still didn't get the right result. If that's not proof that you've got to look past the obvious sometimes, I don't know what is. You still beat yourself up about that one? Good. So you should. But you don't get to tell me that you couldn't have done anything differently with Sharp. Looked harder into his story. You always had a choice. You just didn't want to make it. I'm coming to you now with questions about my dad that have never been answered, not properly. If you're not even willing to listen, then you're just as culpable as the people you put away.'

The words pour out of her with an energy that seems to stun Boudreaux. The agent says nothing. Alice's heart beats bass drum-loud in her ears as she waits for him to snap back to attention, defend his position. Alice wills her own breathing back to a steady rate, but she realises too late the mistake she's made. Admitting the man Boudreaux put away is her dad changes the way he looks at her. She sees it in his eyes.

Something in what she's said has still snagged in Boudreaux's conscience though, because when the agent speaks again, his voice is more balm than barbed wire.

'If you're asking me whether I think Manny Castillo's murder in Florida is linked to one four thousand miles and two years apart based purely on what you've told me, honestly, it feels a bigger stretch than me trying to get back into the suit I wore to prom.'

Still with the unwillingness to look beyond the black and white. Alice is about to berate his narrow-mindedness, but Boudreaux holds up a hand to buy a few seconds.

'But I know a thing or two about losing parents. How you'd do just about anything to keep 'em, or bring 'em back. That being said, if you're asking me to hear why you think there's even the slightest chance we got this wrong, I owe you that much at least. You and your dad. Let's not do this here though,' he says, looking around the street as if seeing it for the first time. 'I've got a thing I can't get out of,' he adds glancing at his watch. 'But if you can come to the office around noon, we can talk.'

Alice goes from boil to simmer in seconds, Boudreaux's unexpected step back sapping the sting from her. A few seconds of silence hang like an uneasy no man's land.

'I can do noon,' she says finally.

'Noon then,' Boudreaux agrees with a slight incline of his head. Backing away slowly a few steps, he gives a polite smile then turns, picking up a brisk pace until he's out of view around the corner.

Alice watches him go, mouth drier than if she'd chewed a handful of cat litter. It's only once Boudreaux has vanished that she feels the aching knuckles from where she's clutching her phone. She takes one big deep breath in through the nose, blasts it back out at twice the speed like she's clearing blocked passages. Nervous fluttering wings in her stomach scale back to more of a twitch.

The change in the agent's tone has surprised her. If he's cocked up on her dad's case in any way she'd expect him to be more confrontational. Less open. Maybe he genuinely believes he did all he could. Then again, what's the saying? Keep your friends close and your enemies closer? She reminds herself that anything she finds in her dad's favour will likely be a black mark against Boudreaux.

At least she has some downtime now to clear her head, pick her questions carefully. At this stage, she doesn't know what scares her more. Getting confirmation that her father is a murderer, or not being able to save him if he's innocent. What follows with Boudreaux might not give her all the answers, but it'll hopefully fill in some of the blanks. That, plus anything else Sofia can dig up, will be the only things that can stop the plungers depressing on a pair of syringes in six days.

Alice starts towards Eva's parked car, but before she's covered half the distance, a gentle vibration ripples through her fingers. Sofia's name flashing on her phone makes her stomach feel sideswiped. It's a little after five a.m. over in New York. The kind of time that rarely goes hand in hand with anything other than dark news.

'Sofia? Are you okay?'

The excitement in the other woman's voice is a living thing, reaching out through the handset, sluicing a fresh wave of adrenaline into Alice like she's mainlined it. Sofia talks faster than a cattle auctioneer, and Alice is reeling by the time she's ten seconds in. This could change everything.

Chapter Sixteen

Tuesday – Six days to go

'McKenzie? How the hell did you find him so fast?' Alice asks, heart thudding against her chest like she's just done a personal best on the track.

Grant McKenzie, the missing eyewitness who had seen her dad on the night of the murder. The man whose testimony was never heard. Regardless of credibility at the time, not having him would have been a blow.

'Part favour, part intuition, part black magic,' Sofia says. 'Asked myself why he'd want to disappear. Could be he was afraid of the cops, could be he had something to hide. Could even be dead for all we knew. But you know me, optimistic to the bitter end, so I figured he'd skipped town somehow. Maybe scraped together enough cash to jump a bus ride. Maybe caught someone on a good day, somebody prepared to give a guy a break, and hitched outta town. He was kind of a regular over at the St Agnes homeless shelter in town. Managed a bed there every now and again, access to a shower. He'd been there the night before the murder, so chances are he looked pretty presentable.'

'Where on earth did you find him then?'

'Orlando.'

'You're kidding me? All this time he's been right there?'

'I know, right? Makes you wonder how hard they actually looked for him.'

Alice mentally adds another black mark in the shitty investigator column for Boudreaux.

'Have you spoken to him then? What did he say?'

'Uh-uh. Only got the intel a half hour ago. I'm going to try and speak to him today or tomorrow.'

'Half hour ago? Do you ever sleep?'

'Overrated,' she says with a hint of mischief. 'Occupational hazard. A mouse farts next door and I'm awake. Figured wherever McKenzie slipped away to couldn't have been that far. Not exactly a man of means, so I looked at cities within fifty miles. Friend of a friend runs a shelter in Orlando, and hooked me up with contacts across a half dozen more, so I called them all last night.'

'And he's staying at one of those?' Alice cuts in excitedly.

'Sort of. He works at one.'

'You've gotta be kidding me?'

'Rocked up at this one a few months after Castillo was killed. Drifted in and out for six months or so, then started helping in the kitchen in exchange for a regular bed. He's been there ever since. Ended up taking a counselling course and splits his time between the shelter and some outreach stuff.'

All too often, becoming homeless is a trip down a one-way street. That McKenzie has managed to wrestle back control of his life is no mean feat. Better still that he's chosen to dedicate it to helping others. All too easy to never glance in the rear-view mirror, forget your own struggles. Albeit very different journeys, Alice can relate better than most to wanting to help those living a life that's wearing them down.

'He goes by Mac these days,' Sofia continues. 'I sent a couple of tweaked versions of a mugshot from when he was picked up on suspicion of stealing food from a 7-Eleven. He's twenty pounds heavier, and a damn sight cleaner, but one of the shelter night shift managers recognised him and made the call.'

'That's amazing. You're literally a miracle worker.'

'Don't thank me yet. He remembers nothing, then we got nothing,' Sofia says, but it does nothing to dampen the Catherine wheels of unexpected excitement spinning in Alice's stomach.

Sofia promises to call Alice the minute she's spoken with McKenzie, and Alice's lighter mood must be plastered all over her face when she gets back to the car. Eva gives her a quizzical look but says nothing until they pull into traffic.

'You're smiling at your phone call, or your conversation with Agent Boudreaux?' she asks, although the wry smile Alice catches suggests she knows the latter wasn't exactly a love at first sight situation.

'Phone call,' she replies, opting not to share specifics. Whatever this is, she feels a need to shelter it from the hurricane that's already ripped through their family. See if it catches light. Nothing personal against Eva, but it takes a lot for Alice to trust, both personally and professionally. With the exception of Sofia, she has a tough outer shell that doesn't open up easily. Sofia's trust has been hard-won. If she's honest, there's an element of embarrassment as well. Who'd want to shout about having a convicted murderer as a parent?

'Just an update on a case,' she finishes.

Eva keeps her eyes fixed forward, briefest of nods acknowledging it for the small talk dead end that it is.

The NCB office is only a ten-minute meander back northwards through lazy morning traffic, following Rue de la Santé up to where it joins Boulevard de Port-Royal. Narrow streets and narrower pavements give way to a tree-lined two-lane street dotted with cafés and stores, every one of which looks quintessentially Parisienne.

Alice lets her gaze roam over the pedestrians who drift along. Imagines a life where she's in town with nowhere to be in a hurry, migrating from coffee shop to coffee shop, pigging out on pastries, strolling along the river. Maybe taking in a gallery. The kind of normal that feels so far removed as to be otherworldly. The daydream is snuffed out by a flare of sunlight off the Seine as they cross Pont Saint-Michel, surface glistening like a disco ball. The bridge takes them onto Île de la Cité – City Island. The French version sounds far better in her head.

It's home to Notre-Dame Cathedral, as well as the Préfecture de Police building that houses the Paris arm of the GALE taskforce. She knows the first part only thanks to Google Maps. Notre-Dame hasn't reopened yet since a fire almost consumed it a few years back. The thought that she might actually get a slice of time to herself to stroll along the riverbanks and see such an iconic building, even if it's swathed in scaffolding, warms her more than the anaemic October sunshine.

Police headquarters is an impressive-looking sandstone-coloured building that looks like an inner-city mansion. Identical twin facades frame an imposing arch, that in turn gives way to a car park beyond. Eva's window purrs down and the guard's face shows a glimmer of recognition as he gives her ID badge a cursory scan.

It has the feel of a castle courtyard to it as they pull into a free parking space, and Alice can't stop staring, scanning the storeys that rise above her, penning her in, tinge of claustrophobia despite the scale of the place. Eva must have noticed her staring and plays the part of tour guide.

'It's big, huh? Used to be the home of the Republican Guard back in the eighteen-hundreds.'

'Hmm? Oh, okay,' Alice says, distracted as much by the architecture as the thought of a potential witness in Grant McKenzie, and the world of possibilities he might stand for. 'It reminds me of the office back home,' she says, flashing a smile, but the joke is lost on her escort.

Alice signs in and is presented with a visitor's lanyard, and they walk along hard tiled hallways for what seems like an age before Eva stops abruptly at an unmarked door.

'This is you,' she says, opening it to reveal a bland space that you'd struggle to swing a cat in. Desk that looks like part of the original furnishings, complete with a high-backed wooden chair with a cracked green leather seat cover that looks polished by a thousand posteriors. A phone sits on the desk, but Alice spies its cable trailing over the back of the desk, although no sign of a socket to plug it in to.

'Thanks.'

'If it were up to me, I would have found you somewhere a little more comfortable.'

The unspoken inference that this is somebody else's decision. A move designed to tuck her out of sight, away from Boudreaux and anyone else she might want to speak to. Boudreaux himself, or somebody higher? Sofia may have sway with some, but not all it seems.

'It's fine,' Alice replies. 'Nice and private. Where do I find Agent Boudreaux later?'

'His office is down the hall from me,' Eva says. 'I'll come get you when it's time.'

'I'd like to speak to Mr Dufort again if that's possible?' she asks. 'Either today or tomorrow?'

'I'll try,' says Eva. 'Can't guarantee today though. Would tomorrow be okay?'

'Yeah, that should be fine.'

Alice is booked on the six-thirty back home tomorrow evening, so worst-case can go straight to the airport from the prison.

Eva leaves to get some work of her own done, closing the door behind her. The combination of worn leather and wooden frame, which looks like it was cut around the time of the Revolution, creaks in protest as Alice eases herself into the seat. She closes her eyes, kneading the bridge of her nose between thumb and forefinger.

Impulse or insanity? Many would likely say the latter, but in a way, this is a journey a long time in the making. Steps along a road to closure of sorts with how her dad's choices have impacted her life.

She pulls her laptop out of its case, thankful that she'd charged it on the flight which saves rummaging around for her travel power adaptor. Before she can switch it on, though, her phone buzzes.

The screen shows an international mobile number, French prefix. Boudreaux must have finished early. Alice injects more energy into her greeting than she feels.

'Hello, Alice Logan speaking.'

The first thing she hears is breathing. Can't be more than a few seconds pass before the voice, but it's enough to make hairs on the nape of her neck prick up. Uneven, rattling edge to it like a smoker about to cough.

'Miss Logan.'

Male. There's a rasp to it, like sandpaper on timber. Unmistakable French accent, although not a voice she recognises. Miss comes out as *Meeees.*

'Who is this?' she asks, hearing the raised pitch.

They ignore her question completely. 'I am just calling on behalf of our mutual friend to say in advance how much he appreciates your help with his case.'

'What mutual friend? Who is this?'

'Our friend in La Santé.'

'What? He ... wait, how did you get this number?'

'We'll be in touch to see what progress you are making,' the man says, and before she can ask again, there's a click, leaving her jabbering into an empty phone.

'Hello? Hello?' she asks, instinct and mild panic driving the questions even though she knows she's talking to herself.

Her heart flutters like a trapped butterfly beating its wings. She hasn't felt this overwhelmed since the day she got the call to tell her Gail had died. That had been like an out-of-body experience. Head spinning like a fairground ride. The steel band of pressure that clamped in place around her chest, squeezing, squeezing, until she thought she was going to pass out. Even now, just thinking about it spikes her pulse.

Whoever that was just now, however they got her number, in less than an hour, Dufort has gone from being a possible asset to a Pandora's Box. One she isn't sure she knows how to put the lid back on.

Chapter Seventeen

Tuesday – Six days to go

Luc Boudreaux is used to being in control, whether it's an interview or an arrest. But Alice Logan has wormed her way inside his head like sand in his shoe.

Jim Sharp's is a name he hasn't heard for a long time. Didn't even know they'd given him his date, let alone it be so close.

It's been four years since he transferred over to GALE. Positioned as an exciting opportunity, a chance to move sideways and up. An opportunity to work all over the world. But he remembers the relief on his old boss's face when he told him he was accepting. Like the class fuck-up was transferring to a new school. The stink of the Higuita case still clinging to him like cheap cologne. He knows that coming here looked to many like he was running away. Heard the whispers as he left. Only knows that he had to put some distance between him and what happened. Some rocks are best left unturned.

He thinks back to the Sharp case. Sure, when they arrested him, he denied all involvement, but if they let off every perp who said they didn't do it, the prison system would be as deserted as a strip mall on Super

Bowl Sunday. With that amount of hard evidence, he hadn't lost any sleep over Sharp's arrest, prosecution or sentencing. There are questions that Alice could ask, though, ones Boudreaux would rather not answer, even if it doesn't change the outcome.

What Alice dropped into his lap earlier has disturbed him. Not to say he now thinks Sharp innocent in the mother of all plot twists, but it's more of an irritation. An itch that needs scratching.

The way she handled herself back there, it doesn't fit with what he'd expect of a daughter about to lose her dad. Right up until the end, she'd been every inch the lawyer. Good poker face, that one. He knows a thing or two about loss. Remembers his own, back in Louisiana. The pain at seeing his life, and those of the people he loved, scattered across the streets in the wake of Hurricane Katrina. It's a lid he doesn't lift too often, but it's given him a connection – however tenuous – to the lawyer.

He has an hour before he meets Alice again; the aforementioned thing he had to take care of first was just an instinctive need for breathing space. Time to reflect, to check, to prepare. Boudreaux settles himself at his desk in the corner of an office that's empty save for a young Ghanaian agent by the name of Abeiku Owusu, GALE's technical equivalent of Gandalf. He prefers Abs for short. He's had his head buried in his laptop, headphones in, for the past hour, so he might as well be on his own.

He calls up Dufort's file first. Not one of his arrests, but he knows a hundred like him. The sort for whom prison is a pit stop. Speed dating for career criminals.

A place just as likely to yield new contacts and offer the chance to learn new skills, as any form of rehabilitation.

The crime he's incarcerated for fits with a typical pattern of escalating behaviour. The lack of prior relationship with the victim isn't necessarily significant. A man of Dufort's temper and track record is as likely to snap at a stranger as an acquaintance. What does bother him are the similarities in puncture wounds and pharmaceuticals, the latter tripping a wire somewhere deep inside his gut.

Boudreaux turns back to his laptop and gets to work. The difference between what he has access to here versus his old life in Florida is night and day. Every member state within GALE has to agree to a practically unlimited data-sharing agreement, compared to the silos he used to work in. Any law enforcement database from those countries, plus whatever icing on the cake Interpol can add, is his to browse through.

He dodges between a half dozen of these databases, but sees nothing to suggest Dufort has ever set foot in the United States to have a personal connection with Sharp. Knowing that over five thousand illegals get stopped on a daily basis along the US borders, this is no guarantee that he has never snuck in through a back door.

Next, he calls up his rap sheet in one window, Sharp's in the other, scanning for similarities. Chalk and cheese. Dufort's arrest record stretches onto a second page. By comparison, Sharp is practically a saint.

Not that small-time offenders are incapable of murder. He's seen enough ordinary people snap like a hungry gator if someone pushes their buttons. If he's learned anything from his years in law enforcement, it's that anyone is capable of anything in the right circumstances, or the wrong ones in most cases.

A question pops into his mind, one he wishes he'd asked Alice, but one he's able to answer with a few clicks. Every file has an audit trail, footprints left by anyone who accesses it. In the case of Dufort's file, it's Eva's name he sees. The young agent clearly has allegiances outside of GALE that Boudreaux hasn't been aware of until now. One to file away for later. Eva's search is listed, along with a string of keywords she must have used, lifted from the crime scene reports.

Puncture

Carotid

Fentanyl

Single wound

Memory loss

The list goes on to almost two dozen words, but that's not what Boudreaux's gaze snags on. Two things. The first is a ghost of a memory, a speck of detail from Sharp's case. Boudreaux had been two weeks into what turned out to be fifth time lucky to kick smoking. What he remembers most is how the patches pulled at his skin, sometimes leaving residue, a smudged outline of where they'd been, branding him with a smoker's scarlet letter.

Jim Sharp had those same marks, although when he'd made a crack about it in one interview, rapport building to tease more detail from him, he'd looked puzzled, denied smoking, claiming he never had. Wouldn't be the first to lie about it. Dufort's front and side mugshots stare back at him, and on the latter, also the same faint outline he remembers from his own experience of giving up smoking. The most tenuous of links between him and the two suspects. A shared vice. Irrelevant to the case, but after this morning's confrontation, any common ground, no matter how stupidly small, feels like shifting sands.

He brushes that aside, forehead crinkling in contemplation as he stares at the second thing. Eva has a reputation for solid work, so what Boudreaux sees seems out of character. If the brief was to look for cases with similarities to Jim Sharp, wouldn't you want to cast the net as wide as possible? Each search defaults to the jurisdiction of the agent requesting it, with the option to add any other locations you see fit. Eva's hasn't been altered from that default, an oversight surely, unless she had specific intel that France was the area of interest.

He stares at the blank white box to the right, the one marked 'all locations'. It's the equivalent of putting a kid in a room with a big red button and asking them not to push it. Not his job to do Alice Logan's legwork, but curiosity gets the better of him. Ten seconds later, he's wishing it hadn't.

Chapter Eighteen

Tuesday – Six days to go

'And I'm telling you to stand down, Agent Boudreaux.'

Boudreaux stares at his boss as if he can bend him by sheer force of will to his way of thinking.

'But sir, I—'

'But nothing. What you're asking is ridiculous. A waste of time, money, and a risk to perfectly sound convictions.'

'That's just it though, sir, they may not be.'

'Nonsense,' his boss snaps back. Pascal Lavigne is the very definition of management. More bureaucrat than ball-busting agent, this isn't the first run-in he has had with him. He was already in situ when Boudreaux joined, having transferred in from *La PP,* the Préfecture de Police, Paris's local force, but is more suited to the desk than the streets. His background is in financial crimes, with a flair for the politics of the role. He concedes it's not something he could do, or would want to do. GALE has been around for a decade now, and the uneasy alliances with local law enforcement have taken most of that time to iron themselves out. Lots of toe treading and posturing for position.

Lavigne reminds him of Frasier Crane. Thick-framed glasses rest atop a balding dome of a head, big enough to have moons orbiting round it. Years of working in a multinational team has sanded most of the edges off his Parisian accent.

'Now whatever this ...' his hands flutter as he searches for the right word, '... this *issue* the lawyer has with you, you deal with that, and only that, are we clear?'

'I can't ignore what I've found,' he says, sidling closer to the line he's drawing in the sand.

'You can, and you will,' Lavigne says, in a tone Boudreaux has heard too many times over the past few years. The one that screams stubborn alpha male.

'Sir, if it was just the Dufort case I could maybe understand, but there are more. Eleven more, across nine countries. You could literally copy and paste the details. Eleven men killed by a single puncture wound to the carotid. Every one of 'em with the same mix of drugs in their system.'

'And all eleven men were convicted in a court of law, a decision you expect me to undermine based on what precisely?'

Boudreaux has never spoken about the Higuita case with Lavigne. Wouldn't surprise him if his boss had done some digging before bringing him on board though.

'There was a case back home,' he says. 'One that looked every bit as nailed-on as these. Turned out we played it wrong. I had it wrong. Looked as tight as any I've seen, but we just got blindsided. I can't let that happen again, not if ...'

He doesn't get a chance to finish. 'You know as well as I do, that any hint of reopening, or even re-examining these cases would be like blood in the water for the sharks that represent these men. They had their chance, and failed to convince anyone. The fact that someone in France, or America, or Outer Mongolia, committed a similar crime is not enough to risk setting these men free. You've seen their records, the other crimes they have committed. These men are career criminals, and I will not be party to their release. Now, I will not embarrass myself by asking my peers in these other countries to listen to this ridiculous theory of yours.'

When he spells it out like that, it sounds far-fetched in Boudreaux's head too. Eleven more men convicted of murder, across nine countries. Boudreaux isn't even sure what he's claiming is happening here. There are only two ways his theory plays out. Either all the other detectives have screwed up in exactly the same way he had with Higuita, or …? Or what? The alternative is even more removed from the plausible, even with all that he's seen and experienced. Occam's razor. That the simplest explanation is usually the best. That the murders are carbon copies, because they were carried out by the same person, travelling from country to country.

How would that even play out? For one person to carry out this many killings and disappear like smoke on the breeze, it beggars belief. Then again, he pictures a world with his own parents still alive. Wonders how far he'd stretch his imagination to think up ways to keep them alive.

'If we're wrong, an innocent man could die in Florida in less than a week. Let me make a few discreet enquiries at least?'

'We're done here, Agent Boudreaux.' Lavigne's attention turns to his phone, a sign that he's done with the conversation. Boudreaux waits a beat to see if he has anything else to add, but he starts tapping away at the screen. He's almost at the door when Lavigne speaks.

'To be clear, I'm ordering you to leave this be,' he says. 'And if I hear from Touissant that Dufort has any more surprise visitors, I'll hold you personally responsible, understand?'

Boudreaux bites back a dozen barbed retorts, settling for inclining his head, not that his boss even looks up to see it. What an asshole, he thinks as he closes the door, a little more firmly than necessary. The sound echoes down an empty corridor and he stands for a few seconds, letting the enormity of what he's just asked sink in.

If Alice's questions have been a minor irritation, then his amended search is a full-blown fucking rash. Boudreaux prides himself on always doing the right thing, but this a tightrope he now finds himself halfway across with no safety net. Share what he's found with Alice, and God only knows what the young lawyer will do with the information. What the implications might be for the other convictions. For anyone else those men might hurt if they were wrongly freed. Keep it under wraps and Jim Sharp joins those that Higuita went on to hurt, like Nancy Killigan, haunting him for the rest of his days.

He heads back to his desk, shaking the mouse to wake the screen. A dozen case files sit open, a dozen flat stares looking out at him as he toggles between them. The rogue's gallery of mugshots includes Dufort's again. A line-up he slots into nicely, but a world removed from the deer-in-headlights snap of Jim Sharp. Boudreaux swats the comparison out of his mind. Can't start wearing rose-tinted spectacles. He has to come at this head-on or risk being clouded by the exact kind of confirmation bias Alice is accusing him of.

A canter through their backstories shows them all to have form. Run-ins with the law for everything from petty theft to attempted murder, prior to them all having succeeded. The kicker, though, is the geographical. Putting Dufort to one side, most of the other eleven are all in different countries. A dozen men sitting in cells, thousands of miles apart. This is both the weak point of his thinking and his greatest worry, all rolled into one.

He knows what Alice will say. That a consistent MO suggests one killer. That Jim Sharp's assertion that he has been set up has been right all along. There's something else that bothers him though. Something he hasn't mentioned to Lavigne. Minor in the grand scheme of things, or so he has always thought. The scuffed outline on Jim Sharp's deltoid muscle, a ghost of a nicotine patch. That hadn't warranted a mention in his case notes, nor in Dufort's, who was a forty a day man by all accounts. Of the eleven new cases including Dufort, eleven mugshots, front and side, he can see matching marks on five of them. Nothing in itself, but the more he reads, the more each case sounds like an echo of the last, and even that small, gossamer-like connection twists into a strand with the lines Alice is dangling in the water, tugging at his conscience.

Quick check of the clock shows little over half an hour before he's due to speak with Alice again. There have been times, after Higuita walked free and before the GALE posting, where Boudreaux had seriously considered leaving law enforcement altogether. His own parents had died in Hurricane Katrina while he was on a tour of duty in Iraq. Boudreaux had thought himself resilient, but the pressure of feeling responsible for Higuita, and the absence of parental support had hit home almost as much as when he lost them. It had been his lowest point in terms of his own mental health. Touch and go whether he walked away from it all, but he'd fought his way back to believing in himself again.

It feels like if he toes the line here, though, that it undermines all the ground he's won back. Damned if he does, damned if he doesn't. His workspace is practically bare, save for a single photo. Him and his folks at their dining table for Thanksgiving when he was fifteen. He stares at his mom and dad's faces, looking into their eyes until everything else blurs around them like a watercolour. What would their counsel be? Easy. Dad would tell him to do the right thing and it'd all work out in the end. He closes his eyes, hearing the words in his voice, just like he'd said them countless times while he was alive. The simplicity of it all, the richness of the memory, makes him smile.

His eyes pop back open and he stands in one fluid motion, bumping his chair against the desk, startling Abs at his desk across the way. Boudreaux walks purposefully towards the door and along the corridor towards the office he knows Eva has booked out for Alice Logan. He knows what he needs to do, and just hopes that this time round, the consequences are easier to live with.

Chapter Nineteen

Tuesday – Six days to go

'No, he didn't mention Dufort by name,' Alice says, heart still puttering away fast enough to make her head swim. 'But guess how many people I know at La Santé that he could have been referring to?'

'I've spoken to the warden,' says Eva. 'He sent guards to the cell, but they found nothing, no cell phone, and no record of Dufort making any calls from the main line the prisoners use.'

Alice is used to being in control, but the call has thrown her. Feels like her grasp on the situation is drifting, like a boat slipping its moorings.

'Are you all right?' Eva asks. 'I can ask Agent Boudreaux to push your meeting back a little if it helps?'

Alice checks her watch. Still thirty minutes before round two with Boudreaux.

'No, I'm fine, honestly. It's my own damn fault for giving him my business card. That must be it.'

'Probably,' Eva concedes. 'And I know this is easy for me to say, but try not to let it get to you. He's not leaving there for a very long time no matter how well things work out for your client.'

'Yeah about that, he's not just a client.'

'Sofia already told me,' Eva admits. 'When we first spoke. But I understand why you wouldn't mention this to Dufort or Boudreaux. Don't worry, I won't say anything.'

'Boudreaux knows now,' Alice admits, still thankful for Eva's discretion.

Eva just shrugs. 'Let me see,' she says, holding out her hand for Alice's phone.

Alice hands it over, watching as Eva snaps a screenshot of her call log.

'I will have somebody take a look at this anyway,' she says. 'Who knows what they may find out.'

Alice is just about to thank her when the door opens without warning. In strides Luc Boudreaux and Alice doesn't like what she sees in the agent's expression. She sucks in a deep breath, ready for a fight, but Boudreaux surprises her. It's not anger in his eyes, more like worry.

'I thought we weren't due to meet till later?' Alice asks, standing to meet him.

'We weren't,' says Boudreaux, turning to Eva. 'Can you give us a minute?'

Eva shrugs, heading out into the corridor without a word, leaving them alone, a few feet apart, in a room that feels half the size it did five minutes ago.

'If you don't mind, I'd like to record this,' Alice says, opening an app on her phone that both records and transcribes.

'In a minute,' Boudreaux says, pulling out the chair opposite Alice's, gesturing for her to take a seat. 'We need to talk first, off the record.'

Alice taps to start the recording and folds her arms. 'With respect, Agent Boudreaux, my dad doesn't have time for games, and nor do I. I need everything on the record. This gets done by the book.'

'By the book?' Boudreaux raises one brow. 'You mean like having somebody carry out an off-books search on our database? That kind of by the book?'

Alice feels the slow glow of warmth spreading across her face, reaching for a quick put-down but coming up short. Boudreaux has his soapbox to stand on with this one. Doesn't mean anything that flows from it is irrelevant or inadmissible though.

'You've never called in a favour?' she asks finally. No point denying it. Weak comeback, but she slides into her seat, sitting as straight as if she had a broom handle down her back. 'However we came by it doesn't change the information, or the questions it opens you, and the investigation, up to.'

'Honestly, how you came by the information is the least of my worries right now.'

There's a roughness to Boudreaux's words. Not the clipped professional tone from earlier. Something has rattled him, and Alice can't shake the feeling that she isn't the sole architect. The two share a moment of silence, Alice trying in vain to read what's about to be shared. Boudreaux looks pointedly at the phone that's still recording every word. Against her better judgement, Alice reaches over, huffing out a sigh to emphasise her displeasure as she taps to stop it.

'What I'm about to tell you, I'm not saying it can never be used, but I need your word that it's contained for now until I give you the go-ahead.'

Not what Alice was expecting. She'd assumed Boudreaux would make her work for any information, fight for every inch. The idea of him opening up, confiding even, throws her, and she finds herself nodding.

'That case you mentioned earlier, Mario Higuita,' he begins. 'I think about that a lot. Probably more than any case I've worked on. What happened there doesn't sit well with me, despite what the inquiry said. I didn't join the force to bend the rules, or let innocent people get hurt.'

Alice is taken aback by how vulnerable he sounds. Wonders how much truth is in the stories she read about him. Would he be opening up like this if he'd been the one doing the bending?

Boudreaux breathes in deep, out through his nose. 'I was as sure as I'd ever been that we had the right man in your dad's case. No doubt in my mind. And that's why I'm talking to you now, because I was sure we played the Higuita case right too. Turned out I was wrong. He walked, and people got hurt. I'm not sure I could live with making the same mistake twice.'

'So you do think there's a link?' Alice jumps in. 'To Dufort I mean.'

Boudreaux appears to consider that for a moment, choosing his words carefully.

'I think there are enough similarities to raise questions. The kind we should have …' he pauses, corrects himself, '*I* should have asked in your dad's case.'

The tightness in Alice's chest starts to unfurl. For all her own cynicism, the seeds that Sofia has planted have taken root, and the lawyer in her has the scent of something. She just isn't sure what.

A tiny voice inside her urges caution, to question why Boudreaux is pivoting so quickly from this morning, from moral high ground to something approaching a neutral no man's land. She's about to ask what has created this olive branch, what's different from this morning, when Boudreaux throws her the mother of all curveballs.

'There are others.'

Chapter Twenty

Tuesday – Six days to go

Boudreaux's words are a circuit breaker, slowing the world around Alice down to a crawl. When she finally speaks, it's borderline hoarse whisper.

'Others? What do you mean others?'

'Other cases like Dufort's,' Boudreaux says, smoothing palms across his jeans.

'But, I don't ...' Alice's brain feels like it's coated in treacle. How can there be more? They would have shown up on the search, surely? 'How many? Where?'

'I can't go into specifics just yet,' Boudreaux says, and it's like relighting a fuse.

'Like hell you can't,' Alice snaps, nought to sixty in under a second. 'You can't dangle that just to tease me, then withhold this kind of information.'

'Keep your voice down,' Boudreaux urges, glancing at the door. What does it matter if Eva is listening, or anyone else for that matter? Let the whole damn world know, she thinks. Let's see you hide it then.

'I'm already sticking my neck out by telling you this much,' Boudreaux goes on. 'I figure I owe you that much, you and your dad.'

'Then why stop there?' Alice asks, caught off guard by the flash of annoyance she feels on her dad's behalf. Surreal enough that he's back in her life, let alone that she feels anything for him or his situation.

'It's complicated.'

'So, spell it out for me, like I'm the judge I'll haul you in front of for obstruction of justice.'

Boudreaux gives her a pained smile. He knows as well as Alice does that jurisdictional lines are already blurred worse than a drunk's vision at closing time. If anything, Boudreaux is the one whose reach stretches furthest.

'The other cases, they're … let's just say the geography is quite diverse.'

'How many are we talking here?' Alice butts in, impatience sparking like a live wire. 'One? Two? A hundred?'

'More than one, less than a hundred,' Boudreaux says, and Alice hears the strained edge to his voice. Whatever this is, there's a cost to Boudreaux that she can't fathom yet.

'All right,' says Alice, trying to reset. 'What can you tell me then?'

'Your original search, they default to the country of origin, in your case France. Eva forgot to add in other countries. I just cast the net a little wider.'

'How wide?'

'Every member state.'

Alice's eyes widen, hungry for every last detail, but her gut tells her to give Boudreaux room to breathe. She's cross-examined plenty of witnesses over the years who need to find the words in their own time. Whatever has Boudreaux so conflicted is still unclear, but there'll be plenty of chances to go on the offensive later.

'Before you get any ideas of calling in another favour, I've had the files in this latest search flagged, so I'll be alerted if anyone accesses them. I see that happening, the shutters come down. I need you to trust me, and if I can help, I will. Agreed?'

That's exactly where Alice's mind had gone to. One quick call to Sofia, and she'd get to see what cards Boudreaux is holding. It may be a bluff by the agent, but instinctively she feels that it's not one worth calling. Not yet.

'Agreed,' she says finally.

'What I can tell you then, is that a number of additional cases popped up,' Boudreaux says warily. 'Same toxicology, same MO for the killings, all of them with massive gaping holes in their memories on the night. All the victims went the same way too. Single puncture wound to the carotid. Victims bled out, quick and messy.'

Alice picks her words carefully, in the spirit of their new-born truce.

'You said it's complicated. Can you at least help me understand why you can't share more?'

'Honestly, as much as my boss is an asshole, he's right when it comes to this, at least for now. The others are all like Dufort. Bad men, who already did pretty bad things before they went down for murder. You wade in claiming any kind of conspiracy theory, their lawyers will have a field day. If even one of 'em gets out when they shouldn't, and they hurt somebody else, that's on me.'

Alice goes to protest, but Boudreaux holds up a hand.

'At the same time, if I do nothing, and there *is* something else at play here, Jim Sharp dies, and well … let's just say if I let something happen once, it can still be an honest mistake. It happens twice, then shame on me.'

'So, you'll help?'

'As best I can,' says Boudreaux, 'but you need to leave this with me. Let me work.'

'For how long?'

'The other countries, I know a few people I can call, discreetly. Give me till tomorrow. How long before you fly back?'

'Tomorrow.'

'You came all the way here just to talk to me?' Boudreaux shakes his head.

Alice shrugs. 'Yeah, my sister can be quite persuasive. Okay, tomorrow then.'

She considers telling Boudreaux about Grant McKenzie, but this new-found truce is still on wobbly legs. By the time they meet tomorrow, she'll have Mac's statement in her back pocket, and for all Boudreaux is being helpful, Alice questions his motives. This could just as easily be about covering his own back, sticking close to Alice so he can see all the angles, shut anything down.

They agree to meet at a nearby café on the corner of Rue de la Bûcherie, back across the Seine, and when Boudreaux leaves, Alice half expects Eva to walk straight back in, like it's a revolving door, but she's left to her own devices.

The enormity of Boudreaux's revelation is just too big and slippery to stand a chance of picking apart by herself. Sofia might be awake, she might not. Alice opts to wait, give the poor woman some hope of a sleep in what little is left of her night back home.

The possibility that these many deaths could be linked. Someone travelling from country to country, killing wherever they went.

What started out as a peace offering for her sister, and closure for herself, has grown more arms and legs than she could have ever imagined. Add in whatever they might get from Mac later today, and Dad might yet stand a chance of seeing the outside of Raiford. There's a part of that that terrifies Alice almost as much as him meeting his maker. The thought of him walking free. Back into the world. Into her life.

How many other cases? How many different countries? She'll give Boudreaux the time she promised, but not much more. If the agent isn't forthcoming with anything Alice can sink her teeth into by this time tomorrow, she might give him another day max, but if Alice gets back on that plane empty-handed thinking he's playing her, there's always the nuclear option. Leak the notion of other cases to the press. Burn the whole fucking lot of them to the ground. Last resort, but if she's honest with herself, that's exactly what she'd do if it were Mum or Fiona in that cell. For them she would do this and more. For her dad, well, that's a ball far too tangled to explore just yet.

Whether it's the early start, or the adrenaline rush that follows Boudreaux's visit, tiredness seems to trickle into every pore, weighing her down like a lead-lined blanket. It's only approaching mid-afternoon but the mental exhaustion of the past couple of days is catching up. A new plan forms. See when Eva can arrange a second trip to La Santé, then head back to her hotel. She can work on her other cases just as easily from there as she can from here, and that will also afford her the chance of a power nap.

Alice contemplates trying to find Eva, but this place is huge. She could lose herself in the maze of corridors without her guide. That plus the lure of room service and rest leads her to settle for leaving a message on Eva's voicemail. She gathers up her things and retraces her steps back to the front of the building.

Outside, afternoon traffic is light, meandering at a pace that suggests nobody has anywhere special to be. Alice opts for the twenty-minute stroll with Google Maps as her guide. The sky is now a patchwork quilt of grey, and she wonders if she'll regret her choice of walk versus cab. After her pre-dawn start and a few hours in a boxy office, the open air is like cool balm against her skin.

The temptation to stop halfway across Pont Notre-Dame is like a physical pull on the brakes. She's almost across, when the railings on the side open up into a small semi-circle, jutting out a few feet over the river, flanked by ornate lamp-posts. What the hell, she thinks. Sixty seconds won't hurt. One moment snatched for herself.

The Seine is a glassy, inscrutable murky green. Ripples radiate out as a breeze drags its fingers across the surface. It's hypnotic, and it's a full minute before she tears her eyes away, staring down the length of the waterway at the series of bridges that criss-cross the River Seine at regular intervals.

Her phone pings. A text from Fiona.

How you getting on?

Alice keeps it short and sweet.

OK. Call you in a few hrs?

Got time for two mins now? Dying to know what's happening!

The day so far has crammed her head to bursting point. All she wants now is to soak in a little scenery on her way to the hotel. She starts to reply again, but stops mid-text. Fiona can wait. Deep breath in through the nose, out through the mouth. Stares back along the river, letting her mind drift like the current. Easy to get lost in the moment in a city like Paris, but she knows she can't dawdle. A quick glance back towards the police headquarters, and she's just about to carry on with her journey when something snags in her mind.

Another look back down the length of the bridge, instinct telling her she's just seen something, and a second later she spots it. Fifty metres back along the route she has just walked, a man leans out over the railings. Looks like he's taking a breather, taking in the view, just like her.

Except a second ago, he was staring right at her. She's sure of it. A frown furrows her brow as she waits, watches. Sure enough, a heartbeat later, he looks her way again. Not a face she recognises. Too far away to make out any real expression, but the way he snaps his gaze away from her makes her all the more convinced he's significantly more interested in her than the view.

Strange city, stranger men. She has no desire to hang around and be hit on by a random guy who's become inspired by the romance of it all. Except this isn't the vibe she's getting. Something more furtive perhaps.

Either way, not something she plans to stick around and explore.

Alice covers the last thirty feet to the end of the bridge, and strides over the pedestrian crossing. She can't help but glance back, and sees the man, hands in pockets walking towards her, not meeting her eye. Her heart, and her feet, quicken pace in tandem. She spies a cab parked up across the road, driver halfway through attacking a sandwich, cheeks bulging like a chipmunk storing nuts.

He sees her approach and starts to wave her off, holding up his lunch in protest, but there must be a sense of desperation about her, and he rolls his eyes in defeat, gesturing her in.

'Merci,' she says hating how un-French her French actually sounds when spoken out loud. 'Hotel Saint Honoré, s'il vous plaît.'

The driver practically slaps the remaining half sandwich onto the passenger seat, as if in protest at what will not be a big fare for him. He flicks a glare her way in the rear-view mirror, pulling into traffic with a grunt of acknowledgement.

Across the road, the man has reached the end of the bridge, and for a split second seems to slow as the taxi cruises past him. There's a fleeting moment, barely the blink of an eye, as her window lines up with him, and their eyes meet. The flash of recognition she sees from him is like an ice cube down her back. She can't help but flinch. Blink and he's gone, a receding shape in the mirror.

No denying though that he recognised her, even if she doesn't have a clue who he is. Who the hell could know her in Paris? Her mind flicks back to the phone call she received. The man claiming a mutual friend inside La Santé. Surely not? How could they have found her so quickly?

She closes her eyes, fixes on his face, commits it to memory. Something else to speak to Eva about. Alice focuses on her breathing, glancing through the rear window, but whoever he is, the man has long since been lost in the sweep of traffic.

She wishes she'd brought her running gear. That's her go-to coping strategy. Her stress ball for the soul. No time for that though.

What the hell has she got herself into?

Chapter Twenty-One

Tuesday – Six days to go

Whatever is going on here, Boudreaux can't escape the feeling it isn't going to end well for him. First things first. Work out how to do the digging he needs without Pascal Lavigne finding out. Of the dozen cases, he knows three fellow agents based in-country, who he trusts to keep his questions off the record. The other ones will require a different approach entirely, one he can't do alone. He knows just the person to tag in, but Abs will take some persuading to go behind his boss's back.

The three he can manage are clustered together in Eastern Europe. Bosnia, Serbia and Croatia. If he can call in a few favours, get the information he needs and satisfy himself that these three align with what he fears, that will go some way to convincing Abs that the remainder need his particular set of skills.

There's one more conversation he'd still love to have, preferably face to face. A visit to La Santé to hear from the horse's mouth. Look Dufort in the eye when he tells him how he didn't do it. Boudreaux prides himself on being able to read people. One thing that gift tells him is that Alice Logan is utterly convinced that something fishy is going on here. It's not just bluster, or clouded judgement on behalf of her dad.

Two problems with that. One, Lavigne is enough of a prick that he'd make good on his threat of lashing out if he tries. Two, Touissant, the warden, is a slimy toad who'd rat him out on the off-chance of currying favour with a fellow dickhead like Lavigne. One to park for now.

Instead he gets to work, picks up his phone and goes fishing. His calls to Croatia and Serbia go unanswered, but the Bosnian number he calls is answered on the third ring.

'Please tell me I ain't your one phone call from a cell?'

It's a voice he hasn't heard in way too long. Four months, maybe five. Hayley Virgo's Texas drawl is as far from native Bosnian as you can get. Hayley joined GALE the same week as Boudreaux. A ten-year veteran of the Texas Rangers, the two of them formed a strong bond from day one, and made for a formidable duo in the field until Hayley was handed the chance to head up the Bosnian field office. Wasn't that they'd drifted apart in the truest sense, just that with the jobs they have, you're never really off duty. Promises of a road trip to Sarajevo were genuine, but timings never seemed to work.

'Without you here to lead me astray, chances of me getting banged up are pretty slim these days.'

'More like if you had me there, you'd not get caught,' Hayley fires back. 'To what do I owe the pleasure? I'm guessing this isn't you telling me you're hitting my town any time soon?'

'I'll get there just as soon as folks behave themselves for long enough for me to leave 'em unsupervised,' he retorts.

'Business it is then. Shoot.'

Boudreaux hesitates a beat, choosing his words carefully. Hayley might be a friend, but she's on a par with his own boss now, and what he is about to ask might not sit well with her, friendship or no friendship. Theirs is a profession of pecking order and protocols, both of which he's going to ask his friend to look past. To hell with it, he decides. Honesty is the best policy. It's what he'd want anyway if the roles were reversed. Hayley can only say no. Worst-case, their history makes Boudreaux confident she won't betray the very fact he's asked for help, even if she declines to give it.

He lays it out for her, warts and all. What Alice has brought to his door, what he's uncovered himself, and while he doesn't sugar-coat the gaping holes in both sides of the argument, there's no mistaking the concern in his voice that something bigger is at play here. A shadow a mile up the road, even if he can't make out its shape just yet.

'Hmm,' Hayley says, letting it all soak in when Luc has finished. 'So look, I'm gonna level with you. I had a call from Pascal a half hour ago. Said you might be getting ideas about ignoring him, reaching out, and that he'd expect the same response as if one of my guys went behind my back.'

Boudreaux shakes his head, biting down hard on his lip to swallow the swear words that try and swarm out at being outflanked by his bureaucrat of a boss.

'Now before you go huffing and puffing,' Hayley continues, 'I know what you're probably thinking. Fuck Pascal, right?'

'You said it, not me,' Boudreaux says, mentally reaching for a plan B on the fly, another way to get the info he needs, and coming up short for now. 'You gonna tell him I called?'

'I'm not,' Hayley says, slow, measured. 'Want to know why?'

'Why?'

''Cos fuck Pascal, right?' Hayley says, sounding like she's savouring every syllable.

'Amen, sister,' Boudreaux says, cautiously optimistic of where this might be headed.

'I will say, though, tread carefully,' Hayley continues. 'You're wrong about this, and he'll nail you to the mast if one of these guys goes free, but I trust you. If you're saying something feels off, then it feels off.'

'You'll help then?'

'I can't let you speak to the prisoner, but yeah, I'll help. Best I can do is have a word with whoever put him away.'

'Hayley, I could really do with hearing whatever happened from the guy you've got banged up.'

'You think he won't speak to his lawyer?' Hayley counters. 'Ask him to find out what's going on? Uh-uh. Can't give these slippery bastards a lifeline to grab on to. That's the offer, take it or leave it.'

'I'll take it,' Boudreaux says without hesitation. He knows his friend is stepping out into moving traffic for him doing even this much, a favour he won't forget.

'Okay, lemme get back to you. Can't promise it'll be today though.'

They make the usual overtures of meeting up, and Boudreaux resolves to make it happen once this, whatever this is, blows over. First Mario Higuita and now Jim Sharp, twin anchors around his neck. Feels like they're only getting heavier, and a change of scenery feels like the promised land right now, even if it's just for a day or two. They're still in small talk mode when he hears the telltale beeps of call waiting.

'Hey, I gotta go,' he says to Hayley. 'Thank you for this.'

'Don't thank me yet,' says Hayley. 'I might not get you anything.'

'Thank you anyway,' he says again, signing off to swap calls.

There's a click and the briefest beat of silence on the line. 'Hello?'

Takes a second for him to recognise the voice. Alice Logan. Somewhere between anger and fear. A few seconds is all he needs to hear, and in the next breath, he's scooping up his keys, running out of the door.

Chapter Twenty-Two

Tuesday – Six days to go

Alice closes her eyes, letting the powerful jet of water slough off the day's fatigue. She could spend hours in here, but there'll be time for indulgence when she gets home. Well, more time than here anyway.

She grabs two towels off the rail, wrapping one around her body, the other turban style around her head. One hour, she promises herself. She'll set an extra alarm so there's no danger of sleeping through. The bedroom is small. Twin beds tucked up against the far wall. The small desk in the corner is barely big enough for her laptop and notebook. Not where she would have chosen if this trip was leisure rather than legal. As long as the Wi-Fi works though, it's perfectly passable.

Alice runs through a mental checklist as she dries herself and slips into jogging bottoms and hoodie. A second trip to the prison today is possible, but tomorrow at a push, depending on when Eva gets back to her. Sofia should have spoken with Mac by seven or eight Paris time. Both out of her control for now. She turns her attention to the biggest development. Boudreaux's revelation about the cluster of other cases.

If this was a courtroom, she'd compel them to share. Basic principles of discovery. Everything up to this point, though, is circumstantial, and she knows it. A judge would laugh her out of court if she suggested otherwise. She needs more. She needs detail, and Boudreaux is the gatekeeper. As thrown as she is by the agent's offer of help, it feels genuine. Not worth testing the fragile goodwill by going around him or behind his back. Not yet anyway.

If she gets the sense Boudreaux is stalling, or worse still, stepping back from his offer of help, Alice needs a backup plan, ideally one that avoids leaking to the press, but that will still be her ultimate fallback. Boudreaux will likely explode if it comes to that, but Alice reminds herself that she owes Luc Boudreaux nothing.

She starts to towel her hair dry, wondering what alternative method there is to root around the other cases. Outside her window, sounds of the city spiral upwards to reach her. A steady hum of engines despite her being off the main road. A harsh horn rips through her thoughts, and she instinctively glances out the window.

The street four storeys below is a narrow ribbon of concrete, a row of parked cars with barely enough space to slip a playing card between them. Off to the left, a moped driver gesticulating at a man who hangs half out of an open car door, his vehicle angled into the road. Maybe he was pulling out, and hadn't seen the moped. Regardless of who's to blame, she doesn't need to be fluent to feel the anger drifting up from both. Road rage is a universal language.

She's about to leave them to it when she freezes, hands working the towel pausing mid-rub. The feuding motorists aren't the only people on Rue Saint Honoré. Four shop fronts to the east, by the junction with the neighbouring street, two men look lost in conversation. One leans against the wall, puffing away on a vape. The other has his back to her, hands in pockets.

Alice does a double take. Impossible as the idea seems, she recognises the slouching man. The baseball cap pulled down to his forehead, wearing the jacket that she last saw heading towards her along the Pont Notre-Dame. She shakes the thought away. You're getting paranoid, she tells herself. Seeing things in the shadows that aren't there. Following her along a bridge is one thing, but knowing where she is staying?

She has just disabused herself of the notion when the man does something that chills her faster than liquid nitrogen. Such a simple gesture. He claps a hand on his companion's shoulder, and as the steam-engine thick cloud from his vape thins, she sees him point at her hotel.

It's as if he's flicked a switch connected to her and Alice jerks back out of sight, heart hammering in her chest. Panic rises like an ocean swell. She focuses on her breathing, telling herself there has to be a logical explanation for it. Another peek around the curtain, and slouchy man is tapping at a phone screen. As he raises it to his ear, the other man looks her way again. Not at her window exactly, but it's enough to spook her. Not as much as what happens next though.

Over on the bedside table, her phone bursts into life, vibrating across the surface, and she bumps her hip against the desk as she stumbles across to grab it. Same number as earlier. Her brain scrambles to make sense of what she's seeing. By the sixth ring, she's back across by the window, phone pulsing in one hand, the other pulling the curtain a fraction wider. Slouchy man takes the phone away from his ear, stabs a finger at the screen, and split second later, Alice's handset falls silent.

'What the hell …?' she whispers to the empty room. Alice slides her back down the wall, mouth as dry as sandpaper. She tries Eva, hating the tremble to her fingers as she taps the screen. Voicemail. Tries a second time, hoping that back to back calls will convey the urgency, but the result is the same.

One other alternative. Someone she never thought she'd run to for help, but she swallows down her pride. If those men know she's here, they could come to her room, and what then?

The knock on the door ten minutes later is all business. A quick triple tap. Alice treads softly over, peering out of the fish eye lens, and lets out a breath when she sees Luc Boudreaux, his face stretched like in a fairground mirror. She slides the chain off the door and can't but help peer over Boudreaux's shoulder when she opens it.

Boudreaux looks round, as if expecting to see someone lurking behind her.

'Expecting someone else?'

Alice doesn't answer. Just arches her eyebrows and gestures the agent in.

'You okay?' Boudreaux ventures, walking across to the window, peering out through a slit in the curtains.

'I'm fine,' Alice says back, a little too quickly to be convincing.

'Tell me again what happened,' Boudreaux asks, leaning against the wall.

Alice takes a deep breath and details her encounter, if it can be called that, with the man on the bridge. How she jumped in a cab, hightailed it back here, and came straight to her room.

'I'd just come out of the shower when I saw him,' she says. 'I was just drying my hair and I heard something going on outside. Two guys yelling at each other. I glanced out of the window, and that's when I saw him. The same man again, the one from the bridge.'

'You're sure about that?'

A pause. 'Pretty sure, yes.'

'Can you describe him?'

'I didn't see his face exactly.'

'How can you be sure then?'

There's a flicker of annoyance, feeling like it's roles reversed, and she's a witness on the stand.

'He was wearing the same outfit. Same jacket. Same hat, blue with big red logo on the front. Couldn't quite see what of though.'

She describes the second man, how they looked across at her hotel. How the mystery number was no longer a mystery. Boudreaux makes a note of the number, promising to check in with Eva and see if she's done anything with it yet.

'And you haven't seen them since you called me?'

Alice shakes her head. 'They must have wandered off while I wasn't looking.'

Boudreaux moves the curtain aside with one hand, cracks the window open, peering both ways. There's an uneasy silence as he scopes out the street. Phone calls notwithstanding, the man on the bridge and the street corner lookout could be Alice's mind joining dots that don't exist.

'Okay,' says Boudreaux finally, 'here's what we're going to do. I'm going to get Eva to put a rush on that number. When did you say your flight home is?'

'Tomorrow.'

'And what are your plans now?'

'Eva was going to try and get me back in to see Dufort again. That and I've got some work to do on my other cases, but I can do that from here.'

Boudreaux just stares at her, and Alice senses he's wrestling with something. When he finally speaks, it's not what she is expecting.

'You won't get in,' he says. 'Or if you do, it'll be me who gets a kicking for it.'

He runs her through the conversation with Lavigne, doing little to hide his disdain for his boss's stance.

'How can you work for a man like that?' she asks when he's done.

'Sometimes I ask myself that exact same question. What else did you want to ask him anyway?'

'What you said about all the others, how they'd hurt someone else in their past. I wanted to see what he'd share. Whether he'd tell me anything that makes a connection with my dad, with whoever might be behind this, whatever it is.'

'Men like Dufort, there'll be a list,' Boudreaux says.

'I've got to start somewhere, though haven't I? Why did I bother coming all this way if not to speak to him?'

'But you already did.'

'And I'm still no further forward,' she says, sounding frustrated. 'It's one brick wall after another, and they're all being put up on your side.'

He huffs out a loud breath, looking off out of the window, as if he's looking for answers. After a moment, he gives her one she wasn't expecting.

'In the spirit of tearing down at least one of those walls, you don't need to head to La Santé to see what kind of man Dufort is. I can show you right here.'

He crosses the room to where she's perched on the edge of her bed, pulling out his phone as he sits beside her. There's a moment as the mattress dips under his weight, making her tip towards him ever so slightly, until their shoulders touch. She feels the warmth of him and, just for a heartbeat, a connection of sorts. A feeling of safety in this unfamiliar city. Then he shuffles along, only a few inches, but it's enough to break the second-long spell.

She shakes the feeling loose, whatever it was, and sucks in a deep breath.

'Let's see what you've got then.'

Chapter Twenty-Three

Tuesday – Six days to go

Alice looks on as Boudreaux opens an app on his phone. The GALE logo pops up, and he turns, shielding his screen as he taps in a password.

'Remote access to our databases,' he tells her. 'Gives us real-time info out in the field. Here's Dufort's highlights.'

He lays his phone on the table where they can both see, and talks as he scrolls.

'He's the kind of guy who's never held down a real job in his life,' he begins. 'Worked his way up through the ranks, and wasn't too choosy about who he trampled on to get there.'

A mugshot pops on screen, a younger Dufort, maybe ten, fifteen years ago.

'Did a stint a while back for aggravated assault. Beat a kid from a rival gang into a coma. Came out and went right back to it. His kind don't rehabilitate. Nothing else has stuck since though, well not until the—'

'I know about the Russian he's meant to have killed to be in there now,' Alice says, 'Viktor Semenov. But if he fits the pattern, there's got to be someone else, someone not much further back.

Boudreaux nods, tapping the screen. The mugshot disappears, replaced with a different picture that makes Alice flinch. It's a young woman. Her face is a palette of purple and jaundiced yellow bruises. One eye swollen shut, the other unfocused, bloodshot. Her nose looks misshapen, a few degrees out of line, like moulded play-dough.

'Elena Georgiou, a young woman who went out for a night with friends, and ended up in a UN field hospital near Nicosia in Cyprus around three months before Dufort was arrested for the Semenov murder.'

Alice's hand goes to her mouth. The poor woman on screen looks half Dufort's size. She slowly shakes her head as Boudreaux continues.

'Witnesses said he assaulted her friend, grabbed her breast, and Elena tried to stop him. He slapped her hard enough that she fell, hit her head on the floor. Fractured her skull, gave her a bleed on the brain. She died on the operating table.'

Alice feels a flush of anger on the woman's behalf. She knows Dufort is a bad man, but putting a name or face to crimes makes them that bit more real.

'How did he not do time for this?' she asks.

'Official version? Witnesses changed their minds. Unofficially, we're pretty sure Dufort's people helped them make that decision.'

'He's an animal,' she whispers, unable to tear her eyes from the screen.

'No arguments from me,' he says with a shrug.

'Could it be someone connected with her that set him up then?'

'If he was set up,' Boudreaux corrects her. 'Doubtful if you ask me. If they could be bullied into changing their stories, they're not likely the kind of people who could kill Semenov to make their point. I'll look into it though.'

Alice nods, pushing back from the table, like she's seen enough. She wanders over to the window, peering out as she speaks.

'Me and my dad, we're not close. Never have been really. But even now, I struggle to imagine him mixed up with someone like this. Someone who's capable of that level of violence. He's a thief and a cheat, but I've never seen him raise a hand to anyone.

'In my line of work, you learn that people are capable of just about anything in the right circumstances,' says Boudreaux.

And what might you be capable of Agent Boudreaux, she thinks, but keeps this to herself.

'Goes without saying I never showed you this,' Boudreaux says, pointing to the file still open on his phone.'

'Scout's honour,' Alice says with a mock salute.

'So, what are your plans now?' Boudreaux asks.

Alice checks her watch. She really wants to call Sofia, see if she's been to see Mac yet, but knows it's pointless. Sofia will call as soon as there's anything to call about. Besides, still no need to tip her hand to Boudreaux on that front just yet. He may be playing nice for now, but how will he react if there's something solid that makes him look bad? Will the version of him that came out in the room just now resurface? Maybe it'd be Alice on the receiving end of the threats next time.

'I'm still working while I'm here, so I'll probably get on with that for now.'

'Is it such a good idea to stay here if Dufort's buddies know where you are?'

'You really think he'll keep at it?' Alice asks.

'With guys like this who can say? Why take a chance though? Let me find you a room somewhere else.'

'But I'm already paid up here.'

Boudreaux waves off her protests. 'I'll speak to them. Least we can do. That way you can work in peace while I do my due diligence.'

'Any news on that front?' Alice asks, wondering if Boudreaux is in a sharing mood.

'Made a few calls, but nothing concrete yet. Let's get you squared away, and we can regroup tomorrow.'

Alice checks her watch. It's a little before four-thirty local time. Nothing she can do back at police headquarters that she can't do within arm's-length of a minibar.

'Okay,' she says at last.

Even this small act of trust feels like a concession she's not quite ready to make. Common sense prevails though. Within the hour, Boudreaux's flashed badge and persuasive promises to recommend the hotel as a base for future visiting law enforcement has secured Alice a refund, and she finds herself in a marginally bigger room at a boutique hotel south of the river in the 7th arrondissement.

Boudreaux leaves her with promises of a meeting at ten the following morning back at headquarters, and Alice grabs an overpriced Coke from the minibar, sliding into the seat that looks out over the front of her new home.

This feels like the eye of a storm she hadn't seen coming. A matter of days ago, her life felt so much more ordered. She has learned to live with her past by stashing it neatly out of sight, like the kind of shoeboxes full of clippings and pictures in a wardrobe that people tuck away. She only delves into hers in the quietest moments of introspection. Few and far between.

No hiding from any of it here though. Dad's reappearance case hasn't so much stirred up old memories, as resurrected them like some kind of Frankenstein's monster. She's trying her best to remain objective. Not let her opinion of the man cloud her judgement. But it's easier said than done. Better if she tries to think of herself as a lawyer, not a daughter.

She takes her time with the drink. Savours it as she closes her eyes and listens to the white noise of afternoon traffic through her open window. The early signs of a pressure headache lurk like monsters under the bed. Don't dwell on Dufort and his mind games, she tells herself. Eyes front. Trust in Sofia, hope for something from Boudreaux, but be prepared for a politician's answer.

There's always another option, a voice in her head whispers. Just pack up and go home. Tell Fiona she tried her best. Maybe her sister would believe her, maybe not. But Alice would know. She prides herself on being better than that. Better than Dad. She reminds herself that she is who she is in spite of him. And that's why she can't walk away. Because it's what someone like him would do.

Alice slides out her laptop, and the first thing she sees is an email from Moira, letting her know that Fiona has called the office a bunch of times. Why wouldn't she just call her mobile? Alice suddenly remembers how she had stopped mid-text on the bridge. Picks her phone up and sees eight missed calls from her sister.

Shit. Knowing the worrier that Fiona is, she'll probably be picturing Alice floating face down in the Seine.

She goes to call her back but stops, finger hovering over the number. How much to share with her? Not that any of this is covered by legal privilege. She isn't representing her dad. More that she needs to control the flow of information for now. No telling what Fiona would do, who she might tell, if she knew about the other cases right now. Then there's the fact that Alice doesn't want to give her false hope. As much as things have moved on from how her dad's case looked yesterday, there's still a long road ahead before it turns into anything useable.

Depending on what Boudreaux and Sofia come back with, another conversation with her dad might be needed too. The thought of it turns the corners of her mouth down. Dad with his meek and mild act, like he's up for martyrdom. She's not ready to play happy families. Not sure she ever will be. She starts a text to Sofia, asking her to reach out to the warden, when her phone starts to ring.

Sofia's name flashes up on screen, as if she's been summoned just by Alice thinking about her. Deep breath. Her heart's pounding like a racehorse's hooves, nerves frayed after the day's events. She prays that it's good news as she taps to take the call, walking across to the window as she does so. In that split second, as it connects, Alice does a double take at a figure that darts behind a bus stop. Bogey men everywhere. In a strange city, thousands of miles from home, she's never felt more alone. More vulnerable.

Chapter Twenty-Four

Tuesday – Six days to go

'Hey, please tell me you got some sleep,' Alice says as Sofia's face pops up on screen.

'Some,' Sofia says. 'Anyway, enough about me. How's the vacation?'

'Just dreamy.' Alice laughs. 'Boat ride along the Seine, being romanced by the local men, you know. You should try it some time.'

'I would but my boss doesn't believe in holidays. Seriously though, how you doing?'

'It's been … interesting.'

'How did it go with your French guy, and Boudreaux for that matter?'

Where to begin? Alice takes her through a potted history of one of the most intense days she's ever experienced. Sofia stays silent, gives her the chance to get it all out. When Alice's recounting finally brings them up to date, there's an audible sigh from the other side of the Atlantic.

'Look, if you need to sidestep Boudreaux, Eva owes me big time. It'll burn her for anything else we need, but I'm pretty sure I can get her to dig into those other cases if we have to.'

Jesus, thinks Alice. What the hell has Sofia done in the past for Eva that she's confident the young agent will put her career on the line for her?

'I don't think we need to go there yet. Boudreaux says he'll have more for me tomorrow. If he's stalling by the time I head to the airport, then we'll see.'

Even as she says it, she knows that'll be a button she'll avoid pushing at all costs. She's taken a liking to the young agent, and there has to be a way to navigate through this without dragging her down. She also wonders if one more day will be enough. What choice does she have though? Fiona has driven her down an emotional one-way street. Feels like anything short of Dad strolling out to start a new life will be a black mark against her. Alice shakes her head. How can a man who literally fucked off and left her to fend for herself waltz back in and wreck her reconstructed life so casually?

'Anyway,' Alice continues, 'enough about me, I'm guessing you have news or you wouldn't have called?'

'I sure do,' Sofia says. 'Let me just dial someone in.' The playful tone Alice hears makes her sit up in anticipation.

After a few seconds a third window appears on screen, and the new face in it, looking every bit as surprised to see Alice as she is to see him.

'Alice, meet Mac.'

Grant McKenzie appears nervous, like he's on trial himself, and the strained smile he gives just makes him look uneasy. He's got a lived-in face, one that's seen more hardship than most judging from the creases etched across his brow. His short hair is borderline military buzz cut, and Alice places him somewhere in his fifties.

'Miss Logan,' he says with a nod. 'Pleased to meet you.'

'You too, Mac,' she says. 'You're a hard man to find.'

'Ain't nobody must have looked too hard,' he says with a shrug. 'I've never been too far away.'

'So I gather. We really do appreciate you taking the time to speak to us though. I'm going to run through a few questions with you if that's all right?'

He nods, reaching off camera, bringing back a glass of water that he takes a long swallow from.

'How about you start by just telling me what you remember from that night?'

Mac waits a beat before answering. 'He wasn't alone, I can tell you that much. My spot was outside Dunkin' Donuts, couple of doors down from the Round Table bar on Seventh. Mr Sharp, he looked pretty out of it when he came out. Had to put a hand out to catch himself against the window before he started walking.'

'And the other guy, when did he show up?'

'Right after that. Mr Sharp hadn't gone but a few steps when this guy comes out after him. Put his arm around and helped steady him a little. I asked 'em both if they had any spare change when they came past. Mr Sharp mumbled something about being broke. The other guy didn't even look at me.'

'What did he look like?'

'Didn't get a great look, not head-on anyway. He was taller than Mr Sharp, maybe around six feet. Skinny, like he could do with a good feed. One of those long over-coats that businessmen wear. I remember 'cos it looked odd, you know, what with him wearing a baseball cap. I remember he was wearing gloves too. Not something you'd expect in the summer.'

'Where did they go after they passed you, Mac?'

'They walked maybe another half a block the last I looked. Got distracted then though. A guy and a gal had come out of the bar, and she was tearing a strip off of him. I looked back but Mr Sharp had gone. Next thing, this big SUV pulls out from where he'd been, and tears off up the street.

'Help me get my bearings here,' says Alice. 'That sends them which way?'

'North on Seventh.'

'North towards Manny Castillo's place,' she says, toggling to a window on her laptop with Sofia's maps open.

This is huge, like shock paddles to the case. A witness who can categorically state that her dad was not alone. Not only that, but one who can testify that he was in such a state that he needed looking after, driving home … or to a murder scene. Her dad was telling the truth, about this at least. The notion of him having even an inch of moral high ground is uncomfortable, like a stone in a shoe, but impossible to ignore. There is, of course, one enormous potential fly in the ointment.

'Sorry to have to ask this, Mac, but had you been drinking that night?'

Mac looks down for a second, then back up at her, giving a slow nod as he speaks.

'I'm not too proud to admit my sins, Miss Logan. Haven't drank now for over five years, but I am an alcoholic. I'll never stop being one till the day I die. But no, I hadn't drunk that night. It'd been a slow week and I couldn't afford nothing.'

He sounds believable now, cleaned up and sober, but a jury back then might not have been so understanding.

'Tell her about the following week, Mac,' Sofia prompts him.

'I had my favourite spots, places I knew were comfortable, less likely to get moved on, you know,' he says. 'Anyway, I moved around some. Didn't go back to Seventh till the week after. Friend of mine tells me I need to watch my back. That someone has been around asking about me, some guy giving off a weird vibe.'

'The guy from that night?'

'Yes ma'am. Of course, I wasn't one for keeping up with the news back then. I hadn't even heard the name Jim Sharp, let alone that he was supposed to have killed someone. Spooked me enough though that I moved spots. Went up the street a little, to a new place behind one of the billboards, where I could keep an eye on the donut store.'

'You went to spy on him? Weren't you worried about why he wanted to find you?'

'I wasn't always on the streets you know. Did five years in the army. I can take care of myself. All these stories you hear about homeless guys getting beaten up, I wanted to see who was coming for me.'

'And did he? Come back I mean?'

'Later that night, I'm hunkered down, almost asleep, when I see it. The guy from outside the bar. He's parked up across the street and gets out. Different jacket, but same cap.'

'Did you see his face this time?' Alice is unable to keep her excitement in check.

'No,' he says with a shake of the head. 'I did get a picture though.'

It's like his words have wired her up to the mains. She sits bolt upright.

'How did you manage that?'

'You learn to travel light on the streets,' he says wistfully. 'More you have, the more there is to carry, or for others to take. Had a few scraps back in the day over stuff that others wanted. Didn't always come out on top neither. The one thing I always kept safe though was my phone.'

'Couldn't pay to use it, but it's the only way I can still see my girl. Her and her momma moved away after I lost my job. Haven't seen her in years. Don't even know where they went, but I've got pictures from before it all went to shit. Happy ones. Kept it charged up whenever I used to get a bed in a shelter.'

'Do you still have the phone now?'

'Not the same one. Mr Spencer, the guy who runs the shelter, gave me his old one when I started working here, but he moved the pictures across for me.'

'Can I see it?'

'Should be with you any second,' Sofia chimes in.

Alice stares at her inbox on her laptop screen, willing a new message to pop up. While she waits, she tackles the elephant in the room.

'Why not take this to the police?'

He cocks his head to one side in confusion. 'I did take it to them.'

'Come again?'

'Not right away. I wasn't exactly watching CNN every day to hear the news, but as soon as I saw the fella's picture in the paper, I called up. Spoke to a guy who said he'd get a detective to call me back.'

'And what did the detective say?'

'Don't know. Still waiting for the call to this day. I tried calling again. Spoke to a different fella who said they were pretty sure they already had their man, but that someone would get back to me. Guess they just decided to pass.'

'Jesus!' Alice exclaims, the enormity of what she's hearing hitting sledgehammer hard. Assumptions made. Evidence missed. Lives ruined.

'I don't suppose you remember the name of the officer you spoke to?' Sofia asks.

Mac shakes his head. 'Sorry, I don't. Long time ago now. Another life.'

There's another question that's bugging Alice. One she knows an appeal judge will ask. One that speaks to credibility again.

'Why did you run Mac?'

'It wasn't just the one time the guy came back,' he says. There's a haunted look in his eyes as he dredges through the sediment of that part of his life. 'I steered clear of the bar after that. Figured he wasn't exactly coming back to give me a roll of hundreds. My buddy Dave said he saw him three more times. I don't know for sure if this guy had anything to do with your case, but I had no desire to find out.'

A soft ping echoes from Alice's laptop, and she jerks forward to check it. Sure enough, there's one from Sofia.

There are four tiny thumbnails. She double-clicks the first, and a grainy photo pops up. Quality isn't great. Neither is the lighting. The SUV is more silhouette than firm focus. Side-on so no chance of a plate. The driver is one leg in, one out, head partially obscured by the door, but there's the hat she's been hearing about. Second and third pics are similar but marginally moved on, like stop motion animation. It's the fourth that's the most revealing.

This one has the guy fully out of the car, looking out across the road towards where Mac had hidden. The ambient light spilling out from the bar makes everything in the foreground a shade darker, but Alice can make out a red blob on the front of his hat. She squints but can't quite decipher the logo.

It's not quite a smoking gun, but it sparks a dozen questions in her mind. Would there be any CCTV from Manny Castillo's place still around that they could check for a similar size SUV? Sofia will have contacts who can work on enhancing the image. What about the call Mac made to police? It's a long shot but there might be a record of it still kicking around. It's starting to feel like Jenga in reverse, extra bricks slotting in to steady the tower.

'Mac, I know this is a big ask, especially after all this time, but how do you feel about going on the record with this, making a statement, maybe even testifying if it goes to a retrial?'

Mac raises his eyebrows, puffs out both cheeks and runs a hand across his beard. Alice clings on to the fact that he's here, now, talking. If he had zero inclination to help, he'd not have even spoken with Sofia, let alone agreed to a transatlantic video call. Big difference between chatting like this, though, and standing up in court.

He may have got his life back on track, but his time on the street has left its scars. A mistrust of authority figures for one. It's stamped across his face like a brand. She lets the silence weigh heavy until it squeezes an answer out of him.

'I'm not proud to say that I've run away from a lot of things in my life. A lot of people too. Spence, that's Dan Spencer who runs the shelter, he's helped me learn to stand up for what I believe is right these past few years. I'll be honest, once they went to trial and I saw how much they had against Mr Sharp, I figured maybe I had it all wrong. Just put it behind me, you know? Maybe that Good Samaritan was exactly that. Maybe he wasn't. The whole thing felt like a sign, you know, that I had to make a change. The man I was back then might not have testified for you, but this one here today sure as hell will.'

Alice lets out a long, slow breath.

'Thank you, Mac,' she says, unprepared for the relief at a win, however minor, chalked up for her dad. Anything vaguely positive towards him feels awkward, out of place.

'I've still got a lot to make amends for in my life, Miss Logan. If I can help save your dad's life, that'll go some way to paying off my balance.'

She would love nothing more than to sit and take a full statement now, but Mac says he has to get back to work. He promises to call Sofia after his shift and agree a time this week to make a formal statement. Alice watches as her new star witness disappears off screen.

'You know we still need more, right?' Sofia says, bringing her back down to earth after Mac has left the call.

'We do,' Alice agrees. 'But tell me this doesn't feel like something?'

Sofia nods, smiling. 'It does. Doesn't make a difference to the ton of physical evidence they still have, though. We need to know what Boudreaux knows to stand any kind of chance of putting a dent in that.'

She's right of course. Mac could have heard her dad's Good Samaritan announce to the world that he was off to kill Manny Castillo, but that doesn't make the blood they found splashed across Jim Sharp just vanish.

For that, she needs help from Boudreaux. No way will she share the content of the conversation she's just had with him. Not yet, but when she's ready to, it has to be face to face. She needs to look Boudreaux in the eye when she asks him about the attempt Mac made to share what he saw. If there's even the slightest flicker of recognition, a hint that Boudreaux was privy to that and turned a blind eye, she'll hold him to account.

For the first time in a long time Alice feels a twinge of something resembling a sense of family loyalty towards her dad. Took years of him being how he is to hack away at whatever bond they might have had. She might never see him as a father figure, but he's starting to look a hell of a lot like a scapegoat here. One who, for once, doesn't deserve the punishment hanging over his head. This isn't about letting him back into her life. It's about saving his.

She vows there and then that if Boudreaux knew about Mac's call and ignored it, she'll make damn sure the agent is tarred and feathered in the most public way imaginable, and to hell with the consequences.

Chapter Twenty-Five

Tuesday – Six days to go

Boudreaux spends the last hour of his working day making calls, reading files. He tries his Serbian and Croatian contacts again, but has to settle for leaving messages asking for them to call him back.

He leans back in his chair and huffs out a loud breath. This is without a doubt one of the most intense days he's lived through. Alice's appearance has thrown him more than he cares to admit. What has always felt like a righteous arrest and conviction as far as Jim Sharp is concerned now feels tainted, scuffed around the edges.

He prides himself on being thorough. On doing what's right. Doesn't always work out that way. Ask Nancy Killigan.

This one doesn't have to go that way though. He can still influence the outcome, for better or for worse. Something he could have done, should have done, back when he was investigating it first time round.

In his heart, he still believes the right man is behind bars. At the risk of sounding like harsh self-interest, if that plays out, it vindicates him. The leap of imagination Alice is asking him to take is off the charts, but he can't ignore this cluster of other cases, however improbable a connection might be.

How would he approach this if he were Alice? The physical evidence feels too strong. No disputing that was Manny Castillo's blood on Sharp's top. Alice's theory then requires them to believe that somebody else put it there. An as yet nameless person incapacitated Jim Sharp, killed Castillo, and dressed it up to look like a disagreement between the two men.

To what end though? Who benefits from that? Castillo had enemies, sure. But Sharp was a nobody in that sense.

What if it wasn't about framing Sharp? What if the end game was Castillo's death, with a convenient gift-wrapped patsy so police didn't look any further? Boudreaux makes a mental note to look back at the case file, see if anyone leaps out as benefitting from Castillo being out of the picture.

Making that link would be step one. If that feels a bit of a reach, the next part is a bigger leap than Neil Armstrong's back in '69.

What then connects Manny Castillo to Dufort or his victim, or to the other ten? Feels like he's walking into an enormous spider's web, cobwebs tangling around him at every turn.

He calls up Jim Sharp's file again, stares at his mugshot, waiting for answers to sprout from the questions he has sown. He stares long enough that when he looks away and blinks, a ghost of the man flickers before his eyes.

There's a knock at the door, and Eva pops her head round.

'Sorry to disturb you. Have you seen Miss Logan anywhere?'

'She's gone back to her hotel.'

Eva turns to leave, but Boudreaux calls her back.

'I like you Eva, I do, but a word of advice? You need to make better choices.'

From the look Eva gives him, Boudreaux can't tell whether she's picked up on where the conversation is heading.

'What bad choices have I made lately?' she asks.

'This job, Eva. You do it properly, and it's all or nothing. We don't get to pick and choose when we follow the rules.'

Eva takes a half step back in, but doesn't say anything.

'Do I need to spell it out for you?' Boudreaux says finally in frustration. 'Whatever marker was called in for you to stick your neck out for Alice Logan, it's done but no more, do you hear?'

Today has rubbed his nerves raw like sandpaper, and it comes out angrier than he intended.

'I don't know what you …'

'Save it. I know it was you that fed her the details on Dufort.'

Eva holds his gaze, a little defiance creeping in around the edges. 'What makes you say that?'

'You telling me it's just coincidence you were the last person to access the file before me?'

'Coincidences do happen. Look at Jim Sharp and Alain Dufort.'

Boudreaux can't help admire her spirit, but Eva is either not seeing the bigger picture, or cares more about doing favours for friends than she does the people Dufort will almost certainly hurt if he gets out.

'And until there's hard evidence that the two are linked, that's all this is. A coincidence.'

'Her father. You arrested him.'

Looks like Dufort isn't the only one she's been looking into. Boudreaux stands up, closes half the gap between them.

'I did, and you would have too if you'd been there. What's your point?'

'I just ...'

Boudreaux knows he's overreacting, taking out frustrations on someone else, but he snaps at the junior agent.

'Just what? Thought you'd switch sides and start putting people back on the streets now, is that it?'

'That's not fair.'

'And neither is assuming I don't care about whether I put the right guy on death row.'

Boudreaux is breathing a little heavier. This is heading down a more personal route, and he needs to rein it in. He ends by giving Eva a slightly watered-down version of the dressing-down he received from Pascal Lavigne, and promises to report her if there's a reoccurrence, then sends her on her way.

It's more bluster than threat. He doesn't want to kick Eva back down a rung on the career ladder. Has no intention of doing so.

Boudreaux stands there long after Eva's footsteps have faded, fatigue filtering through him. Outside, the sun has slipped away for the day, shadows slinking across the sill. He feels the pull of his apartment, a two-bed first-floor rental overlooking Père Lachaise Cemetery. It's like a who's who of famous dead people, final resting place of Jim Morrison, Chopin, Oscar Wilde and a whole host more. Might not truly feel like home, even after five years here, but it's more appealing than the office.

Either way, he hates moments like this, the waiting around for something to happen. For his calls to be returned. For Alice Logan to find something she can wield like a club to free Jim Sharp. And any weapon that helps Sharp, could hurt him.

If that last part happens, it happens. If he's missed something for a second time, he'll almost welcome it, although he isn't sure what it'll do to him. He does what he does to help people, keep them safe. To think there's the slimmest of chances he might be about to cost a man his life.

He grabs his keys and heads out. The fading light shows a cloudless sky, handful of stars barely visible.

The October chill sinks its teeth in, even through his thick padded jacket. A far cry from the Orlando heat he gave up to come here. It's the tail end of rush hour, and he joins the line of traffic that snakes its way across the Pont Notre-Dame, northwards towards the 3rd arrondissement.

The brazenness of Dufort, and whoever those lowlifes are that he's set on Alice, grates on him. The Frenchman is exactly where he belongs. Seeing his influence snaking out like tentacles through the prison gates has irked him though.

Dufont wants to play rough, Boudreaux thinks, let's play rough. He drives past the turning that would take him home without a second glance. To hell with sitting around waiting for someone else to make things happen.

Nobody else knows Alice has moved, including Dufort's men. Anyone who might have returned to lurk near the Hotel Saint Honoré is in for a nasty surprise.

It only takes five minutes until he turns the corner onto Rue Saint Honoré. The hotel entrance is a hundred yards ahead, and up ahead, the street corner Alice said the man had loitered on.

Silhouettes criss-cross the junction, hard to make out detail at this distance. Boudreaux keeps a steady speed, like he's cruising for a parking spot.

Past the hotel entrance, on towards the pedestrian crossing, and he spots shadows in a doorway by the last shop on the left. Two of them. He hasn't thought through the finer points of his approach, other than to fire a warning shot that helps Alice. Maybe it tears a tiny strip of his own guilt away too by doing the attorney a favour.

Boudreaux glances across as he passes, and just as he does, there's a flare of light. The shadow splits into two, both men, one with a phone that's just sprung to life.

Maybe it's bad luck, or maybe he slows the slightest fraction and draws the guy's attention. Either way, he looks up. Can't be for more than a heartbeat that they lock eyes, but it's enough.

He barks something to his friend, and they both burst from the doorway, bustling away and disappearing around the corner within seconds.

Boudreaux's foot twitches on the accelerator but there's a steady flow of people crossing from both directions. He smacks the steering wheel in frustration, and yanks the wheel to the right, bumping up on the kerb.

He's out and running seconds later, pushing past pedestrians. It's them. He's sure of it. Nobody runs if they have nothing to hide. Up ahead, he sees them, zigzagging through the busy pavements. The guy he saw isn't someone he recognises, but he's wearing a baseball cap exactly like the one Alice described.

Boudreaux sucks in big lungfuls of air, arms pumping as he skirts the edge of the pavement to get a better line of sight. Without warning, the two men split, baseball cap darting across the road between traffic. His partner keeps ploughing straight ahead.

Which one to go for? His feet make the decision before his thoughts catch up. A chorus of horns blare as he sidesteps between two cars, reaching the opposite pavement fifty yards behind him.

A rotund man in a parka, head down, lost in his phone, sees Boudreaux too late. He flinches as he pinballs off his half-turned shoulder, pirouetting past a wide-eyed young couple walking arm in arm.

Back across the street, he sees runner number two, his bright red gilet there one minute, gone the next as he skids around a corner and out of sight.

His target turns to check on him, and he's close enough to see the worry written on the man's face. Up ahead, pedestrian crossing lights flicker from green to red. People slow to a stop, massing by the kerb. The man shouts something in French that Boudreaux can't quite make out, and puzzled faces turn to see him, then part like the Red Sea. Baseball cap makes for the gap, even as he continues to close the distance.

The guy is only twenty yards away now, and winces as he sees the car that isn't going to stop in time. He leaps, sliding Hollywood-style across the bonnet of a VW Beetle. As he slips off, his head turns to the side, the peak of his cap catching the windscreen. It spins off, shooting forwards into the road as the car finally stops.

He doesn't even look back, and bounds across to the far pavement. Boudreaux's eyes widen as he sees the waiting commuters start to close ranks ahead of him, unaware of his approach.

'Move,' he shouts. 'Police, move!'

Not technically correct, but he needs results over accuracy. He's a beat too late though, and the gap closes a fraction too much just as he reaches them. He skids to a halt, shouldering his way through. A bus heads towards him as he reaches the front and hesitates. The split-second delay costs him, and it's obvious he won't beat it across.

He grunts in frustration, holding both hands up, swatting one at the rear end of the vehicle as if helping it on its way. The second it's clear, he springs forward, skirting round the knot of people waiting on the far side, but it's as if the city has swallowed him up. He slows to a trot as he scans a sea of heads in all directions.

'Goddamn it,' he snaps to no one in particular as he finally comes to a stop, scowling at the few faces that look at him like he's talking to an imaginary friend.

Ahead it's just a blur of early evening commuters. No bobbing baseball cap to be seen. He realises immediately what's wrong with that thought, and pivots on the spot. The cap. The man had lost it on the road. Boudreaux's sure he did. No way did he have time to scoop it back up. Boudreaux makes his way back just as the lights change, and two opposing sets of waiting people power towards each other like armies advancing.

He scans the road, squinting at the gaps in a dozen pairs of legs. Nothing at first, then suddenly he sees a flash of dark blue fabric, just as a hand closes around the peak of the cap. Boudreaux bustles past a woman in heels tall enough to make him wince, just in time to see a teenage boy smiling as he lifts the hat towards his head.

'Hey!' he calls out. 'Excusez moi.'

Second time lucky. The kid looks towards him, seeing his outstretched hand. He makes no move to hand over the cap, so Boudreaux takes advantage of his confusion and snatches it from him.

'Que diable?' he shouts. *What the hell?*

'Police,' he responds, shaking his head, and whether it's something in his face or his tone, the boy doesn't argue back.

Boudreaux is left holding the hat, and realises he's the only one left on the road now. He hotfoots it across before the flow of traffic washes along the street again, not exactly sure what good the hat is without the owner. What's he going to do, run DNA tests on the sweat soaked into the brim to ID a man whose only provable crime is running from him? He can practically hear the sarcastic put down he'd get from Lavigne.

He turns the hat around, recognising the logo straight away. He's no soccer fan, but he's been in town long enough to know the Paris St Germain badge. Red Eiffel Tower on a blue background, with a gold fleur-de-lis bottom centre. He makes his way back to where he left his car, mulling over next steps, breathing returning to normal after the unplanned workout. Best Lavigne knows as little as possible about this, and anything that relates to Alice Logan. Doesn't mean there are no avenues open to him though. He can't help but scan faces as he walks, more out of habit than expectation. Neither man will be stupid enough to double back to give Boudreaux another shot at them, surely? That's when he glances up and sees the CCTV camera. They won't have to.

Chapter Twenty-Six

Wednesday – Five days to go

Gail has visited Alice in her dreams more times than she can count. Sometimes it's a rehash of happier days. Hanging out at high school, long before New York. Most of them, though, are fuelled by guilt, that feeling she wasn't there when she should have been. The worst so far is a recurring one where she's on the street with Gail. One where headlights illuminate her friend's face, showing the terror of knowing what's coming. The kind where when Alice wakes up, she can still hear the crunch of impact.

This one takes it up a notch. The setting is depressing. Alice is alone in a room full of empty seats. Rooted to the spot as a set of dirty off-white blinds open painfully slowly, and an execution chamber is revealed like an exhibition. Two worlds colliding. Gail's past and Dad's future.

Gail is strapped to a gurney. She looks out at Alice with an unblinking flat stare. Her face is a patchwork of bruises; blooms of purple blend with blotches of jaundiced yellow. A crimson cut carves a path across one cheek. There's no blood though, just angry raised edges of the wound. The sight of her releases whatever has been shackling Alice. She runs to the window, hammering a palm against the glass hard, the reverberations coursing through her like aftershocks.

A masked physician steps up to insert a canula, Alice balls up her fists now, shouting for them to stop, but the sound of her voice is distorted. Like it's travelling through water to reach her.

The doctor, nurse, whoever they are, pays no heed, sliding the needle beneath the skin of Gail's hand. When they're done, they turn to lock eyes with her. She knows them. Sees recognition in those dark pools. Sees their hand reach for the mask, but she knows their identity even before it slides off, floating down to the floor.

Luc Boudreaux seems to study her with something bordering on amusement. Alice resumes her assault on the glass pane, even though she knows the futility of it in her heart.

Even though she feels herself sucking in big ragged gasps of air, the dampened sound fades to nothing, as if someone has hit the mute button. Alice slaps both palms against the window and leaves them there, shoulders heaving as she struggles to catch breath she cannot hear.

Boudreaux glides, rather than walks towards her. It's supposed to be a one-way mirror, but Boudreaux's eyes bore into hers. He seems to know exactly where Alice is, and places his own palms against the cool glass, mirror images of Alice's.

Something swims across Boudreaux's eyes. A look that takes a second to process. A fox about to raid the henhouse.

Alice looks on in horror as the agent's fingers start to move, merging with the glass. Forcing their way through, impossibly, but undeniably emerging on this side as if it's nothing more solid than water between them. Fingers lace themselves through hers, gripping with a strength that makes Alice's own knuckles creak.

There's a pause, like they're trapped in amber, then with a slowness that makes it all the more terrifying, Alice feels herself being pulled towards the glass. Into it. Through it. She can't breathe. Can't even open her mouth now as she emerges on the other side, drawn by her silent dance partner.

Alice's voice echoes in her own head, pinballing around, no way out. Screaming to make it stop. Boudreaux draws her all the way in, locked in the embrace, across to where Gail lies.

Alice tells herself it's not real. Feels like she's about to implode with the sheer force of will she's invoking to try and wake up. It's not real. She knows this, even as Boudreaux guides one hand down to the plunger on a syringe that has appeared in Gail's canula.

'You did this.'

Boudreaux's soft whisper is like silk sliding into her ears, sending a shiver spiralling down her spine.

'You could have saved her.'

A black ooze snakes out of the syringe, disappearing into Gail's hand. Veins darken like a dirty roadmap as Alice locks eyes with her. Sees a single tear well, spilling over her eyelashes. It traces a lazy path down her bruised cheek, hanging for an eternity at the bottom, before dropping onto the gurney.

It's as if the liquid completes a circuit. Alice's world is consumed by a snowstorm of white, and it feels like she's been hurled upwards, but into what, she has no idea. White snaps to black, gives way to shadowy shapes and she's panting, finally able to breathe.

The hotel room around her takes shape in the half-light. For a few seconds, she's still tethered to the dream, to the shocking showreel still running through her mind.

She taps her phone screen, wincing first at the brightness, then at the time. Four thirty a.m. The dream recedes, lingering memory of Luc Boudreaux's face making her shudder as if someone has just walked over her grave. Yesterday was so far from what she'd imagined it to be. A sense that Boudreaux might not be the obstacle that she's cast him as. Alice shakes her head to loosen the last threads of her nightmare. Time to slot back whatever bricks and mortar Boudreaux has chiselled away from her defences.

He is a route to information, a means to an end, Alice reminds herself. Aside from her dad, Boudreaux is the one who stands to lose the most depending on how things shake out. Despite his friendly overtures, attempts at apologies, Alice can't allow him the slightest chink in her armour to exploit. No underestimating what Boudreaux might do in order to save his career, if that's what it comes down to.

Alice swings her legs out, sitting on the edge of the bed for a beat while she works out the kinks in her neck. Sounds like popcorn in the microwave as she rotates both ways a second time for good measure.

By five, she has showered, powered up her laptop, and made a coffee using two of the instant sachets for an added kick-start. It's bitter enough to make her grimace, but needs must. She pulls up Mac's pictures again, zooming in, staring, willing the pixels to snap into better focus.

'Who are you?' she says to the empty room.

Has to be more to this, she tells herself. For Dad to have been in enough of a state to be practically carried along the street, then shrug it off so quickly to overpower a mean bastard like Manny Castillo, feels more of a long shot than Elvis doing a comeback tour.

Alice starts planning out how, and just as importantly when she'll confront Boudreaux with what she learned from Mac. Go bull in a china shop and he'll most likely stonewall. That will mean Sofia finessing contacts back home to rake through the original case file for any sign of Mac's call.

Things like that take time. The one thing her dad doesn't have. The thought makes her glance at the ticker tape running along the foot of a muted TV news bulletin. Wednesday 21st October. T-minus five days.

Is Dad counting down, she wonders. Marking off what's left in hours or minutes? Alice can't help herself. She googles his name again, clicking the news tab. Features from newspapers like the *Orlando Sentinel* and the *Miami Herald* flash up. Headlines pop off the page. Her eye is drawn to one in particular.

D-Day Looms Large for Convicted Murderer.

Below it, Dad's face stares out at her, the same mugshot she has seen in previous articles from a decade ago.

The features around them have weathered and aged, but the eyes have that same sadness to them. She pushes the laptop away, rubbing at her temples with thumb and forefinger.

It's a peculiar feeling, this energy linked to her dad's case that's starting to leak into her system. Flies in the face of everything she felt when Fiona dropped her bombshell two days back. Everything she's felt since he walked out the door years ago.

Shit, Fiona! She didn't call her sister back. The absence of calls or texts since yesterday's flurry is a sure-fire sign of a strop. It's early, but Alice fires off an apologetic text, asking if she's awake. She stares at the screen for a beat, waiting for the dancing dots to appear. Nothing.

She reminds herself of the age gap. Of the fact that Fiona can flip a switch and come at you both guns blazing if she isn't getting her way. Suddenly the prospect of a return home today doesn't feel quite as appealing. This wouldn't be how she'd have chosen to visit Paris, but every day she works from here is one day less of the inevitable arguments with her sister. Alice is pretty sure if she returns with anything less than a full pardon that frees her dad, Fiona will find a way to land at least some of the blame on her.

Hell, she still blames her for telling Mum about the affair. The chain reaction it set off. Separation. Divorce. Relocation. Alice winces at the thought that had she not told Mum about seeing Dad with Mariella, Fiona wouldn't have been back home to meet Trevor. Equally, that parallel universe would have no Jake or Lily, and that's not a world she wants any part of.

She finds the email with her flight details on. Clicks through into the booking and five minutes later, she's on the late flight home tomorrow instead. Moira can work her magic on Alice's diary again, although she'll need to put a call in to one of the senior partners to smooth over the extra day with them.

Settling on her plan of attack, she throws herself into her work. She's quickly lost in the familiarity of it, drafting letters, reviewing case summaries. So much so that she can't say for sure whether the knock she hears is the first.

Time check shows a little after eight. A little early for turn-down service. Alice peers through the peep hole. Luc Boudreaux stares back at her, so directly that Alice flinches, taking a second to compose herself before opening the door.

'Room service,' says Boudreaux, holding up a takeout coffee cup.

There's a moment as Alice reaches out to take it, a flashback to hands reaching out to her through the prison window. She does her best to blink it away, but it must show on her face and Boudreaux frowns.

'Everything okay?'

'Yes, yes, fine. Come on in.'

She takes the cup from Boudreaux as the agent breezes past her.

'Everything all right here last night?' Boudreaux asks, turning to face her. He's clutching a folder, and Alice's pulse quickens at the thought it could contain details on the other cases.

'Hmm? Oh, yes, thank you.'

'I wasn't sure if you took cream, so I brought one of each. That one's black,' he gestures at the cup Alice holds, 'but if you want to switch that's fine.'

'Black's good.'

Whatever this is, maybe a kill with kindness campaign, it bumps up against the walls that last night's dream started the reconstruction of. He's doing this to stay close, Alice tells herself. It's a marriage of convenience. All the same, there's something about him she finds herself warming to in spite of the circumstances.

'So, I figured you might feel safer with a ride to the office. You are coming back in today, aren't you?'

'I can do most of what I need here, but yes, I was planning on coming in to see you, check whether you're in a position to share yet.'

Boudreaux smiles ruefully. 'I'm good, but I'm not a miracle worker. I made a few calls, but I'm not there just yet. Maybe this afternoon. How about you still come in with me? I'll find you a nicer office to use, and as soon as I know what I need to know, I can come tell you.'

Last night's call with Sofia and Mac was like clipping jump leads to Alice's fatigued batteries. She'd love to see the look on Boudreaux's face when he finds out they've found the witness that he and every other officer had failed to. Not the right time though. Better to see what flows the other way this afternoon than to put Boudreaux on the defensive.

'Sure, why not,' Alice says, sipping her coffee as she moves round the room gathering up what she needs.

'There's one other thing too,' Boudreaux says, and Alice turns to see him holding out the folder. Jesus, enough with the tenuous dream parallels. She doesn't flinch this time and she takes it. Plain brown front, thin. Couple of sheets of paper, tops. No markings or anything to signify what's inside.

She flips it open to find three glossy prints. Lays them on the table side by side, a triptych in black and white. Takes a second for her to realise what she's looking at. When she does, her mouth falls open a fraction in surprise.

It's the man from the bridge, the one who watched her from outside her hotel. They're not high-res pics by any stretch, a little fuzzy like when she zooms in with her phone camera. No mistaking him though, even without the distinctive hat.

'Where did you get these?'

'I took a drive by your old hotel last night. Seems your friends had nothing better to do than go back and hang out again.'

'You've arrested him?'

Boudreaux shakes his head. 'One of me, two of them. They got away, but not before they ran past a half dozen cameras. These were the best of the bunch. You recognise him?'

Alice stares for a while before nodding. 'Yes, this is the same guy from yesterday. Do you at least know who he is?'

'Corbin Blanchet. He's mixed up with an organised crime gang that call themselves the Eighty-Niners. Fingers in all sorts of unsavoury pies.'

Alice wrinkles up her nose. 'Sounds more like a sports team.'

Boudreaux shakes his head. 'It's short for seventeen eighty-nine. The year the Bastille prison was stormed. These guys clearly have aspirations of revolution.'

'And that's Dufort's crew too?'

'Mm-hm. Word is that they're more of a subsidiary. Part of a bigger network that operates out of the Balkans.' There's a pause. 'These are bad people, Miss Logan. No telling what they'll do to get Dufort out. If it's okay with you, I'd like to put someone outside your hotel until you go home, just in case.'

Alice almost laughs, but Boudreaux's face is all business. 'Do you really think that's necessary? I mean, they don't know where I am now.'

'No, they don't, but these guys move fast. They shouldn't have known where your first hotel was either, but look how that turned out. I had the warden check Dufort's phone calls since you met him. He hasn't made any. Not a single one.'

'That doesn't mean someone else isn't making them for him.'

'True, but it's a big prison. A lot of people willing to do it for him, but there's more ways than that to get a message out. You've spent enough time with clients who live in these joints. If they want to get their hands on a phone and have the means to pay for it, it's going to happen, and no way can we trace that.'

'So, what's your point?'

'My point is that without that link, we have no leverage over Dufort. No way of making them stop by threatening him. He built the Eighty-Niners himself. Led them for years. If they think there's a chance of squeezing you for information to get him out …'

Boudreaux doesn't finish his sentence. Alice leaves the pictures where they lie, stuffs her notebook and laptop into a bag, and slips into a pair of black flats by the door.

'I'm not going to be intimidated, Agent Boudreaux. Not by them or anybody else.'

That last part comes out a little double-edged. Not that she believes for a moment that Boudreaux is in league with the Eighty-Niners, but it's less likely that anything damaging Boudreaux's reputation will surface if Dufort and his buddies throw Alice off her game. Could be that Boudreaux is cranking that handle a little too hard to see if Alice stalls.

'Alrighty then,' says Boudreaux after a brief pause. 'Let's get out of here.'

Chapter Twenty-Seven

Wednesday – Five days to go

True to his word, Boudreaux finds her a third-floor office with a view out over Rue de la Cité, and Hôtel-Dieu, the oldest hospital in Paris. He excuses himself, promising to come back in a few hours. Alice allows herself a moment to stare out of the window, soaking in the sounds of the city. Off to her right, a sluggish Seine glints through gaps in the trees that border the road.

Her new flight home is a little under thirty-six hours away, and it feels like she's riding a wave of sand down into the bottom of an hourglass. Everything's moving too fast, no guarantee there'll be time to slot all the pieces in place – if she can even find them that is.

Should be no issues getting the plane home as long as Boudreaux doesn't drag things out, but staying here longer doesn't feel like an option. Part of her still thinks this was always an indulgence. As much about exorcising her own demons as placating Fiona's. The two don't have to be mutually exclusive, she tells herself.

This notion of her dad being set up buzzes around her head for the rest of the morning. The further down the rabbit hole, the less their history seems to matter, and the more it's becoming about justice. More lawyer than daughter.

The crux of it, though, is how and why? Things like this don't just happen by chance. Someone has to have picked him for a reason. She hesitates for a moment, then fires off an email to the address Sofia has provided for the warden at Raiford, asking for a video call with her dad later today before she can change her mind. She'll get what she can from Boudreaux, but however much it rankles with her, she's going to have to speak to her father again. Last time was an unexpected shock to the system, an emotional ice bath. Next time she has to leave her baggage at the door. Speak to him like his lawyer, even if she isn't. That thought sparks another. She taps out a message to Sofia, asking if there's any progress on sourcing Dad a lawyer. One ready to act on whatever she finds.

In the meantime, she turns her attention to her new-found French fan club. She's never heard of the Eighty-Niners before, but then again, why would she have?

A quick google remedies that, and she's soon wishing she hadn't been as curious. Page after page of the destruction they leave in their wake. Blurred out bodies on pavements. A burned bombed-out shell of a car by the roadside. They're knee-deep in anything and everything. Drugs, people, money laundering into the tens of millions.

There are some successes for the police, arrests made, assets seized. But the sheer scale of it makes it seem like trying to cut off a Hydra's head. Talk about more than she bargained for.

She slumps back into her chair, stomach on spin cycle. Focus Alice! she berates herself. No time for a pity party. If Boudreaux comes through with details on these other cases, she never has to see Dufort again. Maybe she can get Eva to ask any more follow-up questions that crop up. Another few days and she'll be hundreds of miles away. Another few days and her dad will be that bit closer to ordering his last meal.

Alice tries to take her mind off the idea that an international crime syndicate has taken an interest in her, and turns her attention back to her dad. She grabs a yellow legal pad from her bag and scribbles questions on it, trying to remember how her dad had described the night of the murder. Then it hits her that she doesn't have to rely on her recall. Fiona's text from yesterday. The recording.

She opens her phone, scrolling to the audio that her sister had texted. Before hitting play she gets up to close the door. Can't help but glance out of the window, half expecting to see someone staring back at her from down below. There's a steady flow of traffic, plenty of people passing by, but all with zero interest in her.

She shakes her head, nervous smile at her own paranoia, then settles back into her chair. She listens through once in full, eyes closed, focusing on the answers rather than who's giving them. As much as she tries to squash it down, there's a part of her that can't help but feel a twinge of pity for him, the flatness of his tone at times hammering home the hopelessness.

She's part way through a second pass, this time pen in hand, when something he says sticks in her mind like mud to a wall. She slides the audio back thirty seconds, listening again.

It's his car. He tells her how it hadn't started. How it had wheezed like a forty a day man. Those were his words. That's how he ended up in the bar, waiting for the tow truck. She scrubs the audio back a few minutes earlier. Again with the car, except this time, he says how it's been in the shop for a few days.

Twin tracks appear above both eyebrows as she frowns. Tiny detail. Doesn't change the fact he ends up in the bar with no means of getting home.

Alice tries to slide into the shoes of whoever else could have done this. Assuming Dad's car had been there, and not off getting fixed, what if the Good Samaritan had tried that first? Had anyone examined the vehicle for traces of this mystery man?

It's plausible, she concedes, that this guy might have tried the car, touching something or leaving some sort of trace in the process. A quick check of the arrest report shows car keys but no mention of any search of the vehicle, or what happened to it afterwards.

Everything feels like a long shot, but she can't discount it. One of her law school professors had described reasonable doubt as throwing a ton of jelly at a wall in the hope that some will eventually stick. It can be as much about quantity as quality.

She puts down her phone, hits play and closes her eyes again. Pictures herself back in Fiona's kitchen as he talks. Remembers the mannerisms, the way he licked his lips, the hesitancy between some of his answers.

Nerves or something else? Alice considers herself a good reader of people, especially if she's met them a few times to get a baseline. With her dad, though, she can't quite decide what to chalk it up as. He's already counting down to his last breath, so when it comes to worrying about incriminating himself, that ship has sailed. Could be that he does know more than he's letting on?

Her mind makes a quick-fire series of leaps. What if he's somehow, somewhere, crossed paths either with the Eighty-Niners or someone they're linked to? He had plenty of connections on the wrong side of the law back in the day. The sorts of people who run these organisations rule by a cocktail of fear and respect. What if he's holding out because of fear of what they'd do?

She turns her attention back to the river of sad stories on screen. It's like a motorway pile-up that she can't quite tear her eyes away from. Come back cat memes, all is forgiven. She's lost in that swamp for God only knows how long, when she's saved by the bell, or in this case the chime of her phone.

A single WhatsApp notification glows on screen. Number, not name, the implication hitting home, stomach plummeting like a ship on stormy seas. There's a thumbnail picture visible but too small to see detail.

She reaches for it. Hesitates a beat, then snatches it up, angry at her own timidity.

The image is blurred out, and she taps the arrow to download it. The face snaps into focus and it's like she's just jumped into an ice bath.

The picture shows Mariella halfway down a set of stone steps, eyes averted from the camera. The image has either been cropped, or taken using a zoom lens, a stray arm pokes into shot on one side, a pair of feet further up the stairs behind her.

It's the boy beside Mariella that she can't take her eyes off. Looks the double of Dad from the pictures she's seen of him as a kid. He looks around ten years old. It can only be the brother she's never laid eyes on. Anthony. He looks happy. Happier than she remembers being as a kid. She can't help but wonder how much of that is down to the fact Dad has been in prison most of his life, rather than living under the same roof. A safe distance away and less likely to mess his life up the way he had hers.

Above the picture, she sees with another swoop in her stomach that the sender is typing. Disappears abruptly but no message. She stares at the screen, swallows hard as the typing begins again.

The single note bell tone rings out again. Two lines of text pop onto the screen.

So handsome.

He has his father's eyes.

There it is. The answer to the question that's been prodding her. What does a man sentenced to death still stand to lose?

Chapter Twenty-Eight

Wednesday – Five days to go

Boudreaux feels his patience wearing playing-card thin. His contacts in Serbia and Croatia aren't answering phone calls or texts, and he knows that both of the latter have been read.

He hasn't got time for whatever political bullshit is playing out. Has Lavigne waded in with his tiny size five loafers and stomped all over his enquiries? Told them to stonewall him?

Hayley hasn't brushed him off though. The Bosnian office is still his best bet, but that alone doesn't feel it'll be enough. Hayley has promised to call in half an hour, but until then, Boudreaux decides to take a punt on a few of the others. One tiny step out onto an icy lake. Agents he doesn't know personally, but this has got under his skin enough to make it a worthwhile risk.

He doesn't want to believe a word of what Alice Logan is selling. It's a house built on coincidence, but still, something gnaws at him, a gut instinct tugging him, although towards what he isn't sure.

One thing he knows for certain, he can't let history repeat itself. If Jim Sharp gets the needle in under a week's time, he needs to be able to look himself in the mirror and be proud of what he sees. Doesn't want another ghost looking over his shoulder alongside Nancy Killigan.

Boudreaux pulls up a list of the other cases. Scans the locations. Studies them, the dates of each murder, every conviction. If Dufort's case is part of the chain, it's not out of the question that Eighty-Niners factor in the mix. He is, or was, top of the food chain. Well placed to know where bodies are buried. Enough that they might take risks like escalating the scare tactics with Alice to get him out. Their tentacles wind their way around the world in dozens of countries. A few of these places would be new territory for them as far as his research shows. Doesn't mean it's not them, just another question amongst hundreds of others.

He glances at his phone, seeing a text from Hayley pop up. A non-committal '*Call me*'.

He does as instructed and ten seconds later she answers.

'What have you got me into?' she asks.

'Whaddya mean?' Boudreaux says, feigning ignorance.

'I've had your lovely boss on the phone again, asking me if you've been in touch. Asked me to let him know if you reach out.'

'And?'

'And what?'

'Have you? Let him know I mean?'

'Lavigne is a toad with a Napoleon complex. What do you think I told him?'

Boudreaux can't help picturing an amphibian in a mini bicorne hat. The smile spreads like winter sun over frosty grass.

'You know he probably didn't believe you, whatever you said, right?'

'Yeah, well he's got trust issues.'

Boudreaux laughs this time. 'Seriously though, H, I appreciate what you're doing for me, but don't do anything that puts you in a bad spot.'

'That mean you don't want to know what I know?'

'Now you're just teasing.'

There's a pause, and when Hayley speaks again the humour has gone.

'So, our guy, Jusuf Pasalic, is doing life for killing Osman Kurjak. It's your classic bad guy meets badder guy. This was ...' Her voice trails off for a beat. 'Seven years ago. Anyhow, I've gotta be honest with you, Luc, this one looks pretty solid.'

'They all do.'

'Wait, all? What do you mean all?'

Boudreaux closes his eyes, berates himself for not picking his words more carefully. He leaves enough of a pause that Hayley fills the gap.

'Luc, what is it you're not telling me?'

Screw it, Boudreaux thinks. If Hayley was going to sell him out, she'd have done with Lavigne already.

'Twelve,' he says finally. There are twelve.'

He rattles through the past forty-eight hours at a rate of knots.

'Jesus,' says Hayley when he's done. 'And you're thinking what? That we've got it wrong on all twelve?'

'I don't know, H,' Boudreaux says, weariness wrapping weighty arms around him. He shakes his head, hating the prickle of self-doubt. 'I just know I don't want to get blindsided again like in the Higuita case. I've got to be sure.'

Hayley is silent for a few seconds. 'You're a damn good agent, Luc. We all make mistakes sometimes.'

'Yeah? And when was the last time someone died from one of yours?'

It's snappy, with an edge to it he knows Hayley doesn't deserve.

'Sorry,' he holds up a hand in apology even though Hayley is half a continent away, and can't see him.

'It's fine,' says Hayley, albeit a little quieter than before.

'It's like I'm handcuffed by my own agency,' he says. 'Can't make sure we haven't screwed up cases without kicking over a few rocks. Can't do that without Lavigne saying I'm screwing up cases.'

'Look, you know I'll do anything I can, but first glance, I just don't see the angle here.'

'I know, I know,' says Boudreaux, and for the first time starts to wonder if he's looking too hard for something that isn't there. Maybe it's time to just admit that coincidences do happen.

'Tell you what,' says Hayley, 'let me send over what I got from the local PD on my one. Take a look through. You've got any questions after that, I know the detective pretty well. I can have a quiet word and try to get more detail for you.'

'Amazing. I owe you a drink.'

'Drinks, plural,' Hayley says. 'Anyway, I gotta run.'

'Thanks, H, I really appreciate this.'

He has barely ended the call when Hayley's email pops into his inbox. Boudreaux opens the attachments. Full local case files. He skims them in a matter of minutes, fiddling with sizes, arranging them in matching tiles on his screen, side by side. There's more detail here than he has on the GALE database. Even after a number of years, not all countries have fully integrated their records with GALE systems yet, so there's generally a layer deeper to dig in cases like this.

A low gurgle bubbles across his stomach, reminding him lunchtime is fast approaching. He reaches into his drawer, pulls out a cereal bar and starts munching as he takes a second pass through the files. It's a stretch, he knows it is, but he has to be certain this time.

He takes another bite and stops, mouth half open, snack unchewed, staring at the screen. His eyes flick back and forth between the documents, then flicks open Jim Sharp's file. One line in each standing out, like stumbling over a tripwire that sends sparks flying in his mind. A train of thought that drags him back to the interview room in La Santé. To Alain Dufort, and something that he himself had thrown at him. An improbable link, but a link, nonetheless. One that ties his case to the one in Bosnia at the very least.

For the first time since Alice Logan breezed into town, Boudreaux concedes that this might actually be more than just a Hail Mary. The enormity of that drags him back through the years like a riptide. Past Jim Sharp, all the way back to Nancy Killigan. History repeating. One common denominator. Him.

Fuck.

Chapter Twenty-Nine

Wednesday – Five days to go

To hell with time difference, Alice thinks. The picture of Mariella and Anthony is a message about as subtle as a baseball bat to the shins. She's never met the boy, but already she feels a degree of responsibility. He won't even know he's in danger. Anyone wanting to harm him or Mariella could waltz up to their front door and mother and son would be none the wiser. In that instant she ceases to think of Mariella as a homewrecker. She's just another person whose life her dad has flipped upside down. No time to waste. Her first call is a FaceTime to Sofia.

'Damn,' Sofia says, leaning heavy on the vowel as Alice finishes updating her. 'Just tell me what you need.'

'I don't know what the hell we've stumbled into here, but I need to know they're safe,' Alice says, the words sounding even more surreal now she's speaking them out loud. This is not an angle she saw coming when Fiona had guilt-tripped her into getting involved. Worrying about the safety of the woman who stole her father feels awkward, like she's teetering around in heels way too high. It strikes her that she doesn't have the slightest clue where Mariella actually lives.

'That shouldn't be too hard to find out,' Sofia says. 'You said Fiona has been in touch with her too. Ask her to drop Mariella a message to get her address.'

'I'll call her after this,' says Alice. 'She's been trying to get hold of me since yesterday.'

'Text me as soon as you get it. She told you she was staying with family somewhere near Raiford, right? I'll head down there now, that way I'll be nearby when you get a location.'

'You don't have to do that,' Alice says. 'Would it not be easier to go via local police?'

'Honestly,' says Sofia, mouth twisting as she weighs it up. 'We don't have enough to get them on board just yet. I can sit on her for now, then I've got a few favours I can call in from a guy in Orlando to get her a friendly shadow till this is over if needs be. It's only a two-hour flight away. I'll be there just after breakfast.'

'You're a star,' says Alice, feeling the tide of anxiety recede. 'What time are you seeing Mac for the rest of his statement today?'

'Ten a.m. but don't worry, I can push that back until we get the Fiona thing squared away, or even do it virtually. Has Boudreaux decided to play nice and share any more about the other cases?'

'I'll let you know in a few hours,' Alice says, feeling far from convinced herself.

'You don't need me to tell you this,' Sofia ventures, 'but I'm gonna say it anyway. We could have enough without him. Might be safer for everyone if we run with what we have for now. I found a lawyer I can give this to. Good guy. Mac's statement, his pictures. I hate to think this way about anyone with a badge, but Boudreaux's got an agenda, Alice. He's the only one that benefits from your dad not walking away. What he's doing now, this half-assed sharing, it's a play of some sort.'

'I don't disagree,' Alice says, 'but it's not enough, not this far down the line. We swing and miss too early, it makes us look weaker. I don't trust him either, but it's not about me.'

Even as she says it, the words ring hollow. She knows deep down that however wide the rift between her and her dad, she can't fully untangle herself from the fate he's facing. Not any more. It'd be like trying to strain out the milk from your coffee. Two parts of the same whole since she's pulled on this thread. Sofia looks unconvinced but stays silent.

'I'm going to speak to my dad again later too,' Alice continues. 'I'm not going to mention the picture of Mariella. He's got enough on his plate.'

'Not as if he could do anything about it anyway,' Sofia agrees. 'Depends what time you're calling him, but if you want me to, I can be in the room with him when you do. Much easier to pick up on stuff face to face if you think he's holding out on you.'

'I feel like I'm leaning on you too much here, Sofia,' Alice says, totting up the other actions she's parked with her friend. Mac's statement. Enhancing his photos. Tracking down who he spoke to at the station back in the day.

'Text me the time and the Zoom link. It's all going on your bar tab when you come over,' she replies with a grin. 'Speaking of travelling, when do you go home?'

Part of Alice wonders if one more day will be enough. Feels like this is the centre of the maze. Going back home feels like a retreat of sorts. She brushes the thought away like a stray cobweb. Tells herself to take a step back from the edge. Her life is back in the North East. The one she's built back up from setback after setback. She knows there are limits to what she can do for Dad. This was never about representing him. She can hand this off in the next twenty-four hours. But the further down this path she gets, the more confusing the feelings that slice through her become. She's not about to forgive him any time soon, but there's a hint of pity creeping in at the edges. Like for once, he might not be to blame for something.

'I leave here tomorrow afternoon,' she says. 'Listen, I'm gonna call Fiona now. Let me know how everything goes, yeah?'

She ends the call, closes her eyes and huffs out a loud sigh, trying to smooth the choppy waters in her head. Not for the first time, she regrets leaving her running shoes at home. The thought of pounding the pavements, breathing in the brisk October air by the side of the Seine. Even as she pictures it, shadows creep around the edges, a figure on a bridge advancing towards her. Eyes flick open and she's all too aware of her heart beating double time.

Get your head in the game.

She clears her throat as the ringtone echoes in her ear. Fiona's voice, when it comes, sounds on edge. Alice can empathise.

'Hiya Fi. Sorry I didn't get back to you yesterday.'

'Where the hell were you?' Fi says, in a rush of words. 'I was worried sick.'

'Sorry. Just really busy, it was just all a bit crazy.'

'Did you speak to them then? That agent and the other guy in prison? Spill the beans.'

'Yeah, but there's something I need you to do for me first. I need you …'

'No, no, no,' Fiona says, as if she's telling off one of the twins. 'Spill the deets first, then ask your favour.'

'Jesus, Fi, it's not for me. It's about Dad,' she snaps. 'Well, strictly speaking it's about Mariella.'

'Mariella?'

Alice isn't sure that telling Fiona every last detail will do any good. Doesn't want her sister sent into a tail-spin of panic, but there's no sugar-coating the threat that Mariella and Anthony might be under. She gives Fiona an abridged version of the last few days, leaving out the incident on the bridge and the men outside her hotel.

'Oh my God!' Fiona exclaims when she's done. 'Hang on, I'll message her now.'

As the seconds stretch out, Alice's mind wanders to the conversation she needs to have with Dad later. Just the two of them this time. Even though they'll be thousands of miles apart, the thought of being one on one sends a feeling rippling through her stomach, like wriggling worms.

'Right, done,' Fiona says, snapping Alice back to the here and now. 'Come on then, you said Sofia found that homeless guy. What did he say?'

'He's willing to make a statement,' says Alice, but moves to keep Fiona's hopes from soaring away like a helium balloon. 'There's a photo too, not a great one, but he has a picture that shows the guy he saw. It's a positive start, but we need more.'

'Okay,' says Fiona after a pause, like a kid who's just had their candy snatched away. 'More like what?'

'I'm following up something Agent Boudreaux came across,' she says. 'Other cases similar to Dad's. Might be nothing, but when you spoke to Mariella, did she say anything about Dad spending any time abroad? France or anywhere else in Europe?'

'Europe?' she repeats. 'Not that she mentioned. Why? What's that got to do with anything?'

'Like I said, it might be nothing, but these other cases might have connections to the guy I spoke to in prison here, Alain Dufort,' she says, stripping out detail to keep the tone as light as possible. 'Anything that casts doubt might help Dad.'

'What kind of other cases?' There's a hint of suspicion in Fiona's voice, as if she knows Alice is being sparing with detail.

'More murders,' she says finally. 'I can't go into specifics right now, but these ones happened when Dad was already in jail.'

'Another … wait, what are you saying? That someone has set Dad up?'

'We don't know that just yet, but—'

'But what? What *do* you know? What are you not telling me?'

'Listen to me, Fiona, I'm telling you as much as I know. I'm speaking with Agent Boudreaux again later, but I'm going to be honest, whatever this is, at the moment I don't think it's enough to change things.'

'But what about the homeless guy?' Fiona asks.

'If Grant McKenzie is all we have, it probably won't be enough. We need to do more than just say Dad didn't do it. We need to give them an alternative.'

'Like who?'

'I haven't got a clue. That's Boudreaux's job, not ours.'

'So you're leaving it all up to the guy who put him in there in the first place?'

'Yes.' Alice can't help the snappiness in her tone. 'That's exactly what I'm doing. We're not coppers, Fi. That's not our job. Let's be honest, we're barely his daughters, not after what he did.'

'Speak for yourself,' Fiona spits back.

And there it is, the boil they've never quite managed to lance. Fiona carries on before Alice can argue back.

'Everything is someone else's fault with you, Al. Dad's fault for the divorce. Mum's fault for having a stroke. My fault you came home to look after Mum 'cos I was stupid enough to get pregnant.'

'Fi, I ...'

'I heard you talking on the phone back then, when she was in hospital. Don't even know who you were talking to, but I heard what you said. That I was just a silly little girl who made bad choices.'

Alice remembers the conversation. The day after Mum's stroke when she'd rushed back across the Atlantic to be by her bedside. A call to her then-boyfriend, frustration at Fiona spilling out in what she thought had been a private conversation. Evidently not.

'That's not what I meant, Fi.'

'Oh really? Why don't you explain it to me now then?'

Alice hesitates, feeling the guilty edge to the words she remembers saying back then. She wouldn't have chosen that way to say it if she'd known Fi was listening. The pause can't be for more than a few seconds, but Fiona doesn't give her the chance to walk it back.

'You know what, don't bother. I'll send you the address when I get it.'

There's a click and she's gone. Alice's cheeks flush hot, a mix of anger and embarrassment. Of all the times to pick a fight. Then again, she admits to herself, Fiona hadn't exactly needed to look too hard for one thanks to Alice's pop at Dad. Not that he didn't deserve it, but if she's going to make headway, she has to step back from the line she drew between herself and Dad all those years ago.

If she keeps this up, she might not just lose a parent. Might be a sister as well.

Chapter Thirty

Wednesday – Five days to go

'You interrupted my lunch for this?'

Pascal Lavigne couldn't look less impressed if Boudreaux just took the top of his sandwich and spat in it.

'Sir, look at the …'

'Before I look at anything, how about you remind me what we spoke about last time you were standing there.'

'That was then, before I read the local files. It's not just how these men died, there's another connection too. One I didn't know about yesterday.'

'I'll remind you, shall I?'

Lavigne switches to his schoolteacher tone, one that never fails to irritate Boudreaux, about as welcome as gravel on bare feet.

'Sir, I …'

'I told you, under no circumstances were you to go fishing. I told you to stay away from a list of perfectly good convictions in countries you're not even assigned to work in.'

'Even if you just look at the French case, it's grown arms and legs,' Boudreaux says, feeling the heat rising in his cheeks. 'The guy in La Santé, Alain Dufort, his people are targeting the attorney who represents the man on death row back home.'

'And I'm sure her local police department will be happy to help her with that.'

Boudreaux realises Lavigne hasn't twigged that Alice is in town. He didn't get a chance to tell him when the first attempt to talk about this had been dismissed out of hand. This is going to go down as well as a terminal diagnosis, another stick for Lavigne to beat him with.

'That's just it though, sir, she's here, in Paris.'

Lavigne drops the half sandwich back onto the wrapper with a solid thunk, wipes his hands free of imaginary crumbs and leans back into his chair.

'Then tell her to call the police. A prisoner rattling his cage is not the concern of an international agency,' he says, condescension dripping from every word.

'If he's somehow linked to these others, how is it not our concern?'

Lavigne looks incredulous that Boudreaux is still standing his ground. 'Linked you say? Explain to me exactly how what you've got constitutes a link,' he says, no attempt to hide his contempt, but Boudreaux lets it slide off him like butter from a griddle.

'You know yourself how some countries have dragged their feet when it comes to full integration. Our data only picked up hits based on the wound type and toxicology. What we're missing is depth, interview transcripts, that kind of thing.'

'Yes, yes,' he says, looking bored. 'Tell me something I don't know.'

'I've spoken with someone on the ground in one of the countries. And don't worry, I've played it down,' he says, seeing panic flash in his boss's eyes like gold in a pan. 'They don't know about the others.'

Little white lie. Hayley knows, but she's rock solid.

'Bosnia,' he continues. 'Same as the French case. A man winds up dead in Sarajevo with his carotid popped. The guy they arrest for it had a run-in with local PD a week or two before the murder.'

'What do you mean, a run-in?' Lavigne looks more interested in the lettuce that's fallen onto his desk.

'As in he allegedly beat the shit outta his girlfriend. Put her in a coma for a month. Only witness they had disappeared. Then just a few weeks later the guy gets picked up for a murder that's airtight. The same happened in the other cases too. We've got twelve men serving time for murder in different countries, all of whom should have been behind bars already for either serious assault or murder, apart from Jim Sharp, but nothing stuck. Nothing except the very next one they're suspected of, with the MO they all share.'

'Breaking news, criminals hurt people,' Lavigne says through a mouthful of baguette.

'All of the people these men hurt in the run-up to the murders they're doing time for now, were taken to United Nations field hospitals.'

'Really?' Lavigne looks unimpressed, and Boudreaux allows himself a fleeting daydream where he grinds the remains of the crusty bread into Lavigne's face just to get his attention. 'That's your smoking gun? One small problem. Last time I checked the UN don't operate field operations in France. Your man in La Santé kills that theory.'

'Uh-uh,' he says, revelling in having ready-made answers to fire back at him like a fastball. 'Dufort's run-in was in Cyprus.'

'So, what's your point?'

'My point is there are only so many layers of coincidence we can brush off before we have a duty to look closer.'

The pig-headed stubbornness of the man astounds him. There are ways of doing this quietly that won't upset any apple carts, but it's as if Lavigne has a vested interest in killing any line of enquiry before it's out of the blocks.

Lavigne swallows his last mouthful, licking mayo from his fingers.

'And I'm saying all twelve could be long-lost family members, but it doesn't change the fact that those men who were convicted were put away by solid police work, and even more solid forensics.'

He has a valid point. The hard evidence tells a very one-sided story, but it's blinding him to even the most microscopic of possibilities.

'With respect, it wouldn't be the first time a lab got it wrong.'

'No,' he concedes, but the odds you're talking about of that happening this many times, you'd have more luck buying a lottery ticket.'

'There's always someone who wins eventually.'

Lavigne sighs like a parent who has reached their limits. Boudreaux meets his gaze, spoiling for a fight, but he squashes it back down. Opts for a different approach.

'I've been here before,' he says, calling out the elephant in the room. 'Absolutely convinced my approach was the right way, no one could tell me any different. I wouldn't even entertain the possibility.'

He chews his bottom lip. This isn't something he talks about to many people. Feels awkward to open up to his boss in particular.

'My stubbornness cost a witness her life, and I have to live with that. Doesn't mean I have to let it happen again.'

'And why exactly are you saying these men's lives are in danger?'

'Not all of them,' he concedes. 'Just one.'

Lavigne listens in silence as Boudreaux runs him through Jim Sharp's case, the awful sense of déjà vu that has been squatting nearby in the shadows since Alice Logan arrived in town.

'That's quite the tale, Luc,' Lavigne says when he's done.

The use of his first name takes Boudreaux by surprise. Strips away a layer of the stubbornness he feels whenever they talk. Makes him think he might just have got Lavigne on side. That notion lasts all of two seconds.

'But it doesn't change anything. Doesn't make the evidence disappear like some kind of magic trick. And now you're saying what? That there's this tenuous connection that these men all put people in UN hospitals before they finally screwed up? Different hospitals, different countries.

'Sir, I—'

'What I'm hearing is you screwed up before, and it's making you question your own judgement. Sounds to me like this is more about some kind of penance for you than anything rooted in reality. There's joining dots, then there's creating the damn things out of thin air yourself.'

'You think I'm making this up to suit my own needs?' Lavigne's words have stoked the fire in Boudreaux's gut again. 'All I'm saying is let me follow up on the others. I'll bring everything I find direct to you. I'll be discreet. It just—'

'It stops here,' Lavigne says, slapping a palm against his desk. 'If you wish to reopen Jim Sharp's case, I'll be happy to speak to your old boss at the Orlando PD about a transfer back, and you can do it on their time, but I'm ordering you to stand down on this. Are we clear?'

Boudreaux stands in shocked silence. As Lavigne meets his gaze, he hardens his own, trying to bore some sense into his boss.

'Are we clear?' Lavigne repeats, each word slow and deliberate.

'You're not even willing to try?'

Lavigne doesn't reply. Meets his stare with stony silence.

'When it came out about Mario Higuita, they crucified us in the press. Made it sound like we'd coerced the witness. You want that kind of attention here if this goes the same way?'

'That's a big if from where I'm sitting,' he says. 'Besides, I understand there are plenty who still think you might have.'

The cheap shot makes Boudreaux's blood fizz. Pressure builds in his head, and he clenches both fists by his side, pushing back down the urge to hammer them against the desk.

'And just to make sure there's no room for misunderstanding,' Lavigne continues, 'if I find out after you walk out of my office that you've pursued this any further, you'll be the one under investigation. I took a chance on you when you came across here. Don't make me regret it.'

He pushes back from his desk, stands up and grabs his jacket from the back of his chair.

'Now if you'll excuse me, I've got a meeting to go to.'

Lavigne moves to the door, holding out a hand, gesturing him out. Boudreaux grits his teeth, saying nothing as he storms past his boss. So many things he'd like to say to him right now, but what would it achieve? He double-times it, making a beeline for his own office, door slamming behind him. Goddamn Lavigne and his bureaucratic bullshit.

He walks over to his desk, slapping a hand against his chair in frustration. It spins, slowing to a lazy circle after a second rotation. Lavigne is leaving him with the shittiest of choices. Damned if he does, damned if he doesn't.

Who am I kidding, he thinks. Been damned a long time already.

Chapter Thirty-One

Wednesday – Five days to go

First thing Alice sees on screen is a slate grey wall, the bottom half of a window glowing near the top edge. It's practically luminescent thanks to the contrast with the drab room. The top half of a metal chair peeks over the rim of the table.

'You with us?' Sofia's voice comes from off screen. 'How's the sound?'

'Loud and clear,' says Alice, feeling a flutter of nerves in her chest.

'He should be here any minute. You want some privacy with him first, before you get into the meat of it?'

'Stay,' Alice says. 'He's holding something back, Sofia. Maybe I get him to open up, maybe not, but it's not the same, me being just a face on a screen.'

Sofia pops into view from the left, squatting down, arms resting on the table.

'Whatever you need.'

'How was the flight?'

'Short.'

Alice feels a fresh wave of gratitude. She's always known Sofia is a true friend, but this takes going above and beyond to a new level.

'Everything okay with Mariella?'

'Brought her with me,' she says. 'Told her there'd been threats, just not where from. Soon as she heard I was heading here, she wanted to come speak with your dad too.'

They talk tactics for a little over a minute before Alice hears a shuffling sound from off camera, dragging of shoes on concrete. Sofia stands up, moving out of shot.

'Mr Sharp.' Alice hears Sofia greet him and sees her hand slip back into shot as she pulls the chair out for him.

Her dad ambles into view, leg irons jangling like he's in a chain gang. Alice watches as the guard guides him into the seat, helps him scootch forwards, then threads his cuffs through the steel loop set into the table. Jim Sharp squints as he leans forward to peer at the screen.

'Hi,' says Alice, any semblance of pleasantries feeling alien under the circumstances. In the end she settles for a safe no man's land. 'How're you holding up? They treating you all right?' she asks, searching for the sweet spot between empathy and downright denial of where he is, and why he's there.

'Hey there, honey. They's treating me fine. I ain't got no complaints.'

'Good,' Alice says with a curt nod. 'The lady in the room, that's Sofia Marquez. She's an investigator. She's gonna stick around, help with a little background on some things she's found out.'

'Oh, okay, sure.' Sharp glances off screen, and Alice hears Sofia promising to call the guard when they're done.

'Just so you know, Dad, Mariella's here too. She's just down the hall. Travelled in with Sofia.'

'Ah, she's a good one, that woman. Always trailing up here like that to see me.'

Just the mention of her name seems to relax him, corners of his mouth twitching up in a half-smile, eyes crinkling at the edges. Even his shoulders relax a touch. It's both touching and heartbreaking all in the same moment. It snags in Alice like a dart, unable to remember the last time her mum generated that same response in him.

'I'm sure she is,' Alice says, tight-lipped.

'I worry about her, you know, about how she'll be after …'

'Let's not think about that right now.' Alice tries to keep him focused. 'We've a way to go yet.'

He smiles at that, but it's one that's papering over ever-widening cracks.

'Anyway, Fiona asked me to pull a few strings. Get someone to look into your case. That's where Sofia comes in. She's getting you a new lawyer. I'm going to share a few things with you first though, okay?'

He nods, licking his lips nervously. She wonders if this is as weird for him as it feels for her.

'Okay, honey. But before you start, I just gotta say, I know this can't be easy for you.'

'Don't call me that.'

'Don't call you what, darlin'?' He looks confused.

'That either. Any of it,' she shoots back. 'We haven't played happy families for a long time, and that's not why I'm here today.'

His mouth opens a little but he clamps it shut again, nodding.

'I guess I deserve that,' he says slowly. 'Probably a whole lot more besides.'

She almost laughs out loud with the scale of the understatement.

'And I know you don't gotta whole lot of reasons to help me, but as God is my witness, if I come through this, I will find a way to make it up to you. To all of you.'

The nerve of him thinking that if he gets out of here she'd let him even try. Takes a moment, but she swallows down the resentment she still feels towards him and silently berates herself for letting Fi back her into this emotional corner.

Alice has run a few versions of this in her head before she called. It's a fine line to tread, sharing an honest account of where the case sits and tempering it with enough realism to highlight the holes big enough that the State can drive a bus through.

She runs him through the last few days. The leaps of imagination she's taking with the other eleven cases. How there needs to be a more solid link than the gossamer-thin threads connecting them to him.

When she mentions Mac's name, that not only have they found him, but that they've spoken, his eyes widen in genuine surprise.

'How did you even … what did he say?'

'He remembers it pretty well actually,' Alice says. 'He says he even contacted the police, but that nobody took him seriously enough to follow up.'

'What about the guy from the bar? Did he get a good look at him?'

Alice nods. 'Seems the guy came back another night, looking for Mac. He managed to get a pic on his old phone. Sofia, you got those ready?'

An iPad slides into view, and Sharp leans forward as Sofia swipes a finger across every few seconds. His shoulders rise and fall that little bit faster as he studies the screen.

When Sharp sits back up, his forehead crinkles in confusion. 'You can't even see his face. That could be anybody.'

Whether it's frustration or fear, the edge in his voice is palpable. Like he expected this to be his get out of jail free card. His breathing quickens as he shakes his head. 'This ain't nothing but another nail in my coffin.'

Could just be a trick of the light, but looks to Alice like he's on the verge of welling up. One more blow away from being floored for good.

'What it is, is a start Mr Sharp,' Sofia says. 'A case like yours doesn't get anywhere overnight, but at this stage, you're in a better place than you were yesterday.'

'I'm sorry. Don't mean to sound ungrateful,' he says, addressing Alice. ''S just, when you said you'd found him … all these years. No one apart from Mariella has ever believed me, not really. Only been one way this ends. I guess the thought of that changing is kinda hard to get my head around, you know? It's got me a little on edge.'

He still has something of a faraway look in his eyes. Like he can't quite believe where he's sitting. What must it be like, she wonders, to know your days are literally numbered? Single figures. Just contemplating the notion generates the smallest spark of empathy. Only flares for a second though, before her mind slots back into gear.

'You don't need to explain,' Alice says, although him saying she believes in him makes her want to set him straight. Some thoughts are better left unsaid, for now at least. She waits a beat before asking her next question.

'The quality's not great, but does seeing it bring back anything about him, about the night in general?'

She watches as he looks down at the photos again, running his tongue over his teeth. There's a moment when he leans in an inch, and she wonders if something has registered, but he leans back shaking his head.

'No,' he says, low and quiet. 'Not a damn thing.'

He hasn't aged well in Raiford, and the creases across his face are a roadmap of regrets. He shakes his head again, furrows of frustration scored across his forehead.

Sofia flicks a finger across the screen again, cycling through the four prints. 'I've got someone working on picture quality,' she says. 'Try not to focus on his face. Let your eyes roam around. I'll leave it on while we talk, see if anything comes back.'

'These other cases,' Alice says, 'the ones in Europe. I don't know what to make of them yet. If they're going to be any help, we need more than just a passing resemblance. I need to know what could connect Florida to any of these. What could connect you to them.'

'I don't know what to tell ya,' he shrugs. 'Ain't never been to Europe apart from England, much less know folk there.'

'What about any ...' Alice searches for the right word, '... associates who might have connections.'

The suggestion seems to offend him, and he scowls. 'I don't care what that jury said, I ain't like these other folks in here. I know I ain't always made good choices, but I put all that shit behind me before I ended up in here.'

'I'm not looking to stitch you up here, Dad,' Alice says, holding her palms up. 'It's none of my business and I'm not judging you. All this is about is keeping that needle from your arm, and to do that, I need something solid.'

'You think I wouldn't give it up if I knew anything?' he says, sounding a little snarky.

'All we're saying,' Sofia cuts in, 'is that sometimes the smallest detail helps, things you might not think matter, help us stitch a defence together.'

He slumps back in his seat, eyes closed. 'All's I remember is going into that bar, ordering a few rounds. After that, it's a blur.'

'That's one thing I wanted to ask about,' Alice says, changing tack, hoping to ease up on the gas a little. 'And this is me playing devil's advocate. If I wanted to set you up, why would I drive you to Manny Castillo's place in my own car? Why not take yours so it'd be caught on traffic cameras?'

Sharp opens his mouth to answer, but whatever response he has cued up gets snagged, like hair in a drain.

'I, um, I wouldn't know.'

'It's the kind of question the DA would ask.'

'Remind me what happened to your car by the way?' Alice tosses it in, a casual enough question, but there's a flicker of something. What, she isn't sure, but she waits him out, wondering which of the conflicting versions of what happened to his car he'll churn out this time.

'I … don't know. Probably ended up in the pound.'

'Uh-uh,' Sofia chips in. 'I had a friend in the department check. No record of your car being towed anywhere within the city limits. You see, we're wondering if it's a possible secondary crime scene. Whether this guy went anywhere near it, then got rid.'

'Why would you think that?'

'They tried to find it back then,' Sofia says. 'You'd be amazed at what people let slip between seats, leave in the glove box. It's like an evidential candy store. Doesn't look as if they tried too hard by the looks of it though. Case against you looked pretty strong from the get-go. Could be another thing they've overlooked though.'

'Like I said, I don't remember. Wish I could. Might have had me outta these years ago.' He rattles his cuffs like a ghost with chains, wearing a smile that doesn't quite fit.

'Nobody ever follow that up for you?' Alice asks. 'Not even Mariella? Even if the guy never went within a block of it, it's still a little weird to just forget about it. Mariella could have used it or sold it.'

'I already told you dammit,' he snaps through clenched teeth, more steel in his voice than she's heard so far. It's enough to make her flinch a touch in surprise. A flash of the old dad she knows. 'Wherever it is, got nothing to do with where I am now. Where I'm going.'

The flash of anger fades fast as smoke on a breeze. Zero to sixty in under a second, then back to a standstill.

'That's all I've got for now then,' Alice says brusquely after a pause. 'We'll send Mariella along now.'

Sofia's face pops up on screen as the iPad is swivelled away from Sharp. She promises to call Alice as soon as she's switched places with Mariella. Alice taps send on a text she's quickly composed, seeing the slightest of nods as Sofia reads it.

Something not right. Get Mariella to mention the car.

The drab Raiford room disappears from her screen, and Alice is left alone in the silence of her temporary home, waiting for Sofia to call back. Her dad's reaction at Alice probing around the car has left her with an uneasy feeling. Like she's stepped onto a boat and still hasn't quite found her sea legs. That instant outburst, like dropping a Mentos into Coke.

She reminds herself that reading the emotions of a man due to die in a matter of days is not an exact science. All the same, if he hadn't snapped, she may well have let it slide.

She busies herself with a dozen other emails in her inbox while she waits. Fingers flutter across the keyboard, tapping out a hypnotic beat. Try as she might though, she keeps flashing back to her dad. Gritted teeth and cuffs nipping the edges of his wrists as he leaned into the table.

Everything about him, other than those brief seconds, has been beaten down, all hope wrung out like a damp dishcloth. Could be nothing, but she's never been one to walk away from unanswered questions. The only man who can answer this one is her dad himself. She flashes back to the picture of Mariella and Anthony courtesy of the unknown number. What does he stand to lose by keeping secrets?

Everything.

Chapter Thirty-Two

Wednesday – Five days to go

Alice's patience is paper thin by the time Sofia calls back a full forty minutes later.

'I was beginning to think they'd put you back in the cell with him.'

'I've lived in worse.'

'You'll be telling me next his room service is terrible.'

'Don't even go there.'

'How did it go? Did she mention the car?'

Sofia nods. 'She did.'

'And?'

'And he's not exactly a master criminal.' Alice frowns as Sofia continues. 'So I was a little sneaky. It's unlike me, I know,' she says, doing her best 'who, moi?' face. 'But you're going to want to hear this.'

'Bearing in mind he was found covered in another man's blood I think we'd already established that part but okay.'

'I know you asked me to record our chat with him so you could go back over it if needed, so I thought I may as well do the same for the one he's just had with Mariella.'

'Does he know?' Alice says in surprise. 'Does she for that matter?'

'It's hardly being sneaky if I told them,' Sofia says, feigning offence. 'I just hit record as soon as I opened the call before either of them saw the screen, then left 'em to it.

Alice shakes her head in disbelief. 'Where's Mariella now?'

'Waiting in the car. I told her I needed to speak to the warden about another chat with your dad.' Sofia pauses a beat. 'Look, you trust me, right?' she says, any trace of humour dispensed with. 'You know as well as I do he's holding back. Only question is why. You wanna know why I recorded it? Because when I went to get Mariella and asked her to mention the car, she said she already knew about it. She said it had been stolen a week or so before he was arrested. He'd been stupid and left the key in the ignition, so wouldn't even have been covered by the insurance. She'd asked him about it at the time 'cos she didn't have one, and wanted to borrow his while he was in lock-up.'

'What? But that makes no sense. Why would he tell her that?'

'You tell me. Anyway, I asked her to bring it up in any case. Get this, he tells her he'd borrowed a runaround from a friend, an old Buick he says. That's what he says he was driving that night. Said he must just have forgotten to tell her.'

'What the hell is it with this car? Why would he not have mentioned it to us just now?'

'That's not the best part though. The kicker is the key. The bunch they found on him when they picked him up had a car key on. Not one for a Buick though. One they had was for his original car, a Toyota Camry. You want to tell me why you'd have a key for a car that was stolen on you instead of one for the new car you're driving?'

Alice puffs out her cheeks. 'I'd say it doesn't change the fact that they found him with enough blood to take a bath in, but this doesn't feel right. What else can we do if he won't open up?'

'Honestly, you want my opinion, we go back in now and hit hard. Lay it all out there, that picture you got. If he thinks staying quiet is keeping anyone safe, we need to show him that's what's putting people in danger.'

Alice hesitates, and Sofia's eyebrows arch up in challenge.

'It's the right move. You know it.'

She does. It's more the fact she's not there. Virtual interviews are like a two-dimensional replica of the real thing. No substitute for being there in the thick of it, picking up on the micro-expressions, the jiggle of a client's leg under the table betraying nerves. What option does she have though?

'Let's get him back in.'

Chapter Thirty-Three

Wednesday – Five days to go

'What happened? Y'all forget to validate your parking?' Jim Sharp's eyes dart side to side, from where she imagines her face must be in his screen, to Sofia, somewhere off stage-right.

'Here's the thing, Dad.' Alice dives in head first. 'We know you're holding back. Mariella told us about the car, how you'd said back then that it was stolen.'

'I …' He starts to speak, stops, brain not quite in gear to deal with what's coming his way. Alice doesn't give him a chance to find his feet.

'You told us you'd left it near the bar, that you'd driven it there that day. Now why would you go and tell Mariella something completely different? I know one thing for sure, you're lying to one of us. You did enough of that when I was a kid, so it stops now or I'm off home.'

She pauses, watching his face. It's a confused canvas of creases as he frowns, trying to work out an exit route from whatever dead end he has driven down.

'And before you start spinning me a line here, Dad, I should tell you in the interests of full disclosure, that there are people out there involved in this case who are making threats.'

Her words are like a slap across the face, snapping his head out of the quicksand it's sinking in.

'What kind of threats?'

Alice nods to Sofia, who holds her phone up, showing the picture of Mariella and Anthony, reading the text out to him as she does.

'Mariella! Anthony! Who the hell is threatening them? Those fuckers better not lay a finger on her, or I swear to God …'

'Which fuckers would those be?' Sofia asks casually, like she's enquiring about the weather.

Sharp grunts in frustration, clenching and unclenching his fists. He glares at Sofia, but says nothing.

'C'mon Dad, this is as real as it gets,' Alice says. 'Look at the picture on Sofia's phone. This was sent to me yesterday. I've had men watching my hotel. Whatever this is, it's bigger than just your case. If you won't open up for yourself, then do it for Mariella, 'cos whoever they are, you sure as hell can't protect her from the likes of them, and neither can we.'

His eyes are pools of panic as he sees the picture.

'You don't understand,' he says in a voice half whine, half whimper.

'Try me, Dad, 'cos we're about out of options here.'

The silence stretches out as the timer in the corner counts off first five seconds, then ten. Jim Sharp stares down at his hands, all the fight running out of him like a cracked hourglass. When he finally starts to talk again, the same thousand-yard stare she saw on the screen in

Fiona's kitchen is back, voice flat like the fight has been beaten out of him.

'It's got nothing to do with my case, I promise you, but I … I did something. Something bad.'

'Bad? You're facing the needle for murder, Dad. It doesn't get much worse than this.'

'Before I mean.'

Alice waits him out, not wanting to throw him off his stride.

'You can't tell Mariella about this,' he says, looking at Alice with pleading eyes that would put a puppy to shame. 'She'll never speak to me if she finds out. You might not either.'

'If we find out what?'

'Promise me!'

Even from thousands of miles away, the strain in his voice is a tangible thing.

'You have my word,' Alice says, feeling the familiar fizz of anticipation in her stomach.

'It was little over a week before everything happened,' he begins. 'I'd had a shitty day. Screwed up big time at work. Yeah, I had a regular nine to five, trying to go straight. My boss told me I was in the last chance saloon, and I was in a foul mood. Couldn't go home like that. Mariella and Anthony had it hard enough back then without me putting a downer on everything.'

'Where did you go?'

'Just drove around for a bit, you know. Went to see a buddy of mine over in Kissimmee. He wasn't in yet, so I went into the bar on the corner of his street for a drink while

I waited. Turned out he got held up and I had a few more than I'd planned. You know how it is.'

His last trip to a bar hadn't ended well for him. How much worse can this one be?

'Mariella kept calling, leaving messages asking where I was, what time I was coming home, but I was just in a shitty mood, so I ended up staying out. Musta been around one in the morning by the time I was ready to head home. Figured Mariella would be asleep, and there'd be nobody left up to ask about my day. Anyway, I was hungry and went to grab a burger on the way back, but …'

Whatever highlight reel he's watching as he stares blankly at the table, he's getting to the meaty parts now. Flat tones give way to a throatier voice, battling with what it's about to say. Alice squints at the screen. Are his eyes filling up? Hard to say, the way he's looking down like that.

'Anyway, that's when it happened, on the way to a fucking drive-through.'

'When what happened?' Alice can't help herself.

The two lock eyes. It's as if the universe is holding its breath. When he speaks again, she almost wishes he hadn't.

'That's when I killed her.'

Chapter Thirty-Four

Wednesday – Five days to go

The dozen questions Alice had queued up slip away like cards up a magician's sleeve as she processes what she's just heard.

'Killed who, Dad? Who did you kill?'

The words sound as ridiculous out loud as they do in her head. Ironic seeing as he's a convicted murderer, but the feeling it sparks hits Alice like an avalanche. Something that she hasn't allowed herself to admit up until this point, but she realises now. That she doesn't truly think he's capable of murder. Didn't anyway, until she saw the look in his eyes when he said those five words.

That's when I killed her.

He continues like she hasn't even spoken. 'I could see the fucking golden arches a half mile down the road, and I was staring at them, thinking about what kind of burger to get, and she just … I didn't see the red light, and she stepped out into the intersection and I … I just …'

He sniffs loudly, clears his throat.

'I'm sorry, it's just … hard to talk about, you know? Anyways, I clipped her pretty good and she spun off back towards the sidewalk. I jerked the wheel real hard.

Must've spun a full three sixty, like some kind of damned fairground ride, before I stopped. It was the weirdest thing. I remember the sound when I hit her, but you know what I remember most?

Alice waits him out, stays quiet, gives him space to finish his story.

'When I got outta the car, it was so damned quiet,' he says, shaking his head. 'Like we were the only people in the world. No other cars, no people. I walked over to check on her. Think I'd hit my head on the dash, so everything was a bit fuzzy. Anyways, when I got there, she was … ah, Jesus, her face was all busted up. Bleeding and all, but she was breathing. I swear to God she was still breathing when I left her.'

'You left?' Alice says. 'You didn't wait around for the first responders?'

The shame is scored in every line of his face, like he's branded by it.

'All I could think about was what would happen if I stayed. I'd lose my licence. My job. Maybe even my family. Lost all that anyway. Maybe that's fate. Maybe I'm exactly where I belong,' he says, looking around the room.

'Wait,' Sofia says. 'You said you killed her, but you just told us she was still alive. What happened?'

'I saw headlights coming down the road and panicked,' he says. 'Stumbled back over to my car. God only knows how it still started. Front panels were all busted up. Then I just took off. Stopped a few miles away from home and called 911 from a payphone. Turns out I was too late anyway. I saw on the news the next day that she'd died.

Something about a bleed on her brain. They got her back to the hospital but she didn't make it through the night. You know what the worst part was?'

Worst part? Alice wonders where he's going with this. Surely that's the young woman you left dying in her car, Dad? The corners of his mouth start to twitch, like he's fighting to keep the words inside, squash any emotion down like a trash compactor, but one that's at bursting point.

'Worst part is that I wasn't even that hungry, but she's still dead because I wanted a fucking McDonald's. This is why I stopped fighting. Why I sacked my lawyer and made my peace with what's happening. Feels like the closer this has gotten, it's just the universe's way of levelling the scores. I'm right where I deserve to be.'

'You could have still come forward back then, Dad,' Alice says softly. 'Even after you found out she'd died. You could have come forward.'

She can't quite pick a word to describe what she's feeling right now. Her voice is almost a whisper, calm like the eye of a storm.

'I wanted to,' he says, looking a harsh word away from tears. 'You might not believe me, but I really did.'

But?'

'But I'm a fucking coward,' he says softly. 'Because I was already hanging on by a thread before I got behind the wheel that night. I wasn't strong enough to face up to what I did and survive, so I ran away.'

He's rocking ever so slightly. Hasn't looked at her once since he started offloading. The lawyer in her kicks in. DUI manslaughter over there is a second-degree felony.

Minimum four years, maximum as high as thirty. With a fair wind and a sympathetic jury, Dad could have confessed and been out by now. Doesn't change the revulsion she feels at learning that her father has taken a life, however much of an accident he's making it out to be.

'Who was she?' Alice asks. 'What was her name?'

'Honey, I … I can't …'

His eyes flit around the room, looking everywhere but hers.

'Dad!' she snaps, and the bite in her voice whips his head around like she's slapped him. 'Who was she?'

When he looks at her, there's a depth to his sadness that scares her. He blinks, making no effort to wipe the single tear that streaks south.

In that instant, she knows what he's going to say before the words come out. Hits her with the force of a Category 5 hurricane. A face flashes in her mind, bright and bold, as if Alice had just seen her yesterday. But that can't be, because she's been dead for eleven years.

Gail Lonsdale.

Chapter Thirty-Five

Wednesday – Five days to go

It's like the air has been sucked out of the room. It's all Alice can do to draw breath. His words wrap around her like a python, squeezing her chest in tight coils.

Gail.

Her best friend since high school.

Gail, whose life was snuffed out after a hit-and-run on a trip home to Florida. Driver never found. Case never solved. The injustice of it all has never left her, even more than a decade on.

'Alice, baby, you've got to know if I could take it back I would,' he stammers. 'She was still alive, I just thought …'

Whatever else he's saying fades to white noise. She sees his lips moving on screen, but all she can think about is getting the hell out of there. Her dad is leaning forward, and even though he's thousands of miles away it feels like he's crowding her. Alice shakes her head slowly. Ever so slightly at first, but as she pushes up from the table it becomes more pronounced.

The picture jerks sideways, and Sofia's face fills the screen.

'Alice? Alice, let's take a break. Let's …'

She grabs her jacket, whirls round and is out of the door before she can hear the rest of Sofia's sentence. Feels like she's floating along the corridors. All she can think of is getting as far away from him as possible. Stupid, she knows, bearing in mind there's already over four thousand miles between them, but he's just ripped a scab off a wound that runs right to the core of her.

When she makes it outside, she sucks in lungful after lungful of air, breathing heavily like she's just done a workout. She jogs across the courtyard and out onto the street, no real sense of where she's headed. Just anywhere but here. Memories well up like a hot spring. Happy high school snaps. Her and Gail. Siamese twins her mum used to call them. Joined at the hip.

Felt like she lost a sister back then, not just a friend. The fact that her own dad is the man who took Gail from her is of such a scale that it dwarfs her. Towers over her like a wave about to break, one that will crush her if she lets it.

Alice lifts her eyes from the pavement, realises through the brain fog that she's coming up to the river. There's a flash of panic as she looks around, half expecting to see the same pursuer as last time, but nobody gives her a second glance.

She plants both palms on the side of the bridge, a million miles away from the sense of calm she felt the first time she'd walked along it. Beneath her, the sluggish Seine carries a handful of boats along. Oh to be on one of them, drifting far away from what is becoming an increasingly chaotic situation she wishes she'd stayed well clear of.

Alice closes her eyes. Focuses on slowing down her breathing. Centres herself. Takes a full minute to lose the desperate edge to the rhythm of her heart. She's done. Done with all of this. With him, with Boudreaux, with the whole bloody lot of it.

Where her dad is now, with what's about to happen, feels almost biblical. An eye for an eye. Right now, she can't think of a single reason to do anything other than pack her bag and head home. Let nature take its course.

Fiona. She has a right to know. Needs to understand what this man she's hell-bent on saving is capable of. Not over the phone though. Not after the way the last conversation was cut short. Alice needs to be there, in the room, to wrap her arms around what little family she has.

Family. The notion brings the image of Anthony to mind. Her little brother. Caught up in a river of shit that he didn't choose to jump into. Whatever happens to her dad, he doesn't deserve any of this.

The irony of it all hits her. If she hadn't hightailed it over here to keep Fiona happy, Anthony wouldn't need Sofia to protect him. Alain Dufort would be rotting away in his cell, never crossing paths with any of them. Has she brought this to his door? Alice reaches into her jacket. Pulls out her phone and opens the thread with Anthony's picture on. She's never met him, but knowing that she's played a part in dragging him deeper than he needs to be is like diving into the North Sea. Waves of guilt wash over her, a riptide, but one that pulls her back towards shore. And just like that, the realisation settles over her, even as anger still fizzes in her veins. Anthony. He's the reason she can't wash her hands of it. She can't walk away from this until she knows he's safe. Sofia can protect him for now, but she can't sit on sentry duty forever.

Whatever happens to her dad after that doesn't matter in the grand scheme of things. She's lived so long without him, she can fall back into that groove in a heartbeat. Anthony's picture disappears as her phone starts to vibrate. Sofia's name flashes up.

'Hey,' is all Alice can muster.

'Jesus, Alice, you scared me running off like that. Where are you? You okay?'

'I'm fine,' she says. 'Well, no actually, I'm pretty fucking far from fine. I just had to get out of there, you know?'

She hears a sigh on the other end of the line. 'I hear you. And I hate to do this to you after what you just heard back there, but there's something you should know. Something that happened after you left.'

Alice frowns. 'What kind of something?'

'When you left, the call was still live. Those pictures on the noticeboard behind you?'

'Wait, what? The ones of the guy outside my hotel?'

'Yep,' says Sofia, and it's impossible to miss the excited edge to her voice. 'Your dad thought they were the ones Mac took. He said the hat looked the same, Alice. The hat the guy was wearing in Paris reminded him of the one the guy who walked out that bar with your dad was wearing.'

Alice pauses, picturing the distinctive red silhouette on the cap her pursuer had worn, photos pinned to the noticeboard behind her desk. How Mac had described the guy he'd seen Dad with. Mac's pics are blurry, hard to tell for sure. The ones on her noticeboard are definitely the same shape logo. The Eiffel Tower. The Paris Saint-Germain badge.

'You saying it's the same guy?'

'Impossible to know,' Sofia says quickly, 'but are you gonna tell me that's just a coincidence?'

Alice's heart beats like a bass drum. Sofia's revelation stands firm against the tsunami of emotions swamping her right now. Not for Dad, she reminds herself. He's dead to her. For Anthony. You wanted a connection, she thinks to herself. You got one. Just need to figure out what the hell it means now.

Chapter Thirty-Six

Wednesday – Five days to go

'Leave it with me,' Sofia says. 'I'll work the gang angle, see what ties they have in the US. Whether Gail Lonsdale or her family crossed paths with them in any way.'

Alice opens her mouth to speak but Sofia keeps talking before she gets the chance.

'And before you say your friend wouldn't have been mixed up in that world, I'm not saying she was, but there's gotta be a link between your dad and Dufort somewhere. It's as good a place to start as any. And Alice …'

There's a silence that craves to be filled, but there's a lump forming in Alice's throat the size of a bowling ball, and she can't trust herself to speak as the aftershock of Dad's bombshell hits her.

'I'm so sorry. Sorry for what he did. Sorry you had to find out like that. Whatever you want, whatever you need, I'm here.'

Alice swallows hard. Nods even though Sofia is an ocean away.

'I'll be okay,' she says, knowing that she isn't. Might not be ever again. This will hit home over and over. A wrecking ball to her hard-won headspace. Better make sure it's worth it, she tells herself. For Fiona and Anthony's sake, if not her own.

Alice weaves her way back through the streets, flashing a visitor's pass as she heads back into the courtyard at the Préfecture de Police. She gets Sofia to relay as close to verbatim as she can what was said after she ran out. She's right. Can't just be a coincidence, can it?

'So, the hat thing,' Sofia says. 'PSG are a huge club, but not in Florida. Just feels a little too spooky for it to be nothing. See what you can get out of Boudreaux about the guy from last night.'

Alice finds her way back to her temporary office. She opens the door, about to ask if there has been any progress tracing the call Mac says he made to the local PD, when a voice stops her.

Luc Boudreaux trots down the corridor, stopping abruptly in the doorway when he sees Alice is mid-conversation.

'Sorry to interrupt,' he says, looking a little flustered. 'We need to talk.'

'Can you give me five minutes?' she asks. Partly to finish up with Sofia, but also because she has the urge to press her forehead against the cool plaster, close her eyes, and just breathe.

Boudreaux shakes his head. 'If I don't tell you now, I might change my mind, and trust me, you need to hear this.'

'I'm on with my investigator,' she says, tapping to switch to speaker. 'Okay if she listens in?'

'Your ears only,' Boudreaux says.

'I'd trust Sofia with my life,' Alice shoots back.

Boudreaux chews on his bottom lip, conflict showing in every line of his frown. Alice holds her breath, and it's a full five count before Boudreaux steps forward, slumping into the spare chair.

'What I'm about to tell you,' he speaks slowly, and Alice is painfully aware of how quiet it is in the pauses that punctuate Boudreaux's words, 'it's not easy for me. This could hurt me depending on how you use it. I tell you this knowing that you have every right to want to do just that. But I'm going to do it anyway, because it's what's right.'

'And what do you get out of this selfless gesture?' Alice asks, struggling to keep the prickliness from her voice. Selfless gestures and law enforcement don't go hand in hand in her experience.

'Nothing,' Boudreaux says, and Alice raises an eyebrow in challenge. 'All right, I get to try and show you that I'm not who you think I am.'

Alice stays stock-still. He looks so earnest that she wants to believe him without question. Believe that this is a genuine olive branch. One she instinctively wants to reach for, but she forces herself to take a breath. She's not ready to accept that, not yet.

'And who do I think you are?'

'Someone who cuts corners. The kind that can get people killed.'

He rises to his feet and takes a step toward her as he speaks, and Alice stands her ground, only a few feet between them now.

'That's not who I am,' he says again, softer this time.

She looks at him, at his tired eyes, and for a beat fancies she can read him like an open book. A story she instinctively wants to believe. She bites down on her bottom lip, torn between buying what he's selling and keeping some semblance of a wall up. The few seconds' silence sits heavy as storm clouds, until Alice finally looks away, eyes flicking to her phone screen where she's laid it on the desk. Sophia will be wondering what the hell is going on.

'I'm grateful for the help at the hotel,' she begins, 'but aside from that you've kept your cards close to your chest. Why change that now? Why should I trust you?'

'Because apart from you, I'm probably one of the people that thinks about guys like your dad the most. I come out of this with a clean conscience, I'll take that as a win.'

For all sorts of reasons, these past few days have been tougher than Alice will admit to anyone but herself. Sleep-deprived, hundreds of miles away from home. She carries the past few nights' worth of dreams like a weighted vest. All roads lead back to Boudreaux, to what he set in motion a decade ago.

She swallows down what she wants to say. There'll be a chance after this plays out, whichever way it goes, to have her moment. She reminds herself that this is about a ten-year-old boy now. One who doesn't deserve any of this. She needs to stay focused on him to get through it. Be the better person. Better than her dad.

'Let's hear it then.'

She sits back with low expectations, ready to be disappointed. Sits that little bit more upright when Boudreaux drops in a mention of a link between France and Bosnia. Eyes widening like a kid who's just seen the strings at a puppet show by the time Boudreaux shares the rest.

Chapter Thirty-Seven

Wednesday – Five days to go

'What will your boss say when he finds out?'

'He'll be pissed off, but if this plays out your way, there'll be too much noise for him to do much about it, for a while at least.'

'And if it doesn't?' Sofia asks, speaking for the first time from four thousand miles away.

Boudreaux shrugs. 'Then at least this time I know I tried hard enough.'

An uneasy quiet settles like a fresh blanket of snow, still and silent.

'What if he gets wind early?' Alice asks finally. 'He might put a spin on it to say it's personal for both of us, pull down the shutters. One thing we don't have is time. If I have to work too hard to get the information I need—'

'He won't.'

'How can you be so sure?'

'You're going to have to trust me on that one. I've called in a favour of my own to fix that.'

Alice narrows her eyes but doesn't push it.

'So, this United Nations link, run that by me again.'

Boudreaux runs through the other countries one at a time, rattling through the couple that he knows fit the pattern already. France and Bosnia. From there he bounces into the remaining nine that he has only discovered specifics on since he marched out of Lavigne's office. They read like the reports have been copied and pasted. From the puncture wounds to the tip-offs police received to arrest them, to the fact that their victims were all just as bad as their killers. Only one problem, a big one, that sticks out for Alice.

'This is all well and good, but there's no mention of anything to do with the UN as far as my dad is concerned. Nothing that links him or Manny Castillo over and above the similarities in the murders.'

'True,' Boudreaux concedes, 'but it's a step in the right direction for you.'

No UN link, but the fact that every other man on this list had got away with hurting people in the weeks or months that preceded their arrests. Alice flashes back to her dad's confession. It's like blowing on embers. Stokes up the fire that might yet burn her dad to a crisp if she's ever in the same room as him.

There's still a niggle though. The one that says not to trust Boudreaux all the way, no matter how much she's warmed to him. Now is not the time or place to share what Dad has revealed. She needs to buy Sofia time to do some digging. Also, she's not sure she can bring herself to repeat his tale. Not yet. His confession sits heavy across her soul. Speaking it out loud wouldn't so much feel like airing dirty laundry as wearing it, complete with stenches and stains. There may be a halfway house though.

'Maybe more of a step than you realise,' Alice says, choosing her words carefully. 'There are … things that my dad has shared, things he has done that line up with the profile of the others.'

Boudreaux shoots her a suspicious look. 'He's hurt someone?'

'I can't go into specifics yet,' Alice says. 'But if we need to use it, we will. For now, all you need to know is that he fits the profile.'

'You're telling me now that he's part of the same crew as our dirty dozen but you won't share why or how?'

'You've been asking me to trust you. You're going to need to do the same, for now at least.'

Boudreaux looks far from convinced, but Alice waits him out, and eventually the agent nods in agreement.

'All right, but if he's committed other crimes, I can't guarantee that doesn't come back on him later.'

'Fine,' Alice agrees. 'What's your move from here then?'

'First thing is to get more background on those field hospitals. All these men we know were killed or convicted, they had all put people in hospital first, hurt them badly enough that they never woke up. Someone might have taken it upon themselves to balance the scales. There has to be something or someone at those hospitals that connects them.'

'There was one other thing,' Alice chips in, filling Boudreaux in about the Paris Saint-Germain logo. 'I know it's asking you to stick your neck out, but any chance you could check up on the guy from last night, see if there's any record of him spending time Stateside?'

'Wait, what? You think the guy outside your hotel is your dad's mystery man from the bar?'

'It's a stretch, I know, but that's all he has left,' Alice says with a shrug. 'Speaking of which, now that you're taking a leap of faith, how about sharing the details of these other cases? Give us sight of your files. Sofia can see what she can dig out too. Two heads better than one when the clock's ticking. What do you say?'

Boudreaux rolls his tongue around the inside of his mouth, and Alice isn't getting a good vibe. The no man's land between them might have got smaller, but they're still each in their own trenches.

'Tell you what,' he says finally. 'I can give you names, but I'm not going back into the actual files to show you those. My ID gets clocked going back in, my boss has ammunition that I could do without.'

Self-preservation over selflessness. Alice will take what she can get, but Boudreaux is still making his choice of sides quite clear.

'I might have printed out copies of them that may or may not be in this folder,' Boudreaux continues with a ghost of a smile. 'Trouble is, I can't remember where I left it.' He drops it on the desk in front of Alice, and takes a step back towards the door. 'I'm sure it'll turn up though.'

'Thank you.'

'Anyway, I'm going to press on with this UN thing. Do me a favour, don't head out without telling me. These guys aren't usually this passive. Wouldn't put it past them to do something stupid, and I'm not having that, not in my city. Oh, and this …' he waggles a finger around the room, '… not a word of this outside of us three. That includes your pet agent too.'

Alice and Sofia say nothing, but know that last part is now the worst-kept secret in the room. Boudreaux leaves with a promise to keep Alice in the loop with anything UN related, and leaves her and Sofia in surprised silence.

'Did our good detective just cross over?' Sofia asks after a beat.

'I wouldn't go that far,' Alice says, wondering what label she'd slap on her stance on Boudreaux now. His stuffiness has melted away to the point where she feels relaxed around him. Borderline friendship. She wonders, not for the first time, if she's glimpsed a hint of something more in his eyes. Just something in the way he's looked at her. Her mind strays, wondering if she'd just bumped into him in a bar back home, how he'd look at her then. Whether she'd look at him the same way.

She shakes the thought away, reaching for the file. 'I'm going to dive into these now before he changes his mind. Call me if you get a better version of Mac's pictures, and keep close to Mariella.'

'Make copies, go, now. That way it doesn't matter if he does come back. Better still, take pictures and send them to me.'

Alice laughs at Sofia's on-the-spot ingenuity. 'Thank God you're on my side. That's all I'm saying.'

She ends the call, and two minutes later, after every page has been snapped and sent, Alice sets about soaking up the contents. Page after page of rap sheets. A regular rogues' gallery. Not the kind of guys that her dad's own past suggests he'll have been in bed with, but today's revelation has added an extra dimension. What if it's nothing to do with a shared criminal connection?

What if there is a link, however tenuous, between Gail Lonsdale and the case? Alice knew her as well as she knows herself, but she can't put her hand on her heart and say the same about Gail's family. What if the hit-and-run really is the bridge that spans the cases? Her mind zigzags like a downhill skier.

Still feels like a few steps away, but they're closer. She can feel it. Threads drawing together like purse strings. With that, though, comes the inexplicable sense that she's rushing towards something she doesn't fully understand. Alice is no stranger to running down her opponents in a courtroom from her days as an attorney Stateside, so why is she getting that tingle down her spine, the feel of hunted rather than hunter?

Chapter Thirty-Eight

Wednesday – Five days to go

The walls feel like they're closing in. Alice needs to breathe fresh air again. Clear her head.

She locks her laptop and heads out, closing the door behind her. As large as the building feels, it's still all straight lines and right angles. Corridors peel off the main drag but she follows her instincts and finds herself back at the front door a couple of minutes later.

Strips of cloud line a dirty blue sky, and the breeze flicks through the folds of her coat. The courtyard is littered with a few dozen cars, and with the high walls surrounding it, walking laps would feel like exercise in a prison yard.

Screw it, she thinks. It's still daylight. Once around the block. What's the worst that can happen? Besides, she recalls seeing a food cart that looked like it sells coffee out towards the river.

As she makes her way along Rue de la Cité, her eyes drift across face after face, looking for any sign of familiarity. Nothing, not a baseball cap in sight. The food cart is actually a little tuk-tuk style vehicle, with a built-in coffee machine, and an umbrella extending up and out to form a canopy. The barista wouldn't look out of place back in Tynemouth, surfing the waves off Long Sands beach. Blonde ponytail bouncing around as he busies himself cleaning the steamer wand on his pride and joy. His lightweight hoodie and Bermuda shorts look incongruous among the smartly dressed clientele.

Alice joins the queue, only four deep, and changes her mind three times while she waits.

'Oui Mademoiselle?' he asks in a voice that sounds like he's chain-smoked since birth.

'Decaf skinny latte,' she says with a smile, 's'il vous plaît.'

The words might be French, but the accent is fooling no one, and the barista beams.

'Ah, English, yes?'

'Oui.' She returns the smile, realises that he might think she speaks more than the dozen words she can manage, and switches to English just in case. 'Yes, English.'

'Welcome to Paris,' he says, topping up the hopper with a fresh bag of beans.

Seems that's the extent of his small talk, as he bustles between four coffees, each in various states of readiness, and Alice resumes her scan of the street.

'It's worth the wait.'

The voice comes from behind her. Female, New York in origin, Brooklyn possibly. Alice whips her head round as the woman orders a macchiato. She gives a polite smile that Alice returns out of habit.

'Course it's not quite as good as back home, but sometimes you just gotta make do,' the woman continues.

It's a friendly enough face. Teeth so perfect they might well be veneers, black woollen jacket buttoned up to the neck. Alice puts her around a similar age to herself, with a spray of freckles across pale skin.

'Anything hot and strong will do me right now,' Alice says.

Polite chit-chat, nothing more. She turns back and starts rummaging in her purse when it's her turn to collect. An arm shoots past from behind, close enough to make her flinch, a twenty euro note clamped between finger and thumb.

'Here, let me get this for you. Little treat from one expat to another.'

Same woman again, and Alice turns to study her face a second time. Should she know her? Someone from Boudreaux's team perhaps? The barista swaps the twenty for a ten and two cups, even as Alice answers.

'Thank you, but I'm fine, honestly.'

'Too late,' the woman says, holding up a palm, her change poking skywards from between two fingers.

'Have we met?' Alice asks, frowning.

'We have now,' the woman says, extending out a hand. 'Regina DiMarco. Most folks call me Gina.'

'Alice Logan.'

She shakes Gina DiMarco's hand, firm and cool, then wonders with a swooping dread if this is just a change of ploy from Dufort. Send in beauty instead of beast. Around them, the ebb and flow of people passes them by like they don't exist.

'I gotta be honest with you Alice, can I call you Alice? I just met you, but I do know you, of you anyway.'

'What's that supposed to mean?'

A card appears in DiMarco's hand like she's a street performer. 'When I'm not buying strange women coffee, I'm the Paris correspondent for Fox News. What brings you over to France?'

Alice smiles, but it feels like cracks in plaster. 'Oh, just seeing the sights.'

'Really? DiMarco says. ''Cos I could have sworn I just saw you coming out of the police headquarters up the road.'

Sharp intake of breath from Alice. 'Have you been following me?'

'Following? No. More like waiting. What kind of sights have you been seeing in there?'

Alice feels doorstepped, ambushed, and she goes on the offensive, answering a question with a question.

'And why would you be waiting? In fact, you know what, it doesn't matter. We're done.'

She drops a five euro note on the tiny counter beside them.

'That's for the coffee.'

Alice turns to walk away, but the journalist puts an arm out, barring her way.

'Wait, I just want to ...'

Alice glares but doesn't stop, pushing past the offending limb like it's a pinball flipper, calling over her shoulder as she does.

'I said we're done. I've got to get back.'

'Back to what?' DiMarco pipes up from behind her.

Alice doesn't look back, fixes her eyes on the street ahead and strides away, but DiMarco follows, practically trotting to keep up on shorter legs.

'Everyone's got a story to tell, Alice, and yours is exactly the kind my readers love. Daughter's dash across the channel to save her father from his fate. Just give me ten minutes, then I'll leave you alone.'

Alice looks nervously both ways as she practically power walks across the street towards the safety of police headquarters, but DiMarco is persistent.

'What did Luc Boudreaux have to say?' she asks, a touch breathy now. 'How was it meeting him after all these years?'

Curiosity laced with anger gets the better of Alice, and she stops, turning to confront her shadow.

'How did you even know I was in Paris? And how do you know I've talked with Agent Boudreaux?'

'C'mon,' says DiMarco playfully. 'Have I really gotta trot out the line about journalists and their sources?'

Alice grits her teeth, a dozen other questions rattling around her head, but she's not having this conversation with a journalist, and one she doesn't know to boot. Not now, not ever.

'I'm not your story,' she says, and sets off again.

'No? What about Alain Dufort?' DiMarco says in a voice that's pure mischief. 'He worth reporting on? I hear he doesn't get many visitors, and I figure you won't be wasting your time with anything other than your dad's case. Where does he fit in?'

How the hell does she know about Dufort? Alice is glad she's facing away so DiMarco can't see the surprise on her face.

'What's the deal Alice? You representing him now too, or are he and your dad just old buddies?'

Don't bite, she tells herself. Keep walking. Don't give her the satisfaction.

'You got plans this evening?' DiMarco persists. 'Buy you dinner?'

In response, Alice holds out her arm as she walks past a trash can, letting the coffee cup drop, splashing out through the lid as it hits the inside edge and falls in. If DiMarco has any other smart-ass remarks, they're lost in the hum of traffic, and Alice is left to her own thoughts as she heads back through the archway of the police building.

She's still smarting at being blindsided like that, and all she can think about is who has set this yapping little dog on her heels. If she knows about Dufort, that cuts the list right down. Only two people know Alice has visited him. Eva is one, and Sofia vouching for her is enough to win Alice over. The other, someone far more likely to have his own agenda here, is the person Alice was just starting to trust. Luc Boudreaux.

Chapter Thirty-Nine

Wednesday – Five days to go

'Luc! To what do I owe the pleasure?'

'I can't just call a friend to catch up on old times?'

'Some people could, but not you. We can spend the first few minutes asking what we've been up to if you really want though?'

'Still not one for small talk I see, Nate?'

'Gets in the way of the good stuff,' he says, and Boudreaux can picture the mischievous smile that is undoubtedly accompanying the words.

'Promise the next one will be for old times' sake,' he says, 'but I'm on a bit of a clock here.'

'You must be desperate if you need my help,' says Nate Lawson.

He's underselling himself dramatically of course. Lawson is within touching distance of the New York City Mayoral Office. The former Orlando police chief is one of the few that Boudreaux was genuinely sorry to say goodbye to when he left the States. He was Boudreaux's first commanding officer, as well as a friend of his father's, and he's always seen him as an uncle-type figure. Since he switched one kind of politics for another, his star has just kept on rising. As deputy mayor, he's already bookies' favourite when the incumbent steps aside in a little over twelve months.

'Seriously though,' he adds, 'you know I will if I can. What's up? This personal?'

'Kinda, yeah,' he says, and walks him through his last forty-eight hours.

'Oh Luc, you can't still beat yourself up over Nancy Killigan. That was a solid case against Higuita.'

Right up until it wasn't, Boudreaux thinks.

'That's just it though, Nate. I thought the Sharp case was solid too, and right now it feels like an eighteen-wheeler with the brakes cut.'

'What do you need?' he says, no quid pro quo, no agenda of his own, and Boudreaux feels a rush of gratitude before he even asks the favour.

'Remember a few years before I left, you told me how some guy from the UN kept trying to poach you to cross over and work for them? You still speak to him?'

'We talk from time to time. And he still tries every six months or so. Nice guy though, we play golf a few times a year.'

'Can you put me in touch with him? Something's come up in the case, and there's a link between all of 'em that's cropped up to do with the UN. I just need someone to speak to over there who can help with a little information.'

'Sure,' he says without hesitation. 'I can call him. Depends what you need as to whether he'll give it though. Can't imagine he'll be too keen to share if it's gonna make 'em look bad.'

'Nah, I'm sure it won't. I just need to know whether it's a solid link or not. This isn't me doing defence counsel's work for her. I just need to make that this isn't a repeat of Higuita, for my own sake.'

'I'll call him now and let you know,' Lawson says, and signs off after extracting a promise that Boudreaux will come over for dinner next time he's Stateside.

He's true to his word, and less than ten minutes later, Boudreaux's phone pings with contact details for a guy called Ravi Surjins, Deputy Director for the Office of Mission Support at the UN's Manhattan headquarters just off East 42nd Street by the East River.

Surjins picks up on the third ring.

'Agent Boudreaux, you're quick off the mark,' he says after Boudreaux introduces himself. 'I must have only put the phone down to Nate two minutes ago.'

'Time is rather of the essence, sir.'

'Please, call me Ravi. Now what is it I can help you with? Nate was a little sketchy on the detail.'

He lays it out for him. Jim Sharp, the link to France, how that spread its tentacles out into other territories, and how each of the convicted men had somebody they had recently tangled with end up in a UN hospital. No mention of the shadow of Mario Higuita lurking behind it all. That risks making it sound too personal for Boudreaux.

'It's a long shot, but with a man's life on the line back home, we've got to be sure,' he says, feeling every inch the hypocrite as the detective who'd walked away happy with the original outcome. 'I'm looking for staff and patient lists for the hospitals, either any names that crop up at more than one site, or with links to another.'

He makes a sound like he's blowing out air. 'That's no small task. We have peacekeeping missions ongoing in a dozen countries at the moment. Thousands of soldiers and support staff on loan to us from any of almost two hundred member states.'

'I appreciate that, sir … Ravi, but I'd like to rule it out all the same. Even if we just start with medical staff first, then move on to military after that.'

There's a pause, then he hears him clear his throat. 'Nate said it was a personal favour, I'll see what I can do. One condition though; if anything comes of it, you let me know before anyone else, outside of your own organisation of course. Last thing I need is something blowing up in the media without a chance to get out ahead of it. Deal?'

'Deal,' he says without hesitation. He's not exactly in a position to negotiate.

'Let me give you a name. One of our people you can go to for the actual data. I'll let him know you're calling. It's Doctor Elias Grey. He's one of our senior medical officers who assesses and coordinates deployment of all medical staff for our peacekeeping missions.'

Surjins rattles off a telephone number, and promises his next call will be to Grey. Boudreaux ends the call, feels twin rods of tension running down either side of his neck, and dips his head one way then the other, hearing a satisfying crunch. He grabs a coffee to give Surjins a chance to make his promised call, and moves over to the window that looks out onto the main road.

Boudreaux lets his mind wander as he watches the cars zip by. Couple more days tops to see this thing through with the UN and keep Alice Logan safe while she's in town. After that, assuming this run of coincidences peters out, he'll feel a damn sight safer that he's done his bit, even if that means Jim Sharp keeps his allotted date with destiny. This debt he feels he owes Alice, his penance, will be discharged in part at least. Whether it'll paper over the decade of cracks in his own opinion of himself remains to be seen.

At least, though, it'll let her go back to her family having done everything possible to keep her father alive, regardless of how complicated their relationship sounds. Her heading back to England makes him pause, part of him hoping she might stick around, even just for a day or two. Despite the initial tension between them, he feels at ease in her company. She's smart, principled, and takes no prisoners. The kind of person he'd like to get to know better if circumstances allowed.

Down below, a familiar face catches his eye. Alice Logan hustling towards the entrance at a rate of knots. There's a purpose to her stride, like she's got somewhere to be, and her face is set into hard lines. Movement behind her. Another woman.

Could be someone late for an appointment, but there's a determination on the woman's face, and Boudreaux can see her mouth moving. No sign of a phone or earbuds, so either she's talking to herself, or she's calling out to someone.

Alice looks pissed off, and Boudreaux opens the window six inches just in time to catch the woman calling a familiar name. He could swear he's seen her face before. Who is she and why the hell is she calling out something about Jim Sharp? Alice doesn't react, carrying on as if nothing has been said. Moments later, Alice flicks out an arm, consigning her coffee cup to the waste bin, before she makes a sharp right turn and disappears from view.

The other woman slows as she reaches the entrance, coming to a standstill. Boudreaux almost calls out, but reaches for his phone instead, snapping three quick-fire frames as the woman stares through the opening to the courtyard unawares.

What the hell was that about, he wonders. And what was Alice playing at, sauntering the streets without anyone watching her back? Goddamn it, she's as stubborn as me, Boudreaux thinks. There'll be a chance to ask Alice what just happened soon enough. For now, though, Doctor Grey is the priority.

Boudreaux punches in the number Surjins gave him, and gets through to a bored-sounding assistant who pops him on hold. Sixty seconds later, the silence is broken by an accent that he can't quite place. Brooklyn with a hint of Boston maybe?

'Agent Boudreaux? Doctor Elias Grey. I understand you need some help with a case?'

'Yes, thank you, doctor. Did Mr Surjins explain what I'm after?'

'He did, although he didn't say why exactly.'

Not a question as such, but Grey leaves a gap he resists the urge to fill.

'It might help if I had the context,' he ventures. 'I've worked with some of these people for quite some time, so I might be able to help with any insight you need.'

'I can't go into too much detail with it being an ongoing investigation,' Boudreaux says, little white lie slipping out. It's as far from official as it gets, but if keeping that part to himself gets what he needs from Grey, then he can make his peace with that. 'But you can read between the lines as to how serious it is by the fact we're looking at linking as many incidents as this, across quite a number of years.'

'Hmm, I see,' he says slowly, then 'Can you give me until tomorrow?'

'That would be amazing, Doctor Grey, and I'd appreciate it if we can keep it just between us for now. Could be quite sensitive, you know?'

'Of course,' he says, 'I'll get on it right away. What's your email address and I'll send over what I can.'

'Amazing, thank you so much,' Boudreaux replies, reeling it off then signing off with what feels like the first smile he's had all day. Soon disappears when he remembers what he saw outside just a few minutes ago. No time like the present. Alice needs to realise this is a two-way street. If Boudreaux is putting himself out to help on a case whose success could blow back on him, there's got to be no holding back. No secrets.

He glances back out of the window as she walks past, and the mystery woman is still there, sitting astride a parked-up moped, one of a cluster under the canopy of trees on the corner.

Boudreaux purses his lips, eyes narrowing in suspicion. Time to find out who Alice's mystery woman is.

Chapter Forty

Wednesday – Five days to go

Gina DiMarco's face stares back at Alice from her screen. Her name spits out dozens of results on Google. The few video clips that Alice flicks through are varied in subject, but the key worry here is DiMarco is the real deal. She's got profile and reach. That thought branches out, grows shoots and makes Alice wonder if she might not use this to her advantage should the need arise.

Is this Boudreaux's work? Alice hopes not. She's starting to get on board with the idea of him trying to be a better man. This could derail any notion of that.

It's as if even thinking his name has summoned him. Boudreaux breezes through the door, sliding into the spare chair without so much as a hello.

'So, I've spoken to someone who owes me a favour and got a contact at the UN. A guy by the name of Elias Grey. He's pulling together the list of names we asked for. Likely to be well into the hundreds, so I've got one of my guys standing by to crunch through it.'

'I can still get a copy too though, right?' Alice asks, irked at how tightly Boudreaux is keeping his hands on the reins.

Boudreaux looks a little uneasy. 'Hmm, I don't know. The guy from the UN is a little jumpy about it getting passed around. He's worried in case it turns out to be something and it ends up dragging the UN name through the mud.'

'Well we wouldn't want someone's reputation to get soiled just to save a life, now would we?' Alice's words are like darts, looking for a target.

'Look, I gave him my word, all right. If there's a hit, of course I'll keep you in the loop, but I have to be careful how I trade my favours, or the favours stop coming my way, you know what I'm saying?'

Alice knows the double standards here are glaring. She protects her own sources like a lion defending its cubs. Doesn't stop her from being pissed off with him though.

'Speaking of being careful,' Boudreaux continues, 'I saw you took a walk just now.'

He leaves it hanging, and the stretching silence makes Alice uneasy.

'Um, yeah.'

'I told you, Alice, you need to watch your back. You should have told me. I could have come with you, or sent someone else along.'

'I'm fine,' Alice says brightly. 'Honestly, I just needed some fresh air and a coffee.'

'Must have been a pretty shitty coffee.'

'What do you mean?' Alice asks, feeling the heat in her cheeks.

'I saw her, Alice. That woman who followed you. The one who was shouting after you, saying something about your dad. Who was she?'

'Have you been spying on me?'

'It's hardly spying when it's happening right outside on the street. Now, c'mon I'm playing ball, sharing what I know. What are you keeping back?'

'Keeping back? You're a fine one to talk,' Alice says, anger rising from simmer to boil. 'Only two people could have set her on me, and I'm looking at one of them.'

'Set who? Who is she?'

'Really?' Alice feigns surprise. 'You want to explain to me how else a reporter I've never met is asking me about something I've only known about since Monday?'

The puzzled look on Boudreaux's face throws Alice for a second. 'She's a reporter? Who for? What did she want?'

'Fox. She wants to know what's dragged me over here when my dad's about to meet his maker. Something I didn't even know myself till a few days ago. You honestly expect me to believe this isn't you?'

'Why would I?' says Boudreaux, spreading his arms wide. 'How does that help me, hmm? If there's been a screw-up here, you think I want to be tarred and feathered in public again?'

What he's saying makes sense, but Gina DiMarco didn't just happen past the coffee stand by chance. Alice reminds herself to treat this fledgling alliance with Boudreaux for what it is. A means to an end.

She settles for 'If you say so', hoping it lands a little more sincerely than it felt on the way out.

'I told you before, Alice, I'm trying to help you here. I'm putting my ass on the line by even speaking to that guy from the UN. I could get into big trouble for this.'

'Okay, I believe you,' Alice concedes, feeling anything but mollified.

'You might want to take the side exit when you leave by the way,' Boudreaux says. 'She's still waiting out there last I checked.'

'Okay, thanks.'

'You're really not going to tell me her name then?'

What's the harm in playing this game, Alice thinks? 'Her name's Gina DiMarco.'

'Let me know when you're done for the day. I'll drive you back to your hotel.'

The conversation shrivels up after that, and Boudreaux leaves with a promise to check in with her later. Alice goes back to studying the files on the other cases, one at a time, waiting for something else, anything, to leap out like a jack-in-the-box.

The nagging headache that's drifted in and out all week begins to bump again against her temples like flies against a window. Her mind wanders back to the text from this morning. Mariella and Anthony on her phone screen, walking down those steps, oblivious to who was watching, or what danger they might be in.

On Boudreaux's advice she hasn't tried to interact with whoever sent it. What has toeing the line with him achieved so far though? As long as Boudreaux is flying under his boss's radar, the full extent of GALE's resources will always be just out of reach. It's a different number each time anyway. Single use SIM. Likely to be a case of text and discard.

But what if it isn't? She wonders, not for the first time, if Dufort is holding back, keeping something in reserve that might join the dots faster than she and Boudreaux are managing between them. She has no licence to practise here, but that apparently isn't deterring Dufort or his associates from thinking she can help spring him from La Santé.

She flies back home tomorrow. Five days till Dad's clock runs out. What if she reached out again, to him or whoever is sending these texts? She has cross-examined countless witnesses on the stand, run verbal rings around them to uncover a buried truth. It's what she does best. Who's to say she couldn't tease out some detail from her mystery texter, or Dufort himself without Boudreaux or Eva as part of the conversation? Law enforcement have a way of making people clam up.

Her phone chimes, snapping her out of her thoughts, and when she looks at the screen, she can't help but gasp. It's Dufort's thugs again. She opens the text thread, and sees two new entries. The first is the name and address of a legal firm here in Paris, with a polite but directly worded ask that she share what she knows with Dufort's lawyer. The second is a GIF of a ticking clock.

She swallows hard, fingers hovering over the screen, hesitating for a second, before tapping out a reply.

No progress in my case so nothing to share. Happy to meet with Mr Dufort again to discuss further though

She presses send before she can change her mind, and off it sails into the ether with a swooping sound. Two ticks show it's been delivered, and almost immediately, grey flicks to blue indicating it's been read. Alice holds her breath, watching in morbid fascination as a message at the top of the screen indicates someone is typing back.

Seems to take an age, but when it finally pops up it's short and to the point.

La Santé. Tomorrow. 5 p.m. Speak to the lawyer before you go

Whether it's the text or the tension, her heart and head pound in time. He is willing to meet again. That has to mean something surely? She can leave early for the airport and make a detour to La Santé on the way. No need for Boudreaux to hear anything about it unless it yields something she can use in her dad's favour, and even then, not until Alice has acted upon whatever Dufort might share. The thought of helping her dad still leaves a bitter aftertaste now she knows what she knows. She reminds herself it's not about him. It's about giving a ten-year-old boy a chance.

She texts back one line.

I'll be there

The response comes back her way like a fast first serve, zinging in, pulling no punches.

See that you are, for their sake if not your own.

Alice is still shaken from the quick-fire text exchange when Sofia's name flashes up on screen. A quick tap and the video call kicks in.

'Hey you, how's it going?'

'You okay?' Sofia asks. 'You sound a little flat.'

'Yeah, I'm fine. Just been a lot to process, you know?'

Alice gives her a rundown. The reporter, the texts, Boudreaux's contact with the UN.

'I don't trust him, Alice. I know he says he wants to help, but you ask me, he's playing an angle.'

'I know, I know. But if it wasn't for him, we wouldn't know about the other cases. Don't have to trust him to use him.'

'You think he means it about your dad? About having regrets?'

Regrets. Like the kind Dad has about Gail. His bombshell lurches front and centre again, and for a second, it's an effort to consider Sofia's question.

'Yeah,' she says finally. 'I think he's worried enough there's something to this. Doesn't mean he'll admit to making a mistake just yet though.'

'Let me have a word with Eva, see if she can get her hands on whatever the UN guy sends over.'

'Okay, but tell her to be careful it's all under the radar for him, or so he says, but doesn't mean he can't make things difficult for her. Just make sure she watches her back.'

'Will do. Oh, got a result on those photos as well.'

Really? What kind of result?'

'Guy I used to date is a genius with image manipulation. You want a shot of you on stage next to Beyoncé with Barack Obama on bass, he's that good you'll start to think you might have actually been there.'

'Why do I think you've got one of those framed in your apartment?' Alice laughs.

'So anyway, we still only have an outline rather than a face, and his head was dipped down, but there was enough around the cap for him to clean up. There's a copy in your inbox now.'

Alice pulls up the email and opens the first of four attachments. It's recognisable as the image she's already seen, but at the same time, noticeably different. The contrast between the two is like looking at an image with and without glasses on. This enhanced version has sharper edges, shapes coaxed out of shadow. The colours have been dialled up a notch too. Far from HD sharp, but a significant improvement.

'See what I mean?' Sofia says, snapping Alice out of a stare.

'Mm-hm.'

She's still distracted by the image and calls up the other three. Same frustrating angle of the cap shielding the man's face, but there's no mistaking the frame of an A-shaped logo. What was it Mac had said? A Los Angeles Angels baseball fan?

Alice zooms in, squinting at the red outline. She calls up an Angels logo on Google Images, gaze flicking back and forth between the two pictures like she's at centre court at Wimbledon.

The baseball logo has a halo resting atop it. Nothing like that on this new image. The way the downward legs curve out a fraction, rather than straight out. She calls up a second logo. Compares again. Not the Angels. No, there's no doubt in her mind now. A blurred pattern between the legs. A fleur-de-lis. The same logo as the man outside her hotel. The one Boudreaux chased down.

'Bloody hell,' she whispers to herself.

Mac and her dad can't both be wrong, surely? Something tangible she can take to a judge. Not even close to being enough on its own, but there's definitely a feeling of a piece slotting into place.

The two women share a moment, faintest hint of a smile on both faces.

'That's not all,' Sofia says. 'The call Mac says he made to the station. A friend of a friend of mine knows the desk sergeant who was on duty in the precinct that your dad was held at. He's reaching out to him as we speak. Should know later today, tomorrow at a push, what happened to Mac's tip.'

'Have I told you lately how amazing you are?'

'Ah, there's no quota on that. I'll stick a daily reminder in your calendar.'

Alice toys with mentioning her exchange of texts with the mystery number, and tomorrow's visit to La Santé. Not a question of trust, more that she knows her investigator will worry about the fact she has responded to her watchers. Sofia is one who thinks she can fix anything, protect everyone, and she'll only worry unnecessarily.

Screw it. Not as if she's meeting someone in a dark alley. It's a secure facility, meeting a man chained to a desk. Fear is like dry rot. You let it take hold, and before you know it, it's spread everywhere.

Sofia's parting gift is the name of an attorney who owes her, who will jump in front of a judge the second they think they have enough. The ease with which they've slid back into a working relationship makes Alice nostalgic for her old life in the States. She could still go back. Maybe further down the line, when Mum isn't … She cuts the thought off. Doesn't want to think of a world without the only parent she still loves.

Alice signs off with a promise to let Boudreaux or Eva drive her back to her hotel. In the quiet that settles over the room like a blanket, she lets the waves of information wash over her.

Depending on what Boudreaux and Sofia come back with on their latest lines of enquiry, Alice allows herself to consider the possibility of a stay of execution at very least.

She isn't sure how she feels about anything where her dad is concerned any more. Before today it was a mix of apathy and anger. His confession earlier had been like standing at ground zero when the bomb went off. Now? Now she feels numb. In shock. So what if he'd already have got out if he'd been arrested for what happened to Gail. That does nothing to melt the glacier that had grown between them long before he cleared his conscience today.

Surely when this is all said and done, Fiona and her mum will see him through her eyes. Maybe her sister won't resent her as much for mistakes Dad made. Maybe she'll forgive herself for not living up to what any of her family need her to be.

Maybe.

Chapter Forty-One

Wednesday – Five days to go

The promise Boudreaux extracted from Alice echoes in her head. The more time she spends around him, the more she finds herself warming to him. There's a soulfulness in his eyes. One that speaks of sorrow and sadness. Are her misgivings towards him just tangled up with her feelings towards Dad?

Her stomach growls, reminding her she's barely eaten today. She'll grab something on the way back to the hotel. Dinner in a Parisian brasserie will be the high point of her day, even if it's a table for one in a city for lovers. An idea flashes across her mind of asking Boudreaux if he wants to join her for a bite, talk about anything but the case, just for an hour. She shakes her head, dismissing it as quickly as it occurred, cheeks flushing at the thought of him sat across a table from her. Is it such a daft idea? Doesn't have to be anything in it. Just a glass of wine and a chance to forget the fucked-up father she's spent most of her life trying to pretend doesn't exist.

She wanders along the corridor, following Boudreaux's directions, but when she pops her head through what she thinks is the right door, the agent is nowhere in sight.

Looks like most have clocked off early, and there are only tops of two heads in sight, hunched over screens.

Alice can't help but take in the room as she makes a beeline for the closest. Soaring ceilings and ornate architraves. Plaster ceiling roses encircling lights that could grace a stately home. A far cry from her poky office that feels as claustrophobic as a prison cell by comparison.

The inch of dark hair poking above the screen is revealed to be a young black man in a suit that looks way too expensive for a GALE agent. He wears it well. Lost in whatever is on screen, he doesn't see her coming until she's close enough to touch him. He looks up through glasses that could double as telescope lenses, and her smile is met with a frown.

'I'm looking for Agent Boudreaux. Is he around?'

There's a pause, as if he's trying to decide if she's speaking to him even though she's a few feet away and looking him in the eye.

'No, he's had to head out, but he shouldn't be long. You are the lawyer, yes?'

'Yes, Alice Logan. Nice to meet you.'

She holds out a hand, but again with the pause, as if he's not used to being around people.

'Abeiku Owusu,' he says, eventually reaching out to shake hers. 'But everyone around calls me Abs.'

He smiles, and it's as if his unease evaporates, face lighting up like a tree at Christmas. 'I can call him, or you could wait here.' He gestures to a chair.

Alice hesitates, then makes a snap decision. 'You know what, it's okay. I'll just catch him tomorrow.'

'If you're sure,' he says, glancing back at his screen, clearly eager to dive back into whatever she's torn him away from.

'It's fine, honestly,' she says.

'Okay.'

He's clearly not one for small talk, and makes it clear the conversation is done, at least from his side, by dropping his eyes back down to his monitor.

Alice scans the room for Eva, but there's no sign of the young Portuguese agent either. What the hell, it's not far to her hotel.

She makes a beeline for the exit, stepping out into a courtyard that's draped in the first stripes of shadow. It's another hour and a half until sunset, but the high walls surrounding her act as screens, casting long lines of shadow that slope across the cobbles.

Back out on Rue de la Cité, cars coast past at a pace that's more relaxing ride than rush hour, and casting off the craziness of the last few days, Alice closes her eyes to breathe it all in. The pinch in the air, cool breeze running its fingers through her hair. Grounding herself in the here and now, parking the pressure she's put herself under with this case, just for a moment.

She opens them after a few seconds, blinking away the fatigue from being sat staring at a screen for hours. It's a mile and a half to the hotel according to her phone. She starts south towards the river. No more than a half-hour walk. Maybe even a chance to stop off at a little bistro somewhere and sample some authentic French cuisine instead of room service.

She hasn't gone more than five paces when she stops dead in her tracks. Across the street, around a hundred yards away, two people are up in each other's personal space, maybe only two a couple of feet apart, but their body language screams disagreement. She recognises Boudreaux straight away and drifts towards the road as if she's going to cross. The second person, a woman, has her back to Alice, but a split second later, turns just enough to give a side profile.

Gina DiMarco. The reporter Luc Boudreaux claimed he didn't know. Arguing no doubt over the fact that the coffee stand ambush didn't go as planned. She has half a mind to storm over and tell them both where to go, but a cool head prevails. Courtroom conflict has always been more her style than a public pissing match in the street.

She settles for a grimace like she's just eaten a bad clam, and double times it in the opposite direction. A loop of the building will only add a few minutes onto her journey, and she needs the time to clear her head. She knows now that Boudreaux can't be trusted. Not now, not ever.

Chapter Forty-Two

Wednesday – Five days to go

Alice follows the bend of the river westwards. There's something magical about this time, cityscape transitioning from daylight to dark, and a hundred shades of grey in between.

Boudreaux's betrayal still burns. To think she'd been warming to him. Takes a lot to get past her defences, but he'd been starting to worm his way in. Not now though. She feels like such a fool, as if he's played her from the start. Spun her a line like a stranger at a bar that she's taken hook, line and sinker. Sucker-punched by the sad eyes and the 'I'm not that guy' speech that she wanted to believe.

Footfall behind her is steadily increasing as people drift home for the evening. Alice can't help but scan the faces she sees. Everyone seems lost in their own journey, wrapped up in conversations or eyes down, headphones in. Nobody taking an interest in her.

That feeling is still there though. Like she's a deer in the forest who can't see the scope trained on her. She does her best to dismiss it as she picks up the pace once more.

Hunger beats its drums again as she reaches the halfway mark. The hotel has a restaurant, but when she walked past this morning, it looked dour – dark decor that could be anywhere in the world. The thought of eating there isn't exactly what the notion of a meal out in Paris conjures up. There's got to be a better option. If she has to dine solo, she wants to do it somewhere with character. Somewhere that screams 'I'm in Paris'. A backstreet bistro maybe?

She flicks the map app off screen, diving into Tripadvisor, slowing to a shuffle as she scrolls through a list of nearby options. A couple stand out between here and the hotel. Great ratings, good value, but more importantly judging by the pictures, the kind of vibe she's looking for.

Five minutes later she finds herself outside a place called Le Petit Chateau. Light spills out onto the pavement like a buttery yellow snowdrift. Alice studies the menu tacked up inside a glass frame on the wall, breathing in the scents that drift out as a couple of seemingly satisfied customers slide past her. A waft of warm air washes over her, base notes of freshly baked bread, a hint of herbs and a dozen huddled conversations. Perfect.

The maître d' is a portly man in his fifties who greets her like she's long-lost family. She's whisked into a window seat, a menu, basket of bread, and carafe of water arriving in rapid succession.

The bread is heavenly. Barest hint of warmth, melting the velvety coat of butter. She orders a half-carafe of house red, and not that she's a connoisseur, but it's as good as any she's had back home. Tension seeps out of her like a wrung cloth. This is the first time she's done anything for herself since she arrived, and instead of her default when solo dining of catching up on her emails, she just sits and soaks it all in. Pedestrians shuttle past the window at a pace, giving her the feeling she's in the eye of the storm inside here. A time out to rearrange her fractured thoughts into a semblance of order.

Most of the ambient noise is conversation, rapid-fire French that she can't follow, but in a weird way, that's just what she needs. White noise to wash away her worries.

Her starter comes. Fat slices of juicy beef tomato alternating with thick wedges of buffalo mozzarella. It's gone in minutes, and the plate is whisked away and replaced with a portion of chicken chasseur that could feed a whole platoon. Wisps of steam work their way up, teasing her taste buds before the first forkful even makes her mouth. The chicken is melt-in-your-mouth good, and she takes her time, savouring every bite.

By the time they come to clear her plate, the food has settled, leaving little room for dessert, but she orders an espresso, and heads to the toilet while the waiter scurries off to fetch her drink.

She can't help but admire the subtle decor of the place as she navigates her way to the bathroom. The building is older than it looks, similar period features to the Préfecture de Police, although more understated. A wooden newel post at the end of a short corridor at the back tops an L-shaped staircase which leads down to a basement bathroom. She runs her fingers over the grooves in the carved pineapple shape as she heads down. The stairs open up into a single corridor, two doors either side, plus one that looks to be a storeroom straight ahead.

The ladies is the second on the left, and Alice steps in to see it's a single room, about twice the size of an airplane bathroom. The comparison reminds her that she's around twenty-four hours from boarding her flight home, and the thought of it brings a smile to her face as she reaches for the cord to turn on the light.

It happens with such a speed and ferocity that she isn't even sure what's hit her. Spots of light stud her vision, a swirling Milky Way of stars. She's propelled into the tiny space, head cracking off the tiled wall hard enough that she hears the crack in spite of the cacophony of noise.

Fingers like steel pincers grab at her shoulders, spinning her round. A palm pushes her face against the shockingly cold tiles, squashing her nose and mouth. She tries to turn round but whoever it is keeps enough pressure against her head that it feels as if another ounce would pop it like a cantaloupe.

It lets up a fraction, but there's no respite as something rough slips down over her head, covering her nose. That serves only to intensify the feeling of claustrophobia.

Fingers scrabble at her face, and she wonders for one horrific moment if they're reaching for her eyes. No, they're holding something, coarse material. Even as she opens her mouth to shout for help, it's crammed inside, far enough that it touches her tonsils, making her retch.

The feeling that her food is about to reappear sends her into a heightened panic, fear of choking on her own vomit. For a moment she focuses on that, forgets to fight back, and her attacker seizes the opportunity to manhandle her a little more easily.

She's spun round, whatever they've pulled over her head is yanked down further, covering her mouth completely, then clamped in place by a hand.

In an already dark room, this kills any chance she has of seeing what's happening to her. Alice sucks in desperate nosefuls of air. Smells of sweat and tobacco. She uses her tongue to push the material in her mouth out a fraction, fresh waves of nausea rippling through her body.

She tries to fight back, kicking out, flailing hands clawing the air in front of her where a face should be. But he's too close, pressing her against the wall now, practically chest to chest.

Feels like she is drowning. Barely enough oxygen to stay conscious. The pressure across her mouth disappears. Hands like vices grab both arms, dragging her away from the wall, and her legs buckle as they collide with the toilet. She finds herself awkwardly straddling the seat, but before she can reach up and remove her makeshift blindfold, a weight presses down on her. Her attacker sits across her lap, one hand around her throat, the other, God knows where.

'You scream, you die.'

A heavily accented voice that sounds like its owner eats three square meals of gravel a day. A moment later she feels it. A cold line across her throat. Any notion of struggle disappears in an instant. A weapon of some sort? A knife?

The stillness that follows the past ten savage seconds is a tangible thing. Alice is breathing hard, chest heaving, nostrils flaring, every breath like sucking air through a straw, never enough.

'This is your first warning. Your only warning.' The voice speaks again. Sounds like the W's are swapped for V's. German maybe? It's coming from very close, like he's inches away from her ear, breathing heavily between sentences. 'You have not kept your promise to share what you know. It must be done tomorrow. Nod if you understand.'

She's too stunned to respond. Too focused on breathing. On staying alive.

'I asked you if you understand,' he says again, this time right up against her ear. She feels his breath, warm and stale even through whatever is covering her head.

Alice swallows hard. Gives three quick nods. Hears a grunt in acknowledgement. After a few seconds she feels his weight shift slowly, and the release of pressure makes her want to leap up like a jack-in-the-box but her body won't obey.

'The only thing keeping you alive right now is not seeing my face,' he says very matter of factly, like he's making friendly conversation but there's no mistaking the genuineness of his threat. 'Count to ten before you move.'

She nods again, vigorously this time. Eager to comply, willing to do whatever it takes to walk out of this bathroom. Her chest heaves, desperate to draw a full breath. Feels compressed, like she's been shrink-wrapped. Takes a moment for conscious thought to kick back in, and she starts counting.

When she hits ten, she reaches up with trembling hands and lifts what turns out to be an oversized woollen hat. She spits out a ball of coarse cloth from her mouth, chest heaving like bellows as fresh air floods in.

The bathroom is bathed in half-light courtesy of the hallway. Alice lifts a hand to her throat. Touches where the blade was held to her neck. Goes to stand on shaky legs, but she's running on empty, and slumps back onto the toilet seat.

The muted sounds of the restaurant filter through the floorboards. She's alone. Just the shadows for company.

Chapter Forty-Three

Wednesday – Five days to go

It's a full five minutes before Alice re-emerges. Five minutes of controlled breathing. Of the same words replaying in her head.

He could have killed me. He could have killed me.

It's like looking at a stranger in the mirror. The face is the same, but the eyes are haunted. Wide pools of disbelief. There's the faintest of marks on her neck. No cut, just pressure. She splashes her face, goes to leave, but turns round and sits on the toilet seat again, head bowed in hands.

Shit. Shit. Shit.

The thought of walking back into La Santé alone would be daunting at the best of times, but after this? Even the idea of it sends her stomach into fresh somersaults.

She gets to her feet, leaning on the door frame for a second. It's surreal. Only a matter of minutes since she was manhandled like a rag doll. Now, it almost feels like it happened to someone else. As if she just watched the whole thing from a corner of the room.

What can she do? Who should she call? Boudreaux? He'll tear her a new one for ignoring advice. Sofia is over four thousand miles away, but she's the kind of cool head

Alice needs right now. A far better shoulder to cry on. She looks at her phone. No signal.

The journey back up the stairs feels like hiking a mountain trail. She emerges from the staircase, scanning the restaurant, but nobody seems to care where she's been or that she's back. And it's not as if she can pick her assailant out of a line-up. Not without hearing him speak anyway.

It feels like she floats rather than walks across to the maître d' to cancel her espresso and settle her tab. Outside, the air feels thick, heavy. It's only a short walk back to her place, but she hails the first cab she sees, sliding into the back seat and peering along both sides of the street. No loitering shadows, but her nerves are still jangling.

She grips her phone tight the whole journey, all half a mile of it. Ignores the driver's scowl at his shortest fare of the night and scoots inside, into the relative safety of the lobby. It's not until she's back in her room, chain on, door locked that she lets her guard down. The minibar is house spirits only, but she's past caring. An off-brand vodka on the rocks disappears in two gulps, a second taking its place moments later.

Sofia picks up pretty much straight away. Whether there's a giveaway in how Alice speaks, or Sofia is just subconsciously attuned to pick up on these sorts of things, she jumps right in there.

'What is it? Everything okay?'

Alice composes herself for a second, then unloads. All of it, nothing left out. Sofia listens in silence, letting Alice get it all off her chest. Only when there's a good five seconds' worth of silence does she say anything.

'You need me there, I'm on the next flight out.'

Such a simple statement, but it prises Alice's remaining defences apart. She feels the tears well up. Swallows hard. Gets away with a single sniff as she wipes at the matching pair that draw a plumb line down each cheek.

'I mean it, Alice. This just got real in a big way. I can be there in …' A pause while she works it out. 'Twelve hours. Fifteen tops.'

Alice sniffs again, smiling despite herself. 'I know you would as well, but we'd just pass each other in the airport. Honestly, I'll be okay. Just shook me up is all.'

'Jesus, girl, you're the queen of the understatement. Where was Boudreaux in all this anyway? Isn't he meant to be watching your back?

'He was off somewhere else …' Alice starts but Sofia doesn't let her finish.

'Goddammit!' she sighs loudly down the line. 'What does he say? Can she get anything from CCTV?'

'I haven't called him.'

'Why the hell not?'

'Because he's messing me around,' Alice says, stubbornness rising up, pushing past any fear or anxiety. That reporter I told you about? I saw the two of them talking outside the station. I'm telling you, he's in this for himself, not for what he can do for me.'

'I'd love to say I'm surprised, but hey. What do you think the angle is with the reporter then?'

'I don't know,' sighs Alice. 'Could be to distract me. Could be to tee up a story that paints me to be the daughter blinded by grief after all this time, who's gunning for a decorated agent. He wants to fight dirty, that can work both ways.'

'Isn't that my kind of line?' Sofia says. 'What have you got in mind?'

'The photos we have of his files. He knows Eva helped us, I'm guessing there's some kind of audit trail in these things, so his name will be all over the other dozen. He wants a fight, he's got one.'

'Don't get me wrong, I wish you weren't going through all this right now, but I like this version of you. Reminds me of me.'

They both laugh at that one, and Alice feels almost normal again, as if she hasn't lived through an assault less than an hour ago. Sofia is the perfect antidote to any residual anxiety.

She signs off with a repeat of her promise to share any United Nations info with Sofia, and walks over to the bed with her vodka. She slips out of her clothes and into her stand-in PJs, a pair of shorts and a vest top. She strips back the duvet, sliding her legs underneath, and props herself up with a pair of pillows. What comfort she took from Sofia starts to slip away, like anaesthetic wearing off. Her dad's words start to echo in her head again, each one a slap across her psyche. A shadow flicking by the foot of her door makes her freeze mid-sip, and she pads silently across to the peephole, but the corridor is empty by the time she gets there.

Alice reaches out for the light switch, but thinks better of it. She settles back into bed, but not before she's fished her house keys out of her bag, placing them within reach on her bedside table. A DIY knuckleduster should anyone manage to break in. Anything is better than nothing.

She looks around the room, fighting back the feeling that the walls are closing in around her. Shrinking her world, squeezing her until it feels like every bit the cage her dad is in right now.

She suspects sleep will be a long time coming, and reaches over for her phone, scrolling through social media to numb her overactive brain. Tweets and Insta stories blur into one another. She's about to close the apps down, when she sees something that makes her heart sink.

Pictures of the twins blowing out candles on a chocolate cake big enough to need its own postcode. Shit, their birthday! She's been so caught up in what's been going on that she's forgotten to call them to sing happy birthday.

Not as if Fiona was in any mood to have reminded her either. She pictures her sister silently fuming at the slight. It's way past their normal bedtime, but she flicks through to her contacts anyway. After what's happened this evening, waiting to speak to Fiona about Dad's confession feels like a betrayal. If roles were reversed, she'd want to know as soon as possible.

She counts the rings in her head. By the time it gets to six, she's pretty sure she's being ignored. No point letting it get into double figures, but as she goes to end the call, her sister's face pops up on the screen.

'Hey,' Alice says, feeling every bit as worn down as she sounds.

'Hey,' Fi says, mirroring the cautious tone.

'Look, about earlier …'

'It's fine,' Fiona says. 'Kids had me up since five. You just caught me at a bad moment.'

'No,' Alice says, shaking her head. 'It's not fine that you think I talk like that about you behind your back. What I said back then, I genuinely didn't mean it like that.'

'Well how did you mean it?' Fiona asks, and Alice knows she has to choose her words very carefully.

'I just need to get over myself,' Alice says, 'Trevor isn't the man I would have picked for you, but that's not my call, and it's not fair of me to let it come between us. As long as he makes you happy, that needs to be enough for me.'

'He does,' Fiona says quietly. 'Make me happy I mean. I know we argue, but who doesn't?' She gives a shy smile, one that softens her expression. 'The rest of the time, it's like he makes me feel like I'm all that matters, you know. Like I'm enough.'

That all-consuming, sparks flying kind of love is something Alice has never found herself. Not yet. For a split second, part of her covets what her sister has, just not the man she's found it with. Is that what it boils down to, she wonders? That these niggly moments between her and Fi boil over because of good old-fashioned jealousy? She tries to dismiss it, but the notion won't quite dislodge from her mind.

'Then I'm happy for you,' she says finally. 'I really am, Fi. I just need to tell my face that more.'

That gets a smile from Fiona, one that breaks like a wave across her face.

'I'm sorry by the way,' her sister says. 'For that stuff I said about you and men the other day.'

'Nah, you were pretty spot in to be fair,' Alice says with a wry smile. 'I should get you to screen the next one for me.'

'What about that detective you've met over there?' Fiona says with a sly edge to her voice. 'I googled him. Bit of a dish. Way too good-looking for you.'

'Oh, give over,' Alice says, feeling a warm flush in her cheeks. She quickly pivots the conversation onto safer ground. 'Are the kids asleep? Have I missed them?'

Fiona nods. 'Not by much. They crashed out about half an hour ago. Little sods will still have me up before sunrise though.'

'Bugger. Sorry Fi. I'll make it up to them, I promise.'

'You're all right,' Fiona tells her. 'I told them you're on a secret mission for me, so they think you're some kind of Double O Auntie.'

Nice touch, but it doesn't stop Alice from feeling like she's let them down.

'I'll take them for ice cream at Di Meo's when I'm back.'

'When are you coming home?' Fiona asks.

'Tomorrow.'

'Is everything okay with Mariella?'

'Yeah, I've got someone keeping an eye on them.' Alice pauses, teetering on the precipice of what to share. What happened in the restaurant, that stays with her, for now at least. She's not ready to talk about it to Fi just yet. Wouldn't want her little sister feeling guilty at the thought of having sent her into harm's way.

'There is something I need to tell you though, Fi,' she begins. 'Something about Dad.'

'What?' Fiona asks, frowning. 'What is it?'

'I spoke to him again today. There were some things that didn't make sense, things I needed to ask him about.' There's a hitch to her voice, and she swallows hard.

'What kind of things?' Fiona asks, sounding impatient.

'There's a connection, Fi. Between Dad and all these other men. And I think I know what it is. They've all hurt people. They …'

'He didn't do this,' Fiona counters. 'With what you've found out so far, we can …'

'Not this, Fi. Something else. Someone else.'

That stops her in her tracks. She looks stumped by the statement.

'What do you mean someone else? Like who?'

Alice takes a second to summon the strength to say the words. When she starts, it's like a dam breaks inside her. She manages to get as far as Dad saying Gail had still been alive, when the tears come. Twin warm streams cut lines down her cheeks, and she has to swallow hard between sobs to get to the end.

When she's finished, Fiona sits, hand over her mouth, like she's trying to keep in a scream.

'Oh, Al,' she whispers. 'Oh my God. I don't even know where to start.'

It takes a full minute for Alice to get back on an even keel. She brushes her cheeks with the back of her hand to dry them. She takes a couple of deep breaths, centres herself.

'I can't let myself think too much about it,' she says finally. 'Not yet. I need to finish this with Boudreaux, or they'll come for Anthony. He deserves a better chance than that.'

'This is my fault, I sent you over there.'

'It's nobody's fault, Fi,' Alice says. 'Not ours anyway.'

'Where do you go from here then?'

'Sofia has a lawyer lined up in Florida. She's sending them everything we've found so far, to see what they make of it. That's all we can do really. That and see what else I can get from Boudreaux tomorrow.'

'What about Gail's family?' Fiona asks in a quiet voice.

Alice pauses. Hates the fact that Fiona has thought of them before she has. Doesn't cut herself any slack despite the day she's had. Gail was her best friend. She deserves better, even now.

'I've not spoken to them in years. They need to know though. Sofia will be able to help find them.'

'What will you say?'

'Honestly, I haven't the foggiest. Can't even think straight right now,' Alice says, voice trailing off.

'Sorry, Al,' Fiona says. 'I shouldn't have made you go over there. I just didn't know what else to do.'

'It's okay,' Alice says, and means it. Rather her here than Fiona. An image of her little sister pinned against a bathroom wall frightens her more than what she's just been through.

Alice promises to call Fiona the moment she gets back home, and signs off. She knocks back what's left of her drink. She's never been a big drinker, thanks to seeing the kind of person it turned her dad into. Ironic that she's hitting the bottle now while trying to prove he's innocent. Except he isn't, is he? Even if she somehow helps save his life, innocence is a state he'll never get back to. Whether he's worth saving is up for debate, but there are others that most certainly are. Far better her tonight, than have them turn up at Mariella's door.

Her own transition from lawyer to victim was the work of a few brutal seconds. Such a short amount of time to tear a hole in the fabric of someone's reality. Long enough that it'll stay with her for a long, long time, if not forever.

In amongst the what-ifs of the case, regardless of innocence or guilt, too many people have lost their lives. Every victim of the dozen men who languish in jail. The ones they got away with killing, and even the equally unsavoury guys they killed to earn their sentences. No one deserves to die like that in her book, no matter what they've done.

A rogue thought pops into her mind.

What about the man who could have killed me tonight?

If she'd had a weapon of any kind, how far would she have gone to defend herself? Could she cross that line? Take a life, if she thought her own was in danger? She's heard it said that anyone is capable in the right circumstances, or the wrong ones depending on how you look at it. Would her attacker have deserved it if she had? It's a train of thought she can't bring herself to go down.

What happened tonight cannot become a distraction. She'll box it up, process it later. For now, though, she has to pretend it did not happen.

This will not define me.

This will not define me.

She doesn't dream about her dad tonight. This time, there are far worse shadows stalking her dreams. This time they've come for her.

Chapter Forty-Four

Thursday – Four days to go

Boudreaux skims his cell across the desk in frustration. Twice he's called Alice Logan this morning, same result both times. Straight to voicemail. Add that to the three times last night, and it adds up to an uneasy feeling. Alice didn't expressly state she'd be around today; that was an assumption on Boudreaux's part. It's more the fact she's stubborn as a mule, looking past everything that's happened these past couple of days, and disappeared without a word last night. Feels like a bit of a middle finger after he's gone to the trouble of finding her a safer hotel, offering to be her shadow until she leaves for home.

The fact that Jim Sharp's case is a mirror image of the others in many ways still astounds him. Lightning striking a hell of a lot more than twice. The evidence they found, literally splattered across Sharp, left him in no doubt that they had the right man. What has been unearthed these past few days, though, has thrown him into a tailspin. There's a version of this case that he's never spoken about out loud. A decision he made back in the day. If the UN line of enquiry pays off, it can stay in the past. Even if it doesn't he isn't sure he can bring himself to dredge it up again. Isn't even sure it would make a difference to the outcome. It would definitely make a difference with Alice though.

He's snapped out of his daydreaming by Abs waving at him from his desk.

'Luc, some guy called Elias Grey on the line for you.'

He blinks away the cobwebs, hand hovering over his phone as Abs transfers the call.

'Doctor Grey, good morning.'

'Agent Boudreaux, I hope I'm not interrupting?'

'Not at all. I wasn't expecting to hear from you until much later. What time is it over there?'

'A little after seven. I'm an early riser. I thought it best I call you before I send anything over.'

He sits up a little straighter at the hint there's something worth speaking about that he would prefer to discuss over the phone.

'So, I checked back across the locations you gave me, and listed all the staff. Everyone from surgeons to cleaners. This goes back a number of years, so not everyone is still with us. I've included their names, but finding them, well that's more your forte than mine.'

'Thank you, doctor, I really appreciate that.'

'There are literally hundreds,' he continues, 'but …'

The juiciest titbits are always preceded by a but.

'But?' Boudreaux coaxes.

'I know a lot of these names. They're hard-working, dedicated, selfless people. I find it hard to believe that any of them would be capable of committing any kind of crime. However, there is only one that appears at each of the locations you gave.'

'Who is it, doctor? What's his name?'

He hesitates. 'I will share it with you, Agent Boudreaux, but I wanted to speak to you first, because this man is one of the best I've worked with. A world-class neurosurgeon. He has saved more lives than I care to count. He's … well I'd consider him a friend.'

'I need a name, doctor,' Boudreaux insists, dialling back the urgency that's coursing through him, not wanting to push too hard. Not yet.

'I just wanted to speak on his behalf and ask you to take this information with a pinch of salt. Whatever you think he might have done, please, take it from me, this is a good man.'

He pauses, and Boudreaux waits him out, counting off the seconds in his head.

'Oliver Finlay,' he says finally. His name is Doctor Oliver Finlay.'

'And do you happen to know where Doctor Finlay is working out of at the moment?'

'He's here in New York actually,' says Grey. 'He gave up the field work when his wife took ill a couple of years ago.'

'Do you know when exactly?' Boudreaux feels a fizz of excitement, like it's a game of Tetris and he's watching the perfect block about to drop into place.

'Yes, it was two years past this July, so twenty-five months I guess.'

July two years ago. Two months after the last of his dozen convicts was arrested for a murder they claimed they didn't commit. Doesn't link him to Jim Sharp, but what if he's been looking at this all wrong? What if Sharp is a red herring, and Alice storming in head first has uncovered something unrelated, something darker?

'I'll send the full list now,' Grey continues, 'but please, this man is well-respected throughout more countries than most people visit in a lifetime. If anything comes of this, it cannot come back to me.'

'You have my word, doctor,' he says, mind scrambling around the logistics of proof. How he'll explain away the fact he's a person of interest. Whether there's any way to even link him to anything other than the fact he was in the country when these murders took place.

The little voice inside, the one that has made him what he is, tells him there are ways and means to turn over the right stones. That this could be something career defining. Of course, careers can be defined in more than one way, not all of them good.

'Thank you. I'll keep an eye out for your email.'

Boudreaux keeps his voice level as he says goodbye, but there's no mistaking that hum of energy, like electricity, that comes with these moments. He tells himself he has a decision to make, but even as that notion occurs he sees it for the lie it is. He made the decision the moment he put the phone down.

Chapter Forty-Five

Thursday – Four days to go

Alice's eyes feel gritty, like they've had sand kicked in them at the beach. She checks the sleep tracker app on her phone. Sum total of just over three hours last night, and none of it restful. Dreams of shadows wrapping themselves around her like snakes, squeezing the breath out of her in increasingly small spaces.

She checks the running total of missed calls from Luc Boudreaux, no intention of answering if he tries for a sixth time. The thought of him and the reporter sneaking around, planning God knows what, still roils her stomach. That and the echoes of last night's attack have left her as strung out as she can remember being.

Time to take back control. She starts by drafting an email detailing the full list of a dozen cases that she got from Boudreaux. Next, she attaches all the screenshots she took, before saving it in her drafts folder. One in the chamber should she need it.

She spots a message from Sofia titled 'Good news' and opens it, scanning for context. There's a picture attached as well. She reads the message, breathing a sigh of relief as she finishes, then opens the attachment. It's a familiar shot of Mariella. The same one that was texted to her by Dufort's people, except that this one is a much wider angle, the original picture, before those arseholes cropped it for effect.

According to Sofia's email, it was taken on the courthouse steps during one of her dad's appeals, and is one of the first pages of images in Google if you search for her. So, they haven't been following her after all. Doesn't mean she's safe as such, but it does suggest they don't have eyes on her, or at least didn't when they texted.

It doesn't change things as far as her dad's case goes though. As long as there's a chance of freeing him, Dufort will see an opportunity for leverage, but she'll take all the good news she can get at the moment. It's more about keeping Anthony safe from them, and from her dad, than it is actually freeing the man.

Even the briefest thoughts about her dad bring with them a flash of Gail's face. A sucker-punch snapshot of what he's done. What he took from her. Every tear, every panic attack that followed, all traces back to him.

Alice forces it down like swallowing a lump of gristle. She's torn between spending the morning at the Préfecture de Police, and just working from here before heading to La Santé on her way to the airport.

A big part of her wants to have it out with Boudreaux face to face, but chances are the GALE agent will just put on his poker face and deny, deny, deny. Maybe even spin a line about going out to confront the reporter outside. Also, any sign of losing her cool makes her look like she's letting personal trump the professional, and she refuses to give Boudreaux even a hint of that to point at.

She settles on a compromise. She'll pop into the station to see if there's any movement on the UN angle, then make her excuses and leave early, no mention to Boudreaux of the detour she'll make on her way to Charles de Gaulle. She busies herself with packing up. Doesn't take much. No need to fold the few worn sets of clothes. They're stuffed into her case, and everything bar her laptop is packed in less than ten minutes.

She checks out, books a cab for 3 p.m. That allows time with Boudreaux, then another cab ride to the prison, before finally heading for her flight. She heads into the tiny restaurant, which is surprisingly quiet for lunchtime. Echoes from last night's ordeal in the restaurant lurk all around her like ghosts, and she positions herself where she can see the door, and opens her laptop to make a start.

She's winding down around quarter to three, ready to head outside to wait for her cab to arrive, almost caught up on her caseload, when an unfamiliar number flashes on her phone. Snakes slither in her stomach at the sight of digits rather than a name. She can't help but glance around as she lifts it to her ear.

'Hello?' she says cautiously.

'Alice, it's Eva.'

Alice comes back down a notch at the sound of a friendly voice.

'Ah, hey Eva.'

'Is everything okay?'

'Yeah, everything's fine,' she says, hoping she sounds more convincing that she feels. 'I'm just doing a little work at the hotel. Should be in to see Agent Boudreaux in half an hour or so.'

There's a pause. 'He's not here.'

'What time will he be back?'

'I mean he's left. I saw him earlier, he took a call, and he's gone. Took a few days' leave apparently.'

'What? But that doesn't … that makes no sense. Why would he up and leave like that?'

'I spoke to the agent who took the call first. Said it was some guy called Elias Grey, but he's not sure what it was about. Does that name mean anything to you?'

'Maybe,' Alice says, mind racing away with the possibilities. 'Did he say anything before he left?'

'Not much. Just that he's overdue some time off, and he's heading home for a visit.'

'Home? As in to the US?'

'Yep. We all have to share holiday plans so the boss knows where to reach us if the world starts to burn. He's on the first flight out in the morning to New York for a few days. He'll have his phone if you need to speak to him.'

'Okay thanks, will do. Listen, I've got to go. Think I'll just head straight to the airport, but I just want to say thanks for everything. Whatever favour you owe Sofia, consider yourself owed one by me now.'

'You take care, Alice,' Eva says. 'And good luck with your case.'

Alice ends the call, and places her phone carefully on the table as the anger boils inside like an unwatched kettle. That sneaky, self-serving bastard. Whatever he's got from Grey, he's off chasing it himself, ditching Alice. She seethes with the notion that not only is Boudreaux off pursuing a lead in her dad's case, but that he's cutting her out of the loop.

Question is where is he headed, and why? What could he have got from Elias Grey that jump-started him to take off? She googles the name, coupled together with United Nations in the search bar. The picture that comes up is of a man who could be anywhere between mid-forties and mid-fifties. Hair the colour of pale straw, a pair of thin frames perched on the beak of a nose.

His LinkedIn page tells her he's based in New York City. One train of thought bumps against another, and sparks a connection that makes her mouth open in disbelief.

Sonofabitch, he's going to see Doctor Grey. He's onto something and he's going alone.

An idea starts to form, one that on any other day she might dismiss out of hand, but after the past twenty-four hours, all bets are off. Boudreaux wants to go it alone? Fine. Two can play at that game. A few more minutes of clicking away on her laptop, and Alice picks up her phone, dialling the number on screen. As she listens to the long-drawn-out tone of the ringing phone, it occurs to her that what she's about to do is break the law for the first time in her life. That she should put the phone down before she does anything she'll regret.

She grips the handset all the tighter, smiles as she hears the click of the call being answered, and steps off the edge of the cliff.

Chapter Forty-Six

Thursday – Four days to go

'Can I ask who's calling please?'

'Yes, certainly. My name's Agent Franks with the Global Agency for Law Enforcement. Dr Grey spoke with my colleague Agent Boudreaux this morning. It's just a routine follow-up.'

She sits for a second with only static for company. Rehearses the hastily concocted lines she's hashed together.

'Hello?'

A man's voice snaps her to attention.

'Yes, hello, is this Doctor Grey?'

'Yes, this is he. My secretary tells me you're with Agent Boudreaux. Is everything all right?'

'Yes, everything's fine,' she says, trying to keep her voice low and serious. 'Well, not quite. It's the information you sent him earlier, there's a problem with the file. When Luc tries to open it, he gets a message saying it's corrupted.'

Luc. First name terms to suggest familiarity.

'I was hoping you can send another copy.'

'Oh, okay, yes absolutely. I'll do that right away.'

'One other thing,' says Alice, knowing this part is make or break. 'He had our IT guy take a look and he thinks it might be a problem with our server. Are you able to send to his personal email address instead?'

There's a pause, only half a heartbeat, but it's enough to make Alice squirm.

'Of course, that's not a problem. Let me get a pen for the address.'

She hears him rummage around, her own shallow breathing sounding bass drum loud in her ears.

'Ready when you are,' he says after a few seconds.

Alice rattles off the Gmail address she created moments ago using Boudreaux's surname and a few random numbers.

'We really appreciate this, sir.'

'Glad to help.'

'Oh and if you need to reach him for anything else, he said to use that personal email until we get the problem resolved at our end.'

'Understood,' says Grey. 'Agent … Franks, wasn't it? Am I to assume you're working closely with Agent Boudreaux on this?'

'Hand in glove, sir.'

'So you'll appreciate the sensitivity here? Like I said to your colleague, I'd appreciate a heads-up on anything that will go public, if there's anything to find that is. As I stressed to Agent Boudreaux, Oliver Finlay is a good man. I'd hate to see him dragged through the mud for something he didn't do.'

'I'm all about discretion, sir.'

She bids him farewell, and slumps back into her seat. She has a name. Question is, what to do about it?

Chapter Forty-Seven

Thursday – Four days to go

Roads are starting to thicken like clogged arteries, as traffic starts to build. Alice checks her phone for the umpteenth time since getting in the cab. What should be a twenty-minute journey currently sits at half an hour and counting.

The buffer she left for her meeting with Alain Dufort may not be enough. She toys with texting the number in her phone, saying she'll be a little late, but even the thought of contact with these people cranks up her pulse a notch, and not in a good way.

She glances behind them, seeing traffic stretched out as far back as she can see. Wonders if there's a car back there somewhere keeping tabs on her. She makes the most of the unexpected extension to her journey and logs into the Gmail account she gave Dr Grey. True to his word, there's an email waiting for her.

It has a spreadsheet attached. Names, locations, dates, downloaded from their personnel files. She searches for the name he gave her. Oliver Finlay. Total number of hits corresponds to the number of locations.

Oh. My. God.

There's a PivotTable in a separate tab that shows the total number of people who have been at multiple locations. Finlay is the only one who hits the jackpot every time. She opens up a browser window on her phone, entering a search string for Doctor Oliver Finlay. The face staring back at her is nothing out of the ordinary. Ruffled dark hair like he's just got out of bed. A lived-in face with what her mum would have called kind eyes. The kicker is when she sees he's based in New York these days. Maybe that's what's got Boudreaux all fired up. What if it's not Doctor Grey he's going to see? What if he's going to check out Finlay?

Either way, Alice has what the Orlando PD didn't even bother looking for. An alternative suspect. Someone who came into contact not only with every single one of the murders, but with at least one person who had suffered at their hands prior to their arrests. If that's the who, then how about the why?

Before she can contemplate that, her phone buzzes. Sofia. She goes to answer but hesitates. She's a bundle of nerves, planning and replanning in her head the dozen different ways this meeting with Dufort could go. She lets the call drop, opting to keep focused. She can ring her when she's back in the cab post-prison. Her phone starts up again, soft purring in her hand. Alice huffs out a breath. Some people just won't take a hint.

'I'm nearly at the prison. Can it wait?'

'Depends how long you want me to sit on something this big,' Sofia teases.

Alice purses her lips. Sofia isn't one to mess around, or build things up without cause.

'Come on then, shoot.'

'Turns out the desk sergeant my friend put me on to remembers this one quite well. Apparently, Mac called three times all told. Even mentioned on the last call about his pictures.'

'And this guy is happy to give a statement?'

'Mm-hm,' Sofia says. 'Seems he left the force on less than favourable terms. No love lost between him and his captain. A captain who he says was also aware of Mac's tips.'

'Wait? We're saying that he passed this information to a serving police captain, who completely ignored it?'

'Not quite, and this is the juicy bit. He never told the captain himself. He passed it on to one of the team. Followed it up the next day and they said it wasn't worth chasing up. They told our guy that it was put on ice 'cos they had their man already. Said the captain was okay with that too.'

'Jesus!' Alice exclaims. 'They knew. There was an eyewitness and they knew. They did nothing about it. Who was the officer who he gave the tip to?'

'Who do you think?'

Chapter Forty-Eight

Thursday – Four days to go

It's a peculiar mix. Vindication that her earlier suspicions are confirmed, but tinged with betrayal from someone she had started to believe played with a straight bat.

'What are you gonna do?' It's as if Sofia senses the impact of what she's just said, speaking softly, letting the revelation wash over Alice.

'He has to answer for it.'

'I hear you, Alice, and I'm not telling you how to play this, but we need to focus on helping your dad now. We can go after him later, once this is done, but ignoring a tip won't persuade a judge that the physical evidence is suddenly worthless.'

Up ahead, the workman holding a stop sign flips it round, beckoning her lane past at a snail's pace. Alice stares out of the window as a dozen or more options jostle for position. She knows Sofia is right. Doesn't stop her wanting to go scorched earth and throw whatever mud she can at Boudreaux to expose him for the part he has played in now not one but two miscarriages of justice. That's how Alice sees her dad's case now, regardless of whatever else he's done. However this plays out, due process was not followed. Corners were cut. Moves were made based in part, at least, on assumptions, and those have led to innocent people being put in the crosshairs. If this comes out, it might end up with Dufort walking as well, but if that keeps Mariella and Anthony safe, so be it.

'I know, I know,' she says eventually. 'Honestly, I just want him to account for it. How many other cases might he have done this in?'

'Keep your powder dry for now,' Sofia says. 'Let's see how his UN enquiries pan out, and we'll work out a game plan after that.'

'Yeah, about that ...' Alice figures now is as good a time as any to let Sofia in on her little ruse.

'I've gotta be honest, I did not know you had it in you,' Sofia says when she's finished. 'You do know this could come back and bite you real bad if Boudreaux finds out?'

'Let him try and prove it,' Alice says, feeling the end justifies the means. 'He's off chasing this down by himself. He promised to let me know the minute he got anything. You want to know what I think? Best-case, I think he's keeping one step ahead, so if any of this pans out, he looks like the hero for stepping up and saving a man's life.'

'And worst-case?'

'Worst-case he wants to make sure it doesn't lead anywhere that helps us. Let's face it, he didn't exactly welcome me to town with open arms.'

'You really think he'd go that far? Sabotage things just to keep himself safe?'

'At this point, I'm ruling nothing out.'

'Okay then, so we know who he's going to check out. How do you want to play this?'

Alice is surprised by the level of scheming going on in her head right now, bordering on Machiavellian. She glances at the map on her phone again. Ten minutes from La Santé, twenty-two minutes until her meeting.

'What the hell,' she says. 'Go big or go home, right?'

'What do you mean?'

'I'm coming over.'

'Wait a minute, do you think that's wise?'

'I've got a chance to get in there first,' she says. 'Speak to Grey and Finlay before Boudreaux. I'll be careful. Gets me away from whoever's following me around as well.'

'And what if Finlay is who you think he is?' Sofia asks. 'Tell you what, you go home, and I'll go back to New York.'

'Uh-uh.' Alice shakes her head. 'I'll be fine.'

'The hell you will. If there's even a one per cent chance this Dr Finlay is responsible for all of this, then I'm coming. End of story.'

Alice can't help but smile, one that crinkles her crow's feet. She loves it when Sofia goes all big sister, and truth be told, after last night's events, she'd feel a lot safer with an ex-FBI agent by her side.

'Okay, but I get to pick the Broadway show when we're done talking to the good doctor.'

'Anything except *Cats*,' Sofia says. 'I hate *Cats*.'

Alice promises to text her flight details once she finds out which is the soonest she can book on. In the silence that follows the call, she mulls over her options. Stop at La Santé, and risk Boudreaux staying a step ahead, versus head for the first flight out of here, and risk pissing off Dufort's people.

A highlights reel runs through her mind. Snapshots of the basement bathroom. She touches a hand to the back of her head. Winces at the flash of pain as she probes the lump where skull met tile. To hell with being bullied. To hell with Alain Dufort. She's going to do this on her terms.

'Excuse me, can we just head to the airport instead please.'

Chapter Forty-Nine

Friday – Three days to go

By the time Alice steps outside of Terminal 7 at JFK far later than she'd hoped thanks to a delay at Charles De Gaulle, it's a little after three a.m. local time. Just over seventy-two hours left for her dad. It's warmer than Paris, but can't be much above ten degrees Celsius, and the light misting of rain that jewels the windows of the waiting cabs isn't the welcome she was hoping for. She waits her turn as the caterpillar-like queue of yellow taxis crawls forwards, tired-looking passengers sliding into seats.

The flight passed in the blink of an eye. Nervous exhaustion catching up with her in the relative safety of her window seat. For once her sleep was dreamless, but even though she was out for seven of the eight and a quarter hours, her eyelids still feel lead-lined.

This is the home stretch, she tells herself. By the end of the day, all the cards should be on the table. Really feels like the last chance for her dad, and by association, her new-found brother, Anthony. Alice realises with a start that she's as close to him as she's been in years, geographically speaking. One more short hop flight after this is all done, and she could meet him. Anything's possible. Whether she can open herself up to having that extra layer of family chaos in her life is another matter. Enough maybe just to know he's safe.

Alice has spent the approach into JFK working on a game plan. Doctor Grey has forwarded the original mail he sent to Boudreaux on to the new address. Finlay works out of the same building as Grey, but Alice has been unable to find out much about his personal life from Google or social media. Without the benefit of knowing what Grey and Boudreaux spoke about she's a step behind. One way to remedy that is to speak to Grey first, though she doesn't know how forthcoming he'll be when she can't hide behind a phone call posing as somebody else. There's even a risk that he might recognise her voice. It's a chance she has to take though.

Sofia should be arriving in the city around lunchtime, and they've agreed to meet at a Hampton hotel on East 43rd Street for one o'clock. Plan is to head back there after speaking to Doctor Grey, then spend the rest of the day strategising based on what they find out.

Sofia has been insistent that Alice waits for her before heading to the UN offices, but there's an inherent risk there that Boudreaux will catch them up, if indeed he's not already here. Alice has made educated guesses by looking at the flights the GALE agent could get, and hanging around till early afternoon just isn't going to cut it.

Only takes five minutes to reach the front of the queue, and a driver hops out to put her bags in the trunk. Inside the cab is practically tropical compared to the queue, and the vanilla scent that wafts from a New York Yankees air freshener is borderline overpowering.

Her driver knows better than to make too much effort at small talk with his fares at this time of day, and the witching hour traffic is sporadic at best, so it's a short hop of a little over thirty minutes. They cut across the north end of Brooklyn, and zip through the Midtown Tunnel.

Alice checks her notifications. Stares at the messages she received before she boarded at Charles de Gaulle, all from a new number, but no mistaking who's sending them. All short, but threats aren't all about word count.

Where are you?

You're late

Safe travels. We will come visit you soon

The last one troubles her. It came half an hour before she boarded, as if they knew where she was headed. She glances at the road behind, narrowing her eyes at the few pairs of headlights, but shakes away the thought. She's away from them now. She's safe. She hands the driver a few bills after he hefts her suitcase from the trunk outside the hotel.

Alice is feeling surprisingly alert now, as if she's siphoning energy from the city that never sleeps. She heads into reception, where the night clerk explains she can't check in until 3 p.m., so Alice settles for leaving her luggage in a locked side room, and heads back out into the half-lit streets in search of a diner.

Ten minutes later she's in the Morningstar Café, a twenty-four-hour diner on Second Avenue. The food is excellent. A perfectly cooked pair of poached eggs perched atop a muffin base, smothered with hollandaise sauce, a side of home fries and a bottomless coffee to fill up the tank.

Her booth has a power socket so she charges her phone and laptop as she eats. She passes the next few hours working through the rest of Grey's data. While Finlay is the only one who was at every location, there are a handful who aren't far behind. She has to consider all the angles, be her own harshest critic. Time for another look on Finlay's social accounts. He's not a big poster, mostly work or politics related. The only one that has any real personal insight is a fundraising link for a cancer charity in memory of Alana Finlay. His wife maybe?

His friends list includes a number of those on Grey's list, and she disappears down a Facebook rabbit hole, raking through their lives. They all look so … normal. All roads lead back to Finlay though. His previous profile pictures include a selection of him in what, thanks to the tags, she sees are a mix of the locations he's worked in. Some in his hospital scrubs, standing shoulder to shoulder with some of the peacekeeping troops. Afghanistan, Bosnia, Ethiopia.

Something occurs to her as she clicks through page after page, and she's annoyed it never entered her head sooner. Every victim had bled out. All of them had their carotid punctured. Coincidence or calculated MO? And who would know better how to find the carotid every time than a surgeon?

Feels like things are starting to solidify, like a lake freezing over, almost strong enough to tread on. Almost. She camps out at the diner until a little after eight.

It's a ten-minute walk to the United Nations building. Commuters are out in full force, and Alice feels far more at ease on the sidewalks of the Big Apple than she did in Paris. The UN building looks out over the East River, eclectic mix of member state flags lining the front facade.

With her plans changing so suddenly, there's been no chance to call and make sure Doctor Grey will be in. She'll try him first, then Doctor Finlay, and ask Sofia's forgiveness later.

A man sits behind a wood-topped reception desk that's polished to a mirror-like sheen. He greets her with a smile as she approaches.

'Hi there,' Alice says with a full beam smile.

'Good morning ma'am. Can I help you?'

'Yes, I'm here to see Doctor Elias Grey.'

'Is he expecting you?'

'Ah, no. I just came into town. Last-minute thing, you know. Even just five or ten minutes would do.'

'No promises. Who shall I say is calling?'

'My name is Logan. Alice Logan.' Then, as he reaches for his phone, 'Tell him I'm a friend of Agent Luc Boudreaux.'

He nods, punches in a number, and gives her another polite smile while they both wait. The kind that says I might have to ask you to leave any moment. There's an uncomfortable silence, broken only by others drifting in through security barriers. He half turns away as he starts to speak. Can't make out every word as his voice is low, but she makes out her own name. A pause, presumably while Grey is speaking. The man glances back at her, then away again.

When he ends the call a moment later, she gives him a hopeful smile.

'He's actually not in his office at the moment. He—'

'Do you know when he'll be back? I just need—'

The man holds up a hand to stop her. 'If you'll let me finish ma'am. He's out, but he's nearby. Says he can meet you at the East River Esplanade in about ten minutes, 'bout a half mile from here. Just take a left as far as East 37th, and cut across to the river.'

'Oh, okay,' Alice says, pleasantly surprised. She'd been primed for disappointment or a stonewall, but this is perfect. Gives her time to fit in Finlay as well before Sofia hits town.

'Do you happen to know if Doctor Oliver Finlay is in today too?' she asks, figuring to double down her apparent good fortune.

'Doctor Finlay has been working from home,' he says with a shake of his head. 'I can call him for you if you like, see if he'll speak to you over the phone?'

'No, thank you,' Alice says hurriedly. 'That's okay, I might not need to talk to him if I get everything I need from Doctor Grey.'

Of course she'll be back, but she'd rather give Finlay little or no advance warning. Less opportunity to compose himself if he has anything to hide.

She does as instructed, bearing left onto First Avenue, past a small recreational area, complete with half a dozen kids charging after a football. Along past a strip of fenced-off scrubland, until she hits East 37th. A series of arches marks the entrance to the Esplanade, faded lettering that looks older than Alice herself. Traffic zips past on the road above them, and beyond, the East River slides sluggishly past.

She scurries through the mini-underpass, and it opens out into a small strip of riverfront. One of those places that you can walk the city for weeks and never stumble across. Rows of set-back trees arch outwards towards the water, covering the two-tier paving like an umbrella. Out on the water a handful of boats float lazily downriver as she walks slowly south. Any other time, she'd happily park up on one of the benches with a coffee and just watch the world drift past. One thing this whole mess has done is highlight how little time she devotes to herself. This feels as close as she's come to breaking point since she lost Gail and she'll be no good to anyone, if she burns out.

Quick time check shows two minutes of the ten remaining. Off to her left, a lone jogger bobs up and down with a loping stride, woollen hat pulled down over his ears. Too far away to make out his face, and for a second, she's back on the bridge in Paris, pulse spiking. Looks around and realises for the first time how alone she is here. There's another figure a hundred yards to her right, but they're walking away.

She's got her laptop bag slung over her shoulder, but short of wielding her MacBook like a club, options are limited. Her breathing comes short, sharp, and it takes conscious effort to bring it back under control.

Fifty yards away now, and she swears the jogger is angling towards her. She positions herself next to a bench, a pitiful barrier, but beggars can't be choosers. She clutches her bag as he approaches, and there's a moment when he bounds up the small step to the second tier where she thinks he's going to lunge towards her.

Then she sees the curve of his nose, wisps of pale blonde hair poking out. It's him. Elias Grey. She holds up a hand in greeting and he stops six feet short of her.

'Doctor Grey? I'm Alice. Alice Logan.'

'Ah, Miss Logan,' he says, a touch curt, as if she's here unannounced. 'Sorry, I was mid-run when Zachary called me. I hope this is okay meeting here instead?'

'Oh sure, no problem. I'm kind of jealous to be honest. I run too. This would be the perfect start to the day for me.'

'I do love the river,' he says, staring out over the water. 'Although a start for me is more like five or six. Early riser.'

There's a pause as he continues to stare out across the water. 'Anyway, I know you must be really busy, so thank you so much for seeing me.'

'You said you were working with Agent Boudreaux?' he says, wiping the hat across his damp forehead.

'Yes, he and I have been working pretty closely on this. Might be nothing, but appreciate you helping us check it off our list if that's the case.'

'Not at all, happy to help,' he says, and she can't shake there's something in the way he stares at her, like he's trying to work out where he might have heard her voice before. If he does, he says nothing.

'I've reviewed what you sent us,' she says. 'What can you tell me about Oliver Finlay?'

'Quite a lot actually. I've known Oliver for years. I'll tell you what I told your colleague. Oliver is a good man, with a good heart. He's the last one I'd expect to get mixed up in anything criminal.'

'You'd be surprised, Doctor Grey. In my experience, anyone is capable of killing in the right, or wrong circumstances.'

His eyes widen. 'Killing? My God, who is he supposed to have killed?'

Boudreaux hasn't told him, Alice thinks with a start. Chances are then that he hasn't warned Finlay anyone is interested in him.

'I can't share names right now, I'm afraid.'

'But, what? You think he's done this at each of those places you asked about?'

'Someone has.'

'My God.' He folds his arms, placing one hand over his mouth. 'I just can't … not Oliver, surely? Have you spoken with him yet? Is he under arrest?'

'No, nothing like that. We just want to speak to him. Do you know if he's around today?'

'He's um … he's been working from home for a few months now,' Grey says, visibly shaken by the news. 'I can call him, though, ask him to come in if you like?'

'That'd be amazing, thank you.'

He walks over to the railings, leaning down and resting his elbows on the top one, and Alice moves to join him.

'How did you make the connection with the UN?' he asks.

'Just pure luck.' She shrugs, deciding how much to share with him. 'The murders are already closed cases,' she begins. 'Someone else was convicted in each of them.

If it wasn't for a call my client got, nobody would have even looked for a link.'

'Client? You're not an agent with GALE then?'

'No, sir, I'm a lawyer,' she says, hesitating as she decides how much to reveal. Being more open might encourage him to share more.

'And how is your case linked to the others?'

'It's a long story,' she says. 'Part of which we're still figuring out, but one of the men convicted is my father. Agent Boudreaux and I go way back, so we're working together on this one.'

'Interesting,' he says straightening up. 'Well what can I tell you? What would you like to know about Oliver?'

Alice thinks for a minute, deciding how to approach it. 'What's he like to work with?'

Grey considers this for a moment. 'Intense at times. A very driven, confident individual, but then again, most surgeons are. Nature of the job.'

'Intense how?'

'Just that he's always on the clock. That man works harder than anyone I know, even now, since …'

There's a pause. 'Since what Doctor?'

'Since his wife died. Cancer, few years back now. He threw himself into work to cope. There's even been talk of him going back out in the field this past month.'

'Have you ever seen him lose his temper, Doctor?'

'Oliver?' he says, chuckling. 'That man is cooler than the Antarctic, and believe you me, some of the places we send people to are not exactly holiday camps. You think it's stressful doing surgery in a shiny New York hospital, try doing it in places where you need armed guards to keep the hospital staff alive, never mind the patients.'

He sweeps his fringe back with one hand, and she spots a jagged scar tracing his hairline. He spots her looking and smiles.

'I'm not Harry Potter if that's what you're thinking!'

'Sorry,' she says blushing, 'I'm so sorry. I didn't mean to stare.'

'Honestly, it's fine. This is the reason I stopped doing the role Oliver does, sorry, did.'

'You used to work overseas as well?'

'Long, long time ago.' He nods. 'I had to come back here to recuperate, and been here ever since.'

'Sorry, I really didn't mean to pry.'

'Anyway, where were we?' he says, but before she can answer, she notices his gaze drift over her shoulder.

She turns to see what's caught his eye. Not a what, a who. Two figures approaching at a brisk pace from the north.

'Friends of yours?' she asks, as one of them points, nods, and both pick up their pace. They close the remaining gap with alarming speed, and Grey has seen the change in their demeanour too. He turns to face them, edging to one side in a way that positions him between her and the approaching men. Whether it's intentional or not, she's never felt such gratitude to a total stranger, even as she backs away to the bench a few feet away.

With a jolt of recognition that's like being plugged into the mains, she sees the face of the man from the Paris bridge, minus his hat. Not possible! Yet here he is, barrelling towards her. Feels like she's moving through maple syrup, foot catching on the leg of the bench. Grey calls out to them, no more than twenty yards away now.

'Can I help you gentlemen?'

'Doctor Grey,' Alice says, 'we need to leave. Right now.'

'You can go,' says the man from the bridge to Grey, 'she stays.' Then to Alice, 'Monsieur Dufort has asked us to teach you a little lesson in manners.'

She can't see Grey's face to see if he's afraid, but he spreads out his arms, hands palm out.

'I don't think the lady wants to talk to you.'

'Move,' barks the second man. He's the larger of the two, pockmarked face fixed into a permanent scowl.

'Not going to happen guys.'

The two men look at each other, shrugging, and Pockmark gives a grin that's like a rat baring its teeth.

'Okay' he says, 'we do it your way,' and they both advance, Pockmark angling off to pass on the river side, while Bridge Guy heads straight for Grey. Alice sees the doctor raise his hands, weight shifting onto the balls of his feet, as she pivots around the bench, placing it between her and Pockmark.

'Stupid bitch,' he spits out as he reaches it, grabbing the top wooden slat and hopping over.

Alice squeals and darts further back, bumping against a tree. He reaches for her, fingers brushing against her coat, but not finding purchase. She slides around the trunk, losing sight of him briefly. Hears a meaty thunk, then a loud whoosh of air being driven from lungs, followed by a sound like a sack of grain hitting the ground.

There's another bench behind her, and as she turns to run, Pockmark's arm shoots out again, this time snagging on her hood, hauling her back. The pressure of the seam against her neck makes her eyes shoot wide open.

He spins her round, grabbing a fistful of material, and lands a thunderclap of a slap cross her face. Pinpricks of light cartwheel across her vision, and she has the strangest feeling, as if she's floating, head spinning like a carousel with the impact. She's vaguely aware of his hand drawing back for another blow, knuckles closing into a fist this time. It's all she can do to close her eyes, wait for it to land.

Instead of blinding pain, she feels the hand grabbing her coat loosen. Opens her eyes to see that Doctor Grey has somehow got away from Bridge Guy, and has snaked an arm around Pockmark's neck, pulling him backwards. Behind him on the floor, Bridge Guy is on his side, trying to roll to his feet with all the skill of a tortoise on its back.

Her legs feel like jelly, head still ringing from the blow, and she backs away against the fence. Pockmark reaches around behind, trying and failing to claw at Grey's face. Grey hauls him backwards, away from Alice, and Pockmark changes it up. Instead of fighting it, he starts to pedal backwards, propelling Grey towards the low wall that divides them from the lower tier. Alice tries to call out, to warn him, but only manages one word.

'No!'

Grey can only be inches away from the edge, but somehow manages to spin, like he's doing a judo throw, releasing his grip at the same time, sending Pockmark flying head first onto the lower tier. It's not a big drop. Few feet maybe, but the first thing that makes contact with the ground is the side of his head, with a cracking noise that makes Alice sick to her stomach. Grey turns to look at her, breathing hard.

'Are you okay?' Then when she doesn't answer straight away, 'Alice, are you all right?'

'Yes, yes, I'm fine,' she says, touching a hand to her cheek, feeling the heat.

'Come on, let's get out of here.'

She blinks, soaking in the scene before her. Twice in two days violence has come knocking. Doesn't get any easier to absorb. She sucks in two big breaths, and walks on shaky legs towards him. He holds out a hand.

'Come on, we can go back to my office.'

She takes his hand and he guides her down the steps, drawing her in to him, like they're not strangers who met only five minutes ago. She glances back at where Pockmark lies, not moving. They skirt around Bridge Guy, who shouts something in French at her. Don't have to be fluent to know he's not asking after her health.

'Should we … you know, call the police, or something?'

'Let's get you clear of these two first,' he says, and she's just about to reply, when there's a flicker of movement in her periphery.

They turn together, just in time to see Bridge Guy, somehow risen to his feet, lunging forwards, wicked glint of a blade in his hand. They may have come for her, but there's no mistaking his target now. She feels Grey slip his arm from around her shoulder as Bridge Guy swings the knife in an arc towards Grey's head. He steps into the attack, reaching in to grab the wrist, but he's a fraction too late.

Alice hears Grey gasp as the knife slices across his forearm. It's a wild swing that keeps on going, throwing Bridge Guy off balance, so by the time he's corrected himself, Grey has moved closer to him. Got to hand it to the doc. He's no quitter. Every fibre of Alice's being is telling her to run but she can't leave him, not after he's had her back like this.

Bridge Guy looks to reverse his grip, scything another deadly arc back to finish the job, but this time Grey has closed the gap, grabbing the knife wrist, pushing him back towards the railings. The blade disappears from Alice's line of sight as the two men struggle for control. Bridge Guy huffs out a loud groan as his lower back smacks into the top railing, and the two seem frozen there for a beat. Two dancers locked in step. The ringing in Alice's head finally starts to subside, and she stumbles forward, determined to help her new-found bodyguard.

She's close enough to reach out and touch when there's a sudden jerk, slight shudder for both men, and Bridge Guy's grimace smooths out into glassy-eyed disbelief. Grey takes a step back, flinching as she touches his shoulder. As he does so, Alice sees the matt black hilt of the knife protruding from the Frenchman's jacket. Watches as he drops his own hands to it, fingers fluttering against it, no strength left to pull it out. Whether it's Bridge Guy leaning back or Grey catching him with a shoulder as he turns, the Frenchman now tips a slow arc back, like a seesaw, and falls backwards, head first into the river with a splash that Alice can barely hear over the roaring in her ears.

Grey turns, spittle flecking his lips, drawing deep breaths, in through the mouth, out loudly through the nose. He does a quick check both ways, and she can't help but copy. Nobody but them and their would-be assailants.

'What have you got me into here Alice?'

Chapter Fifty

Friday – Three days to go

'I still don't get why we don't just call the police now?' she says, as they half walk, half trot back towards the UN building.

'We will, as soon as I've seen to this,' he says, gingerly proffering his arm. She knows he was cut, but hasn't really looked at it until now. It's a long diagonal gash across his left forearm, blood still weeping out, drawing lines at a right angle thanks to gravity which makes it look like a grisly crimson hair comb.

'Is there a hospital near here?'

'My place is closer,' he says, wincing as he tests the lips of the wound with a finger. 'I've got everything I need to clean it up there. Besides I can't exactly walk in the office like this, can I?' He studies the wound again. 'Can't need more than ten stitches.'

'What? Oh, no, I couldn't possibly …'

'Not you silly, I'll do it myself,' he says, laughing despite the intensity of the past few minutes. 'I'll get cleaned up and showered, we'll be back in the office within the hour.'

Alice glances back down the Esplanade one more time. Sees the crumpled heap that is Pockmark, exactly where they left him.

'Is he … are they both dead?' she asks.

'Guy on the floor is just unconscious, but yeah, I think his friend may well be. The police will take care of it once I patch myself up. They attacked us, remember.'

Before they head out onto First Avenue, he takes off his hoodie, using a sleeve to tie a makeshift tourniquet just below the elbow, using the hood to soak up the blood that still leaks out.

The adrenaline is definitely starting to wear off for her, as she walks in a daze beside him. She clutches the laptop bag hanging by her side all the harder so as not to let him see her hands shaking.

They turn onto East 38th Street, and he stops outside an expensive-looking three-storey building.

'Which one's yours?' Alice asks.

He frowns. 'Which one? Oh, you think it's apartments? No, it's a house. My house.'

Alice gazes up, wondering how much this would set her back.

'Used to be my parents',' he says, passing her to open the half height wrought-iron gate, and heading up the steps.

She follows him into a black-and-white checked tile hallway, high ceiling giving it an airy feel. It's everything her own place isn't. She could probably buy her own home ten times over for what this cost, maybe more. He leads her into a small but pristine kitchen.

'Sit,' he says, pulling out a seat at the table. He grabs a first aid kit from under the sink while he waits for the kettle to boil, and starts to clean his wound by the sink.

'Cup of hot sweet tea should do it,' he says. 'Helps with the shock.'

'How can you be so calm?' she asks. 'That man in the river, I know it was self-defence, but still ...'

'Before I worked for the UN, I was in the US Army, still as a doctor, but my unit did two tours of Afghanistan. That's where I met Oliver actually. I went over there to save lives, but there's a time when someone is trying to take yours from you ...' She hears a sharp intake of breath and she looks over to see him dabbing at his cut with some kind of antiseptic wipe.

'What was he like over there?'

'Oliver? He was ... just like all of us I guess. Did his duty. Had my back, and I had his. Didn't know what we were going into, so it was all a bit of a shock to the system, you know?' He gives a sad laugh.

'I can't imagine the kind of things you must have seen over there.'

'Yeah, well most of us try and forget as best we can. That's why I keep on saying Oliver is a good guy. You serve two tours with someone, you get to know them pretty well. Whatever you do over there in the heat of battle, doesn't mean that defines the rest of your life.'

'What do you mean? What did he do over there?' She pauses, weighing her words. 'Did he ... did he kill anyone?'

Grey stops what he's doing, staring over at her, lips pursed but saying nothing. That's all the answer she needs.

Chapter Fifty-One

Friday – Three days to go

Grey is about to start suturing his wound, when he looks across and sees the colour drain from Alice's face.

'I can go do this in another room if it bothers you?' he offers.

As rude as it feels telling someone they can't do what they want in their own house, she gladly accepts the offer, and feels the queasy seasickness like sloshing of her stomach subside as he disappears.

Confirmation, albeit second-hand, that Finlay has killed, even in the heat of battle, slots home another brick in the wall. Not to say every soldier becomes a cold-blooded killer, but she knows now that he's capable. She knows he was there in each town. The why still eludes her. Maybe the afternoon brainstorming with Sofia will dislodge something, give her a motive. Somewhere upstairs she hears water pipes groan.

A flurry of hypotheticals swirls around her head. What if he was involved with organised crime, like Dufort's people? All of the others had long rap sheets too, both victims and killers. What if he was somehow in business with them? Could it be that he was treating them off the books, like a back-street clinic for cash? Could he even be selling on pharmaceuticals, or helping them smuggle contraband in or out of the country with his UN connections?

She finishes the last of her tea, rinsing out her mug and refilling it with hot water. Nine hours on a plane, echoes of the restaurant attack and now this? Feels like every muscle in Alice's body has been stretched to snapping point. She puts down her mug, rotates her neck a few times and does a couple of quick stretching exercises.

Sofia. Hot bath. Home tomorrow or the day after, depending on how this plays out with Finlay. The more she hears about him, though, the more relieved she is she won't be going to see him solo.

She wanders into the hallway to stretch her legs. There's a door either side, and she cups her hot water in both hands as she saunters in through the left-hand one, as much out of boredom as nosiness. It's like stepping into a different house. What little she's seen so far is minimalistic, no real character. This is a man cave of sorts, albeit a very cultured one.

Floor to ceiling bookcases line two of the walls. The one behind the door has a series of units attached, housing what looks like a collection of artefacts and trinkets from far-flung places. Butted up against the window is an ancient-looking pedestal style desk, faded red leather covering the surface. It's clear, save for a MacBook, a desk calendar and a letter opener.

His book collection ranges from old, leather-bound volumes, to a shelf of more modern-day paperbacks. Hardly any fiction, she notices. The far wall is a veritable photo gallery, some amazing landscapes and vistas, mixed in with shots of Grey with groups of other people. Dozens of frames, some with more than one picture in. Maybe as many as a hundred images all told. A creak behind her makes her whirl round. Grey stands in the doorway, wearing a pair of jeans and a black V-neck jumper, damp hair scraped back. There's a slight ridge in the material on his left arm, presumably where he's dressed it.

'I didn't mean to startle you.'

'Sorry, I was just … I didn't mean to intrude,' she says, blushing.

'Not at all. My favourite room of the house,' he says, looking around as if it's filled with precious keepsakes.

Suddenly one face on the picture wall jumps out at her, and she moves over to take a closer look. Tousled dark hair, genuine smile, the kind that makes you want to trust the person throwing it your way.

'This is him, right? Oliver?'

Grey walks over to join her, standing so their shoulders practically touch.

'That one was in Somalia, not long after we set up. I didn't stick around long. More of a pencil pusher these days. Oliver ran that place like clockwork, in some really difficult conditions.'

'Do you miss it? Being out in the field I mean?'

'Some days, yes. After my accident, though, being in among the front line every day, I'm ashamed to admit it but it all got a bit much for me.

'Your accident, what happened?'

She leaves it hanging, not wanting to press, but after a brief pause, he starts talking. Tells her about a six-month stint in Somalia in the mid-nineties. How he and four others had been jumped while on their way to a clinic. Two of the group had been killed. Grey was only saved thanks to the bravery of the other two, but suffered massive head trauma.

'How bad was it?' she asks, wondering if it's an appropriate question. Might be something he prefers to leave buried. She thinks better of it. 'I'm sorry,' she says, 'you don't have to answer that.'

'Don't be. Two of my friends didn't walk away from it. I'm still here. I've made my peace with it.' He moves closer to the wall, slipping the picture with him and Oliver off its hook.

'I know he's your friend,' Alice says, trying to mollify him. 'You've seen him under pressure. How do you think he'll react to being questioned?'

'Honestly, I don't know.'

'It could still be nothing. It's just that when you represent clients like mine, you have to turn over every last rock.'

'That must be such a difficult job,' he says, rehanging the picture. 'Pleading for the lives of men who have already taken the lives of others.'

She whips her head around at a version of words she's heard countless times.

'I don't practise over here any more, but why do you think nearly half the country has scrapped the death penalty? No man has the right to take another's life. No one, not even the State. And that's before we even move onto wrongful convictions.'

'And which is your father?'

'What do you mean?'

'Did he do it? Are you just saving his life 'cos you think everyone should be saved? Is it family loyalty, or is he actually innocent?'

She considers this for a moment. 'My dad and I, we have a … let's call it a difficult relationship. Not much to speak of if I'm honest. I've learned some things about him recently that make me think that's no bad thing. But it's bigger than just him. These men in jail, one of them is threatening my brother if I don't find something that clears him as well as my dad.'

'I see,' he says, staring at the pictures of himself on the wall.

'There's that, and as much as me and my dad don't get on, I'm beginning to think he might actually be telling the truth when he says he didn't do it.'

'Don't they all say that?'

She shakes her head. 'Some are quite happy to tell you exactly what they did.'

'Feels wrong to consider Oliver in the same breath as these men,' he says, leaning against a bookcase. 'I know he's no stranger to blood, but I can't imagine him killing another man on purpose full stop, let alone with the kind of savagery you're talking about here.'

'You'd be surprised …' she begins, but the rest of her sentence gets stuck like bugs on flypaper. 'What makes you say that?'

'Hmm?'

'You said savagery, and that Oliver was used to blood.' She turns to look at him. 'What makes you think there was blood involved?'

'Isn't there always?' he says with a confused smile.

'They could have been strangled, suffocated, poisoned …' she rattles off options.

'I'm sure you mentioned earlier that …' he begins, but she blinks away the fatigue that has been wrapping its warm arms around her, to cut him off.

'I didn't say anything,' she says, 'I didn't even tell you the victims were all men. How could you know that?'

He looks down at her with sad eyes. 'I really wish you hadn't asked that Alice.'

Chapter Fifty-Two

Friday – Three days to go

Luc Boudreaux knows Alice has reason to distrust him. Knows there's probably no chance that the young lawyer will ever forgive him, but that sense of guilt and obligation won't stop him from being furious with her right now. Seems like he's not the only person asking about Doctors Grey and Finlay.

'And she went to meet him when?'

'A little after eight-thirty, sir,' says the guy behind reception at the UN building.

'Where?'

Boudreaux hurries out, and along to the East River Esplanade, heart sinking as he sees police tape across the low-arched entrance. A young uniformed officer moves to head him off, but he flashes his badge, and asks to see the officer in charge.

A tall Latino in grey pants and a powder-blue shirt introduces himself as Detective Blanco. He eyes Boudreaux with a healthy degree of suspicion as he explains who he is, and why he's here, saying only that he believes his case is connected to two people who were known to have been on the Esplanade earlier.

'You think they're linked to my homicide?'

'Who's the dead guy?' he asks, soaking in the new info without a pause, but inside his heart is racing.

'Could be a tourist. We got a call from a guy at the ferry terminal over there, he gestures with a thumb over his shoulder. 'Saw two guys fighting. One other person on the Esplanade with them, they think a woman. Another one already on the ground, they think a man, but no sign of him when we got here. One of the guys goes over. We fished him out, but there ain't no bringing him back. Stab wound. Bled out. ID in his wallet is a French driving licence. We're in the process of reaching out to local PD.'

'I got good connections in France,' he says, looking to score cheap brownie points. 'You have any problems, you let me know.'

Blanco gives him a hard, flat stare, as if considering the offer, but instead he says 'These people you think were here earlier, you got names?'

He knows it'll piss him off, but opts to play it tight.

'Uh-huh, but I can't share yet. National Security.'

The miracle catch-all that sends any pissed-off cop down a dead end. He knows it too. Shows on Blanco's face.

'You got a card?' Boudreaux asks, trying to placate him. 'Once I can, I'll give you a call, fill you in.'

Blanco hands over his business card and turns his attention back to his crime scene. Boudreaux managed to get home addresses for both doctors from the guy at reception. Grey is closer, so he'll pay him a visit first. Finlay is more of a hike, out in Suffolk County, Long Island. He'll keep until this afternoon.

East 38th is ten minutes from here. Boudreaux gets his stride on and makes it in seven. He checks off door numbers, raising eyebrows when he sees Grey's place.

'I definitely should have gone to med school,' he mutters, taking in the imposing red brick facade.

He hears the buzzer echo inside, and smiles as the image of a butler opening the door comes to mind. Once the buzzing fades, he's left with the sounds of the city for company. No click of lock or sliding latch. He tries a second time, adding a quick-fire series of knocks.

Boudreaux glances back down the street, wondering where they could be. Maybe they stopped for a coffee? He grinds his teeth at the thought of Alice going behind his back. How the hell did she even find out about Grey? Boudreaux mentioned the UN, but never any names. An off-the-books check by Abs shows Alice's phone as being at this address as recently as five minutes ago.

If it were anyone else, any other circumstances, Boudreaux would slap them with impeding an investigation and ask questions later. But this isn't just any old person. And it's not even an official investigation. Not yet anyway. If this pans out, not even Pascal Lavigne can look the other way.

A faint sound from behind the door. Footsteps, the clicking of a lock. A man appears as it opens, hair damp like he's just showered, wearing jeans and a black sweater.

'Doctor Grey?'

'Yes, can I help you?'

'Agent Luc Boudreaux,' he says, reaching for his badge. 'We spoke on the phone yesterday.'

'Ah yes, nice to meet you Agent Boudreaux. Is there a problem with the information I sent you?'

'No, no, I just … I went to your office to see you, and the guy at the desk said you were out meeting a woman called Alice Logan?'

'Yes, Miss Logan met me while I was out on my morning run. She said you and her have been helping each other with this case.'

Boudreaux pulls a face. 'Not exactly. We do have a shared interest though. Can I ask what you talked about?'

Slow head-shake from Grey. 'She wanted to know a little more about Oliver. She's hoping to speak to him today. I believe she's on her way there now.'

'Where did you see her?'

'She was coming to meet me at the Esplanade, but I made good time, so we ended up meeting on First Avenue. I had to head back for a shower, so we walked and talked.'

'And what time was that?'

Grey glances at his watch. 'Maybe an hour ago.'

'So neither of you made it onto the Esplanade?'

Grey purses his lips. 'No, like I said, we met on First.'

'Okay, thanks,' he says, wondering if Grey is lying, covering for her for some reason, or if she's just left her phone here by mistake.

Quick glance down at his own watch, then back at Grey. He's wondering how to play this when something catches his eye.

A splash of colour where none should be. The contrast of black jumper and pale skin is broken by a single crimson line drawn half way across the back of his hand.

Blood. Got to be fresh as well, else it would have washed off in the shower. He forces his gaze back up before Grey realises where he's looking.

'Actually, would it be okay if I came in to use your bathroom?'

It's an instinctive ask. The kind where he acts while his brain processes what's going on. Something is off here. Alice's phone location. The fact Grey says he came home from a run an hour ago but his hair is still damp now, like he's not long stepped out of the shower.

'Ah, I'm literally just about to head out actually. I should have been back in the office ages ago, so if you don't mind I—'

'I came straight here from the airport you see. I'll literally just be a minute,' he says taking a step towards the door.

Grey doesn't move. He changes tack.

'C'mon, am I gonna have to flash my badge to commandeer your toilet, 'cos I'm not above that right now.'

He looks conflicted, and he reaches out, putting one hand on the door frame.

'Please, doctor, you took the Hippocratic oath, right?'

He takes an age to speak, gives half a glance over his shoulder, then steps back.

'You'll have to use the one upstairs, the downstairs one is broken.'

'Lifesaver,' he says stepping into the hallway.

'Second door on the left,' he says, moving to place a hand on the newel post, waving him past with the other like he's directing traffic.

Boudreaux shoots a grateful smile, taking the stairs two at a time, but leaves the door open when he goes in the bathroom. Due to meet Alice at a location where local PD are scraping someone off the ground, and now bleeding from God knows what kind of wound?

He cocks an ear at the door, listening for anything through the heavy silence that's draped like an overcoat across the building.

Nothing. He counts off a hundred seconds then flushes the toilet and turns on the tap for show. Takes out his phone, prop in a plan that's far from first choice.

He takes the stairs slower this time, hoping that he'll get to the bottom and have an excuse to pop his head into another room. Two doors towards the entrance, a third at the end of a corridor. Kitchen maybe? He's gets within six feet of that one when Grey emerges. There's a distracted energy about him, like he has a purpose but is doing his darndest to mask it.

'Ah, all set?' he asks, with a grin that looks drawn on wonky.

Boudreaux fires back one of his own, tapping his phone screen with the finger that's been poised millimetres away by his side.

'Yeah, I'd best get going if I'm going to catch up with Alice.'

He marks off the seconds in his head. Only manages to count to three before he hears the purr of a phone coming from somewhere beyond the kitchen door.

He knows Grey hears it too. He sees it in his eyes. They widen for a split second, then narrow, a predator fixing on his prey. Boudreaux sweeps back the hem of his jacket, reaching for his SIG Sauer, and the movement triggers Grey. He lunges forward, closing half of the six feet before Boudreaux can draw his weapon. It clears the holster and is arcing up towards him as Grey connects.

He dips low, driving a shoulder into Boudreaux's chest, and he feels fingers scrabble at his wrist. Grey's weight bears down on him, and the world tilts as they topple. Boudreaux reacts instinctively, turning his hips judo style, using his momentum in his favour. They're both going down hard, doing a quarter turn when the thunderclap of a gunshot fills every corner of the hallway.

The two land in a tangle, side by side, and Boudreaux tries for a two-handed grip on his pistol to yank it free. Grey's grip is iron. Boudreaux tries to work out if he's been hit. No pain, except from his shoulder that bore the brunt of his fall.

If Grey was hit, he's not showing it. Boudreaux tugs again, feels his hold give a little. Readies himself for a third attempt, when he sees Grey's free hand heading his way, balled into a fist. No way to avoid it. Best he can do is limit damage, and he tucks his chin to his chest. It's still a jarring blow, but Grey's hurt too. A dry crack, like a stepped-on twig. Grey gasps in pain, and Boudreaux knows he has to capitalise.

Fireflies dance across his vision, but he blinks them away. Grey is marginally stronger than him, but in a dogfight it's not about how much you can bench. He changes direction, moves towards Grey instead of trying to drag the gun away. The doctor is not expecting the switch-up, and his continued pulling, plus Boudreaux's transference of weight, rolls him up and over, throwing one leg across Grey's chest so he's straddling him.

Before he can regroup, Boudreaux takes a calculated risk, his right hand still firmly gripping his SIG, left arm bending at the joint, elbow dropping towards the doctor's nose like a hammer. Grey flinches, and the blow lands on his cheekbone. Boudreaux sees the pain ripple across his face, and as his grip slackens on the gun, Boudreaux gives it his all to wrench it away. Too much as it turns out. It comes easier than he imagined, and his arm whips back, his own grip losing traction, and the weapon clatters across the hard-tiled floor.

Grey reaches up, grabbing Boudreaux's throat, and squeezes. Boudreaux feels a pang of panic, air supply closing, but he powers past it, instinct and training taking over. Damn but Grey's fingers feel like steel claws about to crush his windpipe.

He shifts his weight, sliding one knee up over his arm so it sits between shoulder and neck. As his body twists around, he grabs the hand that's choking him by the wrist.

The edges of Boudreaux's world start to blur, lungs burning from lack of oxygen. One chance, after that this won't end well for him. He throws his full weight backwards, cranking Grey's wrist toward him until it's pinned to his own chest.

The torque against Grey's joint breaks the chokehold, and he gulps at the air in a loud wheezing heave. The respite is short-lived; he grunts out the next breath as he falls back, shoulders slamming into hard tiles.

Boudreaux still clutches his prize though. Hangs on to that wrist for dear life. He's lying perpendicular to the doctor now, Grey's head beneath Boudreaux's calves, arm trapped between his legs. With a guttural bellow, Boudreaux raises his hips as he squeezes his wrist the final few inches towards him, applying agonising pressure on Grey's elbow joint, hyperextending it in a way that nature didn't build it to handle.

He's practised the arm bar a hundred times on the jiu-jitsu mat, but there'll be no tap-out allowed today. He feels the pop a split second before he hears the sickening sound. Grey's scream isn't far behind that.

Boudreaux arches up a touch more, applying the finishing touches. Enough soft tissue damage to take the arm out of commission for months. This is about survival, though, not mercy, and he's taking no chances with his life, or anyone else's.

Alice! He remembers the call to her phone that sparked off Grey's charge. Scrambles to his feet just as Grey makes a clumsy grab for him with his good hand, but there's no real conviction, and he kicks it away easily.

Boudreaux pulls out a set of plasticuffs and rolls him over, ignoring his protests. He cinches them tight, enough to bite into the flesh at his wrists. Next he does the same to his ankles. Satisfied that he's going nowhere, Boudreaux yanks open the kitchen door, eyes widening in alarm as he sees Alice, wedged into a seat at a small wooden table, leaning up against the kitchen wall.

The lawyer's eyes are closed, head bowed so Boudreaux can't see her face.

'Alice,' he calls out, rushing across, squatting beside her. Alice moans softly as Boudreaux tries gently to rouse her.

Quick glance back into the hallway confirms Grey is still belly down, wriggling like an oversized worm. Focusing his attention back on Alice, a large beige patch on her neck catches his eye. Like a large band aid. He peels it back, but there's no injury underneath so he rips it off in one go. Takes him a few minutes to rouse Alice after that. It's as if she's drugged, eyes unfocused and speech slightly slurred.

'Wait, what the … Grey! Where's Grey?'

'Don't worry about him. I got him covered,' Boudreaux says in what he hopes is a soothing tone. 'How are you doing? What happened?'

'He … Grey … I think he's the one,' Alice says, a little of the strength returning to her voice.

'Yeah, I'm beginning to think that myself.'

'This is a mistake.' Grey's voice is laced with pain, drifting in from the hallway. 'Give me a chance to explain, and you'll see.'

Alice peers past Boudreaux. 'How did you find me?'

'That can wait,' Boudreaux says, ignoring Grey and fetching Alice a glass of water. 'What we need right now is a chat with him.'

'He's dangerous, Luc,' Alice says between sips. 'I saw him kill a man down by the river.'

'I saved your life.' Grey manages to sound pissed off at the suggestion it was anything else.

'We'll see about that,' says Boudreaux.

He motions for Alice to stay seated, and does a quick recce of the downstairs, opting to drag Grey across the tiles and into his study. He hauls him up into the desk chair, moving the letter opener lying on the desk. The plasticuffs should hold, but why take a chance? He returns to the hall, standing where he can see both Grey and Alice.

'Can you walk?'

'I'll bloody well walk out of here.'

'You up for a little cross-examination first?'

'Of him or you?' she asks, steely determination creeping back into her voice.

'What's that supposed to mean?'

She leans in close, turning her back to Grey.

'I know you got the tip back when this all started. From McKenzie?' It comes out as an angry hiss.

He opens his mouth, but she cuts him off.

'Don't even try to deny it,' she snaps.

'Alice, I …'

'How could you? I mean really? All that bullshit about not being on the force to see innocent people get hurt.'

'That wasn't bullshit,' he says, 'I—'

'Liar,' she hits back.

'Trouble in paradise?' Grey's voice drifts over her shoulder.

She shoots a cold stare at Boudreaux. This all leads back to him now. Without him, what he did, she might not have been dragged thousands of miles from home.

'You got enough trouble of your own,' Boudreaux calls to him over his shoulder. 'How 'bout you worry about that?' He locks eyes again with Alice. 'Let me explain,' he implores. 'But later. After this.' He gestures with his head at Grey.

She stares at him, conflicted, but knows there are bigger fish to fry, starting with the one trussed up in the chair.

'You better believe it,' she says finally, and looks past him, into the eyes of a killer.

Chapter Fifty-Three

Friday – Three days to go

'Before you start trying to spin whatever line of shit you're peddling here, let me just remind you that I've already got a dead body with your name on it just pulled outta the East River, not to mention what's just gone down in here,' Boudreaux says, sitting opposite a surprisingly calm-looking Grey. Apart from the occasional wince when he shifts in his seat, he could be sitting shooting the breeze over coffee.

'If you mean the man I hurt in self-defence while I was protecting Miss Logan, what would you have had me do?'

Alice feels her stomach turn somersaults at the memory of the Esplanade. Of what could have happened if Grey hadn't done what he did.

Her head is clearer by the minute, the effects of Grey's drugs wearing off like a morning mist burning away in the sun.

'Don't use me to justify murder,' she says through gritted teeth. 'Don't you dare.'

'I saved you.'

'And then you attacked me, so let's call that even.'

'How about we start with that, Doctor Grey?' says Boudreaux. 'If this is all a big mistake, why did you attack Miss Logan?'

The doctor runs his tongue across his teeth, but says nothing.

'You were in Somalia,' Alice blurts out. 'You told me you were there with Doctor Finlay. How many other countries have you been in?'

She walks across to his wall of photographs, pulling down the same one they'd studied earlier.

'You were there with him, but your name doesn't show up on that list you sent. Why is that?'

His eyes follow Alice as she paces along the row of pictures, but still he says nothing. 'You want to hear a theory, Doctor Grey?' She doesn't give him time to answer.

'I'd bet that if we looked closely enough, these pictures place you in a whole lot of other countries too. Maybe even all the same ones as Oliver, but he's the only one that ticked all the boxes on the email you sent. Best-case, you knew what he was up to, and you've been covering for him. Worst-case, you two are in this together, and you've had a falling out, so you're offering him up. That way, you walk away scot-free. How am I doing so far?'

Grey ignores her question, looking over at Boudreaux instead.

'Do I presume backup is on the way, Agent Boudreaux? You've called in the cavalry after you damn near broke the arm of a respected member of the United Nations? Oh, no, that's right,' he tilts his head, makes like he's made some kind of schoolboy error. 'You said on the phone this is on the down-low. That you didn't want word getting out? Fact I've not heard you call this in makes me wonder if that includes keeping it from your own people for some reason?'

'You think I have any issues arresting you, you prick?' Boudreaux barks. 'Go ahead, try me.'

'Arrest me for what exactly?'

'Let's start with the unconscious attorney I found in your kitchen.'

'She'd had some kind of funny turn. I was about to get my car key and take her to a hospital.'

'You lying bastard!' It slips out of Alice in a rush. The gall of the man. As hazy as the memories are, she knows this is far from what happened. Remembers him overpowering her. Everything fading to black.

'And as for you, Agent Boudreaux, we've never met before. I saw a strange man in my house with a gun. I was merely trying to defend myself.'

'Yeah?' Boudreaux strides across, bending down to eyeball him. 'Let's see how that plays out to a jury, shall we? You and I know the truth of it.'

'Since when has justice been about the truth?' he says with something approaching a smile. 'It's about what you can prove, and right now you have nothing.'

'You want to play the wise-ass? Let me tell you what I can prove. I can prove you deliberately kept your own name from a list of persons of interest. I know for a fact you assaulted me. My friend here is pretty adamant she's been drugged, so a tox screen will settle that. I know I've got a guy they pulled out of the East River who I'm betting is responsible for that leak you've sprung from your arm. And I'm gonna double down and say there'll be a trace of him on whatever clothes you've got changed out of. You know how many cameras there are between here and the river? What do you think I'm gonna see when I check the route between here and there? That's enough to get a warrant to search this house in the meantime, and I'm betting we'll find enough to put you and our mystery river guys together.'

Grey says nothing, but Alice can see that some or all of Boudreaux's words have scored a point.

'These things always go easier when you cooperate, Dr Grey.'

'Wait,' Alice says, brow furrowing as she processes Boudreaux's monologue. 'There were two men. The other one …' She looks at Grey, hating the pang of pity ratting on a man who saved her life no matter how you dressed it up. 'He knocked the other guy out.'

'Not for long then,' Boudreaux says. 'The officer running the scene didn't mention anyone else.'

Alice turns to look at Grey. 'Thank you. For saving me back there I mean. I owe you that much.'

He says nothing, but inclines his head a touch in acknowledgement.

'Having said that,' she continues, 'you know more about these cases than you're saying. You want to know what I think?'

'Not particularly,' he says with a dismissive sneer.

'I ask myself why you'd include Doctor Finlay on that list if you were in this together. Sure, you might have had a falling-out, but anything happens to him and it's a risk to you. No, I think he's on that list in your place. He's your fall guy. I think you killed those people. I think you're responsible for all of this. If you killed all of those men, then you're a monster.'

He looks at her like she's just spat in his face.

'I think Oliver Finlay is just an innocent guy, caught up in whatever sick shit you're involved in.'

There's a flash of defiance in his eyes. Enough to set off the finely tuned tripwire in her mind, honed from years in a courtroom.

'What?' Alice asks. 'Was it the part about Finlay, or about you being a sick individual?'

No mistaking it. At the mention of Finlay's name, the micro-expressions are plain as signal flares in the night sky.

'Whatever's going on between you and him, it's over,' she says. 'Luc's right, no matter what happens with all the others, you aren't walking away from what's happened today. Finlay might, but not you.'

'What makes you so sure he's innocent?' Grey says, after a pause.

'You telling us he isn't?'

Deep breath in from Grey, sharp exhalation through his nose. He looks away, eyes flicking over the wall of pictures. Finally, a series of slight nods, as if he's come to a decision.

'What if I were to tell you that he has killed, and I can prove it?'

Alice shoots a glance to Boudreaux, then back at Grey. Boudreaux technically has jurisdiction in any member state, but this is off the books. Even Grey seems to know that.

The elephant in the room hasn't shifted though. Even if he tries to hang twelve killings around Finlay's neck, that doesn't change the outcome for her dad.

'What kind of proof? And what's the motive? What axe did he have to grind with them all?'

'All? No. Just one.'

'What do you mean just one?' Boudreaux asks. 'Which one?'

'Not one of those men,' Grey replies. 'His wife.'

Chapter Fifty-Four

Friday – Three days to go

Did not see that one coming, thinks Alice.

'What's his wife got to do with this?' Boudreaux asks, looking puzzled enough for both of them.

'Wasn't cancer that got her.'

'What are you saying?'

'He did it. Oliver. Killed her and cashed in the life insurance to pay off gambling debts.'

'And you know this how?' Boudreaux asks.

'Because I saw him do it,' Grey says, as nonchalant as if he's making small talk about the weather.

'Wait, you … you actually saw it happen?' Alice asks, feeling ill at ease talking about a woman's murder so casually.

He nods. 'I was too far away to stop it. His house is by a lake. Alana, his wife, she loved to swim before she got sick. She was in remission when it happened.'

He wriggles uncomfortably in his seat, arms still held in place by the cuffs.

'It was around eighteen months ago. He's been working from home a lot for obvious reasons. I went over to talk to him about taking a sabbatical, you know, so he could focus on Alana. He hadn't been the same since her diagnosis. Anyway, when I got there nobody answered the door, so I walked around the side. Saw him in his boat. Had his hands scrabbling about in the water like he was washing up after dinner. I'd covered half the ground when he sat back up. Saw something bob to the surface.'

If he's making this up on the fly, then he's a damn fine actor, thinks Alice. He has that same grim set to his jaw that she's seen in a dozen others who've witnessed something they couldn't prevent.

'He left her floating there a full five minutes while he smoked a damn cigarette,' Grey continues, jaw bunching as he clenched his teeth in anger. 'Had a bird's-eye view when he hauled her in and came back to shore. Threw her over his shoulder like a goddamn sack of corn. I had to listen as he worked himself up to making the 911 call. Everyone at the UN still thinks the cancer finished her.'

'It's a touching story, doctor,' Boudreaux cuts in. 'But if there's a shred of truth in it, why the hell didn't you call 911 yourself?'

'Let me ask you this. Would you vote to convict beyond a reasonable doubt from what the evidence shows?'

'You just said he held her under the water. Who the hell wouldn't convict?'

Grey gives a wry smile. 'You've only got my word for that though. Think about it. Woman whose body has been ravaged by cancer, trying to reclaim a part of her she loved before her illness. Oliver plays the grieving husband who tried to save her. He had on a pair of heavy-duty rubber gloves up to the elbow, so there won't be any physical evidence, scratches, skin under his nails.

And you'd convict on the word of a guy who was a couple of hundred yards away?'

'Cop or no cop, I'd still have called it in,' Boudreaux says. 'Any person with a conscience would. Question still stands, why wouldn't you? You're saying he killed his wife, so why does he get to walk free?'

Alice watches as Grey and Boudreaux have their own private stare-down. The air in the room feels heavy, thick and laced with the weight of whatever he's not sharing. Grey is wallowing deep in whatever this is, no doubt about that. Sounds like there's no love lost between him and Finlay. Surely all the more reason to make sure a man like Finlay gets punished. Anyone who does that to the woman he loves deserves what's coming to him.

Boudreaux starts talking again, but it's like white noise. Alice isn't listening to him, her thoughts racing ahead based on what's she's just heard. When it hits her it's a searing blast of clarity.

'That's it,' she says, as much to herself as anyone. Then a second time, loud enough to interrupt Boudreaux. 'That's just it, he does want him punished, just not by the courts, isn't that right, doctor? He's like all the others, even my dad, isn't he? They all hurt or killed someone, and got away with it.'

Boudreaux opens his mouth to speak but stops, narrows his eyes, and Alice knows the same pieces are slotting home for him. Grey's expression has changed too. The sarcastic, superior edge seems to have softened, lines across his forehead flattening out.

'That's why you killed them all, isn't it?' Alice goes on. 'They were getting away with murder, literally, until you stepped in.'

'And Finlay?' Boudreaux counters. 'If that's true, why isn't he dead too?'

'I think he needs him,' Alice says slowly, working her way through this knotty part of her theory on the hoof. 'I don't think it's a coincidence he's been in every country. I think he's been a fall guy-in-waiting all these years. Fact he's turned out to be as bad as the others is just a bonus. Grey has been in charge of staffing in all these places. How hard is it to make sure you sign up your patsy for the trip, just in case things go bad?'

'You ever been to Florida, doctor?' Boudreaux asks. 'If I was to do some digging, would I find you were there around, say, the same week Jim Sharp was arrested?'

Grey says nothing, eyes flicking between them as if he's studying a chessboard, waiting for them to declare mate. The lack of any protests from him in itself feels telling.

'What happened, Doctor Grey?' Alice asks. 'You're meant to save lives, not take them.'

'You're really going to lecture me on the value of life, Miss Logan?' Grey says, tilting his head like he's studying her. 'You're trying to save the lives of men like your dad who clearly value it so little.'

Knowing what she knows now about her dad, the words ring hollow when she speaks.

'You don't get to judge people you don't know,' she says. 'You don't know whether or not he killed that man.'

'Just 'cos he didn't kill *him*, doesn't make him innocent,' Grey snaps back, real venom in his voice for the first time.

The silence that follows is broken only by the soft drone of traffic outside. The emphasis on *him* is like a flashing neon sign in Alice's mind.

'Now why would you say that?' Boudreaux asks.

'Most people aren't if you dig far enough down.'

'No, you said he didn't kill *him,* that's how you said it. Not him but maybe someone else.'

Alice is painfully aware she hasn't shared her dad's revelation with Boudreaux yet, but any doubts in her mind as to who and what Elias Grey is, are evaporating fast.

'You know something I don't?' Boudreaux asks.

'Off the record,' Alice says, before Grey can speak. She turns to face Boudreaux, 'My dad may have been involved in a hit-and-run the week before he got arrested.'

Boudreaux's eyes widen. 'Is that right? You didn't think to share this little titbit before now?'

'This doesn't come close to what you've done, and that's even before you set that reporter on me. You know, the one you had a little chit-chat with outside? I saw you and her looking all cosy yesterday morning.'

'I was telling her to back off and mind her own damn business!'

'I'm not doing this now,' Alice says, turning her attention back to Grey. 'Of course, you knew what my dad had done. But how? Dad said he'd seen another car that night. Was that you? All makes sense now. That's why you took him for a little drink the night Manny Castillo died. The hat . . .,' she gets up, strides across to the picture wall, jabbing a finger at one frame. Grey with a man and a woman, Eiffel Tower in the background. '. . . you wore the same hat the night you killed Manny Castillo.'

'Objection, your honour,' Grey mocks her. 'Circumstantial.'

'You honestly think twelve members of a jury can't see the picture on a jigsaw just 'cos one of the corner pieces is missing?' she says. 'The police didn't know they needed to look past my dad back then. You don't think there'll be enough once they get started? We've got an eyewitness, Doctor Grey. A man who says the guy he saw could barely walk, let alone pop a man's carotid. If Dad hurt anybody else, then he deserves to be tried for that, and that alone. Same goes for Manny Castillo and all those other men you killed.'

'Have you ever been the victim of crime, Miss Logan?' he asks.

She shakes her head, not willing to share what happened in Paris, but he doesn't give her time to speak.

'Let me tell you what it's like to have your dignity stripped away by people you're there to help. See this?' His eyes flick up in the direction of his scar. 'Tried to help where help wasn't wanted in Somalia. Got this and three days in a coma for my troubles. Those two colleagues in that picture? When I got out of the hospital, I had to look their relatives in the eye and explain why their loved ones weren't coming home.'

'I'm sorry to hear—'

'You can shove your sorry up your ass,' he snaps, tiny grenade of spittle launching out and onto the floor by his foot. 'Until you've lived that, you can save your damn sympathy. I flatlined twice, nearly died on the table while they tried to stop the bleeding in my brain. You think the men who did this were sorry? That all those others were sorry? Uh-uh, counsellor, when you make the choices these people made, sorry just doesn't cut it. Everywhere I've travelled, people are the same. Bullies are universal. Bullies don't have borders. Everyone needs to answer for their choices.'

'And that's what you do?' Boudreaux asks. 'Who holds you accountable?'

'What I do balances the scales,' he says. 'I take no pleasure in it, but every last one of those men had killed without consequence. All I did was dole out the justice they'd managed to swerve.'

Finally, an admission.

'What I don't get, though, is why you didn't just kill them all?' Boudreaux says with a frown. 'If they're all murderers, surely they should be punished equally?'

'Two dead bodies with no one to blame is an open-ended question. One dead body and their killer is enough of an answer to leave me free to do my work.'

'So balance when it suits you then?' Boudreaux fires back. 'How do you decide which one lives and which one dies?'

Grey shrugs. 'I let them decide, in a manner of speaking.'

'In what way?'

'I speak with each of them, give them a chance to show me the kind of person they truly are. The lesser of two evils keeps breathing.'

That night at the bar, Alice thinks, that was him sounding Dad out right before he drugged him, bundled him into his car to go and kill Manny Castillo, and stage the scene. An audition of sorts that Dad didn't even realise was happening. How close was it to going the other way, she wonders? Dad's blood on Manny's shirt instead of the other way around.

'What about Oliver Finlay?' Alice asks, wrenching her thoughts away from what could have been. 'What makes him different?'

'He isn't. Oliver will answer for his actions eventually. The first few overseas operations I ran, it was pure coincidence he was there. After Somalia, after this all started …' He tails off for a beat. 'Well let's just say it didn't hurt to have somebody else who'd been in-country besides me.'

Alice turns to Boudreaux, an uneasy truce having returned following the earlier exchange.

'Is this enough?' she asks. 'Do we have enough to take this to your boss? To make it official?'

'It's enough to take him in for questioning, sure. The NYPD will try and have first bite of the cherry and my boss will have a coronary, but we sure as hell can't let him walk out of here. Let me make a call. You okay in here?'

Alice nods, watches Boudreaux walk out into the hallway, and turns back to see Grey staring at her. Throughout this whole conversation, there's been barely a flicker from him. No sense of guilt or remorse, only a flash of anger at the notion that he's done anything wrong. That he feels elevated above this all, judge, jury and executioner, stokes something inside her. The part of her that reaches back to her own dad, the fact he's paying a price. Just not for the right crime.

'You talk about balancing scales, Doctor Grey. Who balances them for what you do?'

'You think that man by the river would have been happy with a stern word,' Grey asks.

'The only reason he wanted to hurt me is because of a man who you set up. It all comes back to you.'

'Would you defend me, if I was on death row, Alice? Or what about these other men you seem so keen to set free?'

The question cuts to the heart of everything she stands for. It's an absolute. The right to a fair trial, and the right to life, even if it's behind bars. The notion of defending Grey, if he is what she thinks he is, short-circuits her brain for a second, but it's enough that Grey smiles, believing his point made.

'In principle, of course I would. You don't have to be innocent of your crimes for me to fight to keep you alive.'

'How noble.'

'You asked.'

'What now then?' he asks.

'Now?' she raises both eyebrows. 'Now I get my witness to ID you, prove you were in Florida, and get my dad off death row.'

'You know you can't do this without the others following suit, right? They all get out, then anything they do after that is on you. Anyone they hurt, that's on your conscience. Can you live with that?'

'You left Oliver Finlay walking free. How do you know he hasn't hurt anyone else?'

'Oliver is different. He was my plan B. I needed him around in case someone like you came sniffing, but he'll answer for what he did soon enough.'

'In that case, if a dozen men walk free because they didn't commit that particular crime, then yes I can.'

He looks like something she's said has amused him, smile curling up the corners of his mouth.

'What's so funny?'

He looks down at his feet, trussed together, gently shaking his head. Takes his time in answering, and when he does, there's something playful in his eyes.

'The fact you think it's only a dozen.'

Chapter Fifty-Five

Friday – Three days to go

It's as if all the air has been sucked out of the room, and it's like fighting to come out of a deep sleep as she answers him.

'How many more?'

Grey doesn't answer. Instead he looks off to one side, back towards the wall of pictures. She follows his gaze, eyes widening, lips parting a touch in disbelief.

'All of them?' she says in a borderline whisper.

The mosaic of picture frames barely has space for plaster to show through in places. There must be dozens, maybe even approaching a hundred separate snaps. If this is true, he makes Bundy look like a boy scout.

'You've got to be shitting me,' she says, walking across to stand a few feet away. The enormity of what he's suggesting feels too big for her mind to grasp, like trying to hug a sumo wrestler. 'These aren't pictures, they're trophies. Every one of them. A reminder of where you've been. What you've done there.'

She turns to see him twisting his face like he's sucking sour candy. 'Don't use that word, please. This isn't something I enjoy.'

'What the hell would you call them then?' She rounds on him, irritated by his constant attempts to justify and explain away what he is, what he has done.

'There's nothing incriminating about these pictures, Miss Logan, but they are important. They're a reminder that I make a difference in this world. That what I do matters.'

'You're going to want to start practising the past tense,' she says, walking back over to her seat. 'You're not going to be doing much else apart from stare at the walls of a cell for a long time.'

Somewhere from another room, Boudreaux's voice filters back to her, too faint to make out the words. The kitchen maybe? Tiredness tugs at Alice, even though the effects of whatever he used on her have pretty much worn off, these last few days have been a series of waves eroding away her reserves of strength.

'Can I ask a small favour?' Grey motions with his head towards the desk behind him. 'Can I have a sip of that water please?'

Alice isn't exactly enamoured by being in the same room as him, let alone playing nursemaid, and it must show.

'I'd get it myself, but, you know.' He shrugs, smiling apologetically. 'Please.'

She approaches him cautiously from the side. He tilts his head upwards as she lifts the glass across to him, tipping it carefully to give him a chance to swallow. When it's gone, she goes to place it back on the coaster.

'Thank you,' Grey says. 'And sorry.'

She's about to ask him what for, but there's no time as he launches up out of his seat, head connecting with her jaw, and the room snaps to black.

Chapter Fifty-Six

Friday – Three days to go

Alice's head is like a rung bell. All she can do is watch as Grey hikes his arms halfway up his back, slamming them down above his backside, snapping the plasticuffs. She touches the side of her face, wincing. She does her best to push up on one elbow, watching in horror as Grey scoops up the letter opener from the desk, blade catching the light. He hacks at the restraints around his ankles, and they pop with a snap.

'Please, don't …' is all she manages.

The look he gives her is one of confusion. 'I may kill people, but I'm not a killer,' he says, emphasis heavy on that last word. He whirls away, wrenching open a window, and hoisting himself through it as best he can with his damaged arm. There one minute, gone the next, like a magic trick.

'Alice?' Boudreaux's voice seems to be coming from miles away. 'Alice, you okay in there?'

'He's … he's getting away,' she croaks. Forces herself to sit up despite the room spinning. 'Grey's getting away.' Louder this time, and seconds later, Boudreaux hustles through the doorway.

Quick perfunctory check on Alice, then he's past her, gun trained through the window frame. He checks both ways, cursing, and doubles back out into the hallway. Alice hears the front door flung open, and pulls herself up using the edge of the desk, flopping into the same seat that Grey had warmed only moments ago.

By the time Boudreaux comes back five minutes later, Alice is pretty sure she hasn't taken any real damage. There's a click every time she opens her jaw, and the side of her face throbs in time with her pulse, but nothing feels broken.

'Sonofabitch got away. Didn't even see which way he went,' Boudreaux snarls, looking around the room as if he needs someone or something to punch. 'You okay? What happened?'

Alice tells him about the surprise attack, sharing the startling revelation about the collection of pictures that's taken on a macabre new meaning.

'Jesus,' Boudreaux breathes out. 'That's insane. He's insane.'

'That's just it though,' says Alice. 'I think he believes that what he's doing is morally right. Like he's doing everyone a favour.'

They both stand, surveying what was up until ten minutes ago, a run-of-the-mill study.

'What did your boss say?' Alice asks.

'Hmm, I'll not repeat most of the first few minutes. He's pissed at me, but ... he's not stupid either. He knows we need to get out ahead of this now. He's alerted NYPD and he's sending a couple of agents from our New York field office as well.'

'So, what do we do now? Wait here?'

Boudreaux gives her a look that screams mischief. 'Now? We go find that sonofabitch.'

'But how? If you didn't even see which way he went?'

The agent just smiles back at her. 'A magician never reveals his secrets.'

Chapter Fifty-Seven

Friday – Three days to go

Thirty minutes later, they're in a car heading across the Queensboro Bridge, leaving a pair of GALE agents in situ at Grey's house to greet the NYPD.

'What if you're wrong?' Alice asks Boudreaux. 'He could he heading in the opposite direction for all we know.'

Boudreaux taps the side of his nose. 'Like I said, magic.'

'C'mon, you've got to give me more than that,' Alice says, this cryptic approach rubbing on her like sand on sunburn.

'All right, all right, but you have to promise me you'll stay in the car when we get there.'

'I promise.'

'The folks at our New York office have some kind of superuser access to all the public CCTV and traffic cameras in the city. NYPD had a report of a car-jacking a block from Grey's house. Tall white male, light-coloured hair, fifty-something. Sound familiar?

Alice's phone buzzes in her lap. Text from Sofia.

Just landed. Text you when I've got a cab.

Alice fires back a thumbs up emoji. Too much to get into with Sofia if she called right now.

'Anyway, the car he took pinged traffic cameras heading east toward Long Island. I'd bet my badge on him going after Finlay.'

'You really think he'd do that?'

Boudreaux shrugs, changing lanes, engine roaring as he powers past slower drivers.

'Absolutely. He said it himself, Finlay's day would come. Even if we don't get him for all that other shit, he's bang to rights for the East River guy, as well as trying his luck with both of us. The number of photos on that wall, he'll make the FBI's most wanted. Finlay's outlived his use as a fall guy, and this is Grey's only chance to put that right. If you can think of another reason he's heading towards Suffolk County right now, I'm all ears.'

Alice shakes her head. 'Nope, that's good enough for me.'

'How you doing? Boudreaux asks, sounding genuinely concerned. 'Zip tie or no zip tie, I shouldn't have left you alone in there. I'm sorry.'

'I'm okay,' says Alice. She sees Boudreaux shoot a side glance her way. 'Honestly.'

A loud ringing fills the car.

'My tech wizard,' Boudreaux says by way of explanation, before hitting a button on the wheel to take the call. 'Abs, I'm in the car with Alice Logan. What have you got?'

There's a pause, as if the young agent on the other end isn't sure how much he can say now he knows she's there; three's a crowd.

'Hey Luc, so I spoke to your man at the UN, and he confirmed Grey used to fly out to oversee the set-up for each new peacekeeping operation, so he's definitely been to every single country we have a case in.'

'What about him though, Abs? His service record, any hint of anything out of the ordinary?'

'He's been squeaky clean for years,' says Abs, sounding almost embarrassed to not have a smoking gun. Only thing on his record was a thing in Somalia, a run-in with local PD.'

'Somalia?' Alice can't help herself. 'That's where he said he was attacked.'

'Yep, that definitely happened,' says Abs. 'Pretty bad by all accounts. He and a few others had been doing an outreach clinic at a women's refuge on the outskirts of Mogadishu, when they got jumped by a local gang. The others, the ones he was with, they died at the scene. Here's the thing, though. Five months after that, the gang leader turns up dead. They never arrested anyone so not like the others, but makes you wonder with what you've told me about him.'

'And Finlay's wife, did you find anything on her?'

'Official cause of death listed as accidental by drowning, just like Grey said. Nothing on file to suggest the coroner gave it a second thought.'

'Can I ask a question?' Alice says tentatively.

Boudreaux gestures to the car speakers as if to say *go ahead.*

'You've got his full UN service history there, right?'

'Yeah,' says Abs.

'So I'm guessing he was in Cyprus three years ago? Same time Alain Dufort was beating up Elena Georgiou.'

'Um … yep. Spent two months there that summer. Left end of July.'

'Two weeks before Dufort was arrested,' Alice says, the inference plain as day.

'What about Finlay?' she asks. 'Where was he when my dad got picked up by the cops?'

After a few seconds of silence, Abs answers. 'He was in Jordan. Six-month posting.'

'And Grey?'

'He was Stateside,' Abs says. 'Based in New York, but get this, I googled him, and the month Sharp was arrested, it turns out he was keynote speaker at a conference in Orlando, the week before Sharp killed Castillo.'

'Looks like Finlay isn't quite as perfect a fall guy as he thought then,' Alice says. 'The week before is when the hit-and-run happened. Finlay is thousands of miles away. I think this one was spur of the moment.'

'Abs,' Boudreaux cuts in, 'I'm gonna need you to link in with local PD in Orlando. See what we can still dig up around that conference, times he was speaking, where he stayed, that sorta thing. Did he have a hire car? With a bit of luck, from when they'll have checked footage back then, maybe have a list of plates on file, you never know.'

'On it,' Abs says. I've called the local PD near Finlay's place too. They're going to send a car to meet you.'

'You're a star,' Boudreaux says and signs off.

Alice's head spins with the constant barrage of new information, frantically sifting through it to shuffle pieces into the first semblance of order. Boudreaux breaks the silence.

'Listen, I know I already tried apologising to you about your dad, but I … I think what we've got …' he pauses, 'what you've managed to dig up, I think it's gonna be enough. Enough to stall things, at least, give us time to build this case properly.'

'Us?'

'I know I might be the last person you'd have picked to be helping you here, but I want to put this right. I need to put it right.' He pauses, silence weighing heavy.

Alice considers this for a moment. Thinks back to the moment in Grey's study when the ground fell away from her feet, watching as he advanced towards her. Sure that she was never leaving that building alive. Boudreaux is exactly who she would have picked to be here for her.

'Thank you,' she says eventually. 'For saving my life back there. If you hadn't …'

Her throat seems to close, struggling with a speech she hasn't planned.

Boudreaux nods, and Alice turns to stare out of the window again until the lump in her throat dissolves.

'You wanna talk about what happened back there?' Boudreaux asks eventually.

The hum of tyres on tarmac is hypnotic, and Alice stares out at the scenery whipping past. She's trying to ground herself in the present, get ready for whatever comes next, but the events on the Esplanade plays on a loop no matter how hard she tries to cut it out.

The way Grey moved. Didn't hesitate. Slid the knife into the Bridge guy's gut like a key in a lock. Looking back, it should have been a warning sign. Should have been a bloody klaxon that he seemed entirely too at ease with what went down.

As for back at Grey's house, that feeling of her head being packed with cotton wool, and the fuzziness around the edges, had kicked in even before she started joining the dots. It had come from nowhere, and only one explanation makes sense.

'I think he drugged me,' she tells Boudreaux, recounting Grey fetching her a drink, and the brain fog that ensued. She touches a hand to her neck, tracing a fingertip across the sticky residue where Boudreaux had ripped some kind of patch off her.

'That thing you tore off me, what was it? Do you still have it?'

A tug of memory ripples across Boudreaux's face.

'Some kind of patch, like one of those nicotine ones. He put that there?'

'Sure as hell wasn't me.'

Boudreaux reaches over to his phone in the cupholder, taps the screen to make a call, and seconds later a man's voice comes over the speakers.

'There's some kind of fabric patch on the kitchen bench,' he tells the agent back at Grey's house. 'I'm gonna need you to bag it and get it analysed ASAP.' Short and to the point.

'I'm thinking that's how he subdued the others,' Boudreaux says, telling Alice what he remembers from the pictures on file.

'You remember him putting it on you? How fast it worked?'

Alice shakes her head. 'I was already feeling, I don't know, woolly. Maybe he'd put something in my drink too. Maybe he wasn't going to take any chances even if I hadn't made the connection.'

It's a sobering thought. There was no way things would have ended well at Grey's house if Boudreaux hadn't shown up. Makes her fold inwards, content to stare out of the window as mile after mile of the Long Island Expressway zips past.

They cut onto the Northern State Parkway, following its lazy meander through the heart of Suffolk County, before angling north. As they get closer to their destination, the knot in Alice's stomach is wrapped tighter than a ball of twine. She knows this ride-along is crazy, especially after what she's been through, but she needs to see this through, for a whole host of reasons. A brother she's never met. Her sister. Even her dad, despite the fact her feelings towards him are tangled worse than a ball of wool in the hands of a toddler. Most of all though, for herself.

The address they have for Oliver Finlay is on the east shore of Stony Brook Harbor. It's a little after noon as they barrel down Harbour Road, almost missing the turning. The place is enormous, big enough from the front that it could pass for three houses. A central three-storey building, flanked either side with two-storey cousins. No sign of the Lexus that Grey had commandeered. Boudreaux pulls up short of the front door and kills the engine.

'Stay put,' he says, sliding out of the car, checking the clip on his gun, before returning it to his holster.

Alice watches as he approaches the door. Sees him cock his head, reach out a hand and push. It opens without a sound, and Boudreaux disappears inside. Alice's heart is thudding louder than a marching band. The cooling engine ticking like a metronome, as the passenger seat suddenly feels confined, claustrophobic even, the air inside thick and soupy.

She cracks the car door open a foot, popping off her seatbelt, unfolding legs out onto the driveway. Wind rakes its way through half-full branches, clinging on to their canopies. Through a curtain of leaves to the left, Alice can make out the harbour. Same body of water Alana Finlay died in. She takes a few steps towards the treeline, but hesitates, walking backwards until she's resting against the front end of the car again.

Quick glance at the still-open door. No sign of life. No sign of anything. Alice glances nervously back up the driveway. What if they've beaten Grey here? He could pull up any second. She slaps the notion back down. The house is set far enough back from the main road that she'd see him coming and be able to dash inside.

She moves back to her side of the car. Stops, one hand on the roof, one on her door. Takes in the scale of the house, what she can see of the grounds. Wonders, not for the first time, if she'd stayed in Manhattan whether she'd be a partner at her old firm by now, able to afford a place like this. Like everything, that trail of breadcrumbs leads back to Dad's door. If he hadn't cheated, he'd be the one caring for Mum. Buck stops with him however you slice it.

The air out here is a level of fresh she's not used to. The kind of clean that could wash away the stress of these past few days if she only had the time to enjoy it. Despite the tension twisting across both shoulders, she allows herself a moment. Just a few seconds. Closes her eyes, breathes in deep, holds the swell in her chest for a count of three. Feels at least some of the tension melt away on the exhale.

So peaceful. Barely a sound. Then comes the gunshot.

Chapter Fifty-Eight

Friday – Three days to go

Alice's first instinct is to duck behind the car. The crack is muted, coming from somewhere deep inside. Her ragged breaths fog the glass as she peers back through the car window. Her mind splits into parallel universes of fight and flight, tugging her both ways like a riptide. The reality is she can't move, legs caught in a quicksand of indecision.

The world settles back into serene silence, like it was all in her head. Except that it wasn't. She knows what she heard. A glance back down the drive, towards Harbour Road, and the handful of other houses they drove past. Can't be more than forty yards, but might as well be forty miles.

What the hell is happening inside? Has Grey beaten them here? Or is Finlay every bit the monster in disguise that Grey would have them believe? Alice turns around, back pressing against the cool door panel.

'Shit, shit, shit.'

She mutters the mantra as she edges towards the rear of the car, crouching by the bumper. Another glance at the house. Windows like mirrors from this angle. The open door mocks her, daring her to go in.

She's never backed down from a fight in the courtroom, but this is different. Unless it's Boudreaux in there wielding the weapon, any other scenario makes charging in a suicide mission.

Hadn't Boudreaux said the local PD would send someone? Where the hell are they? Maybe they didn't get the memo that this isn't an ordinary house call.

She has to make it to a neighbour, call 911. Light a fire under them. She squats, one knee on the road, one hand on the edge of the bumper, ready to explode up and along the driveway.

Her whole body is suddenly fizzing with energy as the massive adrenaline dump floods her system. She tells herself she'll go on three, but before she can even start the count, a voice as rough as gravel stops her.

'If I have to shoot you, I will. It would be better if you just stand up and come inside.'

No mistaking the accent. French. Familiar. Only one man it can be. Could be a trap, he could shoot her the moment she pops her head up, but what choice does she have? If she runs, he'll pick her off before she makes the road. Stay here and all he has to do is walk around the rear of the car.

Alice peers slowly over the edge of the car again, locking eyes with the pockmarked face she last saw crumpled on the Esplanade. He's leaning against the door frame, handgun trained on her. He motions her over with jerks of his head.

'Inside. Now. Do not make me ask again.'

Not as if she has any other option. He's armed, she isn't. Her legs feel like lead as she walks towards him, and she can't help wondering whether her dad will feel the same sense of dread in seventy-two hours, if she doesn't walk back out of here with a way to set him free.

'I'll do whatever you want,' she says, voice sounding like it belongs to someone else. 'Where's Luc?'

Alice holds her hands up in the universal gesture of surrender as she reaches the doorway. The Frenchman's smile is laced with malice.

'Come, see for yourself.'

Close up, she sees the peach and purple bruising extending from the Frenchman's temple. The skin around it is broken, like it's been roughed up with sandpaper. A memento from Doctor Grey.

Pockmark takes two steps back, opening the door a little wider to let her in and past, into an impressive hallway. Polished cherry wood floors. A sweeping staircase disappearing up and round a corner. A version of her stares out of an enormous mirror on the wall opposite. It's like an out-of-body experience, like watching a cut-price lookalike.

Pockmark doesn't take his eyes, or the gun, off her as he closes the front door.

'Through there,' he says.

'Look, whatever it is you want, we can work something out.'

He doesn't answer. Just grunts, closing the distance between them, poking the barrel of the gun against the small of her back. It's as if the weapon carries a charge, one that jolts through her, goosebumps popping along her arms like braille.

There's a second set of steps leading down into what looks like a living room. A piano stands in the far corner, legs biting deep into thick pile carpet. Enough paintings adorn the walls to make it feel like a mini gallery.

All of this falls away as Alice sees the bloody tableau laid out before her. Boudreaux lies face down. He's not moving, and Alice sees a dark stain on the patterned rug beside him. Is he … dead? A wave of nausea washes over her at the thought of losing him.

No time to fully process this, as her eyes flick left and right. Two chairs either side of a large fireplace, two men. Grey is furthest away, hands somewhere behind his back, bound together Alice presumes. There is a gash above his left eye, thin ribbon of blood running from the far edge of it down his cheek. Alice has a flash of him in a similar position back at his house mere hours ago. Déjà vu.

He looks groggy, as if whatever blow opened up the cut has rattled something lose that hasn't quite fallen back into place. She's about to ask him what happened, when she glances at the second man, and almost squeals at what she sees.

Oliver Finlay's skull has been caved in. The side of it has been bashed up like it's made of papier mâché. Dark red globs of matter cling to his hair. Alice doesn't need a doctor to tell her that Finlay is dead. Who killed him though? Had Grey got here first? Or was this the work of Pockmark, with Grey interrupting them?

Pockmark has given her a full five seconds' grace to soak this in, but he prods her forward again, more insistently this time.

'You sit here,' he indicates the empty sofa.

She moves on autopilot, a hundred questions pummelling her mind. How did Pockmark know where to come for starters?

'I told your people back in Paris, I don't have enough to help Dufort. Not yet,' she adds, hoping the inference that she might still be trying will be enough to mollify him.

He walks behind her, making the hairs on the back of her neck stand up when he leans in close. One hand rests on her shoulder, the other presses the gun against her back again.

'These lies, they are not helpful,' he says, close to her ear.

'I'm not …'

He tuts loudly. 'How do you think I found you?'

It's like he's been eavesdropping in her head, and the question throws her.

'I um … I don't know.'

'The picture you were sent, the one of the woman and the boy. It's incredible what you can do with technology these days. Not my thing. I am, how you say, more hands-on.'

She shudders as he gives her shoulder what in other circumstances could be an attempt at an affectionate squeeze.

'Our man, he added a little extra to the file. When you opened it, it gave us access to your phone – your messages, emails, travel arrangements. Everything.'

He leans heavily on that last word, and the realisation dawns that their dirty footprints are all through her texts, her inbox, the lot. That includes the copy of the UN list she forwarded from the fake address. Finlay's name listed as the standout suspect. She looks over at him again, at the horrific headwound. She may not have delivered the blow, but she did this. She has led them here to him. If she'd just let Boudreaux follow that up, Finlay and Grey might both be in very different chairs right now, in interview rooms. Instead one is a cooling corpse, the other incapacitated and in every bit as much danger as she is.

'Just tell me what to do, and I'll do it,' she says. 'Whatever lets us all walk out of here.'

He laughs at her, as if it's a foregone conclusion that last part is not an option. Maybe it isn't, she thinks, but the longer she keeps him talking, the better shot she has.

'This one,' he gestures towards Grey. 'He complicates things. I need to make a call.'

'Wait, complicates things how?' Alice says, hearing the desperation in her own voice as she sees Pockmark walk towards another set of curtains, plucking a spare tie-back, presumably for her.

'What do you mean how?' he says, scowling. He walks over to Finlay, grabs a handful of hair, and twists his face up towards Alice.

She gasps at the half-open sightless eyes.

'I needed to talk to this one, but your friend over there beat me to it. He was trying to move the body when I turned up. A dead man doesn't get Monsieur Dufort out of prison.'

Finlay would never have done that anyway, but if she tells him about Grey, what's to say he won't still kill them all once he gets whatever he needs? Even now, in the middle of this shitstorm, Alice thinks about Mariella and

Anthony, about how their fate, and maybe still her dad's, rests on both her and Elias Grey walking out of here.

Pockmark walks towards her, gun tucked into his waistband, curtain tie pulled tight between his hands like a garrotte. Alice's brain whirrs through a world of possibilities. No way can she overpower him. No weapons within range.

'Wait!' she calls out, taking a few steps back. 'You've got it wrong. He had nothing to do with it.'

Pockmark narrows his eyes, but slows. 'I warned you about lies, did I not?'

'I'm not lying,' she says, babbling at speed now. 'I'm not. He's been set up. My investigator can prove it. We're close to working out who by. Really close.'

Alice focuses on Pockmark, afraid she might glance at Grey and give the truth away. The Frenchman stops two feet short, letting the cord in his hand dangle as he reaches for the gun again. This time he traces the line of her chin with the barrel.

'You know what we do to liars?' he says, softly. 'If I have to heat one of those pokers up, this is not going to go well for you. Think carefully before you answer me.' He pauses for effect. 'How do you know he was set up?'

'Because she knows it was me.'

Grey's voice sounds stronger than his physical appearance suggests. All eyes turn to him. He has wriggled to sit up a little straighter. Looks fatigued, but his eyes are clearer. Whatever Pockmark did to him, the effects are wearing off.

'You?'

The Frenchman sounds incredulous, the notion that his man has been right in front of him too simple to grasp.

'Do I look any less dangerous than this one?'

Alice's mouth is as dry as an Arizona summer. Even though she knows what she knows, to hear him actually admit it out loud is a shock, like stepping into an icy shower.

Pockmark shrugs. 'Maybe you say what you think will get you out of here. Maybe you prefer the idea of swapping places with Mr Dufort to some time alone with me.'

'I can prove it,' Grey shoots back.

That wipes the cynicism from Pockmark's face. Eyebrows raised, head tilted like he's listening for footsteps. He stays like that for a few seconds, then pulls out a phone. He lifts it to his ear. It's answered within a few rings, and he rattles off something in quick-fire French that Alice can't follow.

He takes it away from his ear, taps the screen, and Alice hears breathing on the other end, and she wonders what the hell is going on. She gets her answer soon enough. Alain Dufort's tone is pure hostility.

'So it's you who put me here.'

Chapter Fifty-Nine

Friday – Three days to go

'I put you where you belong,' Grey says, sounding closer to the smooth arrogance he'd given off back in the city, now his strength is returning.

Dufort responds with a stream of French that proves anger needs no translation. His breathing is heavy now, and Alice imagines his face contorted into a mask of rage. When he speaks again, a switch has flipped and he's calm as a millpond.

'What goes around, comes around, *mon ami*. Maybe not a good idea for a man in your position to be making remarks like that, non?'

'If you did time for everything you've actually done, you'd never set foot outside that place,' Grey counters.

'And yet you belong in here, right beside me.'

'We're not the same, you and I,' Grey says. 'It's the likes of you that made me what I am.'

'Look,' says Dufort, sounding disinterested in what Grey has to say. 'I don't have time for this shit. You said to Bruno that you can prove you are the one, so talk. What proof?'

'Before I tell you anything, what assurances do I have that Miss Logan here walks away? She's not to blame.'

'Do you see the man holding the gun?' Dufort snarls, continuing without waiting for an answer. 'Good, well the only assurance you have is that if you don't talk in the next ten seconds, my friend there will put a bullet in your knee.'

Grey nods, as if he has all the time in the world to consider the offer.

'Five seconds,' comes the voice.

Grey meets Alice's eyes. She wills him to just tell them what they want to know. Now is not the time for games.

'Three … two …'

Pockmark steps over to Grey, crouching a few feet away, extending his arm so the gun is jammed against his kneecap.

Alice can't believe what she's about to witness. Turns her head, looks down at Boudreaux instead. Fancies she sees the rise and fall of his chest against the floor. Even as Dufort counts off the last second, Grey snaps his head up.

'All right, all right. You win. I'll tell you.'

The gun stays where it is, silence stretching out. Alice's own breathing is as loud as Dufort's coming through the speaker.

'I kept something,' Grey says. 'From the bar the night I set you up.'

Alice swallows hard at the revelation. Proof. Concrete proof. If he kept something from this one, what's to say it's a one-off? The thought that there may be hard evidence to exonerate her dad is a lifeline she hadn't expected.

Over by the fireplace, Alice sees Boudreaux's head shift, ever so slightly. The agent groans, fingers of his outstretched hands clawing at the carpet, slow, raking, like he's looking for a handhold.

Pockmark sees it too, and switches the gun across to Boudreaux.

'What's the fucking hold up?' Dufort barks down the line.

Pockmark says something in French.

'I don't give a fuck about him.' Dufort's anger is a rolling cloud of fury pouring from the phone. 'He talks now, or he never talks again.'

Alice stares at Boudreaux. Willing the agent to get up, to stop whatever is about to happen. Grey is the one lifeline her dad has. She looks around frantically, wondering what's happened to Boudreaux's gun. She's still looking for it, when she hears sounds in an order that make no sense. First the grunt, followed by a scream, then the shot.

Chapter Sixty

Friday – Three days to go

The first thing Alice sees is a tangle of limbs. Grey must have taken advantage of Pockmark's distraction and somehow pushed up and out of his seat. He's lying diagonally across the Frenchman, hands still bound behind his back, and face buried by the side of Pockmark's, like he's whispering sweet nothings.

Except there's nothing tender about this embrace. Grey is moving side to side, like a dog worrying a bone. Pockmark's face is a mask of pain, with a dose of disbelief, like this can't be happening.

Dufort's tinny voice still shouts from the phone where it's been flung over by the fireplace. Boudreaux has pushed up onto his elbows now, still dazed, blood trickling from his hairline. But it's the dark dampness on his side that worries Alice most.

It's life on fast forward as she flicks back to Grey, wriggling like a beached fish to keep his body pressed down on Pockmark, who Alice realises doesn't now have the gun in his free hand. Instead he's hammering a fist onto the back of Grey's head, but the good doctor shows no sign of stopping.

As they continue to twist, locked in a bizarre embrace, Alice sees the source of Pockmark's pain. A glimpse of Grey's teeth chomping down on his ear, streaks of blood smeared on his cheek like badly applied make-up.

The speed and savagery has short-circuited Alice, but her mind kicks back into gear now. Every instinct screams run. Sprint out of the door and don't look back. But she squashes it down. Grey won't be able to hold Pockmark forever, and the element of surprise was a one-time advantage. When Pockmark eventually wriggles free it'll be game over.

She looks around frantically for a weapon. Sees the barrel of a gun poking out from under a chair, only a few feet from his head. To get it she'll have to get in close enough that he can grab her through. Whether it's Grey pausing for breath, or the Frenchman gaining the upper hand, there's a brief separation, and Pockmark uses it to slip his left arm between them to protect his ragged ear. His right hand blindly sweeps the carpet.

His fingers brush the gun. She's only got seconds at best before he recovers it. It's now or never. There's a rack next to the fire, selection of pokers lined up. Alice reaches for one, fingers closing around cool metal. She turns, raising it like a club, but it's too late. Pockmark's fingers curl around the grip. He grunts in triumph, swinging it around.

She sees Grey, head twisted to the side, spotting the weapon. He rears his head up for leverage, striking back down like a snake, aiming for the neck. At the same time, he swings his left knee up, a desperate attempt to block the gun. Pockmark tucks his chin down, trying to protect his neck, Grey grinding his head against the Frenchman's face, working at the gap, quite literally going for the jugular.

Feels like she's moving in slo-mo, half the speed of the rest of the room, and she's only covered half the distance when the gun disappears between the two men.

The double pop is muted, but unmistakable. Alice slows, thrown by the sound. Sees Grey's body jerk, legs stiffen. Pockmark's savage smile screams triumph. He scoots out from under Grey, rolling him off. Alice is six feet away, poker in hand, as he brings the gun round to point at her. Six feet but might as well be sixty. Suddenly the poker feels ridiculous.

Alice grimaces at what's left of Pockmark's ear. Looks more like a half-chewed dog treat, and it'll hurt like hell once the adrenaline wears off. His smile widens, impossibly toothsome, and he pushes up to his knees, grunting as he does.

She looks down at Grey, lying on his side, curling up, drawing knees to chest and back down again, moaning softly as he does. Twin red flowers bloom on his gut.

Start to finish, the tussle can't have taken more than ten seconds. The relative silence that follows is broken only by the two men nursing respective wounds, and Dufort's continued shouting. He's practically apoplectic with rage at not knowing, or being in control of, whatever the hell has just gone down.

Pockmark looks down at Grey. Hawks up a big glob of phlegm, and sends it sailing down to splat on Grey's shoulder as he waves the gun at the fallen man.

'By the time I'm finished, you're going to wish I'd killed you, *mon ami*.'

'Don't you fucking dare kill him until he tells us what we need to know,' Dufort shouts.

Pockmark stoops down, picking up his phone and tapping it off speaker mode. For a second, it's as if he has forgotten Alice exists, and she fancies if she stands statue-still, she might yet live through this. That fantasy implodes in a heartbeat, as his eyes drift over to her, flicking once up and down as he listens to whatever Dufort is saying.

The poker quivers in her hand, lowering a touch. His smile makes snakes slither in her stomach. He nods in agreement with whatever is being said in his ear, and she knows, sure as the sun sets in the west, that's she going to die in this room.

'Please,' she begins, 'let me help. I can—'

She never finishes the sentence. His arm whips back up. It's written in his face, in every crease around the eyes, the set of his jaw. She flinches, instinctively closing her eyes, bracing against the inevitable impact. The last thing to go through her mind before the crack of the gunshot is that at least Fiona can't say she hasn't tried.

Chapter Sixty-One

Friday – Three days to go

The first shot is followed by a second, then a third. The poker slips from Alice's fingers.

Makes no sense. Why does she feel no pain? Looks down, expecting to see her top stained red, but instead, there's nothing. Movement, off to one side. A gurgling sound, and she looks up to see Pockmark back down on one knee, clutching the side of his neck, crimson leaking from between fingers at a rate that churns her stomach. A second wound, a few inches above his belt, is a dark blotch spreading across his grey sweater. The gun falls from his other hand, hitting the carpet with a solid thunk.

None of this computes with the last five seconds, and Alice raises both hands to her mouth, as Pockmark topples backwards, still clutching his neck. Even now, with his life leaking through his fingers, she's afraid to take her eyes off him in case he somehow gets his hands back on the gun, but a noise to her right makes her turn.

Luc Boudreaux is still on the floor but has managed to push up to a seated position against an armchair. His gun hangs limply in a weakened grip, and he's pressing his free hand against his side. As Alice watches, he uses the edge of the seat to rise up on unsteady feet, training his gun back on Pockmark.

It's a token gesture though. Already the Frenchman has stopped writhing, slowing like a badly wound clock. Slow blinks counting off the final seconds of life.

'Luc,' Alice gasps, moving over to him. 'You're hurt. Here, sit down.'

'Uh-uh,' Boudreaux says, gritting his teeth against the pain. 'Not yet.'

Alice sees him gesture towards Elias Grey. He's uncurled now, lying flat on his back, one hand holding the now soaked sweater.

'He needs help,' Boudreaux says. 'We lose him, we lose the case.'

Alice pats her pockets, realising her phone is still in the car. Over by Pockmark's outstretched legs, his phone lies face down. Dufort's voice continues a non-stop rant, switching from English to French, then back again, demanding answers. She doesn't say a word, just ends the call and punches in 911 as she moves across to Grey. Takes a deep breath as she walks the operator through the scene.

'Is he conscious?' the operator asks, when they come on to Grey.

'Yes, but he's hurt pretty badly. How fast can you get here?'

'Already dispatched,' the operator says with practised efficiency. 'ETA is around 15 minutes.'

Looking at his face, grey as day-old ash, and the short laboured breaths, Alice doesn't think he'll last that long.

She listens as the operator rattles through instructions as to how to staunch the bleeding. It's far from ideal, but she strips off a pair of cushion covers to use as makeshift gauze, applying pressure as best she can. He winces as she pushes down, but grits his teeth, uncomplaining.

Boudreaux beckons for the phone, and Alice tosses it across. Boudreaux identifies himself to the operator, assures her they'll keep Grey as comfortable as possible, then ends the call so he can make another to his own people.

Alice glances at Pockmark, his unseeing eyes staring up at the ceiling. No threat now, but it doesn't make her any less uneasy being this close to him.

'Thank you,' she says, looking across to Boudreaux. 'You saved my life.'

'Thank me when we're out of here,' Boudreaux says with a weak smile.

'How bad is it?' Alice asks, nodding at his side.

'I'll live,' he says, wincing as he lifts his shirt up. An angry red groove is carved into his skin. 'Skimmed past rather than in. Knocked myself out on the damn furniture when I fell.'

He smiles like they're sharing funny stories over a drink, and Alice finds herself mirroring with one of her own.

Beside her, Grey coughs weakly, making Alice flinch, still on a hair trigger after events of the past few minutes.

'Paramedics are on the way,' she tells him. 'You're going to be fine.'

He manages a smile, but there's a nervousness in his eyes, the way they flit about like flies looking for a place to land.

'I've been on the other side of this enough to know better,' he says.

'Uh-uh, you don't get off that easy,' she tells him. 'You might have helped save us with what you just did, but you need to answer for what you've done.'

'What I've done, I've done in the name of balance,' he says, and she can see the effort that each word costs. The cushion covers she has balled up against his side are soaked through already. She presses harder, seeing his eyes widen as she does. 'Every one of those men deserved what happened. The people they …' He swallows hard. 'The people they hurt, the ones I had to patch up, or worse still break the bad news to their relatives. I am the balance.'

'Fuck your balance,' she snaps. 'An innocent man is going to die because you thought it was your decision to make.'

'Innocent of one crime maybe, but not innocent. I was there that night, parked up outside a 7-Eleven. The others were chosen, picked because of the people they sent to my hospitals to die, but in your father's case,' he says nonchalantly, 'pure coincidence. But I saw what he did. I saw him run like a coward. Followed him home. Gave him the justice he tried to hide from.'

Ever since her dad confessed, Alice has felt a white-hot anger towards him for what he did. Molten. All-encompassing. Something that has seeped into every corner of her mind. Bad enough that he did that to anyone, but her best friend for God's sake. There's something about the savagery of what she's just witnessed, though, that strips away a layer of that. These past few days, she's seen, and felt, enough pain that she's not sure she has the energy to hate that hard. Not any more. What she's left with is sadness. For the friend she lost. For the life Gail could have had. But too many people have died because of Grey. Her dad, whatever his flaws, shouldn't be another. If they save him, he'll have to live with what he's done.

'And he's done the time he would have got if he'd just been arrested for the hit-and-run,' she says after a pause.

'Doesn't bring back the woman he killed though, does it?'

'She wasn't just any woman,' Alice says, blinking as her eyes fill up. 'She was my friend.'

It takes a strength she didn't know she possessed to swallow down the pain that such a simple sentence carries. 'Her name was Gail Lonsdale, and she was my best friend. What price he pays for that is not your call to make. You're a doctor, you're supposed to save lives, not take them goddammit.'

Grey's eyes widen, a sign that this final revelation is news to him. Even wading through waves of pain, he manages a sad smile.

'I didn't know,' he says softly. 'I'm sorry for your loss.'

She says nothing. Just nods, looking down at the floor.

'And knowing that, you would still spare him?'

She looks into his eyes, unable to shake the feeling that he's literally asking her to make that choice. Wonders whether her opinion even matters any more. If Grey bleeds out without revealing what the proof of his guilt is that he mentioned to Dufort, it's all circumstantial. Everything he's said. That happens, and Dad dies anyway. What's to stop Dufort still coming after her? After Mariella and Anthony? Maybe even Fiona and Mum.

She just wants it all to end. To go back to the life she had on Monday morning, but that can't happen however this plays out. There's so much to process and she doesn't know where to start. One thing she does know, though, is that for all Dad's failings as a father, even for what he did to Gail, he doesn't deserve to die. Forgiving him for what he's done is another matter entirely, but his life isn't hers to take. That would make her no better than him.

Alice clears her throat to speak. 'I would. Killing him won't bring back Gail, but that doesn't make it right.'

He seems surprised at her answer.

'So you think serving a few years is punishment enough for taking a life? Our system is broken, and—'

'And what? You're the man to fix it? I don't think so.'

'I won't be around for much longer to play my part,' he says, wincing as a wave of pain washes through him. 'But I don't think you or any other lawyer is going to fix it after I'm gone.'

His pallor is a few shades greyer on the colour chart since she applied the makeshift dressing, and Alice realises with horrific certainty, that he's right. He's not going to leave this house alive. That realisation brings with it a wave of sadness, like a cold spring tide washing over her. Not for him, for the people who could suffer following Grey's death. Anthony. Mariella. Her dad. Tears prickle at the thought of staring through a window as he's strapped onto the gurney, in spite of what he's done. First time she's shed even one for him in years, and she does her best to blink them back before Grey thinks they're for his benefit.

The arrogance of the man, making out like he's doing righteous work, while in reality he's just chipping away at the foundations of everything she strives to protect. Alice feels the anger rise like a hot spring, and it pours out before she can put a cork in it.

'Lawyers do a damn sight more to fix it than you do. You talk about balance? You're proof the system is flawed. Every life you get away with taking just makes those cracks that little bit wider. My dad did a terrible thing, but if I went out and did what you do, I'd be no better than those arseholes sat in prison. You don't bring balance. All you do is bring chaos. You *are* fucking chaos. You want to know what's wrong with our justice system?'

She pauses, but he makes no attempt to answer, seeing it for the rhetorical question that it is.

'You. You're what's wrong. Do I hate my dad for what he did? Yes, but he's served his time, and if you had a shred of the sense of justice you pretend to have in you, you'd see that.'

Grey's mouth is a thinly drawn line, nose twitching as he breathes. He hasn't taken his eyes off her throughout that rant, and his tongue darts out now, wetting lips that have turned a shade of pale blue.

'If it had been another member of your family he'd hit?' he asks, voice strained with the effort. 'Your sister? Your mother? Would you still be asking me to help you?'

She answers without hesitation, nodding. 'You're bloody right I would.'

Even as she says it, there's a flutter inside her chest. Something stirring in her soul. Her answer has come from the heart. From the part of her that realises she hasn't got it in her to hate. Not even her dad, after all he's done. She's always told herself she's a better person than he is. That she'll make better choices. It's never clearer for her than now, when she chooses to want him to live. Anything else, and she'd be every bit as twisted as the man on the floor beside her.

His eyes bore into her for what feels like an eternity. Despite the strength literally leaking out of him, the eyes reignite, and he gives the tiniest of nods.

'I do believe you would,' he says finally. 'And you've suffered as much as anyone. I …' he breaks off, scrunching up his eyes in pain, holding the grimace for a few seconds, and when he opens them again, there's a glassy look to them, like he's barely seeing her.

'Balance is all that matters. I have … to believe … in … that,' words spaced out by the diminishing strength of each breath.

Alice is aware of Boudreaux having moved off to one side, crouching over Pockmark's body, but she feels like if she looks away from Grey now, he won't be there when she looks back.

'But you of all people, deserve that. You lost a friend, you deserve something back in exchange.'

He lifts one hand from his stomach, blood coating the fingers that beckon her closer, like a red glove. Alice leans in, listening to the words that are barely a whisper, and soon, not even that.

Chapter Sixty-Two

Friday – Three days to go

Grey's house is eerily silent now that the last of the CSIs have gone. Alice looks down the hallway, to where Luc Boudreaux is thanking the GALE agents that held the fort while they had been in Suffolk County. After another minute, Boudreaux retreats back inside alone, shutting the door and walking back to where Alice stands, framed in the kitchen doorway.

A little over four hours has passed since they left here to chase after Elias Grey, but could just as easily be four days with the sense of disembodiment that a return brings so soon, while Grey's body is barely cold.

'They've all gone,' Boudreaux says. 'Are you ready to tell me yet?'

Alice is conflicted. Feels like she owes it to her dad to secure what she needs personally on her own. But she wouldn't be stood here with Boudreaux.

'You said I should thank you when we got out of that house,' she says finally. 'If it weren't for you I'd be in a morgue next to Doctor Grey. You saved my life, and I owe you for that.'

Boudreaux shakes his head. 'That doesn't even make us square in my book,' he says. 'I was just doing my job. Doing it better than I did eleven years ago, but you don't owe me a thing.'

Alice feels a little more together since they got back into Manhattan. Far from okay, but emotionally patched up enough to see this through. Boudreaux's heartfelt lack of hubris takes her by surprise, almost unpicking the stitches holding her emotions in check. She nods.

'Thank you all the same.'

Most of the way back, they ride in silence. Boudreaux with his wounds tended to, under strict instructions from the paramedics to report straight to the nearest hospital when they're done here. Alice, still seeing Pockmark's cruel smile, the small round eye of his gun barrel, wondering how the hell she walked out of there without a scratch on her. They didn't talk about Grey's final words though. Boudreaux tried, but Alice wasn't ready. She needed that time to let the storm winds in her head subside. She's ready now though.

What Grey whispered in those final moments is a millstone that hangs heavy around her neck. Proof that he was the monster, not those other men. Not her dad. The knowledge that Dad's life is literally in her hands. For all the times in the past forty-eight hours that she's wished his and Gail's roles had been reversed, there's no real choice in what to do with Grey's dying words. She knows what Gail would do in her place.

She walks towards Boudreaux, passes him, and continues into the study. A brief but sickening wave of déjà vu sends her pulse soaring. The room where she had feared for her life when Grey was unmasked. She focuses on her breathing, gets it back in check after a few seconds.

The wall of photos looks somehow less sinister now that the man who put them there is dead. She remembers what he whispered to her back on Long Island. Hears his voice echoing through her head, and knows it's not the last time she'll hear that. As if her dreams aren't already fucked up enough.

You of all people deserve that, he had said. The balance he had spent years trying to achieve, albeit it viewed through his warped perspective. *And since it was denied to you back then, let me give you a little of it now. A life for a life.*

She's yanked back out of the memory by Boudreaux's hand on her shoulder.

"Alice, we don't have to do this now. Are you sure you're up to it?'

She nods, walking closer to the pictures. 'These aren't just snaps he took to remember the trips,' she says, reaching out, lifting the Somalia frame she had held earlier. She stares at it for a moment. At the younger Grey, the one who hadn't been nearly beaten to death. A version of him that still stuck by his oath to heal, not harm. She replaces it, reaching for one that shows Grey standing outside the Orange County Convention Centre. He's between two smiling people, all three sporting some kind of lanyard around their necks, presumably name tags from the event he was keynote speaker at.

'The murder my dad was arrested for, Manny Castillo. That one wasn't planned. Spur of the moment after he saw what Dad did. He needed someone like Castillo for this messed-up sense of balance he had. Turns out Castillo had sold drugs to some college kids, only thanks to the stuff he'd cut it with, one of them had a reaction and died. There was a story in the paper the same week Dad ...'

She even now, she can't bring herself to say it without feeling the heaviness in her chest. Of being only a few words away from tears.

'When he did what he did,' she finishes. 'Turns out Castillo had walked thanks to an illegal search, so he fitted the bill for Grey.'

Alice flips the frame over, and slides the catches open. The back lifts off, and there it is, just like he promised. Two marks, roundish in shape, not quite a matching pair. Each about the size of a quarter, and look like spots of rust, but they're so much more than that. Alice knows exactly what they are. Knows that each and every frame has a matching pair of blood droplets just like these. Knows that when they test these, they will prove that Doctor Elias Grey had been in possession of a drop of both her dad's blood, and that of his supposed victim, that she's looking at the key that'll open up her dad's jail cell.

'Is that what I think it is?' Boudreaux asks.

Alice nods, not trusting herself to speak.

'Are these some kind of trophies?' he says, shaking his head. Then in more of a whisper, 'All of them?' Boudreaux touches her shoulder again, and Alice's eyes well up, and there's no blinking these tears back. They stream down her cheeks, and she doesn't know if she's crying for herself, or Gail, or even her dad. She lets

Boudreaux wrap an arm round her shoulder, pull her into the most unlikely of embraces. She sinks into him, catching a hint of citrus aftershave. Feels safe.

All things considered, she's in no hurry to move, and for the first time in forever, feels surprisingly at peace with the world.

Chapter Sixty-Three

Monday – Execution day

Alice pulls up outside Nine Streets Coffee shop on Earsdon Road. What little sleep she's been getting these past few days has been plagued with replays of the ordeal at Stony Brook Harbor. Nights she wants to avoid, day-times that have passed in a blur, like she's staring out a car window in the fast lane. How many interviews has it been since Friday? GALE agents and NYPD before they let her fly home, French Police via Zoom since she's been back home in Whitley Bay. Seems everyone wants a piece of her.

A weak sun peers out from behind clouds that hang low, like dirty rags in the distance. It's forecast for thun-derstorms later in the week, and the air has that heavy feeling to it, like a good downpour will wash all the dirt away, start afresh. Alice grabs two lattes to go, and takes a seat back outside at a wooden table.

She's barely had time to take a sip before she sees Luc Boudreaux climbing out of a rental car giving a half-hearted wave as he walks across the road. It looks as awkward as Alice feels. A ghost of a memory flickers in her mind. Him holding her in Grey's study. How safe she felt. This transition from Boudreaux as adversary to something else is taking time, like wearing in a new pair of shoes. Whatever Alice thought of him at first, he stepped up last week. Not only did what was right, but saved Alice's life as well.

'Afternoon,' Boudreaux says, taking the seat opposite.

'I got you one in. Same as the one you had back in Paris at my hotel. Hope its okay,' Alice says, sliding the cup over to him.

Boudreaux takes it but wraps his hands around the cup, not drinking yet.

'Thanks,' he says with a tight smile.

They're both silent for a moment or two, the uneasy truce still sitting uncomfortably on both sides.

'Look, about what you said. Back in New York. McKenzie's tip ...'

'Forget about it,' she says. 'Doesn't matter now anyway.'

'Matters to me,' he says.

'Why?'

'Because I don't want you thinking I'm that guy.'

'You mean you're not?'

'It was blinkers. Nothing more. I did mention it to the Cap, but he told me to forget I ever heard it. What I told the desk sergeant back then, about it being on ice? That came from above me. I was just the messenger. Do I regret it? Hell yes, but there ain't a lot I can do about that now. I just wanted you to know.'

'Why? she asks, feeling the last hints of frostiness from back in Grey's apartment thawing.

'I don't know,' he says, looking a little bashful. 'Maybe I just don't want you thinking I'm a douchebag.'

She looks across at him. Sees what looks like genuine regret in his eyes, and without thinking she reaches out, placing her hand on his.

'Douchebag is a bit harsh. Bit of a dick, maybe, but not a douchebag.'

He drops his eyes to the table, and the laughter that comes from both is light, easy.

A few seconds tick by before she's aware of the heat of her hand on his still, and slides it back with a smile as they both lapse into silence again.

'Apart from that, how are you holding up?' Boudreaux asks finally.

Alice looks away, towards the traffic that zips past along the road. 'I'm okay,' she says as she looks back, wondering if she sounds convincing. In reality it's been a tough week. She's relived the scene out on Long Island more times than she can count.

The senior partners at work, Nicola Shaw and Sharon Finnie, have tried to get her to talk to someone. Even offered to pay for a few sessions, bless them. Maybe she will, but for now, all she wants to do is see this through.

'You?' she asks Boudreaux. 'What's your boss had to say about this all?'

'Mm, yeah I don't think he's going to do me any favours any time soon,' he says with a rueful smile. 'He'll probably wait till all this dies down, then stick me with a series of shitty assignments till he thinks he's broken me back in.'

'You've just taken down one of the worst serial killers on record. Maybe *the* worst. He should be organising a bloody ticker-tape parade for you.'

'Oh, he'll do the smile for the camera part, take his slice of the glory, but he's a weasel. He won't forget that I went against him, no matter how it turned out.'

'What about the crime scene?' Alice asks, surprised that she's held out this long. The lawyer they've hired for Dad has been getting stonewalled so far. Today is the day Dad should have been strapped to a gurney. All they have right now is a stay of execution. Any petition they make to the Court will be thrown back in their face without hard evidence to back it up. Alice promised Boudreaux she wouldn't allow anything to get put on public record until it was more watertight than a submarine, but time is a luxury her dad doesn't have.

'There were seventy-eight frames on the wall. We've typed and matched around two dozen to cases so far, but it's slow-going.'

Even though Alice has seen the wall first-hand, the number is still shocking to hear. She swallows hard. Sees the grave expression on Boudreaux's face. There's more to come.

'Some of the frames had more than one picture in. All in all, we're looking at ninety-six.'

Alice lets out a long, slow breath. 'That's way more than Bundy and Dahmer combined. How the hell did he get away with it for so long?'

'He was careful.' Boudreaux shrugs. 'Most of the countries the UN go to are in pretty bad shape for one reason or another, less sophisticated police forces, some of them not signed up to GALE to link the cases. Even those that are can be slow on the uptake. He picked people that he thought deserved it. People whose victims he had seen and been unable to save. Guys who had it coming. Kill one, set one up. Two for the price of one. That plaster he slapped on you? It's a fast-acting transdermal patch, fentanyl plus a few other goodies to incapacitate, and fuzz up the memory. If you'd had it on much longer, you might not even remember being in his place at all.'

Alice raises a hand, subconsciously touching where the patch had been.

'We're pretty sure that's how he got 'em all. Poor bastards wouldn't have put up much of a fight.'

'Ninety-six,' she says in barely a whisper. 'All because of that beating in Somalia? It doesn't make sense.'

'Makes more sense than you realise,' Boudreaux says. 'I've seen his file. It was bad enough that he never made a full recovery. The beating damaged a part of his brain called the amygdala. Its main job is to regulate emotions like fear and aggression. His was messed up in a way that meant he didn't see risk the same way we do. He wasn't afraid to take these people on. For him, the reward of making sure they didn't hurt anyone else outweighed the risk to his own life.'

'So those men in Somalia, the ones that beat him. It's like what he said to Dufort, they literally made him what he was.'

Boudreaux nods. 'That's why he had the job overseeing the urgent care centres and field hospitals, instead of still being a surgeon. You don't want a man with a messed-up approach to risk-taking out there as your surgeon.'

'The press will have a field day when this gets out,' says Alice.

'Yeah, about that,' says Boudreaux. He looks uncomfortable, and Alice wonders what's coming.

'I just got off the phone with Lavigne on the way here. He's been in with our director today, as well as local PD over in the States and … well I'm just gonna say it. They're burying the cases.'

Alice's eyes widen to saucers. 'They can't! Those men might be criminals, but that's not how this works. And what about the families of the people they've killed? They deserve to know the truth.'

'Word from up on high is it's a pill they're willing to swallow. "Not in the public interest" is the line Lavigne kept spouting like a broken record. Every single one of these guys is a stone-cold killer. They're just not serving the right time for it.'

'They bury this, and my dad still dies,' she says. 'I can't let that happen. I won't let that happen.'

'So there is some good news,' Boudreaux says. 'Probably should have led with this. Your dad is going to walk, but that's the only one they'll move on. The rest stay put.'

Relief floods through Alice, but it still doesn't sit well. Her whole career has been about justice, and this is a skewed version of it, like a picture that hasn't quite been hung straight.

'I know they're not good people, Luc, but this isn't right, and you know it.'

Boudreaux holds his hands up. 'I'm actually with you on this one. Didn't think I'd ever say that, but what went down with your dad, I just can't play in the margins any more, and this is pretty black and white. Grey did it, and we can prove it, but this is way above my pay grade.'

'We can't let that happen,' Alice says. 'I won't let it happen.'

'You don't want to go up against them, Alice. They won't allow it.'

'What are they going to do?' she says, temper unfurling its wings. 'Lock me up too? I'm betting any newspaper I speak to will lap this up.'

'You have to be smart about this, Alice. They have all the evidence locked away in a lab somewhere. Grey was a well-respected doctor, no record. Without the proof to back it up, the kind of claims you'd make, we're talking more National Enquirer headlines than New York Times. Add to that, Lavigne is a vindictive dick with little-man syndrome. I already told him you wouldn't like this, and he made a comment about how the NYPD might be interested to speak to you about the guy in East River. He's just—'

'Those men should be freed and tried for something they've actually done,' Alice cuts in. How can you work for that man?'

'I can't,' says Boudreaux.

Not what Alice had expected, and it saps the heat from her soapbox moment.

'What do you mean?"

'Exactly that. I go back and work for him, he's gonna be as difficult as he can be. Nah, I've been offered a chance to come home, work out of the Manhattan field office.'

'But still part of an organisation that tramples over the law like a stampede.'

'I don't agree with the decision, Alice, but I understand it. I know GALE isn't perfect, but it has done so much good. It can be better. I can be better, and I've got more chance of making it better from the inside than I do by walking away. You have my word, though, that's exactly what I'll be doing. I owe you more than that, but it'll be a start.'

Alice wants to keep the argument going, to quote the Sixth Amendment, how everyone deserves a fair trial, and how these men are being denied that. There's something, though, in Boudreaux's words that moves her, an honesty only seen when someone lays themselves open. She has to admit there's a twisted logic in what GALE are doing, and not for the first time she asks herself how she'd feel if even one of those men walked free and hurt somebody else. There's not an answer that appeases her conscience either way. Credit where credit is due though. He's played this with a straighter bat all the way through than she's been giving him credit for. She lets out a long slow breath.

'Look, I don't think that I'll ever agree with this plan, but that aside, I think I owe you a bit of an apology.'

'Why?' he asks with a frown.

'Because despite me thinking you were the one trying to bury this, you've actually been straight up. I can see that now. That stuff I brought up from your past, the other case, I'm sorry for all of that.'

Boudreaux says nothing for a beat. Just stares off down the road. When he finally speaks, he looks down at the table.

'That case, Mario Higuita. That's the reason I left the Orlando PD. The reason I can't do anything other than what's right. There's so much about that case that was fucked up. I should have—'

'Whatever it is,' Alice says. 'You don't have to tell me anything.'

''Bout time I told someone,' he says, finally meeting her gaze again. 'I figure after what we've been through that I can trust you as much as anyone.'

Alice says nothing. Just leans back to give him space.

'I meant it when I said I've never crossed a line. Not personally anyway. With Higuita, as much as I hated the guy, the witness we found … what they said was true. They were threatened. Told if they didn't testify, that a search of their place would probably turn up a bag of coke.'

That takes her by surprise. So much for playing with a straight bat.

Boudreaux sees the shock on her face and sits bolt upright.

'No, no, I didn't mean by me,' he says, shaking his head. 'My partner, Danny Allan. I heard him swearing at the guy the day he changed his mind about testifying. Told him he'd be paying him a visit soon. I should've done something. Should have reported him.'

His voice tails off as he wallows in the memory.

'Instead I fell for the loyalty card. How us cops should stick together. If we hadn't given the DA that witness, he'd never have filed charges. Never have tipped Higuita off that we were onto him. We should have waited till we had him fair and square. If we had, Nancy Killigan might still be alive. I swore after that I'd be better. Be the kind of cop who should have saved Nancy.'

His body language is all messed up, like he's shrinking into himself.

'If it's any consolation,' Alice says, 'I think that's exactly who you've become.'

Boudreaux opens his mouth to speak, but instead settles for the slightest of nods with a smile.

'Not sure I quite believe that just yet,' he says finally, 'but thank you.'

'You're a good man, Luc.'

'Maybe one day,' he says, with a broader smile. One that reaches his eyes this time. 'Look, I need to get going but check your email. There's a little something there for you.'

Boudreaux rises to his feet, holds out his hand, and before Alice can think too hard about it, she moves in to hug him instead. It must take him by surprise as it's a full second before his arms react, closing around her. She squeezes him tight and feels him reciprocate.

'Thank you, Luc,' she says. 'For everything.'

He says nothing, just holds her for a second or two longer, then finally lets go, stepping back a pace.

'Hey, if you're ever in New York …'

She allows herself to wonder for a beat if there's something there in the invite. Something more than she's allowed herself to open up to for so long.

'Likewise, if you're ever in Whitley Bay again,' she replies with a smile. 'Although now you mention it, I have promised to meet Sofia in New York in a few weeks.'

A smile spreads across his face. 'You've got my number.'

'I've got your number,' she says.

Boudreaux, nods, gives one more smile, then turns and heads back to his car. Alice remembers his comment about something in her inbox and fumbles around in her bag for her phone. Sure enough, there's an unread item there from Boudreaux. He must have sent it when he pulled up.

She scans through the message, noting the other people on copy. The lawyer Sofia brought on board, the Attorney General, and the Governor of Florida himself, Colton Winthorpe. She opens the attachments. Lab reports confirming Jim Sharp and Manny Castillo's blood was found in Grey's apartment. A statement from Boudreaux about what he saw and heard, limited context, and only around Sharp, but it's everything she needs. Everything her dad needs to survive.

She's not used to feeling anything positive where her dad is concerned. It's more about this being the right outcome, than warm fuzzy vibes. All the same, how it's played out, it hasn't just been about saving him. She's saved whoever else Grey might have targeted. Saved a baby brother that she's never met. More than that, by taking the risks she has, she hopes she's managed to halt the constant war of attrition between herself and Fiona.

Baby brother. The most unexpected outcome of this whole wild ride. She's not sure what scares her more at this stage. The prospect of meeting him, or the thought of not. Only one way to fix that. But there's somewhere she needs to be first.

Chapter Sixty-Four

Monday – Execution day

Alice grips the handles on Mum's wheelchair hard enough to turn her knuckles white, as if letting go would see her scoot off into the sea. Beside her, stride for stride, Fiona prattles on about a field trip the kids have next week. Up ahead, the twins shriek with laughter as they storm along the damp causeway towards St Mary's Island.

A halo of seagulls slowly circles the gleaming white lighthouse up ahead. It's like an oversized chess piece, only accessible when the tides allow. Wind turbines are dotted across the horizon, turning lazy circles offshore. Everything seems half speed. After the mayhem of the past week, it's a pace she welcomes.

'Jake! Lily! Not too fast. It's slippy,' Mum shouts, but the kids are having too much fun to slow down.

Fiona suggested, and Alice agreed, that there's little value in telling Mum the whole truth. For one thing, Boudreaux would flip if Mum decided to share the sordid details with her friends over a cuppa. The full story, Grey, and his sickeningly large list of victims, needs to stay under wraps.

Alice has told Fiona though. A split-second judgement call. A feeling that some kind of mortar was needed between the bricks of what they're rebuilding. A gesture of trust. Something to bind them.

They're halfway across when Mum speaks again.

'Must have been bloody awful for him,' she says. 'Being stuck inside, knowing he was innocent.'

The two sisters share a look, but say nothing.

'Leaving him was the hardest thing I've had to do, and the best, all wrapped up in one package,' Mum continues. 'I knew he played around, but I was frightened of being on my own.'

She reaches back, patting one of Alice's hands.

'I never thanked you, you know,' she says.

Alice slows a fraction, peering over Mum's shoulder, frowning.

'Thanked me for what?'

'For telling me you saw him with her,' she says. 'He'd snuck around for years with anyone who'd have him, but I was too bloody scared to leave him. To be a single mother. You seeing it with your own eyes was a wake-up call. Gave me the strength to do it, you did.'

'Mum, I—'

'And I know it hasn't been easy for either of you, what with needing to keep an eye on me.'

'Honestly, Mum, it's no bother.'

'I know what you gave up to come back, love,' Mum replies. 'What both of you give up every day for my sake. And that's what family's all about, isn't it? Putting yourself to one side for the good of the rest. Forgiving each other when you get things wrong.'

Alice isn't sure whether she's talking about her and Fiona, or their dad. She can't quite put into words what she feels towards him right now. There's a molten mass of emotions. Her whole career has been about doing what's right. Holding people accountable, and believing that the system can punish and rehabilitate in equal measures. Dad had looked sickened by his own admission when he told her, but she doesn't know if any amount of remorse will ever be enough to gloss over the scars his actions left.

Alice doesn't answer her Mum straight away. Instead, she lets the wheelchair trundle to a stop, and walks slowly around to face her.

'Whatever I gave up to come back,' she says, crouching down so they're on the same eye level. 'It's not worth half of what I have since I got here.'

She glances along the causeway, at where the twins have stepped off, ankle deep in a rockpool, peering down at the water for signs of life. She looks from them to Fiona. Catches her sister smiling at her. There's a warmth to it that cuts through the October chill. She beams back with one of her own.

'What you smiling at?' Fiona asks.

Alice stares out at the surf crashing off the side of St Mary's Island. Breathes in the damp, salty air, and has never felt more at home.

'Look around you,' Alice says.

They share the moment for a beat, before Alice gets to the question she's been meaning to ask since they arrived.

'I've got a favour to ask, Fi.'

'What is it?'

'Will you come with me?'

'Where to?'

'Florida.'

Fiona narrows her eyes. 'When are you going?'

'Couple of days' time.'

Her sister lets out a short laugh. 'And what am I supposed to do with the kids? Bring 'em along?'

'I've already spoken to Trevor. He's okay to mind the fort for a few days,' Alice says, and revels in the shock on Fiona's face.

'You two BFFs now then, are you?'

'Something like that,' Alice says. 'Figured if he's good enough for my baby sister, maybe I should give him more of a chance.'

Fiona's lunge forwards takes her by surprise, and next thing she knows, she's being squeezed like a kids favourite toy.

'Thank you,' Fiona whispers in her ear. 'And yes, of course I'll bloody come with you.'

Alice feels pinpricks of moisture in her eyes. Blinking them away, she pulls back just as something solid thunks into her leg. She looks down and sees Lily staring up at her. Jake has latched onto Fiona's leg, and both kids screw up their faces into contorted grins. The laughter bubbles up and out of Alice like a mountain spring. Fresh, pure.

For the first time in a long time, she's feels like she's exactly where she needs to be.

Chapter Sixty-Five

Seven days after execution day

The low rumble of the engine is hypnotic as Alice squints over the dashboard at the entrance to Florida State Prison. It's been a full fifteen minutes since she pulled up. No sign of anyone else yet.

Heat comes off the road in waves, bottom of the building walls shimmering like a mirage. Even just looking outside seems to nudge the temperature up in here in spite of the AC on full blast.

'You okay?' Fiona asks from the seat beside her.

'Yeah.'

'You want to try that again like you mean it?' she says with a chuckle, then more serious, 'It's okay to not be okay.'

Okay feels like an alien concept right now. She isn't sure she can remember what okay feels like, let alone plot a way back to it.

'I'm … getting there,' she says eventually.

'What you went through, most people never have to deal with that kind of shit. You know, if you need someone to talk to …'

'I know. Appreciate it, sis.'

They sit in comfortable silence for the next few minutes, and Alice asks herself the same question she's had bouncing around her head since the coffee shop meeting with Boudreaux. Can she live with this? With what's being forced on her? Part of her is glad that Mum didn't feel up to making the trip. Doesn't feel like Dad has earned the right yet to ask for her forgiveness.

A flash of light catches her eye. Sun bouncing off an approaching car. The black SUV turns off the main road, and winds its way towards them. She's deliberately parked in the spot furthest away from the gates so as not to attract attention. Around half the spaces are full, so they don't stand out in their corner spot.

'Is this them?' Fiona asks, words edged with excitement.

'Maybe,' Alice murmurs, fidgeting in her seat.

The SUV pulls into a spot around a hundred yards away. She sees Sofia first, long legs folding out from the driver's side. Both passenger doors open, and a heartbeat later, Alice sees Mariella come round the side of the car. Even from here, Alice can tell how thin she is, like she's not eaten a good meal in years. She supposes having your other half on death row for a decade will do that to you. Behind her, a boy, mop of dirty blonde hair like a flashback to photos of her dad as a kid. Her brother.

'There he is,' whispers Fiona. 'Mariella says he's never stopped asking questions about us since he found out he has big sisters.'

Fiona pops her door open, and it's like a starter's pistol that sends Alice's heart pattering.

'Wait,' Alice says, grabbing her sister's arm. 'I'm not ready. Not yet.'

'But what if—'

'Please sis,' Alice begs her. 'I just need a minute.'

Fiona grumbles, but leaves her door half open and folds her arms like she's sulking.

They watch as Mariella and Anthony join Sofia at the front of the SUV. Mariella's gaze is fixed on the gate ahead, but Alice sees Sofia glance once over her shoulder in their direction. Impossible to read her face from this distance though.

After what seems like an eternity, she sees Mariella's body language change, shifting nervously from one foot to the other, arm curling protectively around Anthony's shoulders. Beyond her, the chain-link fence corridor that leads back to the main building. A series of gates act as checkpoints along the way, and two gates back, Alice sees a pair of figures waiting side by side. Too far away to see faces, but no danger of getting them mixed up.

One wears the short-sleeved white shirt, dark pants combo of a guard. The second, her dad, in the suit he most likely wore when he first walked in. He looks tiny next to the burly guard, skinnier even than he has looked on screen, suit hanging off him like he's a kid trying on his dad's clothes.

The gate trundles to one side, and the men walk through, Dad seeming to take two strides to the guard's one. Alice's eyes flick back to Mariella, seeing her and Anthony taking the first few tentative steps forward. One hand raises in greeting, hesitant at first, as if anything too enthusiastic could make them turn away.

Dad is carrying a duffel bag, the sum total accrued in over a decade. When he sees who's waiting for him, he quickens his pace. Gate number two squeals as it starts to open. Mariella is about fifty yards away, but she's rushing towards him now, dragging Anthony with her. The gate is barely wide enough to slip through but Dad drops his bag, running through the widening gap. The three collide, arms wrapping around each other.

Alice doesn't realise she's crying until the first salty tang of tear hits her lip. She feels Fiona's hand on hers, giving a gentle squeeze, but she can't look away from the reunion outside, not even for a second.

Twin tides wash over her, a peculiar mix of relief, and an unexpected pang of jealousy as she watches the scene play out. The reunion she's watching, the way Dad squeezes Anthony, ruffling his hair. The beam of paternal pride on his face. Something she only ever saw in flashes growing up. Why couldn't he have been the dad she'd needed? Only he can answer that.

The nails on her free hand dig through her jeans, pain of the present keeping her anchored here and now. Dad and Mariella are hugging again, and Alice sees Mariella's shoulders heaving up and down, like she's shaking despite the heat. Beside her she hears Fiona sniffing loudly. Turns and sees that her little sister's lower lip is trembling. She's feeling it too.

Mariella and her dad finally peel away from one another, him reaching out, holding her face in his hands.

They're too far away to hear what he says even if Alice had been outside the car, but whatever it is, it's met with enthusiastic approval by Mariella, who nods her head vigorously.

Dad lets his hands fall back down, retreats a dozen paces to retrieve his duffel bag from a guard who looks about as moved by the scene as a stone statue. Slinging it over his shoulder, he extends one hand to Mariella, the other to his son, and they both reach out, taking his in theirs, smiles beaming as wide as the interstate.

They walk back towards where Sofia waits by the car, and Alice sniffs loudly, wiping both cheeks with her palms.

'You ready?' Fiona asks.

Alice isn't sure she ever will be, but if this past week has taught her anything, it's that life is too bloody short. She doesn't know whether she'll ever forgive Dad for what he's done, the way he was. But there's something about how close he came to dying, and her own brushes with violence, coupled with the revelation of her brother's existence that's made the walls she's built up around her spring a leak.

Only a small one, but it's there nonetheless. A pressure valve that's opening her up to the notion of being a big sister to someone other than just Fiona.

'No,' she replies. 'But let's do this anyway.'

Alice pops her own door open, and slides out into the sunshine. It's an unseasonably hot day for this time of year, and as she shrugs off the cooling cloak of AC, the warmth spreads over her like slipping into a freshly drawn bath.

She closes her eyes, breathes in a lungful, and exhales as she opens them again. Something shifts inside her, seeing the happy faces amble across the road, and she feels a lightness in her chest. Like something heavy has been cut loose, cast off like shedding a skin. Thanks to her, her dad is alive. Despite everything he's done, she still saved him. Became a better person for it. Him walking free today encapsulates everything to do with why she went into law in the first place. He had set her on this path, with his years of shady backroom deals to make a fast buck. Where would she be if he hadn't? Who would she be? Sliding doors.

Over by the SUV, Dad and Sofia are talking. Mariella stands smiling like she's just won the lottery. Alice watches as Anthony's attention wanders. Sees him turn a lazy circle, stopping as he claps eyes on her. She feels a hand in hers as Fiona joins her. The conversation stops as Dad looks over Sofia's shoulder, seeing them for the first time. Even from this distance his body language takes on an awkward feel, like he doesn't know where to put himself.

There's no sprint across the car park the way there was when Dad came out of the gate, and she feels something knot in her stomach. She shouldn't have come. Not today. Maybe not ever. This is a mistake. Her body feels like it's vibrating with nervous energy, the urge to climb back inside the car, building.

Then Anthony takes a step towards her, and it's like a dry desert wind scours all the doubt away. This boy who she's never met, walking towards her with a shy smile on his face, a bridge between the two worlds. This kid who doesn't know her from Adam, but he's been brave enough to take that first step.

She squeezes Fiona's hand, and the two sisters set off towards him. Towards what exactly, she hasn't got a clue, but for him, she's willing to find out.

Acknowledgements

It's been a while since I've had a book out to write any acknowledgements for. Three years to be precise, which feels like a lifetime ago. My last book came out mid-pandemic, under a different name (writing as Robert Scragg) and into a very different world.

A lot has happened in those three years. I've changed agents, changed publishers and even changed the name I write under. There have even been a few moments amongst all that upheaval when I've wondered if I'd see another book published, thanks to the self-doubt and imposter syndrome that seems to follow a lot of us around.

I'm fortunate that I've got more than my fair share of people around me who have helped me along the way, that I now get the chance to say a very public thankyou to – some personal, some professional. The book you've just read has evolved so much since the first draft I finished back in 2022.

First off, I'm eternally grateful to my amazing agent, David Headley, for giving me a new lease of author-life, and finding me and my books an exciting new home with Hodder. I couldn't feel in safer hands.

Phoebe Morgan and the team at Hodder have blown me away with their passion and enthusiasm for Seven Days. They've polished the borderline incomprehensible mish-mash of words I gave them so well that I can practically see my face in them. Honourable mentions go to Alainna, Kate, and Cari who have toiled away behind the scenes.

Then there's the army of booksellers that help introduce the book to you lovely people once it's published – those of you in the north east might recognise that one of the characters in Seven Days is actually named after one of them. Fiona Sharp from Waterstones in Durham is to bookselling what Alan Shearer was to Newcastle United – unstoppable. She's championed my books right from day one, and I'll always be grateful for her support. Goldsboro Books has been one of my favourite discoveries this past year, and the team there are absolute rock stars when it comes to championing authors. My local indie bookstore needs a huge shout out too – The Bound in Whitley Bay (coastal branch of Forum Books). Helen, James and the rest of the staff there work tirelessly to help folks like me connect with readers like you, and they do it with such energy that I'm sure we could power a city if we hooked them up to the grid. Another fab north-east indie I'm indebted to is Drake The Bookshop in Stockton, who are regularly on hand to support local events, hauling mountains of books that would put a powerlifter's back out, all in the name of helping authors.

My Northern Crime Syndicate posse – Trevor, Rob, Judith, Fiona, Chris and Adam – legends and incredible authors in their own right. It's an honour to hit the road with you and talk about stuff we made up in our spare bedrooms.

The Criminal Minds Crew – keeping me sane one alpaca story at a time – pincers up people!

The Circle of Trust – every single one of them are fabulous writers and friends who saw me through COVID one drunken Zoom call after another.

My day job teamies who allowed me to pilfer their names for some of the characters in Seven Days – Nic S, Dan, Sharon, Gail and Trev.

Then there's the family. The Sages who still tolerate having a Geordie as part of their clan, even though I still haven't made good on my promise to take all my wife's childhood hoardings from their loft.

My Mam and Dad who have supported me unconditionally over the years. I wouldn't be where I am today without them, and that's a debt I'll never be able to repay. My Mam can prove this too – she's kept all the IOUs.

No shout-outs would be complete without my ultimate ride or dies – my wife Nic, and my kids, Lucy, Jake and Lily. You guys are what keep me smiling even when the rest of the world sometimes feels like it's going to hell in a handcart.